"Be alert! Look and listen!" Mr. Franklin adjured.

The man was truly dead, no mistaking the awful stillness of him. He lay face up, arms out, one leg straight, the other bent sharply back in a way that would pain any man living. But this man had no life. His head was twisted far to one side, his neck broke in the fall. His hands were curved into claws, as if in the last instant he grasped for life. One shoe had come off, revealing a ragged hole in the baggy stocking on his foot. His clothing bespoke the sham of the proud poor: a patchy coat over a stained bottle-green waistcoat. As for his face, it was stamped with fury even in death, a screaming grimace, the eyes half-open and glassy, the mouth snarling with all its blackened teeth. *I accuse!* It seemed to cry . . . .

But whom?

MURDER AT DRURY LANE

ROBERT LEE HALL

ST. MARTIN'S PAPERBACKS

MURDER AT DRURY LANE

Copyright © 1992 by Robert Lee Hall.

Cover illustration by Jeff Walker.

Library of Congress Catalog Card Number: 92-26154

ISBN: 0-312-95112-4

Printed in the United States of America

St. Martin's Press hardcover edition/November 1992
St. Martin's Paperbacks edition/October 1993

10 9 8 7 6 5 4 3 2 1

For Katherine and Jeffrey, who wanted another story about Mr. Franklin.

*IN WHICH men talk of playacting
and murder . . .*

"S hall I tell a tale of murder, Ben?"

Benjamin Franklin peered at his old friend through his small, squarish spectacles. "Pray, do. Shall it be truth or invention?"

James Ralph solemnly held up a palm. "Truth, Ben, I swear. Ev'ry word."

Mr. Franklin wryly tutted. "Why, then, 'twill be a new thing from your lips, Jimmy. I hope 'twill not badly twist your tongue."

Mr. Ralph laughed, as did I, though Mrs. Margaret Stevenson plainly did not like talk of murder. Her daughter, however, leant forward eagerly, whilst William, Mr. Franklin's twenty-seven year old son, looked smugly pleased to be the agent of Mr. Ralph's presence amongst us.

And how had we come to be conjoined in Mrs. Stevenson's cozy front parlor at number 7 Craven Street, the Strand that chill February evening? A quarter hour ago, Mr. Franklin had arrived after supper to put his feet up by the fender; then I trailed in with my slate and chalk to perch on the stool by his side; next our landlady bustled in with her stitchery, followed by her pretty daughter, Polly, with her book. For some time we four kept silent company, London stirring beyond the curtained windows—when shortly after the big case clock in the hall struck ten William burst in upon us. "Moved to tears, I tell you!" declared he with great melodrama. "Near sobbed out my heart!"

His father lifted his brown, bespectacled eyes from his Addison. "Pray, why?" inquired he.

Polly Stevenson's blue eyes flashed wickedly. "My lord's carriage splashed mud upon your finery?" But this barb made no sting, for the young man in his white powdered wig and gray velvet suit stood in a strange, stupified transport, harkening, it seemed, to angels.

Mrs. Stevenson dropped her stitchery in her lap. "Lud, speak, young sir, for your silence much alarms me."

No sound issued from William Franklin's working lips.

Mr. Franklin glanced at me over the top of his spectacles. "Shall we ever be enlightened, Nick?"

"I pray so, sir," said I leaving my sum undone upon its slate. In truth, though William cared little for me, I held him in great respect and was much dismayed by his manner. Had some calamity befallen?

Mr. Franklin wore his customary brown worsted suit and black, buckled shoes. He sighed. "As my son's voice appears disarmed, mine must slay the silence, *viz.:* he set by the law for the Theatre Royal in Drury Lane, where he saw a play. Some soubrette has stole his heart—and his tongue with it." He lifted an inquiring brow. "Do I hit the mark? Did your enchantress dance in the pantomime?"

"Desdemona," breathed William Franklin. "She played Desdemona." He blinked, as if waking. "But, Father, I did not tell you I went to the theater. Indeed, I have not been in my chamber since midmorning."

"Tut, a thing need not be spoken to be known. A playbill lay upon the floor betwixt our rooms; further, you young rakes of the Inns of Court are great frequenters of playhouses. *Ergo,* you have come from Drury Lane."

William nodded. "Aye, and saw the most bewitching creature there."

"Ha, some sprite or nixie?"

"A girl."

"What, a thing of flesh and blood has done this magic?"

"Of the prettiest flesh."

Mr. Franklin chuckled. "Pray, name the prodigy."

"Mrs. Drumm."

"Drumm . . ." Judiciously, he tasted this.

Polly gave a haughty sniff. "Mrs.?" She tossed her blond curls. "Married, then."

William faced her. "Yes, she is married."

"And yet you call her 'girl'?"

"She *is* a girl, no more than eighteen."

Polly thrust out her chin. "Or twenty? Or twenty-four? Perhaps thirty-six? A very matron, I proclaim!"

"Young and pretty, I tell you." William's arms flew up. "Prettier than you!" he flung in her face.

"Lord, Lord," murmured Mrs. Stevenson, lowering her chin. Her daughter's bosom heaved, whilst Mr. Franklin scrutinized his nails. For my part, I ducked my head. 'Twas an all too familiar scene. Since his lodging at Craven Street with his father (it drew on eight months now), William had seemed smitten with Polly, yet the sharp-tongued daughter of the house always rebuffed him. Thus we had frequently been treated to such moments of parry and riposte, hurtful though no blood was shed. Yet though I ducked my head, I watched, for here was something new: William's affections lodged elsewhere, and Polly provoked to learn it? What news! The young woman's ears had turned crimson, her fingers whitely gripped her book. Did she regret her former disregard of the American agent's son?

Mrs. Stevenson resumed her stitchery of one of Poor Richard's maxims.

Mr. Franklin made a sucking sound betwixt tongue and teeth. "But this is some surprise, Billy. Why did not Mrs. Cibber play Desdemona?"

"Indisposed," muttered the son.

"Ah, as often, I hear. A most frail woman."

"But a most affecting Desdemona!" boomed a new voice, deep and hearty, and a stout, red-faced gentleman huffed into the room.

William's sulk turned to smiles. "I forget myself, Father. See who I have brought with me: your old friend, James Ralph."

Thus came the sixth amongst us.

"Ben!" rumbled this doughty old fellow, wringing Mr. Franklin's hand. James Ralph wore a patchy suit, sagging stockings and down-at-heel boots, and he smelt mightily of beer; yet his fusty appearance in no way shamed him. Bowing grandly to Mrs. Stevenson, he nuzzled her hand, Polly's too, though with elaborate delicacy. "Dear ladies." His rheumy old eyes fell upon me. "Nick Handy, or I miss the mark."

"Yes, sir," said I, rising.

He tapped his brow like a sage, "Learn well of your master." He jiggled my hand like a pump handle.

"But, Jimmy, why did you not come up at once?" inquired Mr. Franklin.

Hoary brows flared like porcupine's quills. "Pah, our hackney coachman proved a pennypincher. Why, I will knock a man's hat cock-a-hoop if he tries to cheat me. I rounded upon him, I made him faces, I made him voices too, the end being he near begged to pay for the priv'lege of transporting me. Ha! But do I hear you talking of the theater? I love such talk. May I sit amongst you? Shall we dissect the bitch? O, I beg pardon, ladies. A life spent amongst curs has made a very dog of me; I bark out o' turn." Polly looked as if she liked such barking, though her mother rolled her eyes. As for Mr. Ralph, he sank into a cushioned chair and beamed at one and all as if he must be the most loved fellow in Christendom.

Mr. Franklin settled back. "Some libation, Jimmy?"

"Small beer will suffice."

"I may make up a toddy," offered our landlady.

"Do so," urged Mr. Franklin. "Your toddy is ambrosia." The woman left us.

William pulled a chair near Mr. Ralph's right hand whilst I sat too. Liking as much as I to hear Mr. Franklin and his friends discourse of scientific matters or deal out London's

WALDO

SBN 10520-0, $3.95

Theroux's first novel is the story of Waldo, graduate of the Bonneville School for Delinquent Boys, lover of ex-starlet Clovis Techy, reluctant Rugg College student, and features writer of such popularity that he is enshrined in a nightclub in a glass "writer's booth."

The brilliant fiction debut of the author of *The Mosquito Coast* and *Riding the Iron Rooster*.

To order WALDO or O-ZONE, call toll-free
1-800-733-3000

news, Polly leant forward eagerly. There came a moment of thought-gathering, flames softly hissing in the grate, during which I reflected how fortunate was I, Nick Handy, to be a chick in such a nest. But twelve years old, I ever thanked the Lord that Mr. Franklin had been sent to London from America. Had he not, I should still be a poor, raddled, boy-of-work at Inch, Printer, Moorfields, and the truth of my birth (for I was Mr. Franklin's natural son) should never have come clear. Mr. Franklin had brought William with him to study law at the Inner Temple, their blackamoor servants, Peter and King, sailing with 'em. We five, adding Polly and her mother, made a ménage of seven at Widow Stevenson's tidy house hard by the Thames, where, though our weather was sometimes cloudy, good sense always brought out the sun.

Stretching his legs, Mr. Franklin regarded his old friend. "So, you met my Billy at Drury Lane?"

"Aye, amooning."

"David Garrick played Othello?"

"Pah, after his fashion."

"What? You disapprove the great Garrick?"

"Disapprove, Ben? Disapprove?" Mr. Ralph treated us to a long discourse in which he conceded that, hum, yes, the actor was perhaps good, frequently excellent, indeed sometime a very paragon; yet he wanted certain refinements to his art, which Mr. Ralph might make if only Garrick would attend. As he spoke a change came upon me, a sort of tingling numbness, an irresistible tugging, so that I acted almost without thinking, as if some power beyond my control bade my itching fingers stray.

Surreptitiously I erased with my sleeve the troublesome numbers from my slate.

I began to draw pictures in their place.

James Ralph faced me; thus I limned him first: his head, round as a pudding; his frayed and patchy wig; his puffed cheeks; his bulbous nose webbed with burst veins; his drooping lips and his lively little pits of eyes, like blackcurrants in a pie. I struggled to capture their look, both merry

and sour, yet I was startled to discover behind the orbs
some dark stirring. Envy? Malice? My chalk found neither
line nor shading for this unsettling note.

"Billy tells us that Mrs. Drumm was Desdemona," I
heard Mr. Franklin say.

"O, Mrs. Drumm," puffed Mr. Ralph. "I cannot proclaim
she was Desdemona, yet she essayed the part."

"Billy is taken with her."

"Do I not know it? Why, in the quarter hour from Drury
Lane I heard nothing but Lucy Drumm. How I prayed for
wax wherewith to stuff my ears!" He patted William's arm.
"Well, I give the woman this: that she died well beneath the
Moor's pillow, with affecting moans. As to her charms, I
concede she is a peach."

"But with a husband," put in Mr. Franklin.

"Such a husband! He keeps close watch on her."

Mr. Franklin's gaze turned to his son. "Take heed then,
William, that you do not come to sword's point over fruit
already picked."

William colored. "I am no fool."

Mr. Franklin pursed his lips. "Would that ev'ry young
man could proclaim such wisdom." For a brief moment his
look probed hard. His son did not always please him. Upon
their sailing from America, William had been all but en-
gaged to marry Betsey Graeme of Philadelphia, the daughter of Thomas Graeme; but, this Graeme being a great
political foe, the liaison had hardly gladdened his father. In
their time on these shores William had spoke little of Miss
Graeme. Yet though Mr. Franklin might be happy his son's
eye roved from its former aim, he was a practical man:
William was of an age to choose a wife, and a married
actress was no candidate for that.

Too, the Franklins were watched. They had many enemies in London. Neither could chance becoming em-
broiled in scandal.

My chalk continued to labor. As it did, the two friends
talked of old times thirty years ago, when Ben Franklin,
printer, and James Ralph, poet, had sailed near penniless

to London. I always liked to hear these tales. Mr. Ralph had
deserted his wife and babe to go adventuring, this proving
but one sample of his fecklessness, for, whilst Mr. Franklin
quickly found work in a London print shop, Mr. Ralph
gadded and whored and lived off his friend's earnings. A
falling out was the end, though 'twas not money that
parted 'em but the bedding of a pretty little milliner. Mr.
Franklin had stayed less than two years, returning to
America in 1726 and settling in Philadelphia to make himself a gentleman in trade, a power in politics, a philosopher
to whom the world paid heed. He had thought to retire at
forty to his beloved experiments, but the call of public life
had proved too great. He was a man who went where he
was needed and so, past fifty, he was driven again across
the seas. Meantime Mr. Ralph had remained in London.
Alexander Pope had lampooned his poetry in the *Dunciad*,
and though he had a small triumph in *The Fashionable
Lady*, the first play by an American to be staged on these
shores, that career too had foundered. He was for some
time assistant to Henry Fielding at the Little Theatre, and
had also worked for Mr. Fielding's newspaper *The Cham-
pion*. "He might have sunk to Grub Street hack," Mr.
Franklin had confided privately, "yet there is wit and te-
nacity in him. He is become an able political writer and
may help us in our aims."

I was glad to hear this, for powerful men opposed Mr.
Franklin; he needed all the allies he might muster.

The gentlemen's talk turned to actresses they had seen
in their youth, especially Mrs. Oldfield, who had played
Lady Modish and Mrs. Sullen. "Two footmen saw her to her
dressing room door ev'ry night," recalled Mr. Ralph, smiling. "O, the women love their airs."

"Do the actresses still long for respectability?" inquired
Mr. Franklin.

"Ha, as much as for fine dresses and rich gentlemen's
favors."

"Why should not actresses be thought well on?" put in
Polly warmly.

"Hush, child," chid Mrs. Stevenson, bustling in with her tray of steaming cups. "Forgive my daughter, sir, for not knowing that gentlemen must be let be in their discourse."

"Tut, you know I always like to hear what Polly thinks," interposed Mr. Franklin.

"If't may be called thought," said William peevishly.

"But your daughter is right." Mr. Ralph grasped his spiced rum. "Many of our she-players deserve as good a reputation as those titled ladies who publicly strut virtue and breeding whilst behind doors they rut like pigs. Do not many actresses take their lovers frankly instead of in a sneaking way? Name me a duchess who may say the same."

"How I should like to see this Mrs. Oldfield," exclaimed Polly.

"You shall not set foot in the playhouse!" declared her mother.

Polly moaned.

Mr. Ralph sipped his toddy. "Alas, 'tis too late to see Mrs. Oldfield, child—except in the churchyard; for she is dead these many years."

"But most lively whilst she breathed," amended Mr. Franklin. "Why, I can hear her still: 'I could no more choose a man by my eye than a shoe; one must draw 'em on a little to see if they fit.' " He winked at our landlady. "Shall I lend this to Poor Richard?"

The plump woman colored. "How you rally me, sir. You know 'twould never do."

"Mrs. Oldfield worked under Colley Cibber's reign at Drury Lane, did she not?" said Mr. Franklin to Mr. Ralph.

"Aye, but old Cibber is dead now too, last year, did you hear? Ah, the world turns, and new men and women tread the boards."

"Yet I am surprised that an untried actress plays Desdemona."

"How else should a young actress prove her skill?" asked Polly.

"With great difficulty," replied Mr. Ralph. "Indeed 'tis a

great trial for any unfledged player to make some mark. When an actress who owns a part cannot go on, 'tis customary to offer another play rather than another player."

Mrs. Stevenson rolled her eyes. "A woman 'owns' a part? And they have plays run up, like suits of clothes?"

"Ha, they must have several so, dear lady, for a player may take ill, as Mrs. Cibber did tonight, or the fickle London crowd may cry down a play."

William nodded assent. "I have seen 'em hiss a play to death."

"As the Penns wish to hiss us out of town, eh, Billy?" put in his father. "But we shall play out our play all the same, and be damned to the Penns. As to owning parts, the actors and actresses jealously guard their roles, eh, Jimmy?"

James Ralph chortled. "Aye, and would cut and scratch, wheedle and plot to keep 'em. Why, they'd sell their souls." His voice lowered. "Some might go so far as murder." He gazed into the fire with that clouded look I had noted. "There is much high temper backstage. As to murder, I do not exaggerate." His gaze lifted with a sly, provoking gleam. "Shall I tell a tale of murder, Ben?"

Thus were we brought to his story.

But first Mrs. Stevenson must go to fetch more toddy, to prime Mr. Ralph's pump, as he said. Meanwhile, we sat in waiting silence, the fire chirping, London breathing beyond the closed curtains, William tapping his finger ends, Polly's eyes glittering like sparks in the lamplight. A small smile played about Mr. Franklin's pointed lips, whilst Mr. Ralph hummed a wheezing tune. As for me, mixed feelings stirred, and my chalk stilled upon its slate. Murder. I had seen it first when I came upon my printing master, Ebenezer Inch, dead in his frost-rimed yard. Then, his wife stabbed in the heart. Then, Mr. Jared Hexham horribly done in, his scalp sawed from his skull. There had been others, which Mr. Franklin had looked into: the strange poisoning of Roderick Fairbrass; Cadwallader Bracegirdle bound, and frozen to death; Cato Prince grappling with burly Mr. Bumpp in the frigid Thames 'til the cruel waters closed over both. I hated to think on these; yet, strangely, I longed for Mr. Ralph's tale. So did Mr. Franklin by the light in his eyes. He sat unbuttoned, at apparent ease, yet a stiffness about his jaw and a mild fiddling of fingers gave the clue: news of murder drew him as the electrically charged glass rods in his workshop drew metal filings. He studied Nature's mysteries to make sense of 'em; he did the same in life. His bespectacled eyes searched, his mind winnowed, his sturdy hands nimbly shook the chaff from truth 'til its kernel fell free.

I too was drawn by mystery. Because Mr. Franklin's blood flowed in me?

I longed to know what drove humankind to dark deeds.

Mrs. Stevenson returned with our toddies. Bending forward 'til his old joints creaked, Mr. Ralph began his tale:

"Well, now," said he, "first you must know that the history of playing is marked by violence: Kit Marlowe dead in a tavern brawl, Ben Jonson imprisoned for murder. The women too? Why, Mrs. Barry stabbed Mrs. Boutell onstage in front of hundreds after a spat over parts, and the great Quin stabbed two men to death in his youth (he was ever a danger when crossed). Yet Charles Macklin, I believe, was the worst; indeed, he once choked Quin insensible for prancing behind his back and spoiling his effects. But to my tale, which I saw with my own eyes. 'Twas twenty years ago, Addison's *Cato* just being played at Drury Lane and all assembled in the Green Room for the afterpiece—*Trick for Trick*, as I recall. I had come to present an epilogue to Fleetwood, though the blind fool never saw its merits. Theophilous Cibber was amongst us. Little Henry Peter Arne too, dress'd as a girl to play Estifania. Other folk as well, amongst 'em one Thomas Hallam, a fiddling fellow who was to do Guzman. The wardrobe was open to all to take what they wished, and this Hallam had pulled from it a black, greasy wig, suitable for his part. There he sat and waited with the rest, a little dark man, arubbing his hands, when all at once in roars Macklin, who is to play Sancho.

'Damn you for a rogue, what business have you got with my wig?' cries he, at which Hallam blanches but stands his ground. 'I am no rogue. 'Tis a stock wig, and I have as much right to't as you.' 'God's blood, you do not!' retorts Macklin, in a rage. All exchange glances; we know the actor's temper. In great haste we urge Hallam to yield, which he does, though with sniveling cavil. Macklin snatches the wig and sits apart, amuttering and atwisting the ragged thing in his hands, whilst in great ill-ease we pray the worst has passed. Alas, it has not, for some worm bores in Macklin, and he cannot let be. 'Scrub! Rascal!' bursts out he anew. 'How dare you have the impudence to take this wig, which you know I have worn these four nights running?' Hallam answers back, 'I am no more rascal than you,' at which, before we can stop him (if any durst), Macklin leaps up. A bundle of sticks sits by the fire. He grabs one of these and lunges at Hallam, who by chance turns his head so as to catch the point in his eye. It plunges deep, and he starts and claps up his hand. 'I am blinded!' cries he. 'Nay,' protests Macklin, gone white, for great gouts of blood are pumping from the eye. He pulls Hallam's hand away. 'Why, the ball still rolls beneath the lid.' Hallam struggles free and, urine being a sovereign remedy, he plucks at Henry Peter Arne in his girl's dress: 'Whip up your skirts, you little bitch, and piss in my eye!' But the boy cannot, so Macklin does so himself, opening his breeches before us all. Suddenly from onstage comes the sound of the fiddlers; the afterpiece must go on. All scramble. Someone steps in for Hallam, and Macklin goes on too and shows a keen edge, as if the stabbing honed his talents. Yet afterward he was aghast; for, seeing his wounded victim sinking into death, he fled in panic out the top of the playhouse and over the London roofs." Mr. Ralph drank deep of his flagon. "And that is my tale of murder."

We stirred uneasily whilst coals sank in the grate.

"He truly died?" came Mrs. Stevenson's voice at last.

Mr. Ralph smacked his lips. "Excellent toddy, mum.

What, die? Yes indeed, within the day. Did I not say so? A pretty tale, eh?" He beamed.

Mrs. Stevenson pressed him. "But how was the wicked man punished?"

Mr. Ralph blinked. "Punished?"

"I shall tell," put in Mr. Franklin; "for I have heard this tale. Though he was taken and tried, Macklin walked free through the influence of friends, with but a token branding with a cold iron. This when penniless fellows hang for stealing a candlestick." He shook his head. "Justice waits not on the friendless."

Polly looked from face to face. "Such a tale!" breathed she.

Mr. Ralph chucked her chin. "O, I have many more, child, which would curl your hair were't not already so prettily done." He held out his cup. "Another if you please, Mrs. Stevenson."

Our landlady went to fetch it.

"Is the theater then truly so wicked a place?" asked Polly, round-eyed.

"No more wicked than the world."

"Then 'tis wicked indeed," asserted Mr. Franklin. "Yet you love it, do you not, Jimmy? Tell of David Garrick. You know him?"

"As well as any. I importune him. I offer the fruits of my labor, which he dismisses."

"Your plays?"

"Are they not as good as most which are enacted? Far better than many. Why, wit and sense sing in 'em."

"A pretty duet. Yet he will not listen?"

"His ear for music is deaf."

"He is rude?"

"No, damn the fellow. I should like to despise him, but he possesses great charm—he says no like a courtier."

"Yet there are many hate him," put in William.

Mr. Franklin tutted. "Envy and malice often march alongside fame to trip it up."

Mr. Ralph nodded. " 'Tis true, many would love to see

him fall—turned-away actors, rejected playwrights, critics, the pack of scurrilous hacks who hop about the playhouse like fleas amongst bedclothes. Indeed of late there seem more than usual vexations at Drury Lane. Pah, am I not the veriest fool to dote upon the dame who scorns me? Yet I do, I must. I mope about backstage; I am there near ev'ry night—or at Covent Garden to see Rich play Harlequin. Indeed there seem more spits and spats backstage at both these days, more brawls and angers."

"And the recent fire, which might've burnt down Drury Lane," added William.

Mr. Ralph's brows drew together above his bulbous nose. "True. If 'twere not for the great reservoir beneath the stage, the Theatre Royal would this moment be charred wood and memory."

"But what memory!" William bent toward his father. "Come to Drury Lane with me tomorrow night. See Mrs. Drumm and judge for yourself if she is not the most affecting creature."

Mr. Franklin pulled his lip. He turned. "What say you, Nick? Shall you go too?"

I thrilled. "O, please, sir."

"And you, Polly—if we may make your mother relent?"

Polly clapped her hands.

"Settled, then." Mr. Franklin started. "My word, 'tis Mr. Ralph to the life!"

His gaze was fixed on my slate.

I felt my cheeks burn. I had not wished him to know I did not add my sums. Too many times of late my pencil had strayed from the lessons it should write to sketches of Mrs. Stevenson dusting, or Polly, or Mr. Franklin's chamber with its high featherbed and shelves of books. Peter's dusky face might appear beneath my chalk, or the slow-rolling Thames with its docks and wherries and tall masts, seen from my back window. I had heretofore hid these fruits of idleness. For weeks I had been tormented by lurking shame as I struggled to school myself from them, so Mr.

Franklin might not think me a wastrel. Yet my miscreant fingers had sinned again, and I was found out.

"I . . . I am sorry, sir," stammered I.

"What? Sorry? For doing well?" He took my slate and held it out to the company. "Look you, Jimmy, is't not your very picture?"

Mr. Ralph peered. "Nay, this is an old man, a corpulent man, an ugly man." His frown devolved to a smile. "But yet 'tis I and no other. Ha, how well you have got my character: the noble, true lineaments and wise aspect. I pronounce it splendid and only wish t'were on a sheet of good paper that I might hang on the wall of my little room, to remind me how grateful the world should be for Jimmy Ralph."

Mr. Franklin gazed at me. "You have worked at this, Nick, and not told?"

I hung my head. "I thought you would not like me at it, sir."

"Not like? Why, 'tis very good."

"It is, Nick, it is!" exclaimed Polly. "Is't not, William?"

William sniffed. "Tolerable, for a boy."

Mr. Franklin pondered. "You shall have paper and pencils and pens," said he at last, "to try your hand when you may. It shall not be with you as with me, who had to battle for what he wished. I shall speed you on your course, though you must see to your lessons first."

A happy glow filled my chest. "O, sir, I shall read ev'ry book and add ev'ry sum!"

He laughed. "I believe you shall."

Mrs. Stevenson returned with Mr. Ralph's third toddy, which he tossed back as if 'twere water before lumbering off into the night, and soon all at Craven Street were abed, I in my little chamber upstairs, across the corridor from Mr. Franklin. Drury Lane! Tomorrow I should for the first time see a play. And the famous Mr. Garrick. And the pretty Mrs. Drumm. I should draw too, as much as I liked.

Murder? I scarce thought on murder. Surely I should see no murder at Drury Lane.

*IN WHICH I learn how to freeze a man to death,
and we set out for the play . . .*

I awoke next day, Saturday, with eager thoughts of the
evening to come. Dressing quickly I went straight to Mr.
Franklin's chamber. Rapping softly, I entered to discover
him naked by the open window playing upon his fiddle. I
had so often seen him at his air baths (as he called 'em)
that I paid little heed. For his part he never ceased his
lively tune but merely lifted a brow to bid good morn. As
was my habit I went to his desk to see what lessons he had
prepared: Addison's *Cato* lay open upon the polished
wood. I waited. To the fiddling the gentleman added a little
jig, which made him puff. He beamed. "How dancing
warms my blood! It gives me life; too, it helps keep that
cruel dame, Mrs. Gout, at bay."

I nodded, though whether his exertions truly mitigated
his gout was doubtful, for he still suffered aching toes. Yet
he had few other infirmities. We had celebrated his fifty-
second birthday on January 17, but he had the vigor of a
much younger man. Stout, he was powerfully built, about
five feet ten inches tall, with sturdy, squarish feet, hands
and head. His brow sloped to a great, bald dome. A fringe
of brownish hair jiggled as he pranced; he most often tied
this back with a plain black ribbon, though on occasion he
wore a wig, three of which rested on stands upon a shelf

next the painting of his little son Francis who had died of smallpox at four. By this stood a painting of his daughter, Sally, who remained in Philadelphia with his wife, Deborah. 'Twas a biting February morn, no fire laid, yet Mr. Franklin appeared to take no note of the chill. Putting by his fiddle, he drew on his dressing gown as my gaze slipped to the bow window fronting Craven Street. Beyond lay the broad Thames bending southwest, with a glimpse of Whitehall and Westminster Bridge. Flecks of morning sun licked the little wavelets where traffic already plied; London's chimney pots had not yet befouled the day.

How pretty a picture! Might I draw it?

As if reading my thought, Mr. Franklin joined me at his desk. He drew from his dressing gown pocket an octavo volume bound in sheepskin. "This was to replace your present diary, in which you write of our days together. Yet as I may at any time have another bound by Mr. Tisdale, this shall be for your drawing. Take it, lad." He pressed it into my hands. "What, no words?"

Feeling the soft, fine binding, I swallowed the lump in my throat. "I am very grateful, sir."

He patted my arm. "Show your gratitude by diligent work. *Labor omnia vincit.* You have talent. I should like to see you pursue it—if't please you."

"O, it shall please me greatly."

"Tut, 'tis what a father owes his son." At this a still, sad air enveloped him. I guessed its source. I had been conceived in America but was born on these shores, and I saw he thought on what he had discovered within months of returning to England: that my mother, whom he truly loved, had been cruelly poisoned. This had happened when I was but four; eight years had to pass before he uncovered the dread fact and brought the murderer to justice. The wound still ached in both our breasts—would it never heal? All this was our secret, which we spoke of to no other. It was, I believed, one reason William was cold to me. I was sorry for William's displeasure. I wished for harmony at Craven Street and had no intent to deprive the older son of his father's affections. Yet William's anger had other sources, for there lay betwixt him and Mr. Franklin some smouldering disagreement. I hoped t'would not one day fan into flame.

In any case I had been welcomed to Craven Street to be tutored by Mr. Franklin. In turn I served as his amanuensis and helped Mrs. Stevenson about the house. Ever I strove to prove worthy.

The day trotted slowly in spite of my longing for it to gallop to speed us to the play. Mr. Franklin set me some ciphering and reading. Too, he began my Latin, long promised. "Any gentleman must know it," averred he, tapping his brow. And so I was introduced to genitives, datives and ablatives, to which I tipped my cap though they proved unfriendly; and to words with genders, though why the body might be called male and the mind female I did not see. Yet I vowed to work as hard at this new task, as at anything the gentleman asked, and set to, gritting my teeth, knowing if I got my Latin I might then have my pencil and soft, new book to make pictures as I pleased. This seemed more than fair exchange.

After breakfast Mr. Franklin settled at his desk to scribble letters to Englishmen who might help him in Pennsylvania's cause, his quill scratching, whilst in his chair by the grate I read *Cato* and strove to make sense of *puer* and *puella*. Often and again I heard my tutor grumble and curse, yet I never minded. In truth I loved the quiet bustle of Number 7 Craven Street—Mrs. Stevenson rattling pans in her kitchen, William starting off to the Middle Temple, Polly humming, King looking in to receive his orders. Mr. Richard Jackson—Omniscient Jackson—stopped by to confer on the progress of the planned *Historical Review*. "This shall tell the truth of our side," proclaimed Mr. Franklin, though I saw by his fretwork brow that the road to truth went amongst hard ways.

Englishmen wished their colonies to be lickspittle lackeys. Mr. Franklin would never submit to that.

But near noon he threw up his hands and called me to his

workshop. Arising, I went with him into the upper corridor, where fingers of winter light played about the wooden floor polished to a fare-thee-well by my busy hands under Mrs. Stevenson's watchful eye. William's was the larger chamber across the way, mine a tiny afterthought of space next his at the back, the two blackamoor servants, Peter and King, residing in the attic above. Mr. Franklin pushed open his workshop door, beyond which lay the spacious chamber behind his own. My pulse quickened, for here stirred a heady air. My glance took in the wooly mammoth's knobby bone, which led Mr. Franklin to speculate that the earth had once been far colder than 'twas now, the little curls of metal upon the broad, pitted bench, which leapt to one of his glass rods when the rod was rubbed with a cloth, the electrical machine, several panes of sash glass armed with thin leaden plates supported at two inches distance on silk cords, which might kill a man by the charge stored in't. Mr. Franklin loved his pen but loved his workshop more, where he might potter and peer, seek and find, in an atmosphere of pure, disinterested philosophy.

He busied himself, for there was always some experiment afoot. He was reviled in his political aims, but in scientific circles he was greatly famed; followers from Scotland to Italy called themselves Franklinists. This was bitter irony, yet the gentleman wasted no spite on't. "William and I have been invited to perform experiments with John Hadley at Cambridge," said he as a brisk rap sounded. "Come."

Polly sailed in.

"Welcome, child," said Mr. Franklin. The pretty daughter sniffed at being called child, but he took no note. "Gather near. I am about to show what the wise men of Cambridge shall soon see. I have done't with spirits but wish now to try other means." Setting forth a large glass thermometer, he drew us close as he began to apply ether to its ball. "Now—blow!" We took turns puffing on the wetted ball—with the result that the quicksilver dropped so rapidly that in but a few moments it proclaimed 'twas near twenty degrees below freezing. Mr. Franklin beamed. "Do we shiver? Yet if you were the ball of the instrument you would be ice." He wore the delight that always accompanied some unveiling of Nature's secrets. "This proves the possibility of freezing a man to death on a warm summer's day if he were to stand in a passage through which the wind blew briskly and were wet frequently with ether. Who has not sucked his finger to see which way the wind blew and found one side grow cold? *Ab uno disce omnes*—from one example we discover the rest. But I hear your mother calling."

Polly stamped her foot. "O . . . !" She marched sullenly out.

Mr. Franklin's eyes fell upon me with a soft, sly gleam that said more was abrewing. He closed the door. "And so, Nick, shall I show you what else I think on?"

"Please, do."

Eagerly he drew a volume of Dr. Johnson's *Dictionary* from a shelf. "Copy this, then, if you please." Setting before me a quarter sheet of foolscap, a pen, a pot of ink, he pointed to a passage.

Though puzzled, I writ as bid, in my best hand:

GRUBSTREET. Originally the name of a street in Moorfields in London, much inhabited by writers of small histories, dictionaries and temporary poems; whence any mean production is called: grubstreet.

"Now," said he when I was done, blotting the ink, "this shall join its fellows." Winking, he drew forth a metal box from beneath the workbench and, slipping the paper in't, shook the box vigorously before spilling its contents upon the bench. This proved many such little squares of foolscap, all alike to my eye and containing the same words I had set down. The gentleman cocked his head. "Find yours."

"Why . . . at once." Yet though I sorted judiciously amongst the dozen or so samples, turning all up, after some

moments of scrutiny I could not distinguish my effort
though I had just writ it. "All look much the same," mumbled I, "all in well-formed letters . . ." I chose one likely
sample. "Might it be this?"

"Mr. Strahan writ that."

I took up another. "This?"

"Mrs. Stevenson's. Can you not see her in't?"

I snatched up another. "This, then, surely."

"You err again. That is Dr. Fothergill's."

"Show me mine, sir."

" 'Tis this."

I peered at the paper he held out. "You are right."

"How do you know?"

"Why . . . because you say so. In truth, I do not know.
How may you tell?"

"You recall my work with fingerprints?"

I nodded. Mr. Franklin had learnt from his early years in
his brother's print shop in Boston, where hands were often
smudged with ink and left their marks in many places, that
each person's fingertips had their own design of tiny curv-
ing lines and small scars, unique to that person. Indeed,
this knowledge had helped him to unmask my mother's
murderer.

"I have made a new discovery," announced he with the
same delight with which he had shown his ether experiment, "that handwriting bespeaks a person's character."

"But we write all alike," protested I, "Are we not taught
to?"

He shook his head. "Many men ride, but none sit a horse
just alike. Bend near . . . look close. See you, the forming
of letters? Observe Mrs. Stevenson's: this fat, solid *o,* and
the loop at the top of the *d* and *t,* the swash of *g* and *y,*
likewise generous yet closed. Can you not read our good
landlady in 'em? There lurks not a bone of deception in
her. There is a simplicity about her which does not admit
of new ideas. Does not her writing bespeak these qualities?"

"I confess, now you point it out, it seems to. And, now I look close, I see that hers is different from this."

"And whose is that?"

"Why . . ."

"Come, concentrate your attentions." His head was near mine as we peered, I frowning, he gently urging. And truly I began to glimpse a person emerge from the writing, as a figure hidden amongst a thicket, at first dimly perceived but growing more distinct. I sensed some impetuosity in the trunks and branches of letters, hurriedly slanted as Mrs. Stevenson's were not. And stubbornness in the grinding of pen upon paper. Some leafy flourishes bespoke pride and pretension. The march of letters said the penman had intelligence, yet some sharp points of the ascenders suggested anger.

" 'Tis William's," said I of a sudden.

"Excellent! Try this."

'Twas but a moment to discover Polly.

My teacher beamed. "You grow expert. Indeed, see her bright, eager character in the sharply formed *r*'s and *t*'s. This is Dr. Fothergill." The sober Scots physician had formed a dry march of precise little letters, like soldiers in a line. After a few more such samples Mr. Franklin gathered the papers and shut the box. "Thus we learn that each person's handwriting is formed in subtle ways by his character; 'tis a sort of mirror. Have I not just proved that an alert examiner might say who writ some missive though the thing be not signed?" He waved a hand. "Yet, is this of use? The Cambridge fellows would proclaim me mad to spend time on't." A sigh. "Still I may perhaps some day write of it, when the Penns have been brought to heel." He led me to the door. "But let us talk on the play. What shall it be? Shakespeare? We have neglected to inquire. Poor James Ralph—I am sorry David Garrick does not see merit in his work, but I do not envy the actor, importuned, and hated when he must say nay. The damned Penns say nay to me. Fie on 'em! How their obstinacy sets me aboil! Leave that. I pray Mrs. Stevenson has prepared some tasty restorative." He hung an arm about my shoulder. "Let us lay seige to a cold joint, eh?"

5:00 P.M. came round at last, time to make ready for the play. " 'Tis to be a new thing, by Mrs. Drumm's husband," informed William, looking in on his way to his chamber.

Mr. Franklin had spent his afternoon with the Honest Whigs at St. Paul's Coffeehouse, whilst in Craven Street— though I would have wished to be with him—I had helped air bedding and sketched between the hanging and bringing in of sheets a tolerable portrait of our landlady at her pastryboard. The gentleman peered up from pulling on new white stockings. "Shall we then see the latest fashion in plays? I pray 'tis half so well-wearing as the Bard." William went to dress whilst his father put on a fine blue velvet suit and waistcoat, and his best wig, which I myself had powdered. "Am I not a peacock?" said he, glancing at himself in his glass. "Yet damned if I do not better like my plain brown stuff." I had early slipped into my good suit, which Mrs. Stevenson and Polly had run up for me, peering at my figure some half dozen times in this same tall glass. I had scrutinized my face too, discovering in it no particular distinction: straight brown hair, wide-set eyes, a mere nose and tolerable mouth, placed upon a body as sturdy as Mr. Franklin's. Yet in my black polished shoes I thought 'twould be no bad thing to be a gentleman with servants and a coach at my beck, and I practiced imperious waves to summon 'em. I did not tell Mr. Franklin of my vanity.

At ten minutes past the hour Peter brought round the gentleman's coach, and he, William, and I descended to it—without Polly. Mrs. Stevenson had stood firm against Mr. Franklin's strongest blandishments, so her daughter now wrung her hands in her bedchamber, whilst our landlady stood like Cerberus at the gates, to prevent her escaping. I felt sorry for Polly. Tomorrow I should tell her all I saw.

We set off in biting air, up Craven Street to the bustling Strand, where we turned right toward Temple Bar. A brief rain had fallen; the cobbles glistened, and the Westminster air had been freshened of its stench of foul drains and coalfires. Shopkeepers—confectioners, linen drapers, apothecaries—were drawing shutters over mullioned windows, yet much traffic still abounded: gigs and drays bumping wheels, beggars and lords jostling elbows, deacons with their eyes on God and cutpurses with theirs on handbags and lace. London was a perilous city. Mr. Franklin kept a cudgel by the seat of his coach in case of attack.

Nonetheless I always liked to travel with him, to the broad Strand, to the narrow alleys round St. Paul's, to the grand houses of the squares. London was the workshop of life. "Learn of her, Nick," Mr. Franklin adjured, "the largest, finest, maddest city in Europe." Obeying my master, I paid close heed.

Our journey was not long. Near Somerset House we turned left into Catherine Street and thence to Bridges Street hard by Covent Garden. Here William called Peter to draw up. "The passage to the theater is close by," said he, debouching, and I followed him amongst a line of carriages, most grander than ours, spilling a stream of tricorn hats, lace collars, and fine satin dresses flowing north. Mr. Franklin clambered out with the aid of his bamboo. Round his neck hung a quizzing glass, all the fashion. Many men peered haughtily through 'em as if at toads in their gardens, but Mr. Franklin was never haughty. Yet he must have his glass: "One never knows when a thing may require close examining."

"Ben!" boomed out a familiar voice, and James Ralph, rusty as ever and as genially disheveled, lumbered up. Puffing, he pounded backs with a raging cheer, a spark in his squinched blackcurrant eyes: a play drew near! "And so you are arrived." Grasping elbows, he urged us forth. "Come! Gird yourself for battle!"

Battle it proved, where we must struggle to gain ground in the crush of jostling ladies and gentlemen flowing into the narrow way to the theater. Over the tops of heads I glimpsed a grand facade lit by dying light: brick and stone-

work and a course of windows blinking back the setting
orange sun. "The King's House," informed Mr. Ralph, "designed by Wren himself. On this site Nell Gwyn stole King
Charles' heart." I wished to ask of this Nell Gwyn but lost
my breath to a stout gentleman's elbow, which sharply
jabbed my chest. Though likewise pummeled, Mr. Ralph
seemed to revel in the fray, slashing his way through as he
pointed out who and what. "Make way, you dogs!" There
were other young fellows of the Inns of Court, whom William greeted warmly. Rakes and gallants strutted in the
finest plumage, sneering betwixt their ruffled necks and
coxcomb periwigs. There fluttered a covey of half a dozen
women grasping small octavo volumes. " 'Shakespeare's
Ladies,' " told Mr. Ralph, "who join to promote the playing
of their god. How they cluck when he is eschewed for some
mere mortal!" Furtive figures lurked too, with sly, watching eyes—plunderers of pockets, and I prayed Mr. Franklin
kept his purse close. Thick in this brew stirred women with
much paint upon their faces and near naked bosoms. They
offered men coy looks and lewd smiles, yet there was
something sad about 'em too. "Punks, fireships, and viz-
ard-masks . . ." drawled Mr. Ralph, brushing the hand of
one such from his sleeve. "Nay, Miss Blogg, I shall partake
of none of you tonight." He drew us quickly past, but I
could not help glancing back at the lost, bitter look on this
dismissed woman's face, though she at once set upon another man. How young she appeared beneath her paint!
Yet ancient history was writ in her eyes; she was of an old,
old tribe. Pity flooded me, and I thought on my own young
life, near doomed but for Mr. Franklin's saving. Would
anyone save her?

Mr. Franklin too peered at the woman. "You know her,
Jimmy?"

"Her ilk. Any man who courts the theater knows 'em.
Their story is much the same: actresses—or wish'd to be.
Some, like Miss Blogg, found early success; she was took
on by Rich at Covent Garden, to sing and dance and show
her figure, for she was pretty. Here now, sir, let us pass! Yet

she possessed no notable talent, one o' the castoff daughters of London, who spawns 'em in back rooms, births 'em in hovels, and discards 'em in alleys. 'Tis a mire! She swam to the surface for some brief time, the rakes dove after and wooed her, but she found no gentleman lover, no protector; thus she sinks. Soon she will drown, and there's an end." Mr. Ralph's eyes grew bright. "Ho, sirs, our goal is near!" He lunged through an opening in the crowd.

Indeed we were close enough to read the large white playbill:

At the
THEATRE ROYAL in Drury Lane
on Saturday the 13th of February
will be performed:
A LORD AND NO LORD
a new play
by *MR. ABEL DRUMM* . . .

More was given: the afterpiece (*Harlequin Necromancer*) and musical interludes: dancing, songs, jugglers. I thrilled. The throng was thickest here, for the most part merry and tolerant of the press—but not all wore smiles. A lean, hawk-nosed man, dressed in satin and full-bottomed wig, stood nearby frowning and muttering amidst a circle of dour, tutting gentlemen, like judges at Westminster assizes.

Mr. Ralph leered at 'em. "Oho, Lord Methuen, here? The play will never please him. Mayhap he will give Garrick something that is not printed on his playbill."

"Of what sort?" inquired Mr. Franklin.

Mr. Ralph lowered his voice. "Because old Methuen has bedded more doxies than any man in London—chambermaids and the daughters and wives of peers. O, he is hot! 'Tis said in the privacy of gentleman's clubs that he must bathe in some woman's charms at least twice a day to cool his fires. Drumm has put Methuen's life upon the stage, that is the rumor. In this Drumm is a fool, for such things, however true, must never be spoke above a whisper; yet he may give us sport. Shall Methuen allow the play be played? That is what we shall see." He chortled. "Life shall take aim against Art."

I glanced at Lord Methuen, lean and sharp-featured. Danger seemed to smoulder in his deep-set eyes, which made me shudder, but I soon forgot him, for a barking voice began to assault our ears. Turning, I saw at the very front of the theater a pair of arms uplifted and a face even more outraged than Lord Methuen's. Eyes flashed hotly in it. Coming nearer, we saw a man stretched on tiptoe upon a box, thin and raging, his hair in wild disarray, his mouth spitting:

". . . Satan does not keep any fitter school to teach his desire and bring men and women to the snare of concupiscence and filthy lusts of wicked whoredom than this temple of sin called playhouse! David Garrick is the devil's tool! He seduces you to tarry at vain idolatry two or three hours when you will not abide one hour at a sermon? Shame! Turn away! Here you learn but to deceive your wives and husbands, to flatter, betray, lie, swear, poison, murder . . ."

He ranted on. "Damn all Methodists," muttered Mr. Ralph as if unswayed, but I was transfixed. The preacher's fervid, accusing look momentarily fixed upon me with such disgust that I was struck breathless before it licked like flame to another face. Was I indeed a wicked boy, as Mrs. Inch had told me in my captivity? Feeling a hand upon my shoulder, I glanced up to find Mr. Franklin peering down. "We do nothing for which we need feel shame, lad." I nodded and forced a smile though I could not entirely rid myself of doubt. " 'Tis an age of factions," sighed the gentleman as he led me by.

"This one dangerous to Garrick," murmured Mr. Ralph over his shoulder, "if't find favor in the Lord Chamberlain's ear."

We were accosted by one more incident before we passed into the doors. There came a rough jostling at my elbow; then a small, crabbed man with a look as sour as gooseberries shot out a hand to thrust a piece of paper at Mr. Franklin. "Here, sir, take't and learn of truth," snarled he out of a lopsided mouth with blackened teeth. He wore a patchy coat over a bottle-green waistcoat. Sprigs of dun-colored hair stuck out from under a dingy wig. His yellow-ish stare startled me, peering, as his reeking breath raked my face. Then he was off, jerking another broadside from his sheaf to wave in another man's view.

Mr. Franklin watched him go. "Busy, busy . . ."

"Only some worm of Grub Street," said William. "Hundreds spew. Pay no heed."

"Nay, I will read me this. " 'Tis about Garrick." Mr. Franklin adjusted his spectacles. "Hum: '. . . a sly tyrant . . . authors discouraged . . . actors starved . . . Shakespeare lacerated . . . true art degraded by mincing, mangling, mutilating, momacking, and castrating into farces, drolls, and mock operas . . .' The fellow makes a kind of music."

Mr. Ralph snatched the paper. "I might make better—or worse—if I chose." He flung the paper away. "Come, Garrick's temple of sin awaits." He led us into the playhouse.

❦ 3 ❦

IN WHICH a play is done to death—
and so is a man . . .

Such crowding! Such a press within! The stench of bodies, the reek of scents, the odor of tobacco, and a hubbub as of Bedlam: wriggling, poking, and crying out, ladies complaining of hats and parasols lost and dresses crushed, gentlemen protesting their honors and swearing they would not come to the playhouse again. Mr. Ralph had previously purchased tickets at Glendinning's in Bedford Street, so we need not stop to buy 'em. Mounting three short steps, we arrived at an anteroom some ten feet wide and twenty long, a sort of staging point whence people took stairs up or down, depending on where they should sit. Ways rose at right and left. "They ascend to the galleries," shouted Mr. Ralph above the din. Ahead lay a wide door through which I but imperfectly glimpsed the stage. "One entrance to the pit," cried Mr. Ralph. "We shall take another way." Beside the pair of mounting stairs were a pair going down. Our guide led—or rather dragged—us to the right hand one of these and, descending where we were near tumbled by those pressing behind, we arrived at a narrow corridor, dim-lit by candles in sconces. "The pit passage," said Mr. Ralph. We turned left. Thirty or so feet along we turned left once more.

The heart of the theater at last. Mr. Ralph gave over our tickets to the doorkeeper, and we went in.

My heart beat fast, and a hotness flamed my cheeks, though I could at first obtain no very clear sense of the playhouse because so many people crowded round me. I noted the great ceiling far above, painted in ornate designs, the babble of voices augmenting to a grander, rounder roar. As those about us scurried to likely vantages, I made out the pit: a dozen rows of fixed wooden benches set before the stage. Outside had been a sign: Ladies May Send Their Servants to Hold Places, and indeed I saw several liveried men giving up seats to their mistresses, who settled like birds upon nests. Mr. Ralph led us to his favorite spot: the fourth row back, near the center. Sinking down with a great, happy sigh, he fanned his face with a little book like those Shakespeare's Ladies had held, *As You Like It*. Yet things were not yet as he liked, for a grimace of displeasure twisted his lips. His seat proved unsatisfactory, and he glared at the gentleman next him as at some usurper and with a disgruntled growling began to edge upon this man, first a twitch, then a nudge. The man was small and thin, and Mr. Ralph's sturdy bottom crept inexorably until the man was displaced by fits and starts and tiny protesting yelps three feet to the left, we following along the bench like some segmented worm. Only when he had achieved the exact center of the playhouse did Mr. Ralph beam with unalloyed pleasure. He spread his arms. "Do you recall it, Ben? O, it has been refurbished with new paint and gilt, but 'tis the same old playhouse we were wont to come to thirty years ago."

"I do recall," smiled Mr. Franklin, "though in younger days we sat much higher."

Mr. Ralph rolled his rheumy eyes. "The gallery! What jolly hours there!"

For my part I was happy to be anywhere in this lively scene. Might I remember all to draw it tomorrow in my book? Mr. Ralph sat to our left, William next him, then Mr. Franklin and I. The benches of the pit gently curved to

follow the curved front of the stage, a broad, raised plat-
form directly before us, at the back of which hung a green
curtain. Indeed there was much green everywhere,
amongst the white paint and gilt. Two pairs of green doors
opened on either side the stage. Box seats also framed the
stage, stretching along the sides of the pit. There the quality perched, lords and ladies, dukes, earls, in their finery
and white wigs, women powdered and patched, gentlemen
peering through their glasses, all in great conviviality as
they gazed down with genial disdain. One face stood out,
in a box quite near the stage: Lord Methuen amongst his
dour company. He sat far back, but I could see black
displeasure stamped upon his brow. Yet I paid him little
mind, for there was much to note. Twisting round, I craned
my neck to take in the two galleries, one above the other.
Faces were visible here too, commoner, coarser: apprentices, students, chandlers, costermongers, shop assistants,
in more rowdy animation than their betters, with a rawer
cheer. What hearty fellows! I glimpsed Peter far up in the
footman's gallery, where servants might sit without pay-
ing—but 'twas another face that most caught my eye, that
of the curmudgeon who had thrust his pamphlet upon Mr.
Franklin. Such a look! He sat at the very front of the first
gallery like some rock eyeing his supper.

I puzzled. If he so despised David Garrick, why come to
the playhouse?

No matter. Wishing to imitate Mr. Franklin's keen obser-
vation. I stayed alert to ev'rything. At the front of the pit
a dozen or so musicians played the First, Second, and
Third Musics, as Mr. Ralph called 'em, airs to divert the
throng; yet these were near drowned by a great echoing
murmur, fans snapping, fellows busily milling, gallants
boasting. Whores plied their trade, wheedling, teasing, displaying their breasts as if flesh went for a penny the pound,
and I saw that the theater provided more than plays and
acting. There were fruit-sellers too, Moll and Bette. One
cried her wares near, and Mr. Franklin purchased me an
orange, wondrously juicy. Hanging from the ceiling were

six many-candled lusters that shed a warm glow over all, so the very farthest gallery seat might be seen equally well as the stage. All London, seemed to be here. Even George II might be if he chose. Mr. Ralph pointed to His Majesty's box, stamped with the royal arms. He sneered. "Empty. The Hanoverian does not deign to grace us tonight. O, why may not Englishmen have an English king?"

"May as well ask why Englishmen may not have justice," rejoined Mr. Franklin.

As for William, he said little but leant forward, his eyes bright, his heart no doubt beating for Mrs. Drumm. I prayed no woman should ever paint so foolish a grimace on my face.

Mr. Ralph seemed to have knowledge of everyone and made many greetings and said who was who. A blunt-faced, thick-lipped man pushed through the door by which we had come. "Oliver Goldsmith," informed our guide, "a man of sense." A stout old fellow stumped in the opposite door, ugly, his face scarred by scrofula. "And that is Dr. Johnson, Garrick's friend. You keep his *Dictionary* in your bed chamber, I believe."

"Nay, it resides in my workshop now."

Mr. Ralph pointed out handsome Lord Edmund Calverly ("in his same box ev'ry night . . ."), Horace Walpole ("up from Strawberry Hill . . ."), Tobias Smollett (*"Roderick Random* lampooned Garrick, but he and Smollett are great friends now . . ."), Lady Linacre, an icy beauty ("seen as much in her box as Lord Edmund Calverly in his—and both without their spouses . . .").

"But, here is some wonder," murmured Mr. Franklin amidst this commentary, "being blind, why comes *this* gentleman to the playhouse?" Blind gave the clue that chilled me. I turned, and there stood John Fielding, principal magistrate for Westminster.

At sight of the great, hulking man I felt the crawling ill-ease I always felt in his presence. Mr. Franklin had befriended him when he looked into the murder of my printing master, Ebenezer Inch, and though Fielding was indeed

stone blind—and had been so since eighteen—he was
feared by all criminal London. Huge, triple-chinned, his
great squashed head resting upon a massive body, he stood
in the door carrying his stout staff of office like a cudgel.
He cocked his head, he was alert, and though his
squinched little eyes saw nothing, he took in much by his
giant ears, like grotesquely curled shells poking out from
his shaggy wig. Those ears seemed capable of plucking bad
thoughts from even a small boy's brain and sending that
boy to Fleet Prison.

Such was his effect on me.

Justice Fielding's indispensable assistant was Mr. Joshua
Brogden, a lively, hopping little fellow who stood by his
side, the chirping cricket-man next the imperious toad.
Seeing Mr. Franklin, Mr. Brogden whispered in one of the
justice's great ears. The ear quivered; there came a
brusque nod, and Mr. Brogden prodded his charge our way,
along the bench. With a great, stertorous wheezing he sank
down next me. His fat hand reached unerringly. It felt of
my face. "Mr. Franklin's boy. I know it be."

"Y-yes, sir."

He clamped upon the back of my neck. "And are you
good? Akeeping to the straight and narrow?"

"O, v-very straight, sir. V-very narrow."

He let go. "See it do not topple you to perdition." He
wobbled his three chins in greeting. "Mr. Franklin, sir."

"Your servant, Mr. Fielding. How d'ye do, Mr. Brogden?
But I am surprised to see you here."

The justice's three chins lifted. "Pray, why? Because I
am come to watch the play?"

"Why—"

"Come, speak your mind! I have no eyes to see it, is that
it, sir? I thought some such." Fielding emitted a contemp-
tuous Pah! "These damned dead orbs do not prevent me
bringing criminals to justice. The Blind Beak is dreaded all
over London. Should blindness then stop my pleasure at a
play? Why, 'tis a great advantage. I listen; I take in the
words of the author, which many fools do not. Too, the

actress of a pretty part is in my mind never less than the perfect picture of what she should be. Nor is a hero."

"Your ears then are your eyes."

"My ears are my ears. 'Tis my *imagination* that is my eyes, for it makes the proper picture of what should be onstage: faces, costumes, effects which Art could never produce. Why, I see the play better than any sighted fellow."

Mr. Ralph bent toward him. "Bravo, Mr. Fielding! Why, I may try shutting my eyes tonight. I have long been blind to this simple means of amending the faults of the theater." He struck his knee. "I am fixed on't! I shall try me this, and if the loss of sight improve the play I may stop up my ears to make it better still."

Justice Fielding glowered at this.

"You are then a frequenter of Drury Lane, Mr. Fielding?" interposed Mr. Franklin.

"Not as I might wish. Knavery steals my time. I have spent more hours in the playhouse to put down riots than to hear a play, and the pleasure of even this night is allied to business."

"O?"

"David Garrick has some trouble, for which he wants my aid."

"What trouble?" asked Mr. Franklin, but no answer came, for at that moment the bill of fare commenced.

The orchestra ceased playing. This signaled a new air, a settling and turning of attention from greeting and gossip to two old gentlemen in forest green who wobbled onstage to light the candle sconces at its sides, the oil lamps at its front. "Bravo, old Dick!" called a voice, at which one of these tottering fellows made a grotesque half-bow. Chairs now sat at the sides of the stage, dandies of the town lounging in 'em with legs outstretched as if at home by a fire. A pair of broad-shouldered, glowering brutes marched out to fix themselves, arms crossed, by the iron grillework at either side the stage. "Garrick's guards," whispered Mr. Ralph, "in case of riot."

I felt a thrill. Mr. Franklin pulled his watch from his waistcoat pocket. "Six o'clock." He snapped the lid. "Time for what we have awaited."

"Come!" called voices, at which a woman in fine dress swept from the left stage door. She was strong-built with a fiery complexion, her deep purple gown swirling as she walked. Snapping her fan, she nodded to the lounging gallants, who seemed to know her well—"Hallo, Kit! How're ye, Mrs. Clive?"—then bowed to the quality in the boxes, who nodded back. Hands on hips, she strutted proud as a peacock to the front of the stage and gazed upon us in the pit as if we were sheep in want of a shepherdess.

All applauded, Mr. Ralph most vigorously.

This woman lifted her saucy gaze to the galleries, which chirped clamoring approval.

Composing herself, she assumed a tragic air and raised a white arm, flesh trembling on its underside. All grew still. Her lidded gaze bade us listen.

Mr. Ralph leant near. "Remember, Ben? First the prologue—though none so fine as I might write?"

This prologue proved a poem of some thirty or forty lines delivered in a sharp, ringing voice, with thrilling modulations. It told something of what we were to see: a new play by a new playwright, Mr. Drumm, heretofore known to patrons of Drury Lane only as actor, a moral story by which we might be instructed in virtue, warned of vice, yet diverted along the way. Begging our indulgence, it concluded:

". . . the Drama's law the Drama's patrons give,
And we, who live to please, must please to live."

Mrs. Clive smiled; her eyes flashed, she snapped her fan and withdrew to much applause.

At once the green curtain lifted, to show that only half the stage had heretofore been visible. The very picture of a drawing room in a grand country house now came to view: pillars and paintings and sofas and chairs and a writing desk and fine cherrywood spinet. Through a window a painted cow ate painted grass. Admiration took my breath, and I thought again on my sketchbook: might I draw this? More, might I someday work in a playhouse to fashion such scenes of my own?

The *dramatis personae* immediately arrived to animate the scene: Lord and Lady Brough and a knowing, compliant manservant named Wink and a maid named Celia and an old gentleman, Mr. King, and his young daughter Araminta, who possessed both charm and lively wit. Too, a friend of Lady Brough's newly arrived from London, Mrs. Stiles, played by that same woman, Mrs. Clive, who had delivered the prologue. The upshot of the story was that old Brough was a rake and a libertine, ever at stratagems to deceive his good, long-suffering wife. His latest passion was to bed Miss King, for whom he was mad, but this sweet Araminta was also pursued by Tom Pitcher, a likely young gentleman just commissioned in the army. The action revolved around a plan to deliver old Brough his comeuppance. In this Mrs. Stiles took the central role, dressing as a man ("Many plays contain such 'breeches parts,' " whispered Mr. Ralph). Garbed thus, and with a false moustache which she was ever atwisting, she pretended to be Mr. Bunty, a sly go-between, who assured my lord he might have Araminta—but only if he paid through the nose. Old Brough was tight-fisted, and much business was made of wringing coin from him. All were drawn into the plot, even Araminta, who led Brough a frantic chase whilst the rest laughed behind their hands.

Between acts the green curtain never descended. Master Holland and Miss Armstrong ("just returned from a tour of the continent!") danced a rigadoon ("never performed before!") whilst behind them in plain view the change of scene was made: the tall drawing room windows and pilasters slid aside, furniture borne off by scurrying green-costumed minions, the back wall of the country house, its cow and grass, vanishing behind a room with a view of St. Paul's, the music of the dance never quite masking a shuffling of feet and scrape of wood and creak of winches and a cry that a toe had near been crushed. I hardly blinked for staring.

Act 2 carried the sly plot further. At its close, juggling twins burst out, Biff and Baff, whose balls and bats flew perilously close to the heads of the men who changed the scene once more. More patrons crowded into the theater. ("Half price after the second act of the main piece," whispered William.) Act 3 was for a time spoilt by ranting, which proved the Methodist we had seen outside, crying against sin, but he was soon carried out, and the play went on. The last act took place at an inn on the Great North Road, where Lord Brough planned to bed his prize but was instead delivered the final blow that brought him low. He cursed, he railed, he bethought himself. Humbled, he acknowledged the goodness of his wife and the error of his ways, repenting whilst in quadruple symmetry he and Lady Brough, and Araminta and her Tom, and Mr. King and Mrs. Stiles, and even Mr. Wink and the maid Celia, who had coyly grappled throughout, embraced and sailed into the wings on courses of wedded bliss.

There came applause, but not the heartiest that might be. There sounded, too, some braying from the gallery that warned of worse to come.

As for me, my first night at the playhouse filled me with many thoughts and feelings. The audience surprised me, for having paid to see and hear a play it had been neither silent nor polite. Rude fellows carried on converse right through, as if the curtain had never gone up. Others bantered with whores. Still others shouted out praise or abuse any time they liked, and three or four times fights near broke out over the merit of a performance or scene or the cut of a gown. Many amongst the quality protested this and cried for quiet, but the gallery hissed 'em, and there was much grumbling on both sides. I glanced sometime at the stage box where Lord Methuen sat amongst his cronies.

Tucked well back, he grew more empurpled as the play went on, as if his face should burst with fury. Yet though his companions glowered as grim as deacons, none ever made protest. The pit grew so restive at the close of act 2, a party of rakes practicing cock-a-doodle-dos, that Justice Fielding stood to face 'em. At this the mischief-makers blanched, and whispers arose from ev'ry quarter, "The Blind Beak!" Such was the power of the sightless man that for full three minutes there came no interruption of the play.

Yet the restlessness resumed, though the actors took it as if they were not shouted at, drowned out, or ignored. When the outstretched legs of the dandies got in their way they stepped over or nimbly danced round 'em. Orange peels flew sometimes, halfpennies, once a lady's slipper, which an indignant voice cried out to have back; yet no missile struck its mark, for the actors ducked and dodged without losing a single line. Plainly the Drury Lane audience expressed its views in lively fashion.

Yet the sense of the play could be got—what there was of't. The acting was by far the finest part, gold made of dross. David Garrick himself played Lord Brough, and I, who knew little of acting, saw at once why he was so praised. Whilst he was on the stage there were few interruptions from the playhouse. Mr. Franklin had in his workshop glass rods which, when rubbed, drew metal filings to 'em. Garrick was like that: he drew one's gaze, making one strain to catch the smallest word. His appearance was not imposing—indeed he was rather short—yet he moved with such grace that one hardly noted his body. And, though his full, round face could not be called handsome, an alertness radiated from it. His rich, warm voice could ring changes on a syllable. And his eyes: I had heard of 'em; now I saw flashing dark orbs beneath commanding brows—what remarkable expression! They drew one to 'em, as if the whole of Drury Lane were reflected in 'em. We lived more fully by grace of those eyes.

I glanced at Mr. Ralph. An entranced smile played about

his lips, and I understood why he was mad for the theater. Hate David Garrick—but love the actor upon his stage. Poor Polly, to've missed it all.

The other players were good, though none with Garrick's magic. Mrs. Clive was clever as Mrs. Stiles (she was clearly a great favorite). Mr. Woodward enacted old Mr. King. Mrs. Pritchard played Lady Brough. Mr. Havard was Tom Pitcher, and Miss Prouty was the maid. As for Lucy Drumm, who had so captivated William, she played Araminta King. William prodded his father at her very first stepping upon the stage and Mr. Franklin nodded to say he took note. From then on he observed her as he might observe some phenomenon of nature, with a judicious little smile that said he should see what to make of her. The young woman was indeed pretty: fine-boned and delicate, with a rose-pink complexion that seemed to owe nothing to art. She moved gracefully, too, and portrayed convincingly the innocent side of her character. Yet Araminta had to show wit as well, in bantering scenes. This Mrs. Drumm did less aptly, with some strain. Irony seemed not to suit her; she seemed rarely to know what was meant to be clever in her lines. The result was awkward, though she was otherwise fresh and charming. Glancing aside, I glimpsed a look of moony entrancement on William's face, but a twitching about Mr. Ralph's full lips said he did not care for Mrs. Drumm. I could not tell what Mr. Franklin thought.

The manservant Wink was done by the playwright himself, Abel Drumm, a dark, lithe man who could screw his face into a livid leer. He hopped and skittered and sneered as he helped to bring his master low, yet he often left off his part to peer anxiously into boxes, pit and gallery, to see how we took it all. Indeed he had much at stake: his performance, his wife's, the very play itself.

And what of the play? Alas, it fared ill that night and died aborning. The first hint of miscarriage was the lukewarm clapping at the end, though one gathering of men in the pit applauded hard and cried how they had loved it. I was glad some did, 'til Mr. Ralph whispered with a rolling of eyes, "Drumm's claque, paid to cheer. Many playwrights hire praise."

David Garrick stepped onstage, still in Lord Brough's wig and breeches. Smiling, he raised his hands and delivered a short, rhymed epilogue, which hoped the play had both pleased and edified us. There was grumbling at this but no outright mutiny, Garrick's lively face beaming as if we gave unalloyed approbation. He then proceeded to announce the following night's bill, a repeat *A Lord and No Lord*.

At this a chorus of "Nos!" burst forth, so loud that Garrick started.

Yet not all in the theater joined in, and the actor kept his smile: "Come, ladies, gentlemen, I say tomorrow night shall be played Mr. Drumm's excellent new play, followed by . . ."

"We shall not have *A Lord and No Lord!*" came a voice from behind.

Garrick faltered. "Why, 'tis an excellent play, and . . ."

"No *Lord!*"

At this a chant of "No *Lord!*" began, picked up by many in the audience, amongst 'em the braying fellows Justice Fielding had earlier silenced, who seemed to look upon this as some new diversion. It became a drumbeat of sound, though not unanimous. William protested: "Let Garrick speak! We shall have the play!" as did some others, but they were few. The crying out clearly had not been spontaneous. It had issued from the gallery, and I turned and peered up, my gaze at once lighting on the man who had thrust the pamphlet attacking Garrick into Mr. Franklin's hands. I was sure it had been his voice which had first denied the play. Now he stood waving his fists and leading the chant with a look of livid hatred. He was ably seconded by strong-voiced fellows around him: "No *Lord* . . . no *Lord!*" They made most vigorous cavil but found avid seconds in Lord Methuen's box, his dour companions now on their feet, ashouting likewise, though their looks askance at the gallery said they were not pleased to be led from there; plainly they had meant to begin the attack.

Yet they cried out strong, and there was for a time war between 'em and the gallery as to who might protest the loudest. A third party was made up of Abel Drumm's claque and William and others who wished to preserve the play, but these were scattered and easily drowned out, and I felt doom gather about *A Lord and No Lord.*

Justice Fielding rumbled, " 'Twas not so very good a play."

And then Mr. Ralph's voice too began to cry it down. I looked past Mr. Franklin. A species of blood-lust twisted his friend's mottled old features so that I hardly knew him. At his joining in, William sank to sullen silence. The cries became a torrent that sickened me. Reason did not abide here, but madness that took joy in tearing down.

"The mob . . ." murmured Mr. Franklin at my side. He sat very still, hands upon his knees, palely grim, his gaze behind his little squarish lenses fixed on Garrick, who kept his coaxing smile, with gestures of supplication, as if sensible men might thus be quieted to deliberation. Did not the actor see it was too late? Mr. Franklin's eyes shifted to the guards posted at either side the stage, fear writ white on their faces. He then looked toward Lord Methuen's box, my lord himself just visible behind his chanting friends. I peered there too, to see the thin, dark man wearing a mask of righteous satisfaction—yet his gaze sometime flicked to the gang in the gallery, at which an expression of puzzlement suffused his face: who had hired this raucous band?

Mr. Franklin also turned to look up into the gallery. The pamphlet man swayed and leant dangerously far over the railing, continuing to shout with fierce fixity of purpose. Spittle stood out on his lips; if he were paid to do his job 'twas work he loved.

At last Garrick yielded. His nodding said so. His hands did too, sinking by his sides. Seeing this, the enemies of the play began to quiet. "As we have said, we live to please," the actor's voice rang over the lessening din, "and as Mr.

Drumm's play pleases you not, Drury Lane shall not suffer it to be played again. Therefore we shall give tomorrow night *The Fatal Marriage, or, The Innocent Adultery*, by Mr. Southerne, which has much delighted you in the past." Cheers greeted this, though William grumbled. Garrick waggled a finger. "Let it not be said that David Garrick denies the voice of opinion. I and Mrs. Cibber, whom you much love, shall, if she is recovered from her distemper, play the mainpiece. Afterward, Mrs. Clive and I shall give you *Catherine and Petruchio*—Shakespeare." This pleased even more. "But that is tomorrow." Garrick affected an easy brightness. "More remains tonight, music and magic. Come!" He gestured (with some small desperation, I thought), and the musicians scurried to their former places and struck up a light air to quench any fiery rebellion that might still smoulder.

Garrick strode off. The green curtain fell on the country inn, and Tom Tinker and Sylvia Cinders danced a pantomime to "The Lamplighter," sung by Mr. Flynn.

We sat back, Mr. Fielding breathing noisily, Mr. Brogden straight as a stick beside him.

"Ha!" exclaimed Mr. Ralph.

"Unjust," muttered William, grinding his hands.

" 'Twas indeed no fair trial," agreed Mr. Franklin. "What are the consequences for the poor playwright, Jimmy?"

"No good ones. We are not paid for our plays. A new play that meets with approval customarily runs nine nights, the third being the playwright's benefit—that is when he takes all profits, less some expenses of Drury Lane, which the pirate Garrick exacts. Yet the benefit can mean a handsome sum, especially if the author's friends fill many seats. A full run proves the play a success; 'tis printed, bringing further profit. 'Tis then like to be played again, to even more profit. *A Lord and No Lord* shall not be played again."

" 'Twas not a good play, but—"

"A crippled thing should be put out of its misery, Ben."

"So cruelly?"

" 'Twas the voice of the people."

"Nay, 'twas the bleating of sheep." Mr. Franklin frowned up at the gallery. "Paid? Well, what is done is done."

I looked into Lord Methuen's box, to find him gone with his friends. I noted that Lord Edmund Calverly and Lady Linacre were also vanished from their respective boxes. Indeed many people came and went, Mr. Ralph informing us that, as Covent Garden Theater lay nearby, patrons sometime skipped to it, and vice versa, if the entertainment at the first did not please 'em.

And then *Harlequin Necromancer* began. This proved a sprightly, witching pantomime, with demons and goblins, and crones in a dev'lish dance. It took place in a graveyard. Mr. Woodward played Harlequin in red and blue motley, who had lost his love to murder (a rejected suitor's poisoned draught; she died amidst tears). Harlequin crept into the graveyard to bring her back to life, which he did in a transformation scene in which the headstones turned into a congregation of resurrected souls who capered at his moonlight wedding. What a lively, happy end. I forgot *A Lord and No Lord*. It made no matter. Was not my first evening of playgoing drawing to a happy close?

But not so, for just as Harlequin and Columbine pledged their troth, a terrible cry sounded at my back, and I twisted round to see a man tumble from the gallery.

'Twas the man of the pamphlets, who had led the shouting down of the play.

He flailed, he gaped. He struck the pit below with a dreadful sound.

🦋 4 🦋

IN WHICH we view a dead man and
sup with David Garrick . . .

A nd yet the pantomime went on. Harlequin wed his
bride and capered, a grand dance by flickering torch-
light concluding all. Some commotion in the pit where the
man had plunged might be heard at our backs, yet few paid
heed; after all, 'twas not some lord had toppled.

But I—I had seen the look on the man's face as he fell:
a mask of fear.

The man might not be dead. 'Twas but twenty feet or so
from gallery to pit. Yet the sound as he struck!—I shuddered to its echo in my brain. My hands trembled. Life and
Art, Mr. Ralph had said. Death and playacted death. I was
more affected by the former.

Frowning, Mr. Franklin peered back in vain attempt to
see what might be. His fingers drummed his knees, his
sober look met mine. "Damn me, Nick, what may this
mean?"

"That a man has fallen," breathed Principal Justice
Fielding by my side. "He will be found stone dead."

Mr. Franklin frowned. "May you be so very sure he is
dead?"

"I have heard a great many deaths. My ears always tell
true."

There remained but a few moments of the pantomime,

which concluded to much applause. When the last goblin had scampered off, Mr. Franklin drew out his watch: 10 P.M. He snapped the silver lid as the audience rose to depart. The evening's entertainment done, some attention began to be paid the back of the pit. Several pairs of eyes in the boxes gazed curiously that way, quizzing glasses glinting from candlelight, and a buzzing circle could be seen gathering. Wearing a look I knew well—grave, urgent—Mr. Franklin strove to peer through the crowd that rose to block our view, but it proved too close-packed, and he muttered under his breath. "Come, Nick." He tugged my sleeve. "Accident or otherwise? I wish to know."

Justice Fielding lumbered up to follow, but Mr. Franklin pulled me with him not to the pit passage by which we had entered but directly back over the benches, clambering with remarkable agility for a man of fifty-two. This was no surprise, for I had watched him leap after a shadowy figure by the rain-swept Thames. He had chased a red-haired stranger near Soho Square as if he were twenty. He had once plunged into icy waters to save my life. In dire moments he summoned the vigor of a lad.

"What, Ben?" came James Ralph's bewildered call, but Mr. Franklin did not look round. Arriving at the railing which divided the lower rows of the pit from the back rows (these under the gallery, held up by sturdy, round columns), he o'releapt it as if 'twere but a stile in a field. I followed on his heels.

This delivered us to the corridor which divided the two halves of the pit, front and back. It was narrow, no more than eight feet wide and crowded with patrons gazing down at the body that lay unmoving upon the floor. Mr. Franklin first peered up, to where this man had sat.

He then looked down.

I forced myself to do so too. I hated to look upon death. I had seen it in the twisted ways by Moorgate, where life went cheap: children expired before they'd sucked a twelvemonth's breath, women wasted by disease, men shrunk to corpses by poverty or gin. The bludgeoner took 'em too, for some little bit of coin or handful of lace. Anger killed 'em, riots, brawls. Despair stole their breaths (it hung 'em in their garters). Wicked guile wrung young girls' necks. And my mother, poisoned. Though I had no clear memory of her, she haunted my dreams, a chalk-white shade, lips silent though I cried for 'em to speak. Cold, so cold!

I shivered, yet I looked down, for I must face the worst. Though I did not know the man, I felt the familiar ringing dizziness and a strange echoing, as if all about receded to a murmur and a blur before this which alone was real.

Death.

I squeezed my eyes tight shut, I made my nails bite into my palms. Be alert! Look and listen! That was what Mr. Franklin adjured. And so I opened my eyes and forged a steadiness in my breast. The man was truly dead, no mistaking the awful stillness of him. He lay face up, arms out, one leg straight, the other bent sharply back in a way that would pain any man living. But this man had no life. His head was twisted far to one side, his neck broke in the fall. His hands were curved into claws, as if in the last instant he grasped for life. One shoe had come off; it lay by his side, revealing a ragged hole in the baggy stocking on his right foot, through which toes with broken, yellowish nails poked through. His clothing bespoke the sham of the proud poor: a patchy coat over a stained bottle-green waistcoat. Some few of the remainder of his broadsides showed inside this coat, but most lay scattered about, mute scurrility. As for his face, it was stamped with fury even in death, a screaming grimace, the eyes half-open and glassy, the mouth snarling with all its blackened teeth. I accuse! it seemed to cry—but whom? of what?

Life itself, of beating him down? How many unfortunate souls had reason to cry the same?

"Dead indeed," murmured Mr. Franklin, grasping my elbow. "Do you smell it, Nick?"

I sniffed. There was the stink of death, for the dead cared not if they pissed and shat. The man had befouled himself, and I wrinkled my nose. Yet there came also the reek of the crowd: breaths, bodies, scents. The leather of tunics and boots. Tobacco. Burnt candle ends. Yet there was, too, another smell that seemed to belong to Drury Lane itself, seeping from the very benches and columns and walls, as if what the theater had known over the years had become part of it, a compound of spite and joy, laughter and tears, triumph and downfall, the grinding together of Life and Art in the pestle of Garrick's playhouse. There was, too, the bittersweet odor of spirits. Was it that of which Mr. Franklin spoke?

The crowd, lords and shop-boys alike, shifted its feet, stared, murmured, but for the moment did nothing. Some smiled crookedly: " 'Twas not I who went betimes," they seemed to crow. Others were pale. A few looked gleeful: a play put down and sudden death—what a story to tell!

Mr. Franklin knelt, knees cracking. He held his quizzing glass to the man's mouth. No mist came. He stood and looked about. His modest gaze bespoke no accusation, but his soft brown eyes seemed to ask questions, and many turned away as if shamed, and the crowd began to thin.

I saw amongst 'em Lord Edmund Calverly and the icy Lady Linacre, whom I had thought gone from the playhouse. Lord Methuen, too, strode up to fix his black, angry stare upon the body.

I felt someone by my side. I looked up.

'Twas David Garrick.

The actor was no longer dressed as Lord Brough but wore a close-fitting white wig and brown velvet suit. His sleeve brushed my shoulder; I saw him nearer than anyone. "Midge," murmured he gazing down. I stared at his famous features, so mobile and expressive: the round face with its fine mouth, flaring nostrils, and eyes that might flash with playacted mirth or fury. Standing still as wax, he seemed to measure out his expression, like a chandler measuring corn, though I fancied that for an instant distaste involuntarily curled his lips.

I read no sorrow in the man.

Everyone now gazed at him. What thoughts crossed his brain?

At last he started and looked round. "Hem . . . ah . . . fell, eh? Mischance. Pity. We must move the poor fellow, what?" He rubbed his hands. "Why, indeed we must. Is there any friend will speak for him?"

No one spoke.

"Dudley Midge," breathed a voice in soft startlement. Lucy Drumm had just arrived, a sylph in lavender dress. Across the close-packed circle her great blue eyes moistly stared at the body, as if 'twas a father or brother who lay ruined. "Dear God . . . !" Slender, white fingers tremblingly lifted to her cheeks, and with her dark lashes and pink, parted lips, she seemed prettier in dismay than ever she had appeared onstage. My heart fluttered. Her air of help-lessness moved me.

William had by then joined us; he too stared at Lucy. Mr. Ralph had come too. Justice Fielding. Pop-eyed Joshua Brogden at his master's elbow.

At the edge of the circle Dr. Johnson, of the *Dictionary*, fixed sharp, examining eyes dourly upon the body as if it bespoke some new definition of death.

Mrs. Drumm's gaze lifted to Garrick in tremulous dis-may. "But what did he in the playhouse, sir? Did you not dismiss him?"

"Dismiss?" Garrick plainly did not like this told to one and all. "Hem, 'tis no secret I booted him out—but, damn it all, any man may buy a ticket! The fellow led the charge 'gainst your husband's play, did you not see? He worked his will; now chance has worked its will on him. He was no friend to life, and it has snuffed him." Garrick darted his glance round once more. "Will no one claim the poor can-dle-end? Pah, then 'tis for the sweepers-up to take him. Giffard," snapped he to one of the green-coated minions who had moved tables and chairs upon the stage and now stood slack-jawed by his side, "call the pauper's men to carry out this thing." The minion departed and, with the look of a housewife chasing dust, Garrick made shooing

motions at the dozen or so patrons still in the narrow
passage. "Come, be off. Think not on this when you recall
Drury Lane. Think of how we please you."

Most moved off—but not Mr. Franklin, who had stepped
well back and stood hands folded over his bamboo, near
invisible in his stillness but taking in all. I slipped to his
side, near John Fielding. The passage did not become less
crowded; departing patrons were replaced by actors agath-
ering: Woodward in his Harlequin garb, two small boy-
ghosts, Miss Prouty, wearing a hard, wry look that stood in
sharp contrast to Lucy Drumm's pale alarm. Mrs. Clive and
Mrs. Pritchard showed their faces, sniffed in distaste and
hurried off. An older woman came to stand by Mrs.
Drumm, and took her hand and chafed it. Lord Calverly
had hung back. As he turned to go his gaze briefly met this
woman's, and there seemed some silent communion betwixt 'em before he went away.

Lord Methuen did not go. Still wearing his haughty scowl
he stepped forward. "You did well, sir," said he into Garrick's face, "to leave off the playing of this play. Had I
known its matter I should have prevented even tonight's
performance (I am friend to the Lord Chamberlain), but as
'twas only this afternoon that I was apprised of its nature
I could not act in time. Yet 'tis libelous. Dangerous, too. To
you. Think not on reviving it."

Garrick blanched. "But, my lord . . ."

"You did not know it injured me?"

"Why . . . I would do nothing to displease my lord.
Injured, you say? Hem, ah . . . why, then," he drew himself
up, " 'tis as dead as this fellow on the floor, and as incapa-
ble of resurrection."

At this Mrs. Drumm softly moaned.

Lord Methuen's sharp jaw lifted. "I shall take you at your
word. Good even, sir." He turned to go, but at this moment
the playwright arrived, Abel Drumm himself, striding along
the corridor. As my lord passed they exchanged a look of
such rancor as might have sent Drury Lane's green curtain
up in smoke, and Drumm made a mocking bow. "Milady

Pox waits upon you, sir," at which Lord Methuen growled and vanished.

Drumm hardly paused. He bore down upon us—yet stopped stone still as his eyes fell upon the dead man. Paling, he made mouths, but mastered himself. He had business with the living.

He faced David Garrick. "I must speak with you," asserted he.

Garrick made to turn away. "Nay, not now."

Drumm scrabbled at his lapels. "But you cannot mean that you will not play my play. 'Twas a faction sent against it. Come, you will never let a pack of braying hounds sway David Garrick. The people loved it! I will not hear of its not being played again."

Garrick's eyes narrowed. Drumm was a black-haired man, somewhat of Garrick's height, with a squarecut face that might have been called handsome were it not for a bruised hollowness to his cheeks and preternaturally deep-set eyes out of which the orbs glittered feverishly. Of some thirty years of age, he had a straight, prominent nose, but his well-shaped mouth was set in a pout. Too, there was some weakness to his chin, and he bore an air of wrongs unjustly suffered. I should not care to be caught betwixt him and Lord Methuen.

Yet though Garrick had deferred to my lord, he did not so to Drumm. He tightened like a bowstring. "You insist we talk now? Very well. My Lord Methuen says your play injures him. Does it?"

"Why, I—"

"Speak."

Drumm wrestled with a placating smile. " 'Tis the tale of a man about town. There are many such, sir."

"Yet there was much particular in't. And now I think me," Garrick's eyes flashed, "did you not once seek my lord's patronage? Did he not deny you? Damn it, have you satirized the man? Egad, a lord? Madness! Whatever the case, your play was cried down by nearly all; 'twas generally disliked. Further, Methuen has the Lord Chamber-

lain's ear, and I want no war with him. We shall play us no
bad plays. We shall not play your play again, and that is an
end on't."

Drumm's mouth worked. His lips trembled, and his face
turned white as bone. He seemed about to lash out—indeed his fist clenched, his arm half raised—but his wife
prevented, darting between the men and pressing her fingers to her husband's chest. "Come, dear, you must pay
heed to Mr. Garrick. No words now, I beg you. You may
speak another time." She tugged at him, cajoling, and his
fists slowly opened. They gripped her arms, and I saw
redness where his fingers dug into her flesh and wondered
why she did not cry out but took it as if 'twere a caress.

Her husband shook her as he must wish to shake Garrick, so that her honey ringlets bounced. "Damn me, but
I . . . !"

She and the woman who had chafed her hands succeeded in drawing Drumm off muttering and cursing as he
went.

There followed an uneasy silence. The pit and boxes
were empty. Light began to dim, candlemen snuffing the
chandeliers they had lowered. Nearby an old woman pried
wax-ends from smoking sconces, whilst other women,
gleaners, moved about the theater snatching up bits of
ribbon, a lady's comb, a ha'penny piece before their
brooms swept up what might not be hoarded for sale. Two
brisk black-coated men abruptly scuttled in and bobbed
their heads and snatched the dead man rudely by feet and
shoulders and made off with him without a word, like
beetles carrying some bit of dung to a hole. Their boots
scraped, and one madly cackled though William seemed to
note none of their antics for gazing after Lucy Drumm.

Garrick bent, picked up one of the broadsides that lay
scattered about, scanned it, wrinkled his nose, let it fall.
Principal Justice Fielding cleared his throat.

Garrick seemed to see him for the first time. "Hem, ah,
sir, you are come! I am pleased for't." He clapped the
justice's shoulder. "Did you like the play? But you could

not, for 'twas a bad play and a bad business. But what am I about? Hem, ah, clear the playhouse! Home, you actors, for there must be rehearsal tomorrow morn, and fines for any who are late. Off, Woodward! Off, you ghosts! Good even to ye, Miss Prouty; ye'll be Celia no more."

Woodward had a piece to speak too. "If Abel Drumm protests the damning of his play," said he, stepping forward, "I protest my salary."

Garrick scowled. "Another time. For now get you to bed—or to a pint of ale, as you will. Go, you all."

Woodward grudgingly yielded, as did the rest. One did not: a plumpish woman perhaps forty, with deep-set blue eyes. She was dressed modestly, her gaze fixed upon Mr. Franklin. It grazed my face too, briefly, before she turned and with an air of quiet dignity, as of a person made wise by life's vagaries, slipped quietly away.

"The drama's patrons indeed gave law tonight, Davy," rumbled Dr. Johnson before he, too, bid good night and trundled off. This left Garrick, Justice Fielding, Joshua Brogden, Mr. Franklin, Mr. Ralph, William and I in the dim-lit corridor.

Somewhere a door banged, and a wind moved through the playhouse like breath in a body.

Mr. Ralph tugged at Mr. Franklin's sleeve. "Come, Ben, all that may be seen is seen."

"But heard?" murmured the gentleman with a troubled air.

John Fielding cleared his throat. "You know Benjamin Franklin, Garrick?"

The actor turned. "I do not, but pleased to meet you, sir." He shook Mr. Franklin's hand. "Yet I *do* know Mr. Ralph, and think that what he tells you is true—all is surely done."

Mr. Franklin's small, squarish spectacles caught a flicker of candlelight. "Do you not intend to speak with Justice Fielding?"

"Why . . . yes."

"Then all is not done."

Garrick half smiled. "Surely that cannot interest you."

"It may," said Fielding. "Franklin is come from America, seeking justice. He is clever and would like, I think, to hear what you wish to tell. Let us have him with us, eh? Come, where shall we sup? My belly cries for food."

Garrick looked from one man to the other.

Mr. Franklin stood very still.

Garrick's hands rose and fell, as had Lord Brough's when he saw all was up. "Very well, to the Shakespeare's Head."

Mr. Franklin turned to Mr. Ralph and William. "Dissect the evening as you will. You are free to go."

Neither looked as if he liked dismissal—but too late, for Mr. Franklin was walking apart with Justice Fielding, Mr. Brogden, and David Garrick. I stood uncertainly.

Mr. Franklin turned. "Well, Nick?" He gestured me to follow, and I lost no time hurrying after.

At the doors of Drury Lane, Garrick paused to confer with a reed-thin gentleman wrapped in the pallid air of the counting house: "How much this night, Lacy?"

"Above an hundred and twenty pounds."

Garrick's fingers fidgeted. "Hem, ah, a decent sum. Is't not decent? We shall not have to close our doors. Yet how did Rich, at Covent Garden? Better? The fellow is damnably clever; the mob loves him. Do we fall out of favor? Fickle London. I was right to kill Drumm's play tonight, was I not? 'Twas a bad play?"

"Very right, I am sure," replied this Lacy, dry as paper, whilst Garrick danced in an agitation of doubt.

Mr. Franklin drew me ahead with him, into Bridges Street. Nearly all the carriages which had crowded here were gone, a half moon sailing amongst tattered clouds. Peter waited with our coach; Mr. Franklin sent him home.

'Twas chill. I drew my scarf tight about my throat.

"And so, young Nick, what thought you of the play?"

"I thought the acting very fine."

"But the play?"

"I know little of plays."

"Come, lad."

"It did not seem so very good a thing."

He cocked a brow. "Pray, why?"

"It was not truly amusing. 'Twas meant to be, but all was forced. The thing lacked lightness. Forgive me, sir, if I say wrong."

He squeezed my shoulder. "You speak as I would—and as many in the audience spoke by their crying down of the play. A mob, yes—but they would not have damned a thing that truly pleased 'em. No, 'twas not good. O, I see why Garrick thought 'twould be, for it has many worthy ancestors, from Plautus to Congreve. But this was bloodless imitation. Mean-spirited too, did you not think? In wishing to satirize Lord Methuen, Drumm made a diatribe in place of a play and lost his sense of humor—if ever he had one. I am glad to find we think alike . . . How did you find Mrs. Drumm?"

"Very pretty."

"Her acting?"

"Affecting, in some scenes."

"But not in all?"

"She did not make me laugh."

"Nor me, I own." A mist rose from damp cobbles as the gentleman leant on his bamboo in the penumbra of a lamp. "She has not the gift for irony. There are some performers can do well with what is in their natures; thus if they are spiteful they enact spite well, if good, goodness. There is a purity about Mrs. Drumm which shines onstage, but I fear the meaner aspects of character fall outside her range. She is indeed pretty. Such alabaster skin, such a budlike mouth. Her youth may give her a following for a time, yet when that flees will she find herself on the streets, like poor Miss Blogg?"

"But Mrs. Drumm has a husband."

"A husband indeed—speaking of whom . . ."

He drew me into a dark mews as Mr. and Mrs. Drumm came walking close beside one another. At first I thought they clung together in chagrin over the cried-down play, but I soon saw 'twas only the lady who clung. Moonlight caught her upturned, pleading face. She gazed at her husband, adjuring, "Please, dear," and pawed pathetically at his arm as he marched along as if she were some importuning beggar. "You must heed. Listen to your Lucy. Your play may be played elsewhere. We may see this through—"

But he only snarled and stomped, she dragging after 'til they turned into Russell Street.

Mr. Franklin tutted. "Devotion is a sad thing, when women make themselves slaves to men who despise 'em." We were about to step out when we heard the soft click of heels, and another person hurried by: she who had stood by Lucy Drumm. This older woman wore a look of deep, searching concern. Never glancing to right or left, she passed like a breeze.

"By her lineaments, Mrs. Drumm's mother," said Mr. Franklin. "Do you not think so, Nick?"

I nodded.

"Does she follow the Drumms?" The gentleman gripped my arm. "But 'tis a parade, for there is Lord What's-his-name."

"Calverly," said I, spying the man at the turning into Russell Street. He seemed stealthily to pursue Lucy Drumm's mother.

Mr. Franklin drew me into the street when my lord had passed. "Does not Calverly have hearth, wife, or friends to occupy him this night? What does he, hanging about?" There came no answer, for at that moment David Garrick, Justice Fielding, and hopping little Joshua Brogden joined us. Covent Garden lay nearby, and we set out, voluble and cheery, as if no man had just died.

I thought not on Dudley Midge.

Shakespeare's visage gazed down from the swinging signboard above the Shakespeare's Head. "And so," said David Garrick when we had passed through its door, "will you, that is, hem, ah, shall you sup with me, gentlemen? Roast beef?" Waving to men who greeted him, he gestured for us to sit at a long wooden table at one end of the room. "I eat nothing before I play a part; Lear starts my stomach aleaping, and Sir Fopling Flutter tumbles it into cartwheels. But afterward it cries to be sated. What say you? Quail pie? A pudding?"

"I should greet a pie fondly," pronounced Justice Fielding, chins wobbling as he sank onto a bench beside Mr. Brogden. Mr. Franklin and I sat opposite. Garrick lowered himself like a squire at table's end.

I looked about. The Shakespeare's Head was both tavern and chophouse, the smell of ale and gravy mingling with the thick odor of pipe smoke from numerous clays. What a jangle of noise! 'Twas near eleven, but the hour did not deter revelers and trenchermen, who struck their pewter with their spoons and called Ho! to the serving girls and burst into song and acted impromptu and juggled (one balanced an egg on his nose) and rallied their fellows and made roistering use of their time. Coats and hats hung on pegs above the wooden booths. Red-faced wenches sweated as they lugged plates and glasses to and fro amidst jibes and pinches and hands traveling beneath their skirts and fondling their breasts as if such familiarity was natural prologue to the fare. This was the theater crowd. I saw faces I had seen in the pantomime (Woodward sat at a far table). There were, too, men I had noted in the pit, amongst 'em the braying cadre which Justice Fielding had cowed. Fops who had stretched out their legs onstage lounged too, as if they had been carried here as they sat, in much the same insolent attitudes, with drooping lids and sneering mouths. I saw fiddlers and supernumeraries and creeping Grub Street scribes. Voices argued the faults and merits of plays at both Drury Lane and Covent Garden. Rich's Harlequin was pronounced superior to Woodward's. Mrs. Clive was proclaimed the queen of comedy. Lucy Drumm was exquisite, but her husband's play!—happy that it had been hissed to oblivion. I could not help feeling sorry for Abel Drumm.

I carried in my right hand coat pocket my journal, in my left my new sketching book. I was but a boy, unlikely to be called upon to express my views, so I drew forth this sketching book and, holding it below table's edge, began to draw: juggling spoons, grandiloquent gestures, a man sawing at a suckling pig whose brown, roasted face was as squint-eyed and crinkled as his own. Yet I listened.

"Will not your wife miss you tonight, Garrick?" rumbled John Fielding when the magistrate and actor had drawn up a bill of welsh rarebit, mutton chops, gammon, broiled chicken, apple puffs, a trifle, porter, and ale.

"Dear Violette," exclaimed Garrick, like Romeo pining for Juliet. "We shall not be separated long. I join her soon in Southampton Street—though we should prefer to be snug in our little villa on the Thames. How inconsolable I should be if anything came between us."

Mr. Franklin smiled. "Should anything?"

"Why, hem, ah, no. Impossible. Since we were married we have not spent a night apart."

"But the afternoons, sir . . . ?" Justice Fielding slyly asked.

"You practice remarkable fidelity," put in Mr. Franklin.

"Not so," protested Garrick.

"I merely mean that instances of the ideal are infrequent in this imperfect world."

"And yet you seek justice in that imperfect world, sir, by Mr. Fielding's report. How, pray?"

"By hard labor in a rocky field, *viz.*: the field of English government, which grows tyrants called proprietors who require a people to maintain an army to protect the proprietor's interests but pay none of the cost themselves. I engage in strenuous harvesting, to make the Penns yield fruit."

"Thomas and Richard Penn? You wish to tax 'em?"

"We do."

Garrick laughed. "No man likes to part with money."

"Right-minded men give it nonetheless, if 'tis fair. We do not seek to take all to market, only to garner what is due."

"Do not think," interrupted Fielding, "that contentious-ness is the whole of Franklin's nature. He is congenial; he has many friends. He is wise, too, and ponders deep. He writes of Nature. He is a fellow of the Royal Society. He invents things."

Garrick looked interested. "What sort, pray?"

Mr. Franklin shrugged. "Practical and fanciful. A stove to give better heat. A musical instrument of glass, played by water."

"Truly? Now, sir, I long to better the lighting at Drury Lane. What would you invent me for that?"

"Nothing tonight—though I might devise something by turning my mind to't. I have much time between my bouts of shaking the tree of state."

Garrick thumped the table. "Why, I am tempted to en-gage you on the spot."

Mr. Franklin smiled. "Haste leads to repentance. Let the idea steep."

Garrick agreed, and there followed converse about Mrs. Clive, whom Garrick called Clivey-Pivey, and other actors, and how Garrick had come to be upon the stage. He had been a pupil of Dr. Johnson, he told us, at Edial; together they had traveled to London to seek their fortunes. Gar-rick was meant for the law, but the death of his father had spoilt this plan. He then set up with his brother as a wine merchant near Covent Garden. Here he met the actor Charles Macklin (he who had stabbed Hallam through the eye) and became theater-struck. He made his debut as Richard III at Goodman's Fields in 1741, and by 1747, famous, he was joint owner with James Lacy of the leading theater in England. Garrick was lively in recounting this. I had always thought Mr. Franklin the most engaging man I should meet, but Garrick rivaled him. Mr. Franklin's charm was quiet, his humor gentle, he being often content merely to watch and listen, whereas Garrick plainly prefer-red to be watched and listened to. He reveled in our atten-tions; he sculpted each detail of his discourse, eyes flashing, voice dramatically modulating, hands carving air.

By this he threaded us upon his needle, and even dour Justice Fielding wore a smile.

But after some mutton and a fine fat hen, the portly magistrate's smile sank to a fretting and fiddling with waistcoat buttons. "Come," grumbled he, "I weary of tittle-tattle. You said you had some trouble. Speak of that."

Garrick paddled his fingers, "Hem, ah, . . ." He seemed to seek lines in a role for which none had been writ. "And must tell of it, I see." A wary peeping. "May I truly speak before Mr. Franklin?"

"Have I not said you may?"

"Then I shall." Garrick leant dramatically forward. "Letters," said he in a hoarse whisper. "I have received me letters, Mr. Fielding."

"Why, so have I, and glad to get 'em."

"Not this sort. Sly letters, I mean. Threatening."

"You are not the first—such letters are a curse o' the time. And what do they threaten?"

"To bring my theater to ruination."

"How?"

"By fire. By scandal."

"Beg pardon," put in Mr. Franklin, "but you must receive many letters which curse you. No offense; I do not say they are deserved. I speak merely of the way o' the world. Seekers will always be about reviling those who have power to say 'em nay. We in the public eye are both loved and hated, licked by the honey-tongue one moment and spat upon the next. I myself have been spat upon." He peered at Garrick. "Surely you are no different?"

"No, and I hate the state!" burst out the actor. "How right you are. Do I not do all I may to please the mob? Do I not give 'em acting such like they have not seen before? Do I not yield to their demands? Do I not bow and scrape before the quality? As for actors and playwrights, a man may hire only so many players and play only so many plays. A man must pick and choose. What a rabble importunes me. And my actors—they are like froward children, ever squabbling, whilst I, Father Garrick, must stride amongst 'em with a 'Now, then,' and a 'See, here' and make 'em come to heel like a pack of untaught pups." Sputtering, he showed not a little of the childishness which he deplored. I thought on Abel Drumm's sour spite, Lord Methuen's fury. Angers and jealousies and misunderstandings truly raged offstage as well as on at Drury Lane.

"Why call good Justice Fielding's attention to these particular letters, then?" interjected Mr. Franklin.

"Because of the fires."

"I heard you had suffered some such recently."

"Why, were't not for Mrs. Drumm the Theatre Royal would be blackened ruins."

"Mrs. Drumm?"

"She discovered the flames in a passage, and we passed buckets and put the thing out, though it ate a doorway and twenty Roman spears and a dozen wigs and hats, all which I have had to pay to replace, before we could drown it."

"Fortunate she was there. Pray, when did this occur?"

"A fortnight and three days ago."

"And how many letters have you received?"

"Some four or five."

"When did you begin to receive 'em?"

"A week or so before this fire."

Mr. Franklin rubbed a circle on the tabletop. "I too should be alarmed."

"I quake in terror, sir. Though 'twas before my time, the playhouse has burnt to the ground once already. And what of 1666, where much of the city sank to ashes? O, I tell you, even the smell of pipesmoke makes me blanch."

"You are insured?" put in Justice Fielding.

"By Sun Fire—though not for all fires: 'except such loss and damage as may happen by any fire occasioned by means of any representation in any play or farce or in any rehearsal of the same.' We show no fires onstage at Drury Lane, I tell you, though Rich at Covent Garden puts theater and playgoers at hazard by his smoke and bombs."

"You and Rich are great rivals?" asked Mr. Franklin.

"He plays comedy tolerably well. I play comedy *and*

tragedy; there is no rivalry. We have had mischief back-stage too."

"Related to these letters, you believe?"

"I do."

"What sort of mischief?" Mr. Franklin had become chief questioner, I noted, whilst John Fielding watched.

"Costumes missing or disarranged," replied Garrick, "playscripts vanished, objects necessary for the right playing of a play misplaced, machinery tampered with."

"Tampered?"

"Found not to work."

"Anything dire?"

"No instance has yet prevented our going onstage."

"But surely some of this is chance."

"Some instances, perhaps. Good God, man, does that make the rest any the less diabolical?"

"I do not doubt you have reason for worry."

Garrick cast a beleaguered look at the magistrate. "The fellow asks hard questions, sir."

"But apt ones. Franklin has refused hire of me, but tonight you have him for free, so answer, sir; take 'vantage."

Garrick sighed. "I bear my breast then. Lay on."

"Gladly. Since by your admission you receive many unfriendly letters, how may you be certain the four or five you name are all from the self-same hand?"

"They have the same insolent tone; their matter is like. O, no mistake, they make a book.

"You said they also threatened scandal. What sort?"

"Why, ah, *scandal,* sir, don't you see?"

"I do not."

"That is the devil of't—the fellow sneaks and implies but does not say."

"Nothing particular, then?"

"No."

"Surely he demands some wrong be righted?"

"Not even that."

"Odd indeed. I should very much like to see these letters. Might I—and Justice Fielding—peruse 'em?"

"Yes, though not now. I meant to bring 'em, but the
death of that man . . . yet I may easily lay hands on 'em."

"I am glad. You have spoke of the writer as a man.
Why?"

"I presumed—"

"Tut, presume nothing, sir. A woman too may dip a pen
in venom. How do you receive these letters? Posted?"

"I find 'em dropped in my way."

"At Drury Lane?"

"Yes."

" 'Tis likely, then, that someone in your employ writes
'em."

"That is what I think—which means the miscreant may
easily set another fire. And know of scandal. You see why
I have been so fretted these weeks past? I thought to ride
it out; 'twould prove no real harm. But yesterday—only
yesterday!—came another fire, or what might have been:
shirts and vestments smouldering in a bin. My wardrobe
woman smelt 'em and doused 'em, but what if she had not?
What if, some night, after all are gone save he who is bent
on harm—? Drury Lane is my life, Mr. Franklin; I cannot
see it ruined." Sinking back, Garrick stared bleakly from
Justice Fielding's squinched, sightless eyes to Mr. Franklin's thoughtful countenance, where spectacles rode low
on his nose. I felt pity for the actor—yet I also saw that he
was two men in one: the first made melodrama of his woes,
whilst the other watched to see how we took his speech.

My pencil struggled to limn this double man. Would it be
possible ever to capture the true David Garrick? Mr.
Franklin thoughtfully poked his glasses higher. As if only
then remembering Justice Fielding, Garrick turned pleadingly toward him. "May you help me, sir?"

"No," said Fielding.

Garrick started. "But, sir—you must."

The justice wiped a foam of porter from his lips. "I
cannot. Look you, I may take a man caught in the act. I

may seek such a man; perhaps I may find him. I may put down riots, as I have done in Drury Lane, at your request. I may, too, keep watch over the licensing of taverns, to keep drunkenness within bounds. But I cannot *discover*. For that you need a different sort of fellow.''

"But, sir—"

"Nay. Even had I means, I have not men to hang about Drury Lane. Parliament allocates far too few. I plead, I argue, I protest, but the prating, periwigged fellows are not to be moved, though the streets crawl with cutthroats and John Bull is not safe in his bed. No, sir, I may not deal with what *may be*. I pray that will some day be the work of such men as I, to prevent as well as to capture and bring to law, but 'tis not so now. I cannot help you. You need a fellow that can see sharper than my dead eyes, and hear half as well. I know only one such man. He sits before you: Benjamin Franklin. Apply to him.'' With another long draught, the magistrate thumped down his glass. "When your theater is burnt to the ground, may't never come to be, then you may call upon John Fielding. For now, Mr. Brogden,'' he noisily shuffled to his feet, "to Bow Street. I want my bed.'' Joshua Brogden rose, bobbed his head, and in a moment the pair were gone.

Garrick gaped. He floundered. "I am damned,'' moaned he.

His gaze fixed upon Benjamin Franklin. "Look you, sir— is't true what Fielding says of you?''

"Others must judge of that. Yet I told true when I said I had time on my hands; and since to waste time is the greatest prodigality I should be glad to spend the excess, which the slow progress of my business lends, to look into your problem. These letters—they possess elements that interest me. Your playhouse too: a little world where dissembling is an art. What better place wherein to practice *my* art, of bringing truth to light? Further, it pleases me to make justice's scales balance. For these reasons I should be happy to be diverted by Drury Lane.''

Garrick stared. "You are a curious fellow, Franklin. But what would you do?"

"Hang about the playhouse, to see what might be discovered."

"And put the wind up our fire-setter?"

"You wish better lighting? I am your man. Introduce me as Benjamin Franklin, inventor, come to see what he may devise to improve Drury Lane. You shall not lie, for I shall turn my mind to that too, and happy to do so, for my brain hates a slothful hour. Thus I shall have reason to lurk about, strike up acquaintance, hear gossip, poke, pry, twist the knife of inquiry, sound the depths of feeling."

"You will find much dissatisfaction."

"There are many love you, I am sure."

"And hate."

"Tut, a man unhated is a man who makes no mark. A man must take pride in those who hate him."

Garrick threw back his head. "Why, damned if I am not proud of ev'ry fool and wretched scribbler to whom I have said nay!"

"Ha, excellent."

Garrick beamed. "I find I like you, Benjamin Franklin."

Mr. Franklin did not smile back. "Will you, after I have been about a while? I never work by half. Do you still wish to make this pact?"

"I will pay good hire for't."

"Let us speak of payment when I have served. If I serve not, then naught is due."

"I like you even better." Garrick thrust out his hand.

Mr. Franklin clasped it.

I watched. The actor appeared as if a great stone were lifted from his chest, his face flushed with joy. He trusted Mr. Franklin—as who save the wicked should not? Yet in that handclasp, in the dim, quiet flickering in Mr. Franklin's deep brown eyes, I did not read the end of David Garrick's worries but the beginning of troubles for Mr. Franklin. He stepped into a tangled wood; from thence, if drawn (for he was bold when seeking truth), he would

stride where signposts did not lead and feet might trip. I
fretted at this, my pencil would no longer draw a line. Yet
I longed to go with him; I, too, loved adventure.

"But, what does the boy?" came Garrick's voice.

I started. His eyes were fixed upon my sketching book.

"Draws," said Mr. Franklin. He held out his hand. "May
I show him, lad?"

I gave over the book for Mr. Franklin to display its pages,
hanging fire whilst the men nodded and said how well I had
got the black-haired serving wench, the fellow with the
great, warty nose, the hound sleeping by the door like an
old, wrinkled wineskin. I fed on this praise as a starved
man would upon a joint.

Mr. Franklin showed the last drawing. David Garrick
peered at it. " 'Tis meant to be me, I think. Yet 'tis not so
apt as your others. You have not gót me, I believe."

"I am sorry, sir." In truth the actor was like quicksilver;
my pencil had been unable to fix him.

"I must go," said Garrick briskly, rising. "My dear wife
waits."

"May I bring Nick to Drury Lane, to aid me?" asked Mr.
Franklin.

Garrick laughed. "Why not? He may draw me better
there."

Mr. Franklin bobbed his head. "Good even to you, then.
I shall begin my investigation on the morrow, if't please."

"It pleases. You do not know how light of heart you
make me. Hem, ah, farewell, Woodward. Good even, Mr.
Bix. Good night, gentlemen, all." And in the manner of my
lord geniality he strode to the door under ev'ry eye: Roscius, as he was called, after the great Roman actor. Did he
ever cease playacting, and if he did whose portrait might
my pencil draw?

The night had grown frosty, Mr. Franklin silent and pon-
dering as we, too, strode out under Shakespeare's gaze,
past the porticos of Covent Garden toward the Strand. The
moon scudded free of clouds. Few people were about.

Across the square a fine coach waited, and I saw a woman's delicate hand briefly at its window.

But where was Garrick? Crossed the piazza so quickly that he was vanished? I thought for a moment he might have climbed into this coach—but why, for he had said he went to his wife nearby? The coach set off, emblazoned on its door: a curling *L*. A cat ran across our path. A drunken man retched in an alleyway. Mr. Franklin thoughtfully watched the departing coach.

❦ 5 ❦

IN WHICH the investigation begins . . .

Bells tolled long and slow over London, and the Craven Street watchman's cry rose ghostlike from the cobbles below Mr. Franklin's bow window as we returned to his dark chamber: "Twelve o'clock and all's well . . ."

The gentleman struck tinder to a candle. "All is not well, Nick," said he, sinking into his chair by the cold grate.

I knelt to help him off with his boots. "The threatening notes?"

"Aye, those . . ." He wore a deep look. "They promise ruin to Drury Lane. The ruin of reputation, too, yet whose? Garrick proclaims the writer did not say, but may we credit this?"

"He lies?"

"He may not tell all. It shall prove some trick to strip the mask of obfuscation which practiced players wear. I speak not only of Garrick. All actors are schooled to portray what they are not." His chin sank thoughtfully upon his breast as I set his boots by his bed. "Midge," murmured he, the candle guttering in a sudden breeze, its wavering light licking fire in Mr. Franklin's small squarish lenses. "Dismissed by Garrick. Dismissed and dead. And trouble with Lord Methuen. And with Abel Drumm. Did you hear Woodward cavil about salary? Actors squabble over parts. Methodists screech of hell, whilst the Lord Chamberlain may at any moment halt a play. Fame, responsibility—heavy burdens." He slapped his knees. "Yet I like Garrick whether or no he gives out the strictest truth, and I shall help him if I may." He rose, bones creaking. "To bed, Nick, to think on this. Tomorrow: to Drury Lane once more, to begin to sweep clean."

"Quickly, tell all you saw and heard at the playhouse!" breathed Polly next morn at the large round table belowstairs, where Mr. Franklin, William, I, Mrs. Stevenson, and her daughter foregathered each day to eat breakfast. (Peter and King ate in their attic room above.) It was just 9:00 A.M. The young woman's eyes danced. "What was the play? The actors and actresses—what did they wear, how did they look? Did they declaim their lines well? And the pantomime, tell of that. Please, O, please, at once." Leaning over the damask cloth, she spoke rapidly and low. Her mother had stepped into the kitchen to bring new-baked bread; and her daughter wished to wring our story from us whilst she was gone. Outside, framed by lace curtains, the widow Stevenson's back yard showed a rectangle of winter-blackened weeds.

"Do you not think your mother should hear all too?" teased Mr. Franklin.

"Methinks the girl should hear nothing," sniffed William. "If she may not go to the theater, she may not hear of it, and there's an end."

Polly moaned.

"Too hard," chid Mr. Franklin. "One may hear a tale, even of wicked deeds."

"I relent then." William bent toward her. "A man died, you know."

"Died? What?" Bustling in with her loaf, Mrs. Stevenson sawed slices vigorously. "Did I not say the playhouse was a wicked place? O, I am glad I kept my Polly from it."

"I misspoke of wickedness," emended Mr. Franklin. "A man fell from the gallery, that is all. Such accidents may happen in churches as well as playhouses." As bid, he and William proceeded to give many details, of the play, the players, the audience, the songs, the dances, the pantomime, the crying down.

Our landlady's eyes glowed with interest equal to her daughter's, yet when all was told she folded her hands like a judge. "Rowdiness and profligacy. Too strong for my girl." She tapped the great mole by the side of her nose. "No, child, I am firm: you must not set foot in Drury Lane."

"O, mother!"

"I have meant to ask, Father," inquired William, buttering bread, "what did David Garrick speak of to Justice Fielding last night?"

Mr. Franklin scooped porridge from a bowl. "Letters," replied he with a small sidewise glance at me, "like to be of little matter."

Near ten o'clock, Peter was sent to bring Mr. Franklin's coach round to the stoop of number 7 Craven Street. Meanwhile, my journal in one coat pocket, my sketching book in the other, I waited close beside the gentleman under a rapidly graying sky. Mr. Tisdale's printing shop was to our right, the broad Thames an hundred yards to our left, aswarm with lighters, barges, and all manner of craft. Opposite this the busy Strand stretched at the top of the street. Poised in fresh morning air amidst the city's buzz, I thrilled, on the verge of adventure once more. I had journeyed on two such with Mr. Franklin. They had led to perils, but he had steered us past 'em, and I was eager for whatever might befall by my father's side.

In twenty minutes we pulled up in Bridges Street once more. "By the by, Peter," said Mr. Franklin peering up at the box as he stepped down. "You sat in the footmen's gallery last night. The man who fell—did you see it happen?"

Peter shook his head. "Only heard the noise, sir. His cry. Some commotion thereafter."

"Keep your eyes peeled nonetheless. There is some business afoot in Drury Lane, which I look into."

Peter showed a small smile. "Again, sir?"

Mr. Franklin patted his servant's polished brown boot. "Aye, once more. I know you will stay alert."

We entered the Theatre Royal, Drury Lane. How different it was from last night: no dire crush of bodies, the anterooms and stairs and corridors leading up and about peopled only by shadows. Yet I seemed to hear the echo of anger, joy, laughter, sobs; the playhouse was strangely alive, breathing, a place where feeling did not die though last night's patrons had gone. Yet some noises were real, for preparations must be made for tonight and nights to come. Admitted by the doorkeeper, we entered at the top of the pit, the stage bare before us, dim-lit. We passed the very spot where Dudley Midge had lain last night. Looking down, I shuddered, though no sign showed that a life had been crushed out on those dark-stained boards. How little mark a man might leave. My journal and sketching book made weights in my pockets, and I patted 'em. I should leave words and pictures to sound my note after the rattle of death.

Above us the old women, the sweepers and gleaners, moved about the galleries as they had the pit last night, in slow, stooping labor.

And then a candleman lit and drew up a chandelier, a laugh was heard, footsteps tapped, and a dozen musicians marched onto the stage, led by a brisk gentleman in a lavender-colored coat, with a baton in his hand. He lined up his troops, rapped his stick, and proceeded to rehearse his orchestra, cursing any fellow who did not keep the tempo as the maestro wished. Strolling to the front of the pit, Mr. Franklin and I stood and listened for a time, he nodding and smiling, for he loved a tune. I heard other sounds behind the music: scrapings, rhythmic footfalls, hammers banging, voices declaiming, and wondered that the orchestra was not set awry by 'em. Yet it was not, for Drury Lane was a workshop where the workmen must tolerate the nudge of one another's elbows to get an evening's entertainment made by 6:00 P.M. After a time the green curtain lifted with a squeal of winches to reveal painters on ladders, working on a country garden scene. I admired their grand design. How petty a thing seemed my sketching book in face of it. Yet that linden tree by the rough stone fountain—might I limn a better, with more real-looking foliage than those faded daubs?

In all this, actors sometime wandered across the stage with little books or pages in their hands, studying lines. Here came the ironic Miss Prouty with her sharp brows. Mr. Woodward. Abel Drumm as sour as last night, muttering. Lucy Drumm's mother. Hoydenish Kitty Clive cast a wry eye upon the garden, then strode off, passing a thin, affecting-looking woman whom I did not recognize. They nodded polite enough, though I saw Mrs. Clive's lips curl with disdain as she walked away. Coughing pathetically into a kerchief, the thin woman moved off with a step as light as a wraith's.

I saw again the plumpish woman who had regarded Mr. Franklin with such quiet interest last night. She stood by the left-hand stage door, very still, watching. Her gaze moved to me for an instant, something flickered in her eyes—and then she was gone. I glanced at Mr. Franklin. Had he seen? If so, he gave no sign.

"Mr. Franklin," came a hearty cry.

We turned as one, for here marched David Garrick from the opposite stage door, to our right. He beamed as he peered down upon us from the footlights. "You are welcome, sir—but, hem, ah, how long have you waited thus, with no one to greet you? Did not the doorman direct you to my office? We must speak. No, damn me, for I must be at rehearsal. Well, I shall deliver you into good hands." The music had stopped. Garrick turned to his orchestra leader. "Have you met Thomas Arne? This is Mr. Benjamin Franklin, from America, who promises to work his magic to make Drury Lane a brighter place."

"You writ 'Rule Britannia,' did you not?" inquired Mr. Franklin with a smile.

"Proud to say so, sir," replied Mr. Arne from above.

"Why, I have took much pleasure singing it. But pray, Garrick, how are we to join you?" Mr. Franklin tapped with his bamboo the curling iron grillework that appeared sharp enough to cut a man. "This barrier to either side your stage looks painful to cross."

"Made so, to deter riots. But you may join us easily enough." He pointed. "Pass out the pit to your right, turn left, go through the door you will find. That will admit you to our precincts."

"As you say, sir."

I followed Mr. Franklin on this path.

We found the door. Beyond it rose narrow stairs, I mounting behind the gentleman who hummed a tune which Mr. Arne's men had played. Thus we passed beyond the world of playgoers into that of playmakers.

"And welcome again," said David Garrick at the top of the stairs, wringing Mr. Franklin's hand. In lower voice he added, "You shall solve my problem, shall you not? I am pleased to think you shall."

Mr. Franklin said nothing to this.

Garrick wore a scratch wig and a suit of ordinary brown camlet. Were't not for his sprightly manner and lively eyes I should have taken him for a banker or merchant, yet the next hours showed him more than actor: a taskmaster too, to make his playhouse run profitably and smooth. For now, he led us proudly in the narrow, shadowy spaces betwixt tall scenes painted on thin wood-and-canvas panels: grand houses, gaming rooms, woodland dales, churchyards. These scenes rode in grooves that traversed the stage; thus they might be pulled out or slid back as needed.

These mechanics piqued Mr. Franklin, who peered long and questioned close on how they worked. There were sliding scenes on the opposite side of the stage as well, so matching pairs might be pulled together to make a back-

ground or pulled partway to provide perspective. We
viewed a grand aisle of cypresses, a dockside tavern. "I
might turn my mind to such a device," mused Mr. Franklin. "What say you to scenes carried aloft, like sails, which
might be unfurled from above?"

"Very clever. Indeed, sir, it likes me." Garrick thumped
Mr. Franklin's back. "I am sure you will do much good for
Drury Lane!" He led us out upon the stage, and I had my
first view of the playhouse from this vantage: the sweep of
pit, boxes, galleries, solemn in their emptiness. How did it
feel, when these were full, to stand before 'em to make
London laugh or cry?

"But here is Richard Cross, my loyal prompter," announced Garrick, briskly turning. "He knows the playhouse as well as I, and must introduce you round whilst I
am at rehearsal. Dick, this is Mr. Benjamin Franklin, inventor, come to design new devices to help enthrall the fickle
mob."

Mr. Cross was a looming, slope-shouldered man with
worried, umber eyes. "New? Do we need new?" His long-
fingered hand barely brushed Mr. Franklin's before he
turned his fretted gaze to Garrick. "Sir, you must to the
Green Room before the ladies draw blood. Mrs. Clive
fumes like sulphur, Mrs. Cibber near faints, Woodward
grumbles of his salary, whilst Drumm cants like Malvolio.
I rehearsed the menagerie as best I might, but they want
your whip." He looked Mr. Franklin brusquely up and
down. "I am very busy, sir."

"The busy man makes no mischief," replied the gentleman mildly.

"Come, Dick," chid Garrick, "you must spare an hour."
Plainly alarmed by impending mutiny, he was about to
speed off, when a niggling voice halted him: "I say, sir
. . . !" and a little man in pale blue velvet scuttled across
the stage toward us.

Garrick groaned under his breath.

His interlocutor wore a strangely yellowish wig, and his
squashed, sallow head sat upon his stiff white collar like a

pumpkin upon a plate. He waved before our noses a sheaf of papers tied with black ribbon. "My play, Mr. Garrick. *Do* read it once more. I have changed it. 'Tis much more pleasing. Quite comic, a merry dance. Droll. Diverting. Moral too, after the fashion. A man and a maid and three plotting scoundrels, and some madcap wits, after Sir Toby Belch. Why, it out-Congreves Congreve. There is somewhat of *The Country Wife*—though nothing to offend the Lord Chamberlain. I have added a dash of Addison, like pepper in the pot. It will like you, sir, mark my word, and—"

"How did you get in?" Garrick cut him short.

"Why—"

"Mr. Fisk!" bellowed the actor toward the back of the playhouse, where the doorman had admitted Mr. Franklin and me.

This old gentleman's bobbling white head came into view beyond the railing.

"Do you not keep watch? Do you not protect me from these importuning nits?" Garrick whirled upon the would-be playwright. "Now, Mr. Wilkes, I have perused your play sufficiently. I have perused its like many times, and I tell you once and for all, they will not do. For wit you give us old saws and in place of sprightly jigs you rattle our teeth in worn-out dances. Take this poxy stew of yours and go. Better: show it to Rich. He may be able to cook something up with it." He flung his hands in the air. "Cannot Shakespeare bring me some new play? I would dig him up if I could." He strode off fuming.

Mr. Arne's men played on. The painters dipped their brushes. Hammers clattered behind the tall flats, and somewhere a saw bit at a board. At the edge of the stage a grinning man in motley juggled plates.

Mr. Franklin looked at his black, buckled shoes. Mr. Cross pulled his lip. With distressed, high-pitched gaspings, Mr. Wilkes staggered off as if he had been mortally stabbed.

"A fly that needed swatting," Cross said of him. "Fools

must be put in their places." He gazed glumly at Mr. Franklin. "Well, what must I show you?"

"A little of this, a little of that. But first tell (for I am a novice), what does a prompter do?"

"Near all, if you must know." Cross enumerated on his fingers: "Obtain licenses, see to the writing out of parts, advise who must play a role, hire supernumeraries, hear lines, direct scenemen. I am at ev'ry performance to repair disaster."

"Does disaster visit often?"

"I have seen actors strike others who pass in front of 'em as they deliver their lines."

"There is then an etiquette to the stage?"

"There is common sense. There is doing what is wise."

"What other disasters may befall?"

"Forgot lines, which I must whisper if the actor does not make up his own—they deliberately forget 'em sometimes, so they may speak impromptu. Ev'ry man fancies himself a playwright. Vanity would capsize Drury Lane, if 'twere allowed."

"But Garrick captains well?"

"And Lacy."

"As to disasters, you have had two fires recently, so I hear. What caused 'em?"

"I do not know."

"A candle left to burn?"

"Mayhap."

"Or set by some disgruntled fellow, like this Wilkes?"

"I cannot say. 'Tis enough we put 'em out. Follow me, sir—and the boy, if he is yours—for your little bit o' this and that may take some time."

The next hour drew us an outline, with much to be filled in. 'Twas like a painter's cartoon: the general form but without color and of uncertain perspective. Many questions remained to be answered, many territories explored; I saw this in Mr. Franklin's hooded look. I felt it in my own wondering thoughts.

Nonetheless, much ground was covered as we said our how d'ye dos, and I ended confident I might draw Drury Lane's map if I could not yet plumb her nature. And what was she? An agglomeration of rooms, passageways, and structures whose center and largest space was the playhouse itself: pit, galleries, boxes, and stage with its sconces, wings, and flats. West of this was the passage from Bridges Street, along which patrons walked. From thence, having passed through the entry doors, they took stairways up or down to their places. North, from Russell Street, wended a narrow alley to the boxes. East, from Drury Lane, lay a passage to the back of the playhouse, by which actors, dancers, musicians, and other theater folk were most likely to arrive, to save picking their way through the auditorium. Rooms and buildings clustered round this central space, to a total of ten parcels of land, amounting to some fourteen thousand square feet, Mr. Cross informed us, ground rent being paid to the Duke of Bedford, who owned the land. We were shown lobbies, offices, dressing rooms, practice rooms, scene rooms, a barber shop, carpenter shop, wardrobe rooms, privies. Ev'rywhere was a bustle of activity. In his shop smelling of shavings and glue, Mr. Johns constructed a grand fountain, "to make a pretty display of water onstage." In the property room, amidst papier-mâché trees and Roman chariots, men on ladders constructed a huge cloth elephant. We met Mr. Samuel French and Mr. John Oram, scene designers, at work on drawings for a palace garden. We glimpsed a practice of a revel of wood nymphs which Mr. Georges Jean Noverre, the Swiss dancing master, oversaw in a mirrored hall.

We met, too, the woman who had seemed to watch Mr. Franklin.

"Mrs. Goodbody, wardrobe mistress," presented Mr. Cross.

Mr. Franklin gazed at her.

The woman stood just inside a chamber crowded with suits and gowns ahanging on pegs and an army of wigs on stands and three seamstresses busily sewing. "Mrs. Comfort Goodbody," amended she, fixing eyes of a remarkable blue on the gentleman. She was perhaps forty years of age, with round, smooth cheeks and an upturned nose and a generous mouth that told she must have been fetching when young. Indeed she was handsome still, with curls of auburn hair barely touched by gray showing at the edges of a close-fitting white cap. She held needle and thread in plump, fine-formed fingers; pins were stuck in her bosom. Something about her deep gaze made me think of my mother. Might Rose Elizabeth Handy have aged to such an one? Yet pride showed too. Haughtiness?

"I am pleased to meet you, Mrs. Goodbody," said Mr. Franklin with a polite bow of head. I looked back as we moved on, to see the woman's steady gaze trace our progress 'til we turned from sight.

We met or observed many more people in our hour: porters, charwomen, candle snuffers, ticket takers, bill stickers, guards, chimney sweeps, coalmen, masons, glaziers, upholsterers, property men, scene shifters, barbers, dressers, singers, dancers, musicians, minor players. The playhouse was a hive aswarm. "How many people must you pay out at week's end?" inquired Mr. Franklin.

"More than an hundred."

"You have been with Mr. Garrick some years?"

"Since he and Mr. Lacy purchased the patent, in 1747."

"How did you come to your job?"

"As actor first—most prompters start so; I still fill in parts, as needed. I acted Lothario's manservant six weeks ago, when Mr. Mossop fell ill."

"You know many parts, then?"

"More than any man—or woman. More than Garrick. I *must* know 'em." We were just then offstage, on the left side, and I was struck how dark it was amongst the great painted scenes in their grooves. How little one could see clearly, but a thin vertical slot of stage, the matching scenes opposite. Nearby sat some oddments of furniture, huddled shadows. Behind us lay one of the great stage

machines, a winch, which might be used to pull Cleopatra's barge or to lower Zeus's thundercloud from on
high, its huge metal teeth held in check by a brake. Mr.
Cross halted by it. "Look you, Franklin, I do not know
what you may improve to make Drury Lane better than it
is."

"The lighting, perhaps? Will you show it me?"

Sighing, the prompter pointed out the side sconces. He
then led us upon the stage (Mr. Arne and his men were
gone) to look up at the six great lusters, many-candled,
which when fired shed a general light over players and
playhouse alike. We walked to the gently curved forestage
to view the third battery in this arsenal: lights in a long
metal trough, the "footlight trap," as Cross called it, which
was filled with oil. Many small saucers floated there, in
each of which rode two candles, backed with tin reflectors
fed by the oil. This device could be raised or lowered by
means of lines and pulleys attached to another winch in
the prompter's corner. "Thus the audience may see the
actor's face, his change of expression. That is why so much
of a play is acted at the front of the stage. Taken all in all,
'tis a good system and wants no improvement, to my
view."

Mr. Franklin merely smiled. "No doubt your view is a
good one—yet where should we be if before he created
Adam and Eve God had judged the earth wanted no improvement? Understand, Mr. Cross, I do not say I may
effect change for the better—but, taking the upper lights,
for instance, might not the audience's attention be better
directed, indeed the whole tenor of an evening improved,
if their glow were sent not so much over the *whole* playhouse, whereby patrons are easily distracted by their fellows, but more upon the players whom they pay to see?
'Tis but my humble thought. You may after all prove to be
right."

Mr. Richard Cross only sniffed.

He showed us the three trapdoors in the floor. Lighting
a lamp, he led us down a ladder to the musty, low-ceilinged

space below, where were more mechanisms for raising people or objects into sight. Mr. Franklin looked, too, at the great round reservoir at the rear, in case of fire, with its pump to lift the water. He expressed a wish to see the very top of the theater, and Mr. Cross trudged before us up three flights of stairs to the attic where we took note of the six great bolts in the floor that held the girondels. There was little else save dust and a door in the sloping ceiling. "Leads out upon the roof, I suppose?" asked Mr. Franklin, regarding this door, whilst I thought on Mr. Ralph's story of the actor Macklin making his escape through it after plunging a stick into Thomas Hallam's eye.

"Do you wish to climb out to poke amongst the chimneypots?" asked Mr. Cross.

"Another day. Shall we descend? No, no, after you. I have but one more request: would you present me to Mr. Lacy? As I will be much about the playhouse, I think I must know him too. Then we may leave you to your business."

Mr. Cross assented. "I do not mean to be uncivil. Perhaps the lighting may be improved. Follow me."

Two floors below, in a corridor behind the stage vista, three offices looked out upon Drury Lane. One proved David Garrick's, another the treasurer's office. The third belonged to James Lacy, Garrick's partner. Knocking, Mr. Cross ushered us in to introduce Mr. Franklin to the gray-eyed, grave-faced man who rose from behind his desk. Neatly arranged stacks of paper bespoke well-ordered methods; all in the office was spare and tidy. Mr. Cross took rapid leave.

Lacy proved the man who had told Garrick of the evening's receipts last night. In his well-fitting suit of clothes, he was as dry to Mr. Franklin as he had been to the actor, polite, matter-of-fact, fixed upon the business of running Drury Lane. He and Garrick divided their labors, he informed us, hands behind his back: "Each does what befits him. I am in charge of the house, from wardrobe to sweepers. Davy does the artistic side: acting, rehearsals, choosing plays—I care little for that." His brow furrowed. "But what do I hear? Davy has hired you, with no word to me?"

"Not yet hired. I am to look about, that is all. I shall make proposals, perhaps, if I believe something may be done. We may speak of hire then."

Lacy said, "Mm."

We remained some moments, Mr. Franklin asking questions about the running of Drury Lane, and Lacy seemed pleased to talk of his methods. I admired how Mr. Franklin drew much from the man by his quiet inquiry, which said nothing could interest him more than to hear what might be told. He tilted his head, he interjected "Os" and "ayes" at just the moments to draw out more. " 'Tis pity a man fell from the gallery last night," murmured he when a silence fell.

Lacy grimly pushed about papers on his desk. "Such a thing does not redound to our good name."

"Not a common occurrence?"

"Indeed, no!"

"His name . . . Dudley Midge?"

"Yes."

"One time employed by Drury Lane, but recently dismissed, I hear. What work did he do?"

"He thought himself an actor. Played some supernumerary parts."

"Swelled a progress, eh?"

"Was a numberer too."

"And what, pray, is a numberer?"

"A check against cheating. There is much temptation amongst doormen and ticket takers to filch money. The numberers count heads, to match against tickets received. 'Tis our way of keeping watch."

"Midge did not count properly?"

"Worse, he was found in collusion with a ticket seller to skim the pot. There were hints too of forged tickets, though we could not pin 'em on him. The first crime was enough. He denied it—he near spit in my face—but we had proof 'twas true."

"And so you let him go."

"Davy did. He never liked the fellow and was glad to toss him out. Midge was mean-spirited, a troublemaker; he scribbled stuff for the Grub Street rags. Such chasers after rumor are a curse! And then he comes last night to cry down a play. O, I am near glad he . . . but, no, 'tis pity he fell, as you say. Why do you inquire so close about him?"

"I merely wondered if some new sort of railing might be designed, to prevent such mishaps. Is your treasurer in? Might I meet him?"

Mr. Lacy ushered us next door, where Mr. Franklin shook hands with the Drury Lane treasurer, William Pritchard, a little pop-eyed fellow, husband to actress Hannah Pritchard, who had played Lady Brough last night. Upon learning of Mr. Franklin's interest in stage mechanisms, Mr. Pritchard eagerly described the ingenious effects he had worked up for the pantomimes before coming to his present position. Mr. Franklin heard this with many Os.

Escaping, we last met David Garrick's younger brother, George, who was subtreasurer. In all these introductions I was presented as Mr. Franklin's "sketch-boy," who must be paid no mind should I be seen ahanging about. "Nick is an excellent hand with pencil or pen, Perhaps you would like him to limn you? Yet not now, for Mr. Garrick waits on us, and I must have the boy with me. Very pleased to meet you. Off with us, Nick. I bid you good morning."

We descended to rehearsal.

Rehearsals were held in the Green Room, behind the stage. 'Twas a spacious chamber with a fireplace and many chairs, so named because it was painted the same grass green as the proscenium curtain and the candle snuffer's livery and much else about the theater. Here players gathered before going onstage to do their roles or retired between acts to fan their brows; 'twas here too that gallants came to pay court to the ladies and wags to banter. Garrick had longed to ban such intrusion, but the public held firm that the back of the stage as well as the front was its right, and his efforts had met with little success. This we learnt later. For now, as I entered quietly behind Mr. Franklin, all was new.

We saw how a play was made. An assemblage of more than a dozen were seated or lounged about the Green Room walls in attitudes ranging from interest to fidgeting boredom. Some I recognized from last night: Woodward, Mrs. Pritchard, Arabella Prouty, Lucy Drumm's mother, Drumm himself wearing a sulking look.

As for David Garrick, he sat in a chair alertly watching two women speak lines.

The women were Lucy Drumm and Mrs. Clive:

MRS. DRUMM: "My lover was upon his knees to me."

MRS. CLIVE: "Mine was upon his tiptoes to me."

MRS. DRUMM: "Mine vowed to die for me."

MRS. CLIVE: "Mine swore to die *with* me."

MRS. DRUMM: "Mine spoke the softest moving things."

MRS. CLIVE: (with a lewd twist of lips) "O, mine had his moving things too . . ."

All laughed. "Bravo!" cried Woodward.

"Very Clivey, Clivey-Pivey," spoke Mrs. Pritchard to Mrs. Clive, who made an elaborate, saucy bow. Mrs. Pritchard fixed a wicked gaze upon Garrick. "You do not think the Lord Chamberlain will disapprove?"

"Eh, hum, what? Why, there's no politics in't." He shot a black look at Drumm. "No, nor no tweaking of some lord, either. The chamberlain will let be. Very good, Kitty. You, too, Lucy."

Mrs. Drumm flushed prettily at this compliment.

"The god of her idolatry, eh, Nick?" murmured Mr. Franklin to me.

Yet Garrick was not wholly pleased and began to stride about. "You see how Mrs. Drumm learns new lines? She is excellent at it, book perfect!"

"Yet a dull book . . ." I heard Woodward mutter.

Garrick seemed not to note. "Why cannot you all do as she does? Do I ask ye to pull toenails? Do I not pay ye for't? Do not your articles promise you will come to rehearsal on time and know your parts or suffer fines? Come, there is a slovenliness about you which calls for strong measures." He halted. "Why, I am apt—yes very like—to close our doors tonight, lest you besmirch the name of Drury Lane."

Protests burst out: "Why, nay, sir . . . no!" and people stirred like fluttering birds. For the first time I noted Lord Edmund Calverly, unobtrusive, by the fire.

Abel Drumm leapt from his corner. "Play *A Lord and No Lord.*" He gazed desperately round for support. "We all know it well."

Garrick glowered at him. "Damn me if I will play your play. Lord Methuen does not want it. London will not have it. I cannot abide it. We have talked of this enough." Drumm slunk back.

Garrick continued to circle, complaining. All watched warily, yet I caught small, quickly effaced smiles, rollings of eyes, secret ho-hums that said most had seen such prowling before and knew it must be waited out. No doubt Garrick was truly angry; no doubt he also calculated his effects. His remarkable eyes darted from face to face. Had he inspired humble, dumbstruck terror? Some mimed chagrin, many hung their heads, but only Lucy Drumm seemed genuinely cast down. 'Twas she he had praised, yet she looked truly fearful he might shut his doors. Her pink, perfect lips were affectingly parted, her skin had gone chalk, her large eyes were fretted by fear. How small she was, thin-armed, vulnerable, and I had a sudden unsettling intuition of triple forces buffeting her: her husband; Garrick; the spite and petty squabbles of the stage. Could such as she survive 'em?

"Why, Mr. Franklin," exclaimed Garrick, "I did not see you amongst us." With a sunny change of mood, he led the gentleman round, to greet the wry Woodward, Catherine Clive, the formidable Mrs. Pritchard, Mossop, Havard, Davies, Holland, Yates, even the visiting Lord Calverly who

looked on with one or two other men about town. Abel
Drumm shook hands in a crabbed way, whilst his wife
made a quick, deferring curtsey. I was named as Mr. Franklin's sketch-boy, who would be often with him. We also
met Susannah Cibber, the wan-looking woman who had
crossed paths with Kitty Clive as we arrived at the theater.
Both were London favorites, with great followings, and
rivals for important parts, we learnt. Mr. Franklin was an
inventor from America, Garrick explained, who was come
to see what he might do for London. "Welcome him, expect to see him about; offer any assistance you may." He
looked round. "Now . . . I relent; I shall never shut up Drury
Lane. Tut, could you believe I would? But we must perform
better!" He stretched out a hand. "Let us show 'em how to
do't, Mrs. Cibber, eh? Come."

Thus the rehearsal recommenced, Mrs. Cibber and Garrick showing the way well, for they were excellent together: matched souls. Others stepped in as needed. Mrs.
Settle, Mrs. Drumm's mother (for that was who she proved
to be), played the small part of a visiting aunt. Her Lucy
had hardly a larger part, summed up mainly in the words
she had spoke with Mrs. Clive. I puzzled at this, given the
importance of her role last night, but William had said she
performed it due only to Mrs. Cibber's illness, who
would've played it except for her distemper. Mrs. Drumm
had known the part; she had filled in—did that not explain
all? I wondered: had her husband penned Araminta for
her? He glowered and grumbled in his corner, though he
was not the only simmering pot, for I saw in numerous
sharply watching eyes that many an actor would gladly
pounce upon a part if another failed in it. Miss Prouty and
others sneered sometime when they thought no one
watched. As for Mr. Franklin, he leant on his bamboo, his
attention apparently fixed only upon the performers,
whilst his brown eyes slyly roved. Did Lord Edmund Calverly and Mrs. Settle exchange a glance? Did Woodward
always mock? With what awe Lucy Drumm studied Mrs.

Cibber's ev'ry move, to learn how she produced her effects. Sometimes Mr. Franklin's hand squeezed my shoulder, as to say: did you see that, Nick?

At last, near half past one, Garrick pronounced himself
tolerably satisfied and dismissed his players with adjura-
tions that each be prompt at the theater tonight.

When they were gone he came to Mr. Franklin. "Did I
not tell you they were froward children?"

"You guide 'em well."

One player had hung back: Abel Drumm. He sidled up to
Garrick. "Beg pardon, sir—but do you not think my wife
might better play Nancy? 'Tis a larger part, and the crowd
loves her better than Miss Prouty."

Garrick frowned. "Miss Prouty does Nancy sufficiently
well, Mr. Drumm."

"But is 'sufficiently well' enough?"

"What? You protest my judgment in this too?"

"I . . . that is, my wife thinks she might essay the part
better."

"She has said so, has she?"

"Not in so many words, but—"

"The idea, then, is yours?"

Drumm made mouths. "What if it be?" said he in a rush.
"You have shown my wife some favor in allowing her to
stand in for Mrs. Cibber, and—"

Garrick held up a hand. "Mr. Drumm, it is right that a
husband speak up for his wife, especially a wife so reticent
as yours; indeed a wife is in her husband's charge. But you
push her forward too much. She played Araminta de-
cently, yet I do not judge her ready to play more at present.
She is pretty. And affecting. I go so far as to say the mob
smiles upon her. I have noted that she always knows her
lines. She has ambition but wants practice. Practice her,
Mr. Drumm; train her more, and then I might be moved to
enlarge her scope. Now you must excuse me, for I wish to
speak to Mr. Franklin."

"But—"

"Good day, Mr. Drumm."

Drumm's eyes smouldered. He marched off.

"Damned fellow!" growled Garrick as we followed the actor from the room.

⚜ 6 ⚜

*IN WHICH more threats are heard
and a neck is nearly broke . . .*

David Garrick's mullioned office window looked down the playhouse passage, east over the roofs of the wardrobe and scene room and other buildings that lined this passage, to Drury Lane, where coaches, chairs, and the London throng could be seen wending their way under a lowering sky. On the walls were pictures by Hogarth and Reynolds and one of Garrick as Benedick. There were, too, many pretty china plates in blue and white, which the actor collected, he said.

City bells tolled 2 P.M. as Mr. Franklin settled into a chair before the broad oak desk. Garrick perched as bright as Puck on the forward corner of this desk. "Well, sir, you see our playhouse. Mr. Cross showed you all? You spoke to Lacy? Pritchard? My brother, George? What progress do you make?"

"But little, as yet. I see a crooked path, I peer at a vista in which much is indistinct. May I have the threatening notes which have been delivered you?"

"You mean to take 'em along?"

"To peruse at my leisure."

"Hem, ah, might you not do so here?"

Mr. Franklin peered. "You have reason not to let 'em from your hands?"

"Why, ah, no . . . I shall . . . yes, I believe . . . indeed, here they are." Unlocking a desk drawer, Garrick drew forth some sheets of foolscap tied with black ribbon. He passed 'em over.

Untying the ribbon, Mr. Franklin ran his eyes briefly over each sheet. "Common paper," judged he, "which might be had anywhere at twopence the twelvesheet. I know much of paper—I owned in Philadelphia a shop which sold such goods: books, pens, ink. "You find these about the playhouse, you say, dropped in your path?"

"I do."

"Addressed to 'The dev'lish David Garrick.' Mm. The ranting Methodist who had to be put out last night—have you much trouble with such fellows?"

"There are always those who protest pleasure."

"Pah, I hold a man should keep his religion in church. Yet these letters seem to accuse you of sin. Do you sin, Mr. Garrick?"

The actor flushed. "I do not."

"Come, never?"

Garrick's fingers fiddled. "Hem, ah, as ev'ry man sins. I am petty. I lose my temper. Perhaps I too much desire the approbation of the throng, but—"

Mr. Franklin waved a hand. "I ask for no catalogue; 'twas a question in passing. 'I myself am indifferent honest, yet I could accuse me of such things,' etc." He smiled benignly, whilst I wondered, What was in those letters?

Mr. Franklin adjusted his spectacles. "You still wish me to look into this matter?"

"I do."

"Then tell of Dudley Midge."

Garrick spread his hands. "There is little to be told: one of those scrivening fellows, a Grub Street hack, dealing out rumor, lies, and scandal. That the reputation of hardworking men should find itself sucked by such leeches—!"

"Midge worked for you?"

"As numberer. Sometime ticket taker. He acted too, small parts."

"So Lacy said. And was let go for—?"

"Stealing."

"Of which you had proof?"

"Indisputable: the corroboration of the man with whom he was in collusion; records too, of tickets sold but money missing—a petty skimming, but small crime may lead on to greater; we had to toss him out."

"He did not go gracefully."

"He spat, he spewed."

"Threats?"

"Of a general sort: 'You are a superserviceable scoundrel, I shall see you in hell'—that ilk."

"How long ago dismissed?"

"Some two months."

"Seen at the theater since?"

"Not backstage. I banned the creature."

"But may've watched plays from pit or gallery?"

"May have."

"He counterfeited tickets too?"

"We have had, off and on, such vexation."

"But no sure proof Midge took part in't? Where did he live?"

"I do not know."

Mr. Franklin pursed his lips. "Your partner said you had especial reason to dislike him."

"I dislike all such Grub Street scourges."

"But he aimed particular barbs at you?"

"I confess he did."

"How do you know he writ 'em?"

"They appeared in newspapers signed with a name he sometime used: Mr. Wrye. Their tone and manner were his. O, he penned 'em, all right."

"And so you dismissed him. And so he is dead."

"Dead," echoed Garrick as footfalls passed in the corridor outside. Faint music sounded, and the sky beyond the panes grew blacker with cloud. "Why do you inquire so close about Midge?"

"Because he may have writ the threatening letters. Surely you have thought so too?"

" 'Tis true they began to come after he was let go—but, I tell you, he has not been backstage to deliver 'em."

"Perhaps a confederate did it, then."

"Good God, who?"

"With whom was he close?"

"No one loved him. He drank sometime with Abel Drumm; neither holds his liquor well. That was another reason to dismiss Midge, for he came often drunk to rehearsal and one time near spoilt the play by swooning amidst Mrs. Malaprop's lines. We had to drag him offstage."

"All knew he drank?"

"His reek and reeling proclaimed it."

"Yet many drink. You?"

"But little. It diminishes my art."

"Then I am glad you are temperate. By the by, did anyone apply for Midge's body?"

"Not that I know."

Mr. Franklin shook his head. "Truly friendless, then. Well, some poor fellows are not made for friendship. Abel Drumm—has he friends?"

"He insinuates himself here and there. As to friends, he is tolerated."

"You do not like him. Why do you allow him amongst your company?"

"Because he has some skill. You saw him do the manservant in his play last night. He is apt, a quick study, excellent at makeup and disguise. He acts sly roles well. He pestered me to play Lord Brough, but that would not do."

"He is ambitious?"

Garrick laughed without humor. "What actor is not? 'Tis my most trying task, to keep ambition in bounds. The old declaiming style, with solemn sawing of the air," he enacted this with jerking arms, "whilst all other players stand round and watch 'til their turn comes to make the same unnatural droning must give way. Actors must learn to put the play above reputation. Many hate this, but I will have all parts subservient to the whole."

"Pride is indeed hard to quell. Drumm may not have your favor, but what of his wife—young, pretty, affecting? Might not she one day make a name as grand as Mrs. Cibber's?"

Garrick considered. "May be. She is green, yet Mrs. Cibber was green once too—why, I myself grew from a twig. Lucy Drumm has made a beginning. She wants fire (did you note how Mrs. Cibber seemed lit from within as she acted?), yet I do not say it is impossible Mrs. Drumm might one day burst into flame."

"Is she ambitious too?"

"Her husband has ambition enough for both."

"Drives her, does he?"

" 'Twas he convinced me she should step in for Cibber last night. Lucy Drumm is worth much to him: husbands receive their wives' salaries, their right under English law. Drumm himself is not likely to climb the heights—his benefits draw small crowds—and after last night his career as playwright is deader than Dudley Midge. My judgment is that his future lies in his wife, if he can mold her."

"She loves him?"

"I believe she truly does, pathetic woman."

For my part I recalled Lucy Drumm clinging to her husband in Bridges Street last night. I thought, too, on poor Miss Blogg, plying her trade. Was this the choice many women must make: a bad life unwed or a worse one married?

"Pathetic . . ." echoed Mr. Franklin. "What of Lucy Drumm's mother, Mrs. Settle?"

At this Garrick smiled. "Would that all my company were so easy of management. Esme Settle is one of our dependable small players, content in minor roles, a sturdy footsoldier. She made a grave misjudgment in throwing together Abel Drumm and her daughter, but Drumm's career was then on the rise. I wonder if she regrets the match."

"Women must practice strategems in this world."

"Damn 'em when they practice 'em upon me!"

"Is there a Mr. Settle?"

"Enough to beget a child. An actor at Goodman's Fields, I believe, but long out of the picture. Dead or run away, I could not say."

"Mrs. Settle is handsome still."

"Some gentlemen pay her court. And she has her 'gallant in the wings,' as they say. Why, in the dim light backstage you might mistake her for her daughter."

"Might you?"

A sudden brisk rap at the door was followed by pretty face peeping round the jamb, and a woman stepped in, slender, dressed à la mode in becoming pale lavender. She was small and light of step, with high-piled copper-colored hair, tiny pearls at her shell-like ears, sparkling eyes. She came forward, sprightly. "Dear hussbandt," her voice was soft and accented, "I do not viss to dissturb you. I am stopped in merely to ssay I vill be go-ink now, to avait you at home."

"Dearest Eva!" Garrick hurried to embrace her. "My wife, Eva Maria, Mr. Franklin." He gazed at her dotingly. "This, dearest, is the ingenious Benjamin Franklin, of Philadelphia, who is come to design machines for the betterment of our theater."

Eva Maria Garrick held out her hand. "Happy to meet you, Mr. Frank-leen. I hope you vill please my hussbandt."

The gentleman kissed her fingertips. "If it pleases *you*, ma'am."

I, too, was presented.

She cocked her head at me. "A sketch-boy? You vill draw mine hussbandt?"

"No, dear," said Garrick, "he is here to draw the playhouse, to help Mr. Franklin at his task."

"But you musst draw mine David, boy. Sso handsome!". The woman pecked her husband's cheek. "You vill come home before you play tonight?"

"As fleet as Hermes, dear."

Her bell-like laugh sounded as she departed.

"Charming," said Mr. Franklin when the door had shut.

"She is from Vienna," informed Garrick, "a dancer, though she gave up terpsichore when we married. She helps me about the theater; she makes my home a haven. She is the light of my life."

"You have told her of the threatening letters?"

Garrick blanched. "Never! I would not trouble her. You must not speak to her of them."

"As you wish." Rain began to patter at the windows. "You must be off; so must Nicolas and I. One last matter: *A Lord and No Lord*—you truly did not know it lampooned Methuen?"

"I would never have played it, if I had."

"Yet the crying down was begun not by Methuen's partisans but by Dudley Midge, with many in the gallery to help him. A claque?"

"Midge hated me. He vowed revenge."

"Yet revenge on that particular night? By crying down Drumm's play? Where would he get money to pay a claque?"

"I do not know."

"Leave that. The two guards who stand either side your stage—"

"Melville and Flint?"

"Trustworthy?"

"Utterly."

"And quick?"

"Of limb more than mind."

"Quick limbs will do. Alert 'em. Have 'em rove about the playhouse, to keep an eye out for mischief—but they must not put the wind up anyone."

"I shall swear 'em to secrecy." Striding to the rain-wet window, Garrick made irresolute mutterings in his throat.

Mr. Franklin waited.

The actor turned at last. "I must tell you, sir, that . . . hem, ah, Midge likely did *not* write those letters." He pulled a folded paper from his waistcoat pocket. "This came this morn."

Mr. Franklin held out his hand.

Garrick palely relinquished the paper.

"Where found?" asked Mr. Franklin.

"Slipped under my door, before I unlocked it when I arrived at ten o'clock."

"There were people already in the playhouse?"

"Many, as usual."

"Why did you not give this to me with the rest?"

"Because . . . O, you must read it for yourself." With a violent motion Garrick snatched his greatcoat from a peg. "I must go. My wife awaits." He flung himself from the room.

Mr. Franklin looked after him as rain began to strike the window hard. He opened the letter. "Ah," breathed he. "So." He tucked it away with the rest.

I must wait to know its contents, it seemed.

Stepping into the corridor, we descended the stairs.

I thought on Garrick's mercurial nature as we went down, but this soon fled my mind. We stopped in the narrow space between two painted scenes in their grooves. Onstage a swart, moustachioed man balanced on a taut-strung rope, see-sawing, waggling his arms. He juggled plates, one, two, three, then hopped from leg to leg, and I gazed in wonderment at his skill—when there came a whirring and clatter at our backs, followed by a woman's cry of dismay. The letters had named mischief. We discovered mischief indeed.

Mr. Franklin and I turned. In the dim-lit offstage area hovered Arabella Prouty, not ten paces away, hand to her mouth, though she did not see us but stared at something else.

Following her gaze, I saw entangled in the great winch near her a scarf, its loose ends still atremble as if it had just been caught there. Curses onstage drew my attention to discover the acrobat on his back, struggling to rise but unable to do so. The winch had let go his rope. The painters scrambled from their ladders to help him.

I looked to Mr. Franklin. His sharp gaze told he had observed all. With a quick glance at me, he strode solicitously to Miss Prouty. "You are in distress, ma'am?" asked he.

Her fingers chafed her throat. Words came gaspingly: "I had the scarf here . . . 'twas for a part . . . I merely tried it on . . . yet it became entangled . . ." She fixed a look of horror upon Mr. Franklin. "Why, it might've snapped my neck."

He peered at the scarf. "But it did not." He patted her arm. "You are fortunate." Going to the winch, he disentangled the cloth, whilst I watched his eyes trace the weights and lines and brake, which had somehow torn free to tumble the rope-dancer to the ground.

I looked about to see if anyone else was near but could discover no one in the shadows.

Mr. Franklin handed the scarf to Miss Prouty. "Take this. Wear it only when you enact your part." He hurried upon the stage.

I followed. Two lit chandeliers provided a flood of light. Unable to rise, the rope-dancer moaned in ashen agony. Mr. Lacy had arrived, grave-faced, rubicund George Garrick too. Between 'em and some workmen they contrived a litter to bear the injured acrobat away.

Mr. Cross glowered nearby. "Might you design some machine to prevent *this*, Franklin?" snapped he before stalking off at the tail of the procession.

We were left momentarily alone, even the painters gone, save for a single old woman moving amongst the pit, bending, gleaning, breathing a tuneless sing-song as she crept. Mr. Franklin gazed out to the first gallery, from which Dudley Midge had fallen. "Tempers run high. More aboil than usual? Fire seems a theme, Nick. Falling too. Let us take care we neither slip nor burn. For now," he threw an arm round my shoulders, "to Craven Street, where we may think on all that we have met."

* * *

The rain continued throughout the afternoon, a steady patter, dripping from eaves and running amongst cobbles toward the broad, brown Thames, whilst we stayed snug at Craven Street. A leaking at the front parlor window much vexed Mrs. Stevenson until Mr. Franklin stopped it with wax, at which she declared him a wonder and returned happy to her gooseberry tart. Plainly the gentleman did not wish, or was not yet able, to speak on our morning's venture, for he settled at his desk and, muttering now and then an "Aha!" or a "There, you shall see!," scratched vigorously with his quill, reminding me that though he was forced to wait upon the Penns he dug diligent as a mole beneath their feet, scribbling letters to men who might befriend his cause.

He writ, too, to his good wife Deborah and his daughter Sally, to give 'em London's news. At this a deep thoughtfulness fell across his face and he sat tapping his quill against his brow. It was many months since the gentleman had left home.

One peculiar circumstance greeted our return: William had sent his man, King, to see if a shirt he had ordered of a haberdasher in St. Martin's Lane had been sewn, but the blackamoor had not come back. He being absent two hours, William stomped and chivvied outside his father's chamber.

"O, I should be in no hurry to return to you either," Polly tweaked him as she brushed past with an armful of linens. She laughed as she descended the stairs, but I wondered if she was truly so light of heart, now William's fickle affections had lit on Lucy Drumm. I observed this exchange crossing from my chamber with my Latin.

William halted me with a rough grip. "What do you stare at, boy?"

I lifted my eyes. His expression was furious. Customarily I would have lowered my gaze and murmured "Nothing, sir," but long-smouldering resentment struck tinder in my breast. William's haughty visage never once had smiled at

me. I pulled my arm free. Why should he so despise me?
Had I ever done him wrong? Did I not treat him with ev'ry
respect? Emboldened by months of safety at Craven
Street—and by Mr. Franklin's example, who always raised
his voice against oppression—I lashed out: "I met Lucy
Drumm this morn, and you did not! I touched her hand! I
watched her rehearse a part!"

William stared. He bent into my face. "What do you
say?"

My voice faltered at once. "I . . . I spent five hours, s-sir
. . . with Mr. Franklin . . . in Drury Lane."

He turned abruptly and stalked into his father's chamber.

I felt hot and cold all over, yet I must see the result of my
words. Creeping, I peeped round the jamb to discover William so near his father's desk it seemed he might topple
upon it, whilst Mr. Franklin gazed up coolly, pen in hand.

"Why, yes," the gentleman was saying, "I stopped round
Drury Lane. I took Nick with me. Mr. Garrick has asked me
to study what I might devise to improve the lighting of his
playhouse, and I see fit to comply. Did I not tell you of my
intent? O, then I am very sorry, though there is much I do
not tell, if I do not think it suits. Yes, we met Lucy Drumm.
We met other actors as well: Mr. Woodward, Mrs. Clive,
Mrs. Cibber; we saw 'em rehearse for near an hour, Garrick
too, very fine. I shall be spending more time at the playhouse—but I do not think it wise you accompany me, for
that would mean neglecting your studies at the Inner Temple, and I should not be pleased at that." William made
some protesting sound, but his father held up a hand. "No,
Billy, I am adamant in this. Attend plays at night, if you
will, but save your days for study." Rising, Mr. Franklin
gazed sympathetically at him. "I too have sighed at a
pretty face, but the woman you sigh for is married, you
must remember that."

"Married women take lovers!" spat William at this.

Mr. Franklin started, and I sought to read what was writ
in his look: anger, disappointment, the realization, per-

haps, that his son walked a divergent path? Yet was not I the result of the union of a man who had loved outside his marriage, and that man Benjamin Franklin? His troubled gaze found me where I stood just inside his door. I flushed. Mrs. Stevenson's big case clock ticked loud on the landing below, ships' bells sounded mournfully out upon the Thames, whilst Mr. Franklin looked for a moment older, the dying afternoon light making his bald brow dully glow and marking out the lines about his eyes.

He peered back at his son. "Indeed they take lovers. And is't your plan to become Mrs. Drumm's?"

"Why, I . . . that is not what I meant . . ."

"Think what you mean, then. Men's acts exact their toll." He sank into his chair. "And now I must return to my letters."

William's fingers twitched at his sides. He looked like saying more but turning on heel, strode out.

The breeze of his passing chilled me to the bone.

King still not returning as the afternoon wore on, Mr. Franklin began to fret as did Mrs. Stevenson and Polly. For my part I missed the sweet, sad songs King was wont to croon in the attic room during his times alone. They would drift downstairs, a strange consolation. Now, nothing.

Mr. Fránklin stopped Peter on the landing. "Do you know ought of King's defection?"

"Nothing, sir," replied the blackamoor, "and yet—"

"Come, speak."

Peter hung his head. "He was not happy. He talked of running away."

Mr. Franklin looked grave. "And has done so, it seems. Well, we shall send inquiries round. We must try to save him from this course." He sent a searching glance. "Was he not well treated here?"

Peter made a movement but no sound, and I saw from his woeful look that he did not think we should bring King back to Craven Street.

*　*　*

Mr. Franklin and William had their moments of falling out, but they customarily fell in soon after. Whatever William's faults—his rashness, his foppery, his headstrong nature—Mr. Franklin loved him. Watching this drama of father and son, I thought that both were in the wrong: Mr. Franklin wishing too much to guide his twenty-seven year old son, William too much discounting his father's wisdom. At any rate, by six o'clock they were friends once more—though contriving to be so by avoiding speaking of what had passed between 'em at four. They sat by the fire in Mrs. Stevenson's front parlor whilst the skies wept softly out o' doors and hooves clopped soggily in Craven Street.

I sat with 'em, drawing in my sketchbook a map of Drury Lane, as Mr. Franklin had directed, struggling to remember all rooms, passageways, stairways and put 'em where they fit.

"You lawyers have long been friends to acting," said Mr. Franklin, at his ease, feet up. "Indeed, you put on plays yourselves, I hear."

William laughed. "In former days; lately we study law. But you are right: good Queen Bess saw the first playing of *Twelfth Night* in Middle Temple Hall, with Shakespeare himself in Malvolio's crossed garters."

"Ah, I should like to've seen it."

"And I."

Rain softly hissing outside, the men talked of how the playhouse had grown to what it was, whilst I, who had been fed on few books and little teaching, ate this history as a starveling gnaws scraps. How the world had changed from that rawer time, when traveling troops played in inns and public squares. They talked on the Globe Theatre, sadly burnt to the ground, Ben Jonson's comedy of humors, the masques at the new indoor theaters, which he and Inigo Jones designed for Charles I. But His Majesty lost his head to Puritan zeal, and there followed the suppression of the playhouses lasting 'til the Stuarts were restored. Theater revived—in 1660 Charles II issued official patents to men named Killigrew and Davenant, to operate two officially licensed playhouses, these patents devolving by various turns upon Garrick and Rich, the great rivals of our day— but it still must keep watch, for zealots suspicious of its morality longed to shrivel it to a paltry reed that could whistle no significant tune. Even the Crown feared the stage and had passed a licensing act. Its named purpose was to safeguard decency but its real aim was to protect public men from satire's lash. Under it the Lord Chamberlain had unlimited powers of censorship; all plays must be in his hands a fortnight before they were acted, and he might delete lines at his whim.

No wonder David Garrick feared this official's power and bowed and scraped before any man who had his ear.

"Actors no longer own shares but are salaried these days, eh, Billy?" inquired Mr. Franklin.

"They are."

"Tell of these 'benefit nights,' of which I hear."

"Most important to any actor. At the end o' the season, in March or April, a player or playwright is given a night when all profits (minus the expenses of operating the theater) fall in his pocket. The actor's friends throng. London supports its favorites. That is his 'benefit.' "

"So 'tis truly bad for Abel Drumm that on his night few come to support him?"

" 'Tis."

"And that his play was cried down. But, look you, he might take it to Rich, might he not?"

"No. Rich likes Drumm less even than Garrick, so I hear. How dreadful that his wife has such a husband."

Mr. Franklin kept silent on this. He turned to me. "And how goes your map, Nick? Why, excellent!—'tis much as I remember it." His finger traced lines. "What a maze, in which one might become lost. Apt for a game of hide-and-seek, eh?" He rose. "But, as I am to meet Jimmy Ralph for supper at the George and Vulture, I must dress. Your Addison, Nick. The law, Billy. Farewell."

William rose too. "I suppose your map is a decent

thing," sniffed he, glancing over my shoulder. "Damn King for deserting me!" He mounted the stair.

"I have picked Mr. Ralph's brain, Nick," said Mr. Franklin upon his return at eleven, "—all he knows of Roscius and Drury Lane. Sad to learn that so many believe they have reason to hate Garrick: spurned playwrights, slighted actors, envious rivals. Gossips serve up rumors, whilst the mob laps Grub Street's curdled milk as if 'twere cream." He sighed. "Fame will always have its enemies." He dropped into his chair. "Off with these boots, eh? Damn Mrs. Gout! King has not returned? Well, I shall advertise for him tomorrow. Indeed, I may advertise for more than King . . ." Kneeling, I helped tug off his boots beside the half-warm grate. "We have had no time to talk, Nick," said the gentleman when his feet were free. "What do you make of Drury Lane?"

" 'Tis another world, sir," said I.

He wriggled his toes. "A 'distracted globe,' where much is rotten, eh? Do you recall that as we stood by Dudley Midge's broken body I asked if you smelt something? Spirits. Garrick confirms that Midge drank much. Is his toppling accident, then, caused by tippling?"

"Do you think so?"

"I do not know what to think, that is the devil of it. But you have not seen the threatening notes. Fetch 'em from my desk."

Doing so, I read 'em on my low stool under Mr. Franklin's patient gaze. They proved strong meat, railing against Garrick as "a blight upon the English stage," and "a worm in the bud of promising careers." He was "a base, proud, beggarly, white-livered, glass-gazing rogue," and "a knave and a coward," and such like and more. Fire was threatened, and mischief and scandal, yet the notes—all save one—were as Garrick had described 'em: strangely general, demanding he must be more generous with actors and playwrights, easier in his terms, less tight-fisted, etc. " 'Tis as if the writer were chary of naming specific terms for fear of revealing his face," said I.

"Or *her* face, Nick. What do you make of the last letter, the one received this morn, which Garrick near did not give over?"

This was indeed another matter. "It alludes to a woman, his secret mistress," said I.

"But is there truly such a woman? That is the question."

"Can there be, given his devotion to his wife?"

"Desire may be a powerful suborner of sense. Did you note how he paled at the thought she might learn of these threats?" Mr. Franklin made a tent of fingertips before his mouth. "But does this prove he has a mistress?" His brown eyes flicked to mine. "Yet if so, does she ride in a coach emblazoned with *L*?" Slapping his knees, he pushed himself to his feet. "Such speculation is moot if 'twas Dudley Midge writ the things, some ignorant minion dropping 'em in Garrick's way. But if Midge did not write 'em," he gazed out at rain-drenched London, "if the scribbler still lives and plots—what the devil is his aim?"

"Or hers, sir?"

He softly laughed. "Or hers. Faugh, I want rest! Poor Richard says early to bed makes a man wise." He yawned. "To your bed then, Nick, I to mine, to seek wisdom in sleep."

*IN WHICH I draw a dead man, and we
pursue scandal in Grub Street . . .*

W e are invited to dine, Nick," informed Mr. Franklin
when I went to his chamber early next morn to see
what lessons he set out.

In some surprise I glanced out the bow window. Rain had
washed London clean of her customary pall, she standing
out in stark midwinter beauty, rooftops etched in black,
the sun piercing Hungerford Market with icy rays from a
frosty sky. Huge sails glided majestically upon the Thames
like curtains in the theater of life. "*You* are invited to dine,
sir, you mean?" replied I as I laid out on his bed one of the
shirts which Mrs. Stevenson had freshly pressed.

"Nay, we two. This was left whilst I supped with Mr.
Ralph." He held out a paper. "Read."

I took it. In a small, neat hand was writ:

Sir:

I hope you recall Comfort Goodbody, for I am she, of
little account though (humbly) not unwise and perhaps fit to help you in some small way. Indeed I
should be happy to aid the man who has revealed to
the world so much about the electrical fluid. Too,
Poor Richard sits by my bedside to keep me com-

pany on frosty nights. But to business: without intent
I overheard converse betwixt you and David Garrick
which told that you wish to learn more of Drury
Lane, its history, its denizens, the secret currents
that blow in its corridors. She who quietly serves
knows much, and I have served the playhouse many
years. In short, let me now serve you. Should you and
your boy sup with me tomorrow eve, I promise you
good repast and better stories.

A note to number 52 Wild Street, shall set the
stage.

> Yours in All Sincerity, etc.
> Comfort Goodbody

" 'Tomorrow eve' is tonight. What make you of it,
Nick?'' asked the gentleman as he began to pull on his
shirt.

"Mrs. Goodbody has sharp ears."

One inquiring eye peeped above the neckpiece. "And?''

"She is clever at piquing a man's interest."

He tugged the shirt down. "More?''

"You shall sup with her tonight, I think."

He smiled. "Shall I?''

I smiled back. "You cannot resist the bait in this trap."

He laughed. "How you come on, Nick! But it is true, I am
caught by her bait. Stories? A good repast? We shall answer this call. Now, decline love, as the ancient Romans
did."

"*Amo, amas, amat, amamis, amatis, amant,*" pronounced I promptly.

"Excellent—and sufficient Latin for today." Taking my
sketching book from his desk, he leafed through its pages.
"Hum, apt—though your drawing of Garrick somewhat
misses the mark. Yet I like your map of Drury Lane." He
peered up. "Might you draw more: a portrait of Dudley
Midge?''

"But . . . he is dead."

"Yet you saw him three times, *viz.*, in front of the playhouse, in the gallery, expired upon the floor. Come, jog your memory—might you not limn him?''

I closed my eyes, and indeed a picture of the man's features floated up like a dead fish in water: his lopsided mouth, blackened teeth, scaly scalp, the spiteful stare from his yellowish eyes. For an instant Abel Drumm's mean expression was superimposed on Midge's, though they looked nothing alike.

I opened my eyes. "I believe I might try, sir," said I.

Beaming, he thrust the sketchbook in my hand. "Make your attempt, then, before breakfast, whilst I pen a note to Jimmy Ralph. He has consented to help guide our *Historical Review* into print, to right the slanders against Pennsylvania; he will prove some aid to our cause."

With no more ado, tucking his shirt into his brown breeches and drawing on his long maroon dressing gown, he settled at his desk whilst I lit tinder in the grate. To the sound of his scratching quill I sat in his chair by the fire and struggled to transpose Dudley Midge from memory to paper. 'Twas not easy. I made many false starts and must rub out a dozen lines; yet gradually, as a veiled London way resolves out of clearing morning mists, Midge began to take form, not only his brow and nose and unshaven jaw but his furtive nature too. What vengeful eyes! As I worked I thought on the playhouse. How many corridors we had yesterday traversed, stairs mounted, doors opened, vistas explored; with, always, the stage at its center: capitol, throneroom, privy chamber. The citizens of this nation were sweepers and dressers, scenemen and painters, playwrights and actors, all with diverse aims and territories, of which each cried, " 'Tis mine!" Yet they must intermingle, rub elbows, knock shins, black eyes; they must come together to make a play.

And sometimes to murder?

I carried my book to Mr. Franklin. "The best I may do, sir." I held it out.

He peered. "Why 'tis Midge to the life—or the death. Excellent." The sound of Mrs. Stevenson kneading dough thumped from below like the beating of a drum. "Let us down, to stoke our fires with hot porridge and bread."

At the round table belowstairs William chanced to give out that Mr. Franklin and I would be spending much time at Drury Lane, at which Polly wriggled and moaned and begged for news whilst her mother rolled her eyes and tapped her mole.

Fleeing interference, Mr. Franklin wrapped himself in his long, brass-buttoned coat, pulled his round beaver hat on his balding head, and we took coach, he carrying two envelopes in his hand. "I fear for King, adrift," murmured he, tapping these papers as Peter drove us into the Strand. He held up one. "Thus I have writ an advertisement, to see if someone has took him in."

I was glad, for I had many times observed the turned-out slaves, known as St. Giles Blackbirds, ashivering and begging by the road. "I hope good comes of it, sir." This turned my thoughts to John Donne, whose *Meditations* made part of my lessons. "No man is an island." In my short life I had felt enough of loss to hear with trembling the toll of the bell which Donne described. Loss of King stirred my soul, and I hoped we might rescue the little piece of Craven Street that had slipped free!

"What is in the other envelope, sir?" asked I.

Mr. Franklin's eye brightened with the light which warmed it when he was on the trail of hidden truth. "More advertisement, directed to those who populated the Theatre Royal's gallery two nights past. What did they observe of Dudley Midge's toppling? I wish to know."

"Then you believe he was pushed?"

"I think that more than one person is happy Midge is dead." Rubbing the envelopes together, he sang "Under the Greenwood Tree" as he gazed out at the surging morning traffic of the Strand.

The view out David Garrick's office window, down the playhouse passage, was much as yesterday, St. Paul's looming grandly in the east. Garrick wore his tight white wig and was likewise as yesterday, animated, with that volatile manner that made me think of Mr. Franklin's experiments, as if the actor were electrified, though with a fluctuating spark, alternately positive then negative, one moment cheery and welcoming, the next seeking almost guiltily to flee. He greeted us heartily, yet almost at once lost his smile and began to dart about, avoiding eyes, fiddling with playscripts, saying he had much to do and must be immediately in the Green Room and was sure we could be left to our devices, since we had leave of all the playhouse.

Mr. Franklin assured him that we would be happy to pursue our ends by ourselves.

Looking relieved, Garrick had his hand on the brass latch when Mr. Franklin called, "Before you go, may I inquire of one or two matters?"

Garrick halted with an insincere smile.

"You have alerted your two guards?" asked Mr. Franklin.

"As you advised."

"As to the incident of the highwire man—"

"Signor Boldini."

"He is well?"

"Alas, broke his hip."

"I am sorry to hear it. Yet may one wonder . . . did someone break it for him?"

Garrick held his short, sturdy body very still. "Both Lacy and Cross said you witnessed the incident."

"Did they?"

"Little goes unremarked in Drury Lane. But what can you mean? Who should wish to harm Boldini? He is here from Naples but a week."

Mr. Franklin spread his hands. "Mischief was promised; mischief has been delivered. But there is more: Arabella Prouty stood just offstage. Her scarf became entangled in the winch that held Boldini's wire, the failure of which—or deliberate unlocking—might easily have broke her neck."

Garrick looked truly alarmed. "Dear God!"

"How long has Miss Prouty been with your company?"

"Two years."

"Her character?"

"Sharp-tongued sometimes, but—"

"A good actress?"

"You saw her. How do you judge?"

"Favorably. Might she one day make a name as great as Clive's?"

Garrick's fingers twitched at his sides. "Might."

"Who would wish her harm? Come, who?"

With a gray look Garrick relinquished the door latch, "Damn me, I do not know." He began furiously to pace, his hand coming to rest upon a large folio volume which sat on a reading stand beside his desk, his thumb caressing the worn vellum binding as if he sought some strength or clearer thought inside it. I read in his furrowed brow doubts about giving Benjamin Franklin so free rein.

"Shakespeare?" inquired that gentleman.

Garrick peered up broodingly. "Yes, the *First Folio* of 1623, edited by Hemminge and Condell. I prize it above all else."

"Above your wife?"

"What? Never above her. Nothing is above her."

"The last threatening note suggests otherwise, but we shall talk of that another time. As to your book, any man should prize such a volume—though I hear that Shakespeare is sometimes forged these days."

Garrick slapped the vellum. "This, sir, is real!"

Mr. Franklin only nodded. "Speaking of plays, have you a copy of Abel Drumm's at hand?"

"I am sure . . . somewhere . . ."

"Might I take it?"

"Why? 'Tis a dead thing. 'Twill never be played."

"Yet I should like to anatomize the corpse." Mr. Franklin stretched out an arm. "Come, can you find it?"

Fussing amongst papers, Garrick drew forth a sheaf of

foolscap bound in string and passed it over. " 'Tis in Drumm's own hand, and good riddance to it."

"No new threats have come?"

"No, thank God. I truly must go." At the door he showed a face pitifully livid with hope. "Mayhap 'twas Midge writ the notes after all, as you suggest? Yesterday's shot only fired by some minion? Why, that would mean there shall come no more threats, and all that is left for you to do is to improve my playhouse? Egad, I sincerely wish it!" He rushed from the room.

"One may wish," murmured Mr. Franklin, pursing his lips, "but one must also delve." He took my arm. "Come, goodman delver, with your sketchbook as your spade. Let us delve together."

The morning passed in several small scenes, first with Mr. Pritchard, the treasurer, who, like the prompter, Richard Cross, had been with Garrick and Lacy since they purchased Drury Lane's patents in 1747. This rendered the meek, pop-eyed Pritchard expert in all aspects of the playhouse's finances. I sat to one side of his small, neat office, with its shelves of ledgers and view similar to Garrick's over the rooftops, discreetly drawing in my sketchbook what I could of the treasurer's puckered brow and pursed lips with their dry little curve, whilst Mr. Franklin chatted genially, making it seem mere pleasant whim that had brought him to knock, to be gratified with more talk of the machines Pritchard had designed for Drury Lane before he fell into numbers forever. The man was again delighted to speak of his devices—indeed all such mechanisms: the ropes and levers and winches and rising platforms and sinking platforms and pulleys that lifted cherubs upon clouds. His gray look gradually altered to sunny animation, so that in a quarter of an hour Mr. Franklin had from him a well-ordered description of all the mechanical aspect of Drury Lane. As I drew, I listened. When Mr. Franklin had all he wished of machines, he led the talk to salaries, learning that there was a treasurer's book telling of monies in and monies out. By seemingly artless stratagems he soon had this book open before him, Mr. Pritchard explaining entries with an eager tongue and tracing with a ready finger any matter which might puzzle his pupil. Through all this Mr. Franklin's eyes shone. "Truly?" he exclaimed, and, "Explain this, if you will," thus carrying Mr. Pritchard to doormen and numberers and how Drury Lane knew it was not cheated, and from thence to counterfeit tickets and Dudley Midge. Mr. Franklin was shown proof (though it was made to seem Mr. Pritchard who insisted on producing it) that Midge had withheld funds.

"A petty skimming," pronounced the treasurer sternly, "but not to be winked at."

"Indeed, no. Why, never any winking."

As I drew my last line, the treasurer's wife, Mrs. Hannah Pritchard, burst in in a rustling green dress and a little hat perched upon her head like a dinghy riding the sea. She was a famous tragedy queen, and formidable, of so large a girth that next her husband she seemed a barrel next a stave.

With little ado she peremptorily drew him off to act as her knight in some matter in which she believed she had been slighted, though how the little man could right what the grande dame could not I did not see.

When they were gone Mr. Franklin rolled his eyes and hummed before pulling from his pocket a folded paper, which he waggled with a knowing look. Opening it, he went quickly to the treasurer's book, to place the paper next some writing therein. "Not the same, see you?"

Bending near, I saw that this paper was the last threatening note. I nodded. "Indeed, sir, the treasurer's neat script has not the note's broad scrawl."

"We may conclude something from that." He put away the paper. "Your portrait of Pritchard, come. Ha, excellent! Draw more; let us have all the animals here."

Going out, we turned right along the corridor, to descend to the stage—but as we reached the stairs a small sound caused me to glance round, and I saw Lucy Drumm's mother, Esme Settle, backing out of David Garrick's office. Something about her manner made me pause on the top step whilst Mr. Franklin continued down. She was indeed handsome, near as pretty as her daughter, but she wore an anxious look; she seemed to be pleading.

The actor himself appeared, though he had said he went down to the Green Room. "Impossible," murmured he to the woman in some urgency. "Impossible . . ."

Mrs. Settle bit her lip.

Garrick touched her arm. "No," said he firmly before he ducked back into his office. Mrs. Settle looked grave.

And then I was upon the descending curve, Mr. Franklin several paces below. I felt shamed for having observed this scene not meant for any eyes.

Mr. Franklin spent some time looking at the floats that rimmed the stage and squinting at the side sconces. As before, sounds of the theater in preparation accompanied us: the slapping of paint, the scrape of flats, the declaiming of lines. The gentleman wandered about, one hand stroking his jaw, murmuring, "Indeed, I think I might . . . O, it could be done . . ." as he scrutinized candleholders and oil lamps and scowled at the six great pendant lusters, now lowered so their candles might be lit at 5 P.M. "And these . . . how might we . . . ? Look you, Nick, draw me this . . . and this." With a finger he marked the air to show what he wished, I scribbling furiously. He tilted his head at my result. "Hum, it wants refining, but we may do that at our leisure. O, I love a workaday problem! Why, I should've made a happy joiner or blacksmith."

"Never a blacksmith, sir."

"Ha, and you are right, for I would've hammered horse shoes with heels, to see how the creatures walked in 'em. But, hush—"

Above the din of the playhouse we heard an angry voice. We stood far to one side, by the left-hand door, in shadow, so that from most points in the playhouse the stage must appear deserted. The pit was empty save for two figures far

at its back, near the spot where Dudley Midge had broke
his neck: Abel Drumm and his wife, the husband berating
the pale, thin young woman, whilst she stood with an arm
tremblingly held up by her face, as if he might strike her.
"You would never have walked upon the stage were't not
for me," growled he with a black look. "Did I not bring you
to Garrick? Did I not train you? Did I not push and contrive
to put you where you are? Do I not speak up for you, since
you are too meek? Would that you had the Clive's tongue.
But you do not. A girl such as you *needs* a man like me.
And now you say I go too far? Stupid woman!" He flapped
his arms. "Why, you are as good as Cibber, younger, prettier." He grasped her hard, whether in passion or fury I
could not say, and peered into her face madly. "You should
have her roles, if blind Garrick could only see. O, damn the
man."

"But, dear—" faltered his wife.

The husband shook her hard, and hating his cruel fingers
digging into her soft flesh, I made a betraying movement.
Drumm shot a furtive look at the stage—"What?"—and
dragged his wife away whilst she gazed back like a poor pet
bird on a string. Had her frantic eyes glimpsed me?

When husband and wife were vanished, Mr. Franklin
drew me upon the stage. "The playhouse is so designed, I
see, that the topmost row of the gallery may hear what is
spoke here; contrariwise, a voice from the pit carries easily
to us. Have you heard of the whispering gallery, in St.
Paul's? Indeed one might make study of the movement of
sound. We walk in an ocean of air, Nick. What else may its
currents carry to us?"

I wondered the same, but was startled out of my thought
by the rising up in the pit of one of those black-garbed
gleaners who bent and stooped her way with hooded eyes.

Mr. Franklin regarded the creature. "What do they see
and hear, Nick? I make note to inquire."

The gentleman had sent Peter to Wild Street, with word
that we would sup with Mrs. Goodbody tonight. We

stopped by Drury Lane's wardrobe, but if he hoped to find the woman there, with some hint of what would come, he was disappointed, for only an undermistress greeted him, Miss Cray, small, birdlike, curtseying a dozen times beneath her stiff white cap. She allowed him to poke as he wished amongst the garments closeted in rows and folded with the scent of cedar in chests and drawers. We saw Gloriana's gown and Shylock's ragged hair amidst the high white wigs of tragedy. " 'Tis free for all to take, anythin' they needs, for any part," informed Miss Cray as two girls sewed nearby.

"Ever locked?"

"Never. Not that there ain't some finery worth astealin', but the actors and actresses takes pride in havin' their own coats and gowns, and dressers to keep 'em and put 'em on for 'em. Many a actress gets gowns from some fine lady who has worn 'em once and would not be seen in 'em again, but a actress who has no such patron may borrow things here, if she wish, at any time."

"Tell of the head wardrobe mistress."

"Mrs. Goodbody?"

"She is good to you?"

"Very kind."

"Has been here many years?"

"More'n a dozen. Was a actress herself, once, I b'lieve."

"Indeed?"

"Yes. Though many poor girls who do not last upon the stage turn to the streets, Mrs. Goodbody has kept herself respectable these many years, and proud to do so."

"I see," said Mr. Franklin, and we strolled on, seemingly at random, though after a time I saw a pattern to his steps, as if he had in mind my map of Drury Lane, and was pacing it off, corridors, stairways, scene rooms, practice rooms, storerooms, offices, fixing it in memory. He stopped in the offstage gloom to peer at the great winches and pulleys, especially the one which had failed Signor Boldini to break his hip. We then climbed by candlelight to the dark, musty, low-ceiled attic, where I helped push open its sloping roof-

top door. Climbing five rough wooden steps, we stood to
gaze out over 2 P.M. London. A brisk wind blew as Mr.
Franklin leant upon his bamboo. Smudgy mounds of cloud
climbed above Westminster and the long, shining west-
ward curve of the Thames. "How I love the city, Nick,"
said the gentleman as air whipped his brown fringe of hair
about his head. " 'Tis a place of both good and evil—yet I
think if 'twere less evil I might like it less. But we shall
eschew paradox. Yonder lies Grub Street." He pointed
northeast. "Let us hie us there, to ask of Dudley Midge."

Though Peter was returned from Wild Street and might
have drove us, we went by foot. It was some distance, but
Mr. Franklin liked walking. "It both fends off the gout and
improves the wind." This pleased me, for I liked to see the
city. Heading past Lincoln's Inn Fields, Holborn Hill, New-
gate, and Cheapside, I noted playbills for both Drury Lane
and Covent Garden stuck on many walls, as well as for
Sadler's Wells, Spring Gardens, Ranelagh and like places
of diversion, where dancers, puppets, talking cats, contor-
tionists, seven-foot giants, the "baby in the bottle," and
other oddments were set out in view. Billstickers scurried
to slap up the newest fare, and as we approached our
destination Mr. Franklin pointed out runners dashing into
coffeehouses and bookstalls with the corrected bills for
tonight's performances. Taking up one, he sniffed it. "Ink.
Smell, Nick." He held the paper toward my nose. "Another
reason I love London, for its rivers of good, black ink."

Grub Street proved a narrow, cobbled lane reeking of
this ink, men leaning in its doors with ink on their hands,
men rushing along it with ink on their aprons, ink marking
the dun-brown winter grasses by ink-smeared stoops. Inside, the great presses, with their screws and tympans and
friskets, were worked by burly, grunting, inky fellows,
whilst lines of new-printed sheets were strung like handkerchiefs to dry. Mr. Franklin had made his fortune by his
printing shop in Philadelphia; ink flowed in my veins too,
from my time at Inch, Printer, where my good master

Ebenezer Inch taught me to love the craft. Here, midst the sturdy creak of the presses, my fingers itched to take up the composing stick to set some lines once more.

" 'Tis the age of the word, Nick," proclaimed Mr. Franklin as we went. "London pants for news—though more than half that is set in type is lies. Why, I am told that same Dr. Johnson, whom we met in Drury Lane, has invented speeches supposed to be uttered in Parliament." He laughed. " 'Tis not my idea of invention, yet his words may improve on those truly spoke, and as I too have hood-winked the mob, let me not complain." He pointed out several samples of that other Grub Street inhabitant, the scribbler: men disheveled and ill-garbed in frayed collars and scuffed boots, with an air of meanness about 'em and hunger in their eyes, who rushed into this shop or that, or sped their scraps of paper from door to door, to market 'em like costers crying marrows: "Scandal! Aspersions! Unwonted praise!" This was the busy tribe from which Dudley Midge had been yanked by death.

Stopping by a stall, Mr. Franklin bought two or three newspapers, which he perused. "See you? We learn in the *Daily Intelligencer* that last night Garrick and Mrs. Cibber 'seemed to warm and animate each other to such a degree that they near burst into flame.' Yet, hear now, in the *Advertiser:* 'Poor, wan Mrs. Cibber was so languid in last night's performance that she near fainted away during Garrick's rantings.' One is puffery (paid for by Drury Lane?), the other, spite. And who is to choose between 'em?"

"One must watch and listen and follow his mind."

"You will never be admitted to the ranks of scribblers if you advocate such sense! 'Pretty Miss B was seen departing Lord M's chambers four nights together in a closed carriage.' Pah. 'Lady R has hastened back to town from her country seat to do battle with Miss D for her husband's affections.' There are a dozen more such barbs, hundreds in a week. Titillation, Nick. Lies and rumors in a potent brew, to intoxicate London."

"Poison her, rather?"

"Apt. But in it we see why talk of scandal frightens Garrick. It might any man. London battens on a man's reputation, chews it, sucks the bones, and casts about hungrily for the next ragged morsel. But to Midge—" The gentleman inquired in many shops, showing the drawing I had done. I was proud to hear praise of the likeness. Most said they recognized the face ("O, he hangs about . . .") if not the name. A few knew him as Midge, but to others he was Mr. Wrye or Mr. Scatter or Mr. Mince, for he used various *noms de plume*. At each stop Mr. Franklin also showed one of the broadsides which had flown from Midge's toppling body.

In the offices of the *Grub Street Journal*, on the second floor overlooking the yammering street, Mr. Maggers, editor-in-chief, a squat, toadlike, sour little man, squinted at the drawing laid upon his littered desk. "Aye, 'tis Dudley Midge." He peered up from under belligerent brows. "Why the devil d'ye wish to know?"

'Twas just past three o'clock.

Mr. Franklin placed the broadside next the drawing. "Pray, did you print this?"

A scowling glance. "I did. Just three days past. I ask again—"

"I am, sir," said Mr. Franklin sadly, "the poor fellow's brother."

The gentleman had not prepared me for this, but I composed my face into bereft solemnity, so I might be thought the grieving nephew.

"Brother, eh?" growled Maggers suspiciously. "Here, now, why 'poor'?"

"He is dead."

The editor showed neither surprise nor regret. "Come, what's this to do with me?"

The printing room resounded beneath our feet. "He gave the impression, sir, that you owed him," Mr. Franklin leant forward slightly, on tiptoe, "money."

Maggers turned red. "What? He gave it wrong, then, sir.

Or you lie. I owed the fellow nothing, damn him. True, he writ this and that for me, and was a good hand when something low and mean was wanted, to twist the knife, as you might say, but I paid him in ready cash. I owe him nor no one a ha'penny—least of all a man who says he is his brother."

"O, I have no mind to dun you."

"Then—?"

"I wish only to ask some questions."

Maggers grunted assent, at which Mr. Franklin proceeded to tell with a sanctimonious air that he and his brother had been estranged of late, but now that he was dead Mr. Franklin wished to know somewhat of him. Where, for example, had he lived?

"How should I know if his own brother does not?"

"Was he not in your regular employ?"

"No."

"A free agent, then."

"That's it, free. What better than free?"

"O, free is good, free is excellent. But the money flowed both ways sometimes? He paid you?"

This brought a renewal of apoplectic suspicion.

Mr. Franklin pointed to the broadside still on the desk. "He paid for this, for example? Surely you did not print it out of kindness?"

"Aye, he paid me, but he acted as agent for someone else, he said."

"Pray, whom?"

"I did not ask. A man who wishes to express his opinion may do so if he please, and there's an end. I do not pry."

Mr. Franklin struck his breast. "O, prodigious! Should not any man have printed all he wishes? What matter if't be motivated by spite or gain? And if falsehood and calumny mark it, why blink? Aworrying over such trifles partakes of scruple." He poked Maggers's chest hard with his bamboo. "A woman might also write? And pay?"

"Here, now!" The editor scrambled up. "As to that,

women will always have their say. 'Tis past time you were gone, Mr. Midge."

"O, my name is Benjamin Franklin."

"But—"

Mr. Franklin smiled. "You print lies, I speak 'em—no harm." He scooped up the broadside from the desk. "Come, Nick, to fresher air."

He drew me out—yet when we were below, he halted me half-hidden in the ink-smeared doorway of the *Grub Street Journal*. "Aha," exclaimed he softly. "See you? I thought I glimpsed him from the window."

I peered round the edge of the jamb to see slope-shouldered Richard Cross, the Drury Lane prompter, just emerging from the *Public Advertiser* across the way. A black tricorn hat cut hard across his brow. He looked dourly preoccupied.

Stepping out, Mr. Franklin accosted him.

Cross jerked in startlement. "Franklin. What do you here?"

"Place advertisements, what else? And what do you do?"

"What I do near ev'ry day: deliver the notices."

"Like Dudley Midge?"

"Eh?"

Mr. Franklin flapped his arms. "He, too, flew in this air?"

Cross snorted. "I do not 'fly' here, sir, I do business. As for Midge, I do not know what you speak of. Drury Lane wants me. Good day."

"Good day, sir." Mr. Franklin tipped his hat to the prompter's stiff, receding back. He winked. "How fine to be so wanted. Yet I do not disparage Mr. Cross; a hard-working man earns my approbation. Speaking of which, let us work too."

In the following three-quarters of an hour we placed in several newspapers his advertisement for King; in addition: a note saying that Mr. Franklin of number 7 Craven Street, the Strand, wished to speak to anyone who sat in Drury

Lane's first gallery Saturday night. "Having planted, we must wait for harvest."

As we turned back toward the Thames I noted another sort of establishment, a shop which printed salacious books, displaying boldly in its window several titles: *The Maid Upstairs, Night in Old Rome, The Virgin Debauched*, and others, along with engravings which left the contents of these books in little doubt.

Mr. Franklin glanced at this shop. Giving thought, he stepped in and showed the gaunt, sallow man behind its counter my drawing of Midge. "Aye, he writ somewhat for us," said this man. "A dab hand, he was. Dead, you say? O, a sad day for lit'rature." He gave forth a keening cackle.

A moment later we turned out of Grub Street.

🦋 8 🦋

*IN WHICH Mrs. Goodbody tells the life
of a woman—and much else too . . .*

Wild Street lay just east of Drury Lane, three minutes
walk from the playhouse. Though the moon was hid
by cloud, no rain fell when Peter let us down in shadow at
the corner of Wild Court just as the watchman cried eight
o'clock. I knew this spot, for 'twas here more than thirty
years ago that Watts's Printing House had employed a
young man, aged nineteen, setting foot in London for the
first time to seek his fortune.

That man was Benjamin Franklin.

Mr. Franklin had told the story often, but I knew Wild
Court for a darker reason: 'twas here that he and I had
been followed by the mysterious Mr. Quimp when we
sought the murderer of Ebenezer Inch. Quimp was the dire
force behind much of London's crime, and the memory
made me warily scan the night. Twice Mr. Franklin had
thwarted him; twice he had been warned never to do so
again, but though naught had come of these warnings, I
could not dislodge the idea that the evil man kept an eye
on my father, and that he—just, standing for all that was
good—was bound to cross Quimp's crooked path once
more. I shuddered in the shadows.

Yet my fear sank as number 52 came in view, a narrow,
red-brick building of three stories, with a cheery light spill-

ing from a pair of windows on either side its white-painted door. If a woman's house proclaimed her character, Mrs. Goodbody was trim, scrubbed, orderly. Window boxes, bare in February, proclaimed a love of flowers in spring.

A maid opened to us, shy-eyed, little older than I. Curtseying, she led us to the front parlor, where the mistress of the house stood at her mantel lighting two tallow candles in tall pewter sticks. Mrs. Goodbody turned. Her blue eyes took us in. She was somewhat over five feet tall, her figure plump and pleasant in a dark green dress with a white satin underskirt; she wore no wig, but a little ribboned cap on neatly backswept hair, brown with reddish tones: all simple, clean, unostentatious. I judged her somewhat past forty. Folding her hands, she stood silent a moment, and I had the sense that she examined us with scrupulous curiosity, nothing overbold, interested yet willing—indeed restrained—to wait; above all not wishing to make any move which might jeopardize . . . what? In this I recognized the expression Mr. Franklin wore often. I glanced at him. He showed a little smile, head slightly cocked, his attitude the mirror of hers.

The moment broke. A fire crackled merrily. "I thank you for coming, Mr. Franklin," said Mrs. Goodbody, stepping forward.

" 'Tis mine to thank you for inviting me, ma'am," replied he with a small bow, "and for inviting Nicolas too."

"O, I could not leave out the boy, since Mrs. Clay spoke of him so warmly."

Mr. Franklin blinked. "Mrs. Martha Clay?"

I too was surprised.

"None other, she of Bradford Street, sister to Ebenezer Inch. Do not be amazed. She sews, I sew; and there is a confraternity (should I say consorority?) of sewing women who make their way through life by their needles. They talk as they sew. She has spoke of you often. I am grateful to offer what I may to the man who flew his kite to prove lightning and electricity are one, and at some risk hunted down the murderers of my dear friend's brother."

Mr. Franklin inclined his head. "I do what I must."

A smile. "O, not too much modesty, Mr. Franklin. If the cock may crow for believing he brings the dawn, you may crow for deeds you truly do."

The gentleman bowed. "I shall remember me to crow now and then in your presence."

"And welcome—if't be not too loud."

He rose and fell on his toes. "Your letter hinted that you, too, should like to crow, sometime."

The woman's expression changed. I had sensed that she and Mr. Franklin fenced, though the aim of their parrying puzzled me. Her plump face altered to a kind of angry listlessness, and she showed barely restrained disgruntlement as she trailed a finger along the back of a chair. "Many women should like to crow," said she. "Many ought, for they have talent and voice, with much to say and do. Yet most are stifled. 'Stay in your place!' men command. They rule the roost."

"You are such a woman?"

"Now you tempt *me* to immodesty."

Mr. Franklin spread his hands. "Honesty, rather. I prize it above the polite lies I am met with at too many firesides. Come, crow."

Mrs. Goodbody seemed to measure him. She made a small, impatient gesture. "The best I may say is that I have sharp eyes and a brain. I can walk without stumbling."

"A fine skill where the path is rough. I myself stumble often."

"O, I do not mean to say I never—"

"All trip, at times."

"You see how the world runs."

"And try to teach it to Nick. Truly, ma'am, I should like to hear of your life."

"Tush, 'twould not interest you."

"It would, I say."

There came a searching look. "Betsy," called Mrs. Goodbody to her maid, who had hovered in the door, "bring the Spanish brandy. You would drink some brandy,

Mr. Franklin? And a syllabub for the boy. But I am impolite. Sit you down. You, Nicolas, too, here by the fire where 'tis warm." We did, on the sofa. She took the brocaded chair opposite. I sensed an eagerness about her, as if she had much to tell, with here, at last, a worthy man to hear. Yet beyond this I knew not what to make of the woman. She was sure, she knew her mind—yet there was something agitated about her. She sat quite still, seeming as easy as a duchess in a drawing room whilst the fire made flickering shadows, her broad face handsome—pretty, in fact, now I saw it close, with a fleshy pinkness and generous mouth and sharply slitted nostrils; her plump fingers rested calmly in her lap, yet she leant forward, her ample breast heaving with a kind of breathlessness. I longed to limn her in my sketching book.

Betsy brought brandy. Pouring two glasses, Mrs. Goodbody raised hers. "To your very good health, sir."

Mr. Franklin lifted his. "To yours—and to 'stories.'"

Faintly flushing, the woman lowered long lashes over her glass.

"Excellent brandy," proclaimed Mr. Franklin.

My syllabub warmed me with its mild tinct of rum.

"Now, come, ma'am," the gentleman urged. "Your life."

"You will have it, will you?" Brass irons caught the firelight as Mrs. Goodbody seemed to gird herself. "Well, then . . ." Her fingers stroked her glass. " 'Tis many a woman's story—to a point. The long and short is that my father was a profligate Yorkshireman, likable (I am told), an upholsterer by trade but a dreamer, stage-mad, who fancied himself the next Congreve or Addison, as the comic or tragic spirits inhabited him. These spirits struck him alternately, depending upon his fortunes: up or down, though the course of his life bent increasingly down. In any case his occupation—and my mother's, for she had been a dressmaker—had the result that I could thread a needle before I could walk and run up a gown or a seat cushion by the age of ten. My father had learning too, and so I read and spoke French and Latin, in which he gave me regular cate-

chism, very stern, when he was sober. I was a prodigious
student, not from any great love of study but out of boredom. I sewed a great deal, to help my mother in the family
income when my father was on his scribbling rampages,
where gin and ink commingled to produce one of his slap-
dash masterpieces, which few would read and no one play.
I would prop a book before me as I sewed. Thus I spent my
childhood, reading and stitching, not a bad one as I see it
now. We were sometimes hungry and often cold, but I was
not thrust out upon the streets like many a poor girl. That
came later . . .

"After some time my mother died of a pleurisy. I was
thirteen, my hands now sewed alone. And they sewed a
great deal—even to bleeding, late into the night—for 'twas
I who must support father and his gin-and-ink life. A street
brawl took him three years later, at one of the Fleet Street
taverns frequented by poets: a blow, a brief wasting away,
then dead within a week, with my few last coins dug out of
my purse for a pauper's grave. The preacher droned, earth
was thrown onto the wooden box—and what was to
become of me?

"You may guess. The look in your eye says you do. O, I
ask no pity; I have risen above what I was. 'Twas the
streets, Mr. Franklin. You ask for honesty? I give it you.
The streets, where I was debauched by military rakes and
bloods, who promised love to a desperate girl. O, they gave
love: they thrust their idea of it into me, then marched on.
I soon saw how I would end. Did I not have evidence on
ev'ry corner: ruined women, pleading, begging, with hundreds froze to death each winter, or pocked by disease, or
murdered for threepence, hags at twenty, corpses at
twenty-two? Gazing into the cracked mirror of the little
room I lived in, I tore at my hair and sobbed. What had life
meted out? Was I not pretty? Did I not have a brain?

"This thought stopped me. A brain. Should I not use it
to save my life?

"But how? At once my father's dream flooded upon me:
the playhouse. Do not laugh. I had no illusions about my

abilities; indeed I had no idea if I had any. But the play-house was all I knew that might offer salvation (father had took me many times). How ironic that the dream which had destroyed him should lure me. How naive I was. Yet my plan was not wholly without merit: I was pretty and could speak well, and sing. Was that not all that was wanted? In my foolishness I believed so and eagerly began to prepare, sewing the finest dress I could out of scraps, to present myself at my best.

"I set out for Drury Lane.

"It was then managed by Colley Cibber, before he sold the patents to Fleetwood, who sold 'em to Garrick. Old Cibber was a good manager (he died just last year, you know), and he saw in me . . . something. He had been often importuned by my father; he had read one or two of his plays. 'Goodbody has at last produced a masterpiece,' said he when I presented myself. 'Tut, he's dead? Read me some lines.' I did: Polly Peachum, in *The Beggar's Opera*. I sang a song too. 'Very pretty,' pronounced Cibber and that night, more out of generosity (or, perhaps, a wish to bed me, though he never did) than any belief in my talents, had me sing the same between the second and third acts of *The Conscious Lovers*. Many hands clapped, the rakes ogled me for I wore a dress cut very low, and my career was launched.

"Yet I soon learnt that the men about town, young or old, married or otherwise, looked upon actresses as little better than whores. I was thus fair game and found the Green Room each night crowded with flattering, ardent gentlemen who wished to buy me supper as payment for bedding me. How their eyes flashed, how their lips whispered promises to care for me forever! But I had heard such promises before, and seen where they led. O, I was tempted, I longed to be loved. But I mistrusted and slipped free and bided my time and earned the name of Cold-Heart, which made me valued as a tough nut to crack with sweet meat inside. I was pressed hard, yet I saw how it was: I, a woman alone, dared not follow her heart but must count out my life, like a miser his pennies. I had but one treasure. I must give it to the right man. Whom? As to whether or no he were married, that made little difference. Not that I did not long for the respectability conferred by the name of wife, but that could not be my first consideration. I would be a mistress if I must—did not some men set up their mistresses well, and love 'em, and settle goodly sums on 'em too? See how well I had learnt to cipher, by the age of sixteen?

"As to keeping myself by acting, I saw after some months at Drury Lane that I should never supplant Peg Woffington. I had not the gift. I should play maids and visiting nieces and dance a dance or two betwixt the acts before my youth faded—and then where would I be?

"I must find me a gentleman.

"And so I campaigned. To those who seemed possible I made myself agreeable, sometimes even yielding for a time. But this man or that proved as fickle as the rest, as falsely flattering and eager to move on when another, less importunate voice whispered in his ear. O, that a woman might philander with a like impunity! We would teach men how to love.

"And yet I found what I sought: Sir Robert . . . but I shan't pronounce his full name, for he is dead these six years past. Married, but not to me. A gentleman, loyal after his fashion, who truly loved me, I believe. And so I adopted the life of the mistress, she who waits, and when her lover arrives gives him what he wants: a little conversation and then herself. I chafed at this. You, Mr. Franklin, may go out into the world unfettered, but imagine yourself restrained by law and convention so that you may act only through another. He is no better than you, no more able or intelligent, yet the world says you must dance to his tune. Imagine being proclaimed wicked for stepping into a coffeehouse unescorted. Imagine being stood before the magistrate because you do not yield your salary to your husband, who may fritter it on drink and then beat you when he comes home. At least I kept my salary, and my new life was not all bad. The world came to know of my alliance, and, as Sir Robert was powerful as well as wealthy, the rakes soon cried off. I even earned a species of respectability: actresses envied me my gentleman, and he proved my judgment sound, for he bought me this house and when he died settled upon me over a hundred pound a year, which keeps me well."

"Then you have no need to work at Drury Lane?"

"No."

"Why do you?"

"Because I love it. The playhouse has been my life. I have artistry with the needle; 'tis that in which I take pride, with no man to correct me or say me nay. In it I stand alone. And so when I left the stage I went to the wardrobe. Garrick is fortunate to have me."

"He is indeed. But you call yourself Mrs. You then married—?"

"No one. I was loyal to my lover many years; I wed him in my mind. Too, he took this house for me under the title of Mrs. I have kept that title."

"I see."

She regarded him. "Well, what do you think of my honesty, Mr. Franklin?"

His brandy was gone, though in hearkening to her story I had hardly sipped my syllabub. " 'Tis very honest," said he. "A remarkable story. From a remarkable woman," added he after a pause. This unadorned directness struck me, and I peered at him. He had his jocular moments; this was not one. As in those times when he spoke of my mother, his dear, lost love, he seemed now, gazing at Mrs. Goodbody, as naked of soul as when he capered at his air baths. How he examined the woman!

I did likewise: her rosy cheeks, her ripe solidity, the pride gleaming like twin lighthouse beams from her eyes. Yet something mean lurked in me, mistrust. Mr. Franklin liked her? Well, I did not. Why, I could not say; but I conceived in that moment an enmity which I husbanded with shameful joy, like the stolen hoard of some thief.

Wicked Nick.

* * *

This ill feeling was mitigated by the warmth of the fire, my lulling syllabub, talk. It became Mr. Franklin's turn to tell his tale, which he did, I taking pleasure in hearing again the details of his boyhood in Boston, his apprenticeship at his brother's printing shop, his first writings, his early sojourn in England; then setting up for himself in Philadelphia, marrying his Deborah, followed by hard work which was capped with success in business, politics, philosophy, 'til he became world famous for his electrical discoveries and was chosen (though he thought to retire to experimentation) to represent the Philadelphia Assembly in its dispute with the Penns. He displayed a wry smile. " 'Tis hard to walk both high and low roads. I am praised by men of science whilst at the same time spat upon by the Whigs for a dangerous republican. As for the Penns, when I meet 'em their countenances twist in anger and vexation, and at the Board of Trade, where I plead my case, reason is heard with fear. My fairest representations are thought the result of superior art. I have much to overcome."

"Yet you find time to help others."

"I fill my hours of waiting."

"Tell of your wife."

"Why . . . a good wife."

"Your daughter?"

"I miss my Sally."

"Indeed, you are far from 'em."

At nine o'clock we were led into a small, paneled dining room, where an oval table was laid with a white damask cloth and bone china and six candles in a polished brass holder. Sitting down, we begun with a West Indies pepper-pot soup, which I had never tasted before, nor Mr. Franklin, for he praised it highly; then came fish, a large pike; then roasted chicken with chestnut stuffing, all this with tipsy parson and boiled carrots and plenty of Madeira wine. Mrs. Goodbody drank little, and Mr. Franklin was, if not abstemious, at least judicious about his glass. Near ten o'clock came welsh rabbit, all concluded by apple puffs and a cream trifle which I felt disloyal finding at least as good as any I had eat at our good landlady's board.

Mrs. Goodbody asked for my history, and I told of my captivity at Inch, Printer, triple murder, families rent asunder. At this her eyes clouded and she uttered sympathetic sounds. I stopped short of revealing that I was Mr. Franklin's natural son, yet her gaze moved speculatively from his face to mine, and I wondered if she guessed.

If she did she said naught on't. Plainly she was saddened by my blighted childhood, but I still did not give myself leave to like her.

Sipping claret, Mr. Franklin praised Mrs. Goodbody's cook.

"I thank you. Mrs. Nunn has as skilled a hand in the kitchen as I at my needle. I found her in the streets. She was apt; I trained her. It pleased her to do tonight for more than one."

"You have not much company?"

Mrs. Goodbody gazed toward the curtained window. "No."

"Found your cook in the streets, you say? That is like discovering a diamond amongst coal."

Mrs. Goodbody was sharp: "Much that seems coal merely wants polishing. I gathered my maid from the same heap. The world would call them fallen women. I call them beaten down. Would that I could take in more."

Mr. Franklin merely inclined his head.

"But what of your circumstances in London?" asked Mrs. Goodbody. "Is your landlady's cook as able as mine?"

"She herself cooks. She would let no one else in her kitchen."

"Is she good to you?"

"Very zealous about my well being."

"And has a daughter, I believe?"

"Mrs. Clay informed you well. Yes, Polly, a bright girl whom I give books to read, though her mother frowns at the practice."

"You are right to educate her."

"I am glad you approve."

Shortly we repaired to the parlor, by a fire blazing with newly laid oak. There followed a desultory moment in which, settling themselves with more stir than seemed necessary, both Mr. Franklin and Mrs. Goodbody appeared to be laying wood for their own fires.

The woman first struck tinder: "Now, sir, what do you do for David Garrick?"

"Look to invent some improvements in his lighting and machinery."

"Come, that is all?"

"What else might there be?"

She smoothed her dress in her lap. "Rumors abound, Mr. Franklin. About letters that speak threats." Her eyes gleamed. "Do you say you know naught of these? And that Garrick has not asked you to discover who writ 'em?"

Mr. Franklin regarded her out of a great stillness. He spread his hands. "I adjured honesty from you, ma'am. I owe you the like, and so I tell you (trusting my words will not escape this room) that you speak aright. I *do* seek the author of those letters. How did you know?"

A small shrug. "Adding numbers gives a sum. You investigate both nature and murder—so said Martha Clay. Now you are come to the playhouse with more freedom than Garrick gives other men. There you poke about farther than any mere mechanic."

"You cipher well. You believe you may help me in my task? That is why you invite us here tonight?"

"May I speak before the boy?"

"Anything."

"Then, yes, I invite you to offer my help—though that is not all the reason." Her breast rose, fell. "I long to be part of some endeavor of consequence. When I listened to Mrs. Clay tell in what danger you found yourself from this Hexham and the dreadful Quimp, I thrilled. Give me danger, Mr. Franklin. Peril, if need be. Only let me do something in this."

Her breast heaved once more, and her passionately glittering eyes contrasted with her housewifely figure. The fire sparked and licked, sending round the room dancing shadows that might have been the shapes of the adversaries with whom our hostess longed to grapple.

Mr. Franklin tutted. "Peril is no pleasure," said he. "Yet I welcome such alliance as you propose." He reached out to take her fingertips. "I welcome a new friend."

"I long to be such a friend." But she withdrew her hand.

Mr. Franklin seemed not to note. "Then let us begin."

"Have you perused the threatening letters?"

"I have."

"What do they say?"

"They promise mischief at Drury Lane, fire, scandal. Why is not clear. Some general displeasure, it seems. They are couched in a calculated vagueness, as if the writer knows that too much specific may reveal his name. The most I may say is that they seem from some turned-away playwright or slighted actor."

"But there are hundreds such."

"Garrick has many enemies, I am told."

"The prudes despise him, and would shut down all playhouses."

"A certain Methodist preacher, for one?"

"For one. But what scandal does the writer promise to make?"

"To reveal an indiscretion."

"Garrick's? With a woman?"

"Yes."

"But, what woman?"

"The letters do not say. Tell us of Mrs. Garrick."

"Why . . . she is pretty; charming. A man who wished a wife to cater to ev'ry wish could do no better than she. She was a dancer—though after she married never danced except to her husband's tune. Eva Maria Veigel was her name, trained at the Imperial School of Ballet in Vienna. She took the name La Violette for the stage, enjoying a great vogue on the Continent. She arrived in London under a cloud of mystery, to escape enemies some say; here she fell under the protection of the Earl and Countess of Burlington. Rumor has it that she was Burlington's mistress, but I do not believe it. In any case Garrick became smitten, so much that he once dressed in women's clothes to slip a love letter into her sedan. They have been married ten years now, and a happier union might not be known. They own a house in Southampton Street and a villa by the Thames. Mrs. Garrick is a perfect helpmeet. At the theater she reads plays and advises about costumes. At home she is ever ready to serve her husband a cup of tea or a dish of chocolate or to take off her apron to slip under his head when he dozes. She is the one person in whose presence he never playacts, and they have not spent a night apart in all the years of their marriage."

"But in the daytime he might dally?"

"He is devoted to his Eva Maria."

"Many 'devoted' men take mistresses."

"You, Mr. Franklin?"

The gentleman spilt Madeira on his breeches, at which Mrs. Goodbody called her maid. In the busy wiping up, the answer to her question was laid by.

"I believe he loves her, and she him," went on Mr. Franklin when the maid was gone, "—and yet Lady Linacre comes often to the playhouse when a play is not played."

"You suggest—?"

"I merely observe."

Mrs. Goodbody pondered. "Yes, I have seen her there. But many ladies are devoted to David Garrick."

"He is invited to their homes?"

"Often. Garrick dearly loves a lord."

" 'Tis the lords' ladies of whom I speak. Yet as to lords, what is Lord Linacre's character?"

"Very bad. Selfish, wanton, cruel."

"Is he seen much about the playhouse?"

"Some."

"Sir," put in I.

He turned. "Nick?"

"I have forgot to tell you, but—" I described the moment I had observed between Garrick and Mrs. Settle.

"He refused some request? Agitated her greatly?" Mr. Franklin bent his gaze upon our hostess. "A closer view of Esme Settle, if you please."

"A minor actress, as was I, and very good at what she does. Never favored by the mob but yet dependable—one always needs a nurse to Juliet or slave to Cleopatra. Her story is much as mine: she found herself at fifteen under seige and was soon with child. The father, Settle, married her and then ran off, to Barbados I believe, never to be seen again. Esme Settle was determined her babe should not suffer her fate. She found a niche in the theater and has been there since."

"Might she and Garrick have formed a liason?"

"I do not think it."

"Why?"

"Because she is Lord Edmund Calverly's mistress."

Mr. Franklin's eyes lit. "Aha, so that is why he hung about! And why we saw him in the street Saturday night, seeming to observe the woman. Indeed she is attractive; 'tis easy to see why Calverly is taken with her. And has my lord a wife?"

"The mother to two golden-haired children."

Mr. Franklin shook his head. "What a net is wove at Drury Lane. As to Mrs. Settle's daughter, Lucy Drumm—"

"Brought up in the theater, as I told you, home to plotting and spite. One would think she would know these well, yet her mother has protected her, perhaps too much. The child is strangely innocent. She submitted to her upbringing; now she gives the same subservience to her husband. Too many women—even those of gifts—are taught to think so little of themselves they welcome beatings to keep 'em in their place."

I winced at this. I had been often beat at Inch, Printer, but I had never learnt to welcome it; my spirit had been inflamed rather than quenched by hard treatment. Yet thinking on Lucy Drumm—her wide, affecting eyes awaiting her husband's commands, her pale skin, thin arms, and neck like the stalk of a flower, easily snapped—I understood Mrs. Goodbody's bitterness at a world where children were blighted before they had bloomed.

"Tell of Lucy's husband," asked Mr. Franklin.

"There is tragedy—or farce, as you will. The marriage was arranged two years ago, when Abel Drumm was a coming actor, thought to be the next Macklin. We all saw he itched to get his hands on little Lucy, but her mother insisted marriage must be the way. Drumm chafed, he burned, he yielded; the bargain was struck. Foolish mother. Drumm has bad habits, but she overlooked 'em and now she must regret. He drinks, he games. He has twice been thrown in the Fleet for debt. He writes vile stuff. At the playhouse he grows more disagreeable by the hour. O, he acts some parts well—he has a talent for makeup and odd characters—but I do not think Garrick will countenance him much longer. Soon he'll be out o' the playhouse; he'll more than ever need his wife, then. She shows some gift for the pathetic, which always moves an audience; she could become a favorite."

"If put forward."

"What a fine life Drumm might have, dissipating whilst his wife labors! As it is he receives her salary and spends it as he likes."

"English law."

"It must change."

"Much must change. You said Drumm writes vile stuff. What?"

"Books in which men and women appear no more than rutting animals. 'Tis by such low scribbling that Drumm augments his income when he falls into debt."

I recalled the print shop in Grub Street, which had displayed such books.

"But, damn it, why did the fellow choose to lampoon Lord Methuen?" asked Mr. Franklin.

"Because Drumm is a fool. He cannot contain his anger.

He importuned Methuen to be his patron. Methuen turned him from his door. Drumm writ his play in spite."

Mr. Franklin shook his head. "A man out of bounds, I do not like it. To mistake that Lord Methuen might support him, then publicly to attack him, which could have no good result. It shows want of reason."

"Truly, there is something mad about him."

"Drumm and Dudley Midge—were they acquainted?"

"Midge? They had dealings of some sort, for they had a row two weeks ago, so loud I was drawn from my wardrobe. 'Twas over money, I believe."

"Did you hear particulars?"

"None. When they saw me near they fled in fury."

"Midge was liked no more than Drumm?"

"Much despised."

"Midge's friends?"

"None, that I know."

"He tippled?"

"Rum, gin, beer."

"Lived where?"

"I do not know." She tilted her head. "Why do you ask? You think the man's toppling was foul play?"

Mr. Franklin examined his hands as a log sank into sparks in the grate. "I come to believe so." He looked up. "How greatly you help me, with your deep knowledge of the playhouse."

Mrs. Goodbody shuddered. "Murder? Dreadful! And you wish to know more of Midge? Inquire after him at Sadler's Wells. He worked there too sometimes."

"I shall do as you say. Now to Arabella Prouty."

"Why she?"

Mr. Franklin described the incident of the slipped winch.

"Dear God, you think 'twas deliberate? And aimed at her?"

"The scarf would have snapped her neck. The thing goes beyond mere letters. Fires were promised, fires spring up. Mischief was promised, it comes too. The revelation of scandal may follow."

"Miss Prouty . . . I like her; not all do, but she holds her head up well. She is of an age with Lucy Drumm; indeed I believe they are within a year of one another, twenty-two, and play much the same roles. Yet they are worlds apart in spirit. Lucy is self-effacing, a wan goose. Miss Prouty is bold, with a willingness to put herself forward."

"She asks no man to speak for her, you mean?"

"Her tongue can bite, but she is generally approved, a protégée of Kitty Clive's, who sees in her a kindred soul."

"Has she a lover?"

"Has had, I believe—though I think there is not one now."

Mr. Franklin stroked his jaw. "As to the rest of 'em at Drury Lane: Lacy, Cross, Arne, Noverre, the whole pack— are they loyal to Garrick?"

"So far as I know. O, they have their spits and spats, but—"

Furrows lined the gentleman's brow. "Yet all these questions may come to naught. Is there any real crime? 'Tis elusive as smoke: letters from an unknown hand, fires which may be carelessness, the near fatal strangling of a young woman which might be chance, a toppled man who may've fallen only because he drank too much."

"But you suspect."

"I suspect."

Mrs. Goodbody drew herself up. "Then I shall put my mind to't too. I shall watch and listen."

"But not so much that you fall into peril. I should hate to lose so fine a friend so soon." The clock struck eleven. "So late? I fear that Nick and I must go." Rising, Mr. Franklin bowed and kissed her hand. "Thank you for your hospitality. Excellent food too. And your compliance in helping me in my whim."

" 'Tis no whim, sir. Drury Lane must be saved from fires—and murder."

He bobbed his head. "Indeed it must."

With this we stepped out into biting night air, and shortly our coach was swaying and rattling along the dark

London streets, with only an occasional lamp to light the way.

I felt Mr. Franklin increasingly agitated by my side. He burst out: "Think of being a woman, Nick, and being so bound! She spoke true, did she not? A mind like hers, restrained? And to be forced to find your only joy in your needle and thread? 'Tis truly a crime." He moved to other thoughts. "Hum, new actresses must some day supplant Mrs. Cibber and Mrs. Clive in the city's affections, eh?"

"The new must replace the old."

"Aye, but who shall they be?"

To this I had no answer. Mistrust of Mrs. Goodbody still ate at me.

I tossed fitfully in bed at twelve.

❦ 9 ❦

IN WHICH handwriting leads us on,
a creeping woman shows what she has found,
and a dying actress talks of love . . .

There fell more rain in the night, but the heavens
wrung themselves dry by morning, and I awoke to
dripping eaves and thin gray cloudless light seeping
through my casement window overlooking Mrs. Stevenson's back yard. For a moment I lay quiet before creeping
out into the cold. My notebook and sketchbook were by
the burnt candle end on the small stand by my bed. In the
first I writ what passed in my days with Mr. Franklin (six
such volumes filled with shorthand reposed on shelves in
his chamber beside two dozen of the Royal Society's
Transactions). But in my sketchbook I had begun to tran-
scribe a different view of life, and much as I might love
words I thought I might love pictures more. This gave me
pause, for Mr. Franklin guided my writing; yet in drawing,
though he could sketch out a thing tolerably well, I knew
in my heart I did it better. Was there some betrayal in this?
It wrung me to think so. Yet Mr. Franklin praised my work.
His eyes lit when they fell upon my gallery of Drury Lane
faces. Had not my drawing of Dudley Midge served him
well? These thoughts assuaged me and, eagerly taking up
my sketchbook, I began in gray dawn light to limn Mrs.
Goodbody whilst her round face and watchful eyes and
hair neatly done up under her simple white cap were fresh

in my mind. She came with effort but grew clearer until she stood tolerably well-made upon the page. Squinting, I tilted her this way, that. Had I caught the intelligence in her look? Her eager, restrained longing? Yet I hated those keen eyes that seemed even now to quiz me. They were kind, no denying, but I hated Mr. Franklin's liking her. Was he not thus disloyal to my mother? To me?

Dragging on my breeches and shirt and black buckled shoes, I trudged in no very good temper across the landing to his chamber.

I found the gentleman in his maroon dressing gown in his cushioned chair by the fire, a large volume in his lap. The latched window showed that his airbath was done. "Good morrow, Nick," greeted he. "Later than usual. Asleep?"

"Drawing, sir," said I.

"O?"

Reluctantly I showed him Mrs. Goodbody.

He looked long. "Why, 'tis very like the woman." He tapped his brow. "This gives me a thought . . ." Yet instead he pointed to his book. "Betterton's *History of the English Stage*. How strangely artificial were Restoration plays! Indeed many that are writ and done still are: true feeling masked by seeming indifference. Wit bubbles, the manner is all—they produce great delight. Yet in real life the manner cannot be all. Longing and spite lurk behind the mask. Do you know of volcanoes, which seem to sleep yet suddenly wake, to spew destruction?" He gazed out the bow window. "What may happen in the human sphere, when true feeling, long restrained, bursts forth?"

"People then burst, as volcanoes do?"

"And spill into murder?" The gentleman sighed. "Mayhap." He shut his book. "Now, look at this." He took up a newspaper, its ink still wet, as I could see from the smudges his fingers made. "The *London Chronicle*—Peter went round to pull the first copy from the line." He tapped his advertisement seeking knowledge of King. "May this produce some result, for 'tis two long days since we have seen him." He turned to another page: " 'To any person attending His Majesty's Theatre Saturday evening; if you witnessed the toppling of a man, Mr. Benjamin Franklin seeks word with you, which he may make worth your while. Carry your news to No. 7 Craven Street, the Strand.' " He set the paper by. "Honey to lure flies. O, there will be some false buzzing, yet I hope to hear the buzz of truth as well."

"Speaking of truth, sir—you looked to see if Mr. Lacy had writ the threatening notes. Have you satisfied yourself that Mrs. Goodbody did not write 'em?"

He gazed at me. "Why, you are right." How his look probed. "I have her invitation to dine. And right you are too, to remind me that no person stands above suspicion." He rose. "Let us go, then; we shall do't at once." He led the way to his workshop, where he lay out upon the pitted workbench the packet of threatening letters, alongside Mrs. Goodbody's note. 'Twas clear at once that her neat, rounded script partook of none of the jagged quality of the letters Garrick had received.

Mr. Franklin continued to examine me. "Satisfied, Nicolas? Would't not be a sorrow to discover the good woman was our criminal?"

I effected a nod.

"But yet I wonder that, being so keen, your mind does not ask more: whether Abel Drumm writ the letters. Is he not a far more likely suspect?"

"But you do not know his hand."

"O, I do. I have the copy of his play, 'writ in his hand,' as Garrick informed us. Have you forgot it? The lapse is no doubt due to your suspicion of Comfort Goodbody. Truth to tell, I have already compared Drumm's writing. See with your eyes." Bringing the playscript from a cabinet, he set it beside the threatening notes.

I looked. What I saw gave me unaccountable chill. I had learnt that ev'ry person's writing showed idiosyncracies—flourishes, errata, signs of agitation, haste, even pride. Yet this had no idiosyncracies; 'twas, in its precisely formed letters, strictly by the book, as if a master of penmanship had writ it as an exercise; it bespoke no personality. And it was many leagues from the mad rush of letters in the threatening notes.

"Abel Drumm did not write the threatening letters, then, sir?"

The gentleman did not look pleased at what he must reply. "Not by this evidence." Gathering the papers, he slipped 'em into a drawer. "See you the result of study? How might we have guessed that our inquiry into handwriting should help to disclose our quarry?"

"It has not disclosed him yet."

"No, but it helps us to winnow, lad."

At ten o'clock we set off once more for Drury Lane, through a London freshened by rain. At the door Polly pouted that she was not allowed to accompany us. "Were she a young man, her mother would not prevent her," muttered Mr. Franklin to himself. On the way he tried me in my Latin, but I faltered in my response.

He raised a finger. *"Tu ne cede malis, sed contra audientior ito.* Virgil. 'Yield not to adversity, but press on bravely.' Latin will come if you meet him half way."

"I go more than half, but he skips out of reach."

A warm laugh. "O, he skipped from me too! Yet I caught him. You shall too."

'Twill be a hard race, thought I.

Soon enough we were at the playhouse. I began to feel at home here. I liked the bustle, the sense of aim: an arrow notched in a taut-strung bow, to strike at 6 P.M. when the green curtain should rise.

We first came across Dr. Samuel Johnson, who hung about to see his old friend, Garrick. He was a strange combination of the kindly and the satirical; I knew not what to make of him. A staunch Tory, he did not care for "upstart colonists," as he called 'em.

"I, sir, come from America," said Mr. Franklin to this.

Dr. Johnson only sniffed. "That, sir, I find, is what a very great many of your countrymen cannot help."

Mr. Franklin took no umbrage. He praised the *Idler*, which the doctor writ for the *Universal Chronicle;* he drew him on about David Garrick.

The scrofulous old man smiled to recall their journey to London. "I had twopence half-penny in my pocket, Davy had three half-pence in his." Yet there seemed some envy of his friend's success. "Hmph, the world praises Roscius, whilst I drudge, busying myself in detailing the signification of words."

"Not all praise him."

"Davy has his shortcomings, it is true. He flatters himself that he can write plays as well as act 'em. He wastes himself in bowing and scraping before the gentry."

"In the latter I think that you are right."

Dr. Johnson flared. "Hear me, sir, I have known David Garrick longer than you have done, and I know no right you have to talk to me on the subject." With this he strode off.

Mr. Franklin merely smiled. "I like this Johnson. I always like a man who speaks his mind."

We next met Richard Cross, the busy-fingered prompter. From him we learnt bad news: a scene of the Pantiles, just built and painted, had somehow slipped its screws and fallen, striking Mrs. Cibber. Fortunately it had injured only her arm, barely a scratch; but so shaken was she by the event that she had been chaired home to Scotland Yard, and should not go on this night. Cross scowled. "And we must now scramble to substitute *The Fair Penitent,* Garrick as Lothario, Clive as Calista. I pray I get these new bills out in time." He rushed off.

Mr. Franklin met my eyes. "More mischief? Damn it, who is the maker of it?"

We were in the shadowed world just offstage, amongst the giant scenes in their grooves. We could hear from the front of the house Mr. Arne rehearsing his orchestra. Mr. Franklin touched my arm, and I looked. Onstage, from out

the scenes on the opposite side, came Arabella Prouty,
alone, carrying some "lengths"—copies of lines and cues
for parts. Her tawny hair swept back, her sharp nose fixed,
she strode in deep concentration, practicing the lines
which she held out dramatically, and there seemed some
deep signification in her tone:

"How hard is the condition of our sex,
Through ev'ry state of life the slaves of men!
In all the dear, delightful days of youth
A rigid father dictates to our will,
And deals out pleasure with a scanty hand.
To his, the tyrant husband's reign succeeds;
Proud with opinion of superior reason
He holds domestic business and devotion
All we are capable to know, and shuts us,
Like cloistered idiots, from the world's acquaintance
And all the joys of freedom. Wherefore are we
Born with high souls but to assert ourselves,
Shake off this vile obedience they exact
And claim an equal empire o'er the world!"

Miss Prouty gave this speech a breathing life.

"Bravo," pronounced Mr. Franklin, stepping into view.

The young woman started.

"Practice for tonight's play?" inquired the gentleman,
coming near.

She reddened. "The play has changed . . . and . . . that
is—" Her chin lifted. "If you must know, sir, I practice a
part not my own."

"Whose, pray?"

"Mrs. Clive's. Calista."

"What?—you think that something may prevent her
doing it, as injury has prevented Mrs. Cibber's playing
tonight?"

Miss Prouty bit her lip. "There are many accidents of
late. No, I do not think anything will prevent Mrs. Clive.

Mrs. Clive is impervious. Yet I like to try her roles. I could play 'em."

"I am certain of't. What you just read gives proof, for you spoke from the heart. Calista speaks as you feel?"

"If you must have the truth, she does."

"Happy the circumstance when an actress may play her own convictions."

"I *will* play 'em. Some day."

"I pray so." He tilted his head. "I pray too that there have been no more incidents like that with the scarf?"

The young woman touched her throat. "I take great care."

"Was it only accident, ma'am?"

She swallowed hard. "Spite always lurks in the play-house."

"Aimed at you?"

"I speak in general."

"But has such mischief occurred to others? Mrs. Drumm, for example?"

"I do not know."

"You are friends with her?"

Miss Prouty sniffed. "The truth is, I despise her."

"Sweet Lucy Drumm?"

"Sweet as treacle, cloying as honey! I cannot bear a man who toadies; no, nor a woman, neither."

"Her manner toward her husband, you mean?"

"How can she let him treat her thus?"

"May be she has no choice."

"Some women may bend to men because they say they have no choice, but *I* shall never plead that. And now, sir, I must go." She strode off.

" 'Tis a day for honesty," said Mr. Franklin, watching her go, "or what may pass for it."

The morning proceeded in hints and suggestions, though what they might lead to was unknown. They were like the strokes of the painter first sketching his scene; how each line fit to delineate the whole was not yet plain. Mr. Franklin inquired—subtly, so as not to arouse suspicions—who besides Susanna Cibber had been about when her arm was injured and received for reply so many names that it grew to seem a great crowd must have been gathered. "Pah, impossible," grumbled he. "Memory is one quarter truth and three-quarters lies. Who lies, Nick? None claims to've been truly there when the flat fell, though he avows that ev'ryone else was."

He roamed about, taking measurements and poking into corners, as an inventor of devices must. Running into Garrick, he drew him off where they might speak alone. "More letters received?"

"No. My second day free of 'em, thank God."

"I am glad to hear it. But we must converse on the last letter you gave me, if I am truly to help."

Garrick dithered. "If we must . . . but yet . . . just now I shall . . . excuse me." He whirled away toward the Green Room but turned back. "I have forgot, there is a gathering at Lord Edmund Calverly's this afternoon, at two. You are wished to be present. Shall you? Let us take coach together. We may speak privately then."

Mr. Franklin inclined his head.

Garrick fled.

"Skittish as a rabbit, eh? Oho, Lord Edmund Calverly! We shall see what we shall see."

Over the course of the next hour we observed Noverre practicing his dancers, George Garrick and James Lacy earnestly conferring, Pritchard scratching in his volumes of accounts, the actors Mossop, Havard, Davies, Holland, the actresses Mrs. Pritchard, Clive, Yates. I sketched as many as I could. During a stop in the Green Room we overheard Woodward further press Garrick for better salary. Rudely denied, he danced a bitter caper. "Tom's acold—but Tom's no fool. Tom is longed for in Dublin, and Tom may go to Dublin." He gave Garrick a meaning look, "What will his old master do then?" before he capered off. Mrs. Settle was present, in the role of Calista's sister. I looked for some sign of what had passed between her and

Garrick, but he hardly glanced at her. Her daughter Lucy had a tiny role, no more than three lines, at which Abel Drumm grumbled in a corner.

"Get you from the room, sir!" exploded Garrick at this, "I cannot abide such sniveling!" Drumm crept away whilst his wife chafed her hands. Her eyes flitted to the door. Follow her husband? Stay? Garrick's peremptory stare decided her; she stayed. How like a reed she was, bent by the latest wind. Too, reeds might break.

As for Arabella Prouty, she watched all from her place by the fire with a curl of contempt on her lips; Arabella Prouty would never break.

And what did Mr. Franklin make of what he saw? Little if anything, it seemed, for he watched with a fatuous smile as if he had not a thought in his brain. Mr. Franklin could act too.

He led me from rehearsal. By the east passage entrance we encountered James Ralph, who grinned madly as he waved a sheaf of papers in our faces. "A new play, Ben. You will call me fool. You will say I am like the moth at the lamp, for I dash my head against the glass once more. Yet this play—this!—shall make my name. Why, 'tis a very pet. London will be aroar: Jimmy Ralph! give us more of him! But what do you here?"

"Work for Garrick, to make the lighting better."

"What? He does not deserve so worthy a fellow."

"But he deserves *you?*"

"Ha, you have me there." Mr. Ralph rolled his eyes. "Would that Peg Woffington still trod the boards. She would be excellent as Mrs. Bellars in my play. She and Garrick were lovers once, did you know? I go to see her this very noon, and you and the lad must go with me. Come, do. 'Tis opportunity to meet one of the great shes of the stage. Poor Peg suffers a great decline and may soon be with us no longer. Play the truant. Be a madcap, Ben."

Mr. Franklin turned to me. "What say you, Nick?" He tapped his old friend's arm. "I must be back at the playhouse by half past one."

"If you are not, I am not the finest playwright in London."

"You are surely its greatest braggart. Well, then, we shall go."

"Excellent. Give me but half an hour, to press Garrick with my play."

"I wish you well." His friend dashed off. "Hum, half an hour? Let us seek a new perspective, lad."

He led me through the empty auditorium and up silent stairs to the first gallery, to the very place Dudley Midge had sat before toppling. Why had not Mr. Franklin told Mr. Ralph about the threatening letters? Some mistrust of his friend's loose tongue? 'Twas dim where we ended, the great lusters unlit. The gentleman stood very still, gazing out at the benches below, the boxes, the stage. "And there sat Lord Methuen," murmured he amongst the shadows, "and there Lord Calverly, and there Lady Linacre, and there we, beside Justice Fielding and Joshua Brogden."

"Just there," echoed I.

"And there the stage." He stroked the brass bar at his waist. "This railing is tolerably high, and Midge no more than five and a half feet tall. How did he come to go over? Did he stand for one last tipsy denunciation? Lean too far? Or did a pair of unfriendly hands give him the push?"

I started at a noise from the gloom.

Along the row shuffled one of the chars, head down, gleaning with a busy sweep of fingers beneath the benches. She carried over one shoulder a short-handled broom, over the other a worn satchel, like a bladder. With her scrabbling hands and black dress she seemed some huge creeping insect.

Mr. Franklin turned to her. "Good day, ma'am."

The woman peered up. "Aye?"

"Do you always sweep here?"

" 'Tis my territory."

"A man fell from this spot Saturday night."

"Did 'e?"

"What I wish to know is: did you see him fall?"

She wheezed something like a laugh. "I have no part in the playhouse when th' play is on. I comes after."

"Then did you find anything—?"

A shrewd screwing up of her yellowish eyes hinted the answer might be yes.

Mr. Franklin pulled some coins from a pocket. He chinked 'em. "Show."

The wizened woman eyed the coins.

"Three shillings," said Mr. Franklin, "no more."

She scrutinized him but seeing that what he offered was all she would get, she groped in her satchel, drawing forth a cambric handerchief, a worn lady's shoe, a broken watchchain, a small pewter flask. "This," said she, holding out the flask, "I finds under the bench, at this very spot, Satiddy night." They made the exchange, she dropping the coin into her satchel with the rest of her treasures, and Mr. Franklin examined the flask. It was rectangular, an inch wide, four across, about six inches high, with a cap attached by a small chain. Common, marred, dented, it gleamed inauspiciously in the shadows. Unscrewing the cap, he sniffed. "Spirits. 'Twas empty when you found it?"

The old char cackled. "Aye—though if 'twere not, t'would ha' been soon."

"You do not know who left it?"

"Th' likes o' me sees neither play nor playgoers, I told ye."

"The likes of you has eyes sharp enough to see what she wishes." He dropped more coin into her palm. "Keep your eyes peeled in Benjamin Franklin's behalf. Watch for accidents. Watch too for men—or women—who slip pieces of paper under doors. Shall you do this?"

She bit the coin. "This buys my eyes." She moved on.

"Come Nick." Pocketing the flask, Mr. Franklin led me from the gallery.

Backstage we looked for James Ralph but spied Lady Linacre instead, with her long swan's neck and icy hauteur. She was dressed in handsome blue taffeta and strode purposefully. Mr. Franklin met my eyes, jerked his head, and we followed discreetly, upstairs to the corridor containing Drury Lane's business offices. Which door she had entered (for she was nowhere in sight when we arrived) we could not say,

Suddenly Mrs. Garrick came tripping behind us, peeling off her gray kid gloves as she walked. "Good day, Mistair Frankleen," greeted she in her musical voice.

"Mrs. Garrick."

"Good day, sketching-boy."

I bobbed my head.

With no more ado the small, pretty woman rapped gaily at her husband's door. Calling his name, she was about to sweep in—when out he popped like a jack-in-the-box and drew her rapidly away, chattering how pleased he was to see her, at which she laughed her bright laugh.

This laugh echoed as they vanished down the opposite stair.

Mr. Franklin fixed his eyes on Garrick's door. "No faint hearts, Nick." He essayed a purposeful step and might have discovered Lady Linacre inside had not James Ralph prevented, popping up the stairs the actor and his wife had just descended. His face was livid with outrage. "Damn Garrick! Instead of greeting my play with smiles, he hems and haws and says, yes, perhaps he may find time to read it. May find time! If I were a lord, he would give me ten days should I require it, and thank me for the pleasure. But he shall read it, oh, yes; and when he does, why, then . . . but, come, Ben, Nicolas, to Peg Woffington, the happiest whore of the age. Her honest laugh will cheer us."

In a dirty, ill-sprung hackney coach which threatened to unseat us ev'ry moment, Mr. Ralph expatiated so long and with such relish upon Peg Woffington, that by the time we reached her house in Lower Grosvenor Street we had her history and character, *A* to *Z*. Born in Dublin of a penurious bricklayer, she had lost her virtue by the time she was twelve. But she was a striking beauty, full-cheeked, full-lipped, melting-eyed, and determined to rise out of poverty. As it had for Mrs. Goodbody, the stage proved her means. She began as one of a troupe of rope-dancing Lilliputians under the tutelage of a "driving French bitch," as Mr. Ralph put it, and after long years of struggle, honing her skills, rose to fame, first in Smock Alley, Dublin, then with Rich at Covent Garden. She loved men's company, in drawing rooms, taverns, beds; she made no bones of this.

"And was, one time, Garrick's mistress?" inquired Mr. Franklin as our coach flung his spectacles into his lap.

"Aye," replied Mr. Ralph clinging to the door handle, "before he was married. He and the Woffington set up housekeeping in Bow Street. The affair lasted three years. 'Twas Peg who ended it. Garrick wished to curtail her liberties, but she would not be bound, and so 'twas fare-thee-well. She has taken lovers since (I flatter myself I might have been one such, had I pressed my suit). Her present alliance is with one Colonel Caesar, a queer dog who likes not to be known. Peg was famous in breeches parts, where a woman plays a man. An excellent story is told of her and the Clive. Peg sweeps into the Green Room in Harry Wildair's breeches and coat. 'By God, half the audience truly thinks me to be a man!' crows she, to which the Pivey, never one to mince words, retorts, "And the others have seen with their own *eyes* that you are not; aye, and felt with their *hands*, too."

Mr. Ralph's whoop of laughter brought us to the stoop of a large two-story townhouse on the left side of the street. We got down, rapped the brass knocker, and a maidservant showed us into a chill parlor where the same Colonel Caesar Mr. Ralph had spoke of greeted us. He was a little, gray, moustachioed man with large, wet eyes, and looked ev'rywhere but at our faces as he murmured near inaudibly that he was very sorry his dear Peg was not well enough to come down, though she had given orders that all who arrived must mount to her at once. "You know how she likes to see you, Mr. Ralph." With a sad flurry of hands, he said he did not believe he would join us, for he had . . . O, many things he must attend to, and he cast about fretfully to see what these might be whilst we mounted stairs to an airy bedchamber overlooking the street. In a large feather-bed propped up by four or five pillows sat a woman bizarrely rigged: face white with powder, cheeks rouged, lips reddened, patches by the nether lip and the right eye, kohl darkening her lids, and great false lashes, like huge fans, avidly batting. Her great, spotted breasts near lolled from her gown making her seem some huge, grotesque doll. But the doll lived and lifted her plump hand, which Mr. Ralph scurried to kiss.

Mr. Franklin kissed it too.

The hand beckoned me; it stroked my hair. "Pretty boy," came a rasping voice, followed by a spasm of coughs. "What a fine man you will make! Would I were younger so I might teach you a thing or two about life. But who are these handsome fellows you bring me, Jimmy?"

Mr. Ralph told of Mr. Franklin's political aims and electrical discoveries.

Her lashes fanned. "Electricity. I have read how it titillates. Pray, is it any use in love?"

Mr. Franklin smiled. "None that I know, ma'am. As for titillation, beware, for such titillation may kill."

Her arm waved tragically. "I need no killing. I die, do you know that?"

"Never!" exclaimed Mr. Ralph with booming vehemence.

"Nay, my beauty is gone," sighed the Woffington. "Life departs soon after."

Indeed she was wasted; her paint could not hide it. Yet there was spirit in her, coquetry. She pressed Mr. Ralph for news of the stage, which he gave. She cursed Susannah Cibber, Kitty Clive, Hannah Pritchard: "Upstarts! They do not know the tenth part of acting that I know. Why, I have played Doll Common, Mrs. Sullen, Rosalind, Lady Macbeth. I have wrung laughter and tears—may they say the same? But I have always preferred the company of men. Women prattle of nothing but silks and scandal."

"Hard to be an unmarried actress, was it?" asked Mr. Franklin.

"La, 'tis as hard for a woman to keep herself chaste in the playhouse as 'tis for an apothecary to keep treacle from flies; ev'ry libertine buzzes about her honey-pot."

"But a woman may seek a protector."

"And find one. Why, the Duke of Bolton gave Lavinia Fenton four hundred pounds a year as long as she slept with him, and he ended discarding his wife for her." Peg smoothed her coverlet. "An estate and beauty joined are of wondrous power: they make one not only absolute but infallible; a fine woman's never in the wrong."

"Yet the husband comes to own all that is hers."

"True. But if he owns much himself, then she has the use of it and may take a lover if her spouse displease her." She wheezed a laugh. "But you speak true, marriage was not my way. I wanted my life to myself and have had it and pleased to say so. I regret nothing except perhaps that I did not meet *you* sooner, Mr. Franklin."

"I am flattered, ma'am." The woman began to heave great coughs, and we departed soon after.

"Is she not grand?" breathed Mr. Ralph as our coach once more rattled our teeth.

"None like her," agreed Mr. Franklin with a firm grasp of his beaver hat.

I had been promised we should visit Sadler's Wells this evening, to learn more of Dudley Midge. In the meantime Mr. Franklin went off to Lord Edmund Calverly with David Garrick, I home with Peter. The afternoon proved dull. Polly and William were out, Mrs. Stevenson to market. The case clock in the hall marked time with grinding slowness. Yet I looked forward to the oddments that would be served up this evening. As for Drury Lane, it stuck in my thoughts as I drew in Mrs. Stevenson's warm kitchen. Its acting was not all on the stage—but who played false behind the scenes? And why?

☙ 10 ☙

IN WHICH Mr. Franklin spends an afternoon amongst lords and ladies, and we go to Sadler's Wells . . .

Sir, what are you about?" cried Mrs. Stevenson in the entranceway as Mr. Franklin returned just past five-thirty. "My knocker has been rapped so often and so loud that I have been unable to sew or sweep or cook. Rude men have importuned me. Where is Benjamin Franklin? they say. They have things to tell, they say—and they must have money for 'em. What a to-do!"

Mr. Franklin chafed winter-chilled hands. "Did any claim to bring news of King?"

"They would speak only of the playhouse."

"To the devil with King!" huffed William, thumping downstairs. "Did I not treat him well? Leave him to the streets, I say."

Mr. Franklin pulled off his greatcoat. "You are too hard, Billy. I pity the man. Would that I might've done more for him—he had a brain; I had begun to teach him to read."

"You did a very great deal for him," said Polly, joining us. She plucked at Mr. Franklin's sleeve. "Come, why do men wish to speak to you of what they saw at Drury Lane Saturday night? Do you look into murder again? Tell us, do." She fairly danced in her eagerness, but her mother clutched her bosom.

"Murder? Dear me, not again, Mr. Franklin; say 'tis not

so. Seek whatever you will with the Board of Trade or King George himself, but do not bring murder to my door."

"I do not, dear lady." He firmly patted her hands. "Yet I must do business. If more men come, tell 'em I shall hold court tomorrow morn, from ten 'til noon, and that is an end on't."

Mrs. Stevenson muttered at receiving so little satisfaction, but Mr. Franklin staunchly mounted the stairs. I followed. From the landing I glimpsed William slip out for his night on the town. To worship Lucy Drumm at Drury Lane? Little good it should do him for all the part she had in this evening's play.

In his chamber, chill from lack of fire, Mr. Franklin changed his clothes. "Poor Polly. She has a lively mind and should benefit by deeper experience of life. But I will keep close counsel—he who lets the cat out of the bag loses the cat. Now, Nick, we must be off to Sadler's Wells. Prepare you: warm coat and scarf and close-fitting woolen cap. Bring your notebook and sketchbook and a well-sharpened pencil. Hurry, lad."

In ten minutes we were abroad once more, Peter our loyal steersman: up St. Martin's Lane to Broad Street; from thence to High Holborn, then north on Gray's Inn Road toward Finsbury, where my dear mother was buried. 'Twas huddling cold. We pulled the traveling rug close, and I thrust my mittened hands deep in my pockets.

Mr. Franklin leant back. "Shall I relate what passed this afternoon?" This is what he told:

I took coach with Garrick; he keeps a fine rig. On the way he pointed out his house in Southampton Street, "though I much prefer my villa at Twickenham. You must visit there soon, to see my riverside pavilion, where I will put up a statue of Shakespeare so I may worship my god ev'ry day."

I inquired after Lord Edmund Calverly: "Why does he wish to meet me?"

"To know one of the most interesting men about town."

"Though I am an American?"

"True, there is prejudice against you, but he does not partake of't."

"And my lord's character?"

"Why, the most upstanding of men."

"With a wife and two babes, I hear."

"The prettiest children you might meet."

I wondered that, liking children so much, Garrick and his wife had had none. "Calverly dotes on the theater?" asked I.

"Does."

"And finds a mistress there?"

Garrick cleared his throat. "Hem, may do."

"Come, Mrs. Settle, is't not?"

"Well, then, I believe so. The pair makes no bones of it. Surely you do not judge 'em for that?"

"Nay, sir. I am myself too much subject to errata to pass judgment. Besides, 'tis the custom to take a mistress. Why, I am told many a wife positively longs for her husband to do so, so she may have her lover with free conscience."

Garrick made a face. "Too cynical, sir."

I watched him close. "Or too true?"

"Hmph, what people do does not make it right."

"Now who judges? Come, sir, speak of things as they are. You have asked for help, but I cannot give it if you pretend false virtue. Truth, sir. The last letter you received implies you have a mistress. Tell me 'tis a lie, and I shall inquire no more. Yet if't be true—"

Garrick fiddled with his hat. "Damn Fielding for setting you upon me. Well, then—I *had* a mistress." He gripped my arm. "But that is done, I swear." He sank back in misery. "At least I wish that it were, for the damned woman demands that we go on."

"Lady Linacre?"

He stared. "How do you know?"

"I have seen her much about the playhouse. Her coach stood in Covent Garden the eve we supped at the Shakespeare's Head. This very morn she came to you."

"You observed that? Then you saw my dear Maria near discover her in my office. Dear God, how that affrighted me!" He shook his head. "I tell you, though my lady looks fragile as a petal there is something hard as flint about her. Does she more hate or desire me? I cannot tell."

"How did the liaison begin?"

"I was entrapped."

"Ha, come, sir."

"I do not lie. I am in many fine houses; the *ton* wish to entertain David Garrick—and to have me entertain 'em; I play 'em Abel Drugger, Andrew Aguecheek, Lear. Lady Linacre invited me to South Audley Street one afternoon, for a gathering of men of music, painting, art. She is a patron of such fellows, through her husband. I hardly knew her. O, I had seen her in her box, watching, and found her beautiful: an exquisitely made toy, though I had no designs on her. At her gathering, which I attended in all innocence, she drew me apart into another room, and in five minutes, by those flutterings and flattery at which women are expert, made her intents known. I thought on my dear wife. I said no, I could not yield, must not. Yet she was practiced. She burned for me, she pined. Her husband would never know, nor my wife. 'I wish only one hour with you, dear Mr. Garrick, to fulfill me.' She pressed herself to me, she offered her lips—and in short I succumbed. Her guests were quickly dispersed by some excuse, and in her very bedchamber we fell upon her silken sheets and made the two-backed beast. O, she was expert in that as well, a very courtesan, and made me promise to come to her again, which by then I longed to do. Other men have mistresses, said I as I rode home to Southampton Street; why not David Garrick? Yet misgivings tormented me: my wife's little face peering trustingly up into mine, the music of her voice, our perfect life. And then there were the lies I must in future tell. Was this David Garrick? Last there was my art. Could I give all to the stage if I must playact to disguise an affair? No, 'twas too ignominious. Yet once more I lay with Lydia Linacre and went again and again to her house. She had me, it seemed. I grew sick at heart; this must stop. Then came the first of the threatening letters, to which I paid little heed, for a dozen such volleys are loosed ev'ry week. But the fire of which you heard broke out, and then more notes came, hinting at scandal. Fear of exposure spurred me. I did not love my mistress; she had grown in a few weeks clinging, peremptory. I sent word I would see her no more. What a burden was lifted! Yet I reckoned without her nature (I have since learnt that she has cast aside many lovers—but never before she is done with 'em). Her pride is wounded, her ire aroused. Thus she watches, follows, knocks, enters, demands. I have wondered if she herself writ those letters, to punish me."

"Yet they began to arrive before you repulsed her. Too, why would she threaten to expose herself?"

Garrick fell back. "You are right."

"Did her servants see you at her house?"

"No. I always entered by a back way, in disguise."

"Her husband?"

"Never about."

"You know him?"

"A little."

"What is he like?"

"A libertine. A crony of Lord Methuen."

"The man satirized in Drumm's play?"

"The same. They share a taste for gaming and brothels. They are dangerous too—each has wounded at least one man in a duel, Linacre fatally."

"Another reason to cry off his wife. Might he have writ the letters?"

"Pistols at twenty paces are Linacre's style."

"Yet there were strong hints in the last letter that someone knows what you have been about."

Garrick kneaded his brow. "You see why I fear? It is for the sake of my dear Maria that I wish to prevent discovery. How it would wound her! O, I curse the day I met Lydia Linacre."

These were our last private words for a time, for we drew up before Lord Calverly's fine manse. Debouching, we climbed marble steps and were in a moment in a handsome drawing room amidst a gathering of men in velvet suits and ladies with jeweled wigs piled high, all struggling under a brittle air of artifice. Garrick was the most artificial of all, but he had superior means. He set aside the gloom of the carriage. He enacted a carefree soul, sweeping in, beaming, so that even the shopworn *mots* of the dullest nit gained luster by being spoke to him who laughed at them so genially. Indeed all were soon smiling and laughing; ill-ease was banished. Garrick brought me along, presenting me. (Might some of these men take my part against the Penns?—the thought crossed my mind.) Garrick knew his role perfectly: he is after all only an actor, but he must pretend that no one, least of all himself, could ever discover that he is not well-born. There was something sad in this. That so talented a fellow must play the monkey!

Yet I too play a game, and must often smile when I long to grimace.

As to Lord Edmund Calverly, I found him gracious and sensible. "England must make concessions to the colonies or lose 'em," said he, which I was glad to hear. He seems happy in his home. His two girls, four and six, ran in pursued by their governess who was greatly chagrined that they had slipped her charge. They must see Papa, they must! But instead of reprimanding the clamoring poppets, Calverly gathered 'em to his breast and presented 'em round before he bid 'em go. How charming the moment, how touching his care. His wife looked on, her fingers laced at her waist, a grave young woman with large, dark eyes. What to make of her expression? Love for her husband? She showed some strain, I thought— understandable if she knows of his liaison with Mrs. Settle. We spoke briefly, and I found her modest and intelligent, but with an air of tragedy. She is not happy, Nick.

Lady Linacre was present. Garrick blanched to see her, but she was discreet; she hardly spoke to him. I watched her eyes rove. They are of a peculiar light blue: ice in ice. They fell on me, they took me in, they weighed. I was presented, but she showed little interest in an unknown American and soon coldly extricated herself.

Her husband was there too. I tell you, I do not think I have met a man with a crueller face! Not that it is ugly. Though marred by smallpox, it is well-formed, with coal-black eyes, a fine nose, and a mouth crafted for sneering. He marched about like a soldier. Lord Methuen was present as well, and this haughty pair stood apart in their shiny boots and laughed at private mutterings whilst they measured the women as Lydia Linacre had measured me.

I was glad to spend some moments with my old friend, Dr. Fothergill. We talked of botany, Clive's triumphs in Bengal, the playing of the guitar, which the latest manual instructs in.

Toward the end Garrick consented to perform, and the company drew into a semicircle about him. He looked down, breathed, gathered his powers— and launched himself into the dagger scene from *Macbeth*. How prodigious! He stared, he trembled, he intoned, making me think the dagger truly hung in air before him, yet his art suggested that the thing

was at the same time a would-be murderer's guilty
imagining. To produce such contrary effects—why,
'tis genius! There came applause, praise, the struggle
again with wit. The spell of the afternoon was broke,
and we departed soon after.

"Ah, Franklin," Garrick moaned when we were
once more alone in his coach, "if you guessed my
affair with Lydia Linacre, how many others, more
about the playhouse than you, may've done the
same? How many hands may've writ those letters?"

"Too many," agreed I, but there was little more to
say on the bewildering matter.

I thought on Mr. Franklin's narrative as we jounced along
to Sadler's Wells. I saw in't two companies of players: the
actors at Drury Lane, and the titled men and women who
played out scenes of public virtue and private vice in the
drawing rooms—and bedrooms—of the town houses making up the new, grand squares of London. I saw connec-
tions between these two companies. Garrick made one, for
he stretched himself betwixt both, and I felt in him (and in
some of the wealthy merchants who were Mr. Franklin's
friends) a blurring of the line marking out citizen from
nobleman. Abel Drumm's play made another connection,
for it had come near the truth of a man in the higher of the
two spheres. This sphere sang a siren song. Garrick set his
course for it; so did Abel Drumm, with his desire for success and fame. Both men wanted a name greater than that
they had, and might indeed climb to it, by hard work or
stratagems. But what of a woman who wished to do the
same? She could rise only by marriage—or by finding a
lord to be her lover.

Amidst these thoughts we left London's narrow lanes to
move out upon the New Road, heading north under a black
sky where no stars shone. Fields surrounded us, looming
folds of shadow. Our coach lamp so feebly cut the inky
night that I was glad when light from some farmhouse or
inn said we kept to the proper way. Highwaymen might

lurk even this close to the city, and I had no wish to find this the occasion of meeting one.

"Sadler's Wells, sir," said I to Mr. Franklin, "why so named?"

He smiled. "Because of its history. 'Tis in the high north ridge, next the New River, the location of many springs. Many years ago one Dick Sadler kept a music house there. His workmen uncovered an old well, part of an ancient festival site, and upon being advised that its waters might be restorative, the man determined to convert his establishment into a watering place, where a course of libations was advertised to cure the dropsy, jaundice, scurvy, green sickness, ulcers, virgin's fever, what you will. Whether or no these claims were true, the thing proved a success, Sadler laying on gardens and arbors, where patrons might be entertained by singers, tumblers, and rope dancers whilst they waited for the waters to purge 'em. The place has had its ups and downs; at one point 'twas little more than a house of bawds and tricksters, I am told, where the high point was the Hibernian Cannibal, who for five guineas ate a chicken live, feet and feathers. But it has new managers now, Rosoman and Hough, and is licensed under the minor theater act. The wondrous waters are no more, though one may purchase ale and beer." He grew alert. "We slow. Have we arrived?"

We had. The creak of our wheels ceased, and I heard faint sounds of music and laughter coming from a barnlike wooden building with light spilling from two small windows like slitted eyes on either side its door. We got down, Mr. Franklin beckoning Peter to join us. Crossing a coppiced garden, I caught the soft sluicing of water from the New River and glimpsed through an arbor the lights of London far away downhill.

Then we were indoors amidst heat and noise. Mr. Franklin paid two shillings for us, threepence so Peter might stand in back with the other servingmen. 'Twas a small house: a pit and boxes and one low gallery, in a horseshoe curve. The show had begun, so we had to squeeze to find places at the far left side. Sadler's Wells was a far cry from Drury Lane. It sported no titled patrons that I could discover, being made up of footmen done up as beaux, apprentices with oaken cudgels, slatterns and city rakes. Yet there was a raw cheer to the throng, an unbuttoned joy. Red faces, clay pipes, blackened teeth split in grins, pints of ale lifted high, and a circus onstage: that was Sadler's Wells.

Mr. Franklin leant near:

"Here hat with hat, ribbon with ribbon vies;
Wig threatens wig, and eyes contend with eyes."

I nodded. The show was no play as at Drury Lane but a succession of acts marked more by vigor than grace. There were Miss Jenkins, who danced with rapiers pointed at her throat and twirled so madly that her skirts lifted immodestly high; the 'Dutchman,' who did a headfirst fall from the ceiling, miraculously landing on his feet; Mr. Carey who played triple peals and bob-majors by the bells on his head, hands, and boots; Miss Grice, who leapt a somersault through a hogshead of fire; Michael Maddox, the rope dancer, who played the violin, trumpet, and drum, tossed a coach wheel, and concluded by firing a brace of pistols, at which two dead woodcocks flew from the wings. How we laughed and clapped! There were singers, too, and an entertainment called "The Americans Triumph over the Savages," a sort of pageant, comically absurd, with outlandishly dressed Indians put down by wooden muskets.

Mr. Franklin nudged me. "I would be better entertained—and vastly more pleased—if the savages were certain officious Englishmen I meet about Whitehall. Come, Nick." He drew me out.

The corridor was chill and deserted save for a hoary old ticket taker. Mr. Franklin inquired where he might find Thomas Rosoman, and we were led with wheezing breath to an office at the back of the house.

This proved a small cell, cramped and untidy, with papers and ledgers piled precariously ev'rywhere. It had a narrow window at the rear, where one might look out over the pit, to watch the stage. A willowy gentleman of middle age was doing just this as we entered.

Shutting the wooden panel, he turned to meet our gazes.

"Do they like it?" inquired he sharply. "Do they?"

"*I* do," replied Mr. Franklin.

A gesture of impatience. "Nay, but do *they?*"

"I believe so."

"But how d'you *know?*"

"I sat amongst 'em. They never saw better."

"*You* never saw better, you mean. What is your name?"

"Benjamin Franklin. Of Philadelphia. This is my boy, Nick. You are Thomas Rosoman?"

Nodding, the man stared as to say, come, out with your business.

Mr. Franklin wished to know about Dudley Midge, he said. "I am told he worked here."

"Midge?" Rosoman scratched his chin. Mr. Franklin produced my sketch, and his eyes lit. "Fly." He tapped the face. "Why, 'tis Mr. Fly. Not his real name, o' course. But called himself so and was billed so, and that was all I ever knew him by. Midge, you say? Well. He imitated a fly, you see, with a darting and buzzing and licking of hands. Very comical."

"One of your acts, then."

"Was."

"But has not been for a time?"

"O, many weeks."

"What do you know of him otherwise?"

"Nothing—save that he was one o' those scrambling fellows who leads his life by hit or miss. Not a pleasant man. I have some memory that he labored in Grub Street, though I cannot say for sure." A final burst of music sounded from the stage, followed by the noise of patrons cheerily departing. "They *did* like it, didn't they? Will they come back? But why do you ask about Fly?"

"Because he is dead. And there are questions about his dying."

Rosoman blinked. Rummaging amongst a pile of papers at the foot of his desk, he plucked forth a folded scrap of paper. "Then I may toss this out."

"What?"

"A note, delivered to Fly when he worked for me. I had forgot 'twas here (my office may look ill put-together, but I know where to find a thing when I need it). Fly didn't show to do his turn that night; he never showed ever, and I forgot the paper." Crumpling it, he was about to toss it in a bin when Mr. Franklin spoke.

"May I have it?"

" 'Tis yours."

Mr. Franklin received the wrinkled scrap. "Who delivered it?"

"Some dirty-faced boy; London crawls with 'em like a dog crawls with fleas. Who gave it him?—I know not. What the devil!" The door had crashed open, and Mr. Carey of the bells burst in, followed by Miss Jenkins hot on his heels, brandishing her rapiers, with which she pursued Carey frantically round the desk until Rosoman grabbed her by the waist. "Here, now!" There followed screaming and counterattack: "Hound, bastard!" cried Miss Jenkins in Rosoman's grip. "Bitch, slattern!" fired back Carey and stuck out his tongue.

"Cease!" shouted Rosoman. "Stop at once!"

They did not stop. Rolling his eyes, Mr. Franklin drew me from the melee.

The last of the patrons were moving out into the night as we approached the exit. Unfolding the paper in the light of a sconce, Mr. Franklin perused it.

I too read in a scrawling hand:

I watch in my place, you
in yours. What do you learn?
I must have intelligence, else
why do I pay you?

Deliver, damn you!
Meet me in the Garden,
tonight, eight o'clock.
Do not fail.

It was not signed.

I looked up into Mr. Franklin's eyes behind their square-lensed spectacles. "There is more, Nick, do you see?" He turned the paper over to reveal two addresses: 108 Grinder's Court, and Sadler's Wells, Finsbury. "What do you make of't, lad?"

"For one, sir, the boy who carried it could read. The places he was to seek out were writ for him."

"And?"

"He tried the first but did not find his man. That is why he came to Sadler's Wells. When he discovered the fellow was to be here, he left the note."

"And what of 'Garden'?"

I faltered. "There are many gardens in and about London."

He nudged me. "Come, spelt with a capital *G?* It is surely Covent Garden." He tucked the note in a waistcoat pocket. "We will pursue this tomorrow. For now: to Craven Street to warm my feet, for Mrs. Gout nips at my toes." He tapped a boot with his bamboo. "I hear you, madame, I feel you!—dear God, she chivvies worse than any fishwife."

Rumblings and screechings still resounded from Thomas Rosoman's office as we rejoined Peter for the journey home.

❦ 11 ❦

*IN WHICH I hear footfalls at night,
and we visit a dead man's chamber . . .*

I awoke at the click of a latch. I swam up out of sleep. Had I dreamt it? No, for there came now the soft thud of a door being shut, then the creak of stairs as someone mounted to the second floor of number 7 Craven Street. Accompanying these footfalls sounded the chime of Mrs. Stevenson's case clock: 3 A.M. Blind in the darkness, unconscious of cold, I sat upright, all ears, with a prickling at the nape of my neck. Upon our return from Sadler's Wells Mr. Franklin had retired to his chamber. William must be abed. Polly. Her mother. Peter slept upstairs. Who came at this hour? King, returning? Happy to hope so, I dropped bare feet to the wooden floor and, feeling my way to my chamber door, cracked it open.

Wavering candlelight rose up the stairs, spreading near, pushing back the shadows. Mr. Franklin, in greatcoat and beaver hat, crept into view like a housebreaker. Looking neither right nor left, he went straight to his room.

Softly I shut my door. Softly I crept back under the thick comforter which Mrs. Stevenson had sewed for me. I shivered. Where had the gentleman been? He was used to confiding in me, yet in this strange going-out he had not. I chid myself: do not expect to be told ev'rything! Yet it took many moments before sleep tugged, caught, and drew me down to an uneasy bourne.

In the morning I wondered if I had dreamt the vision, the more so as I found Mr. Franklin at his air bath at the usual hour, as cheery as ever to be up with a day's work ahead.

"Did you sleep well, sir?" asked I placing a length of alderwood on the blazing tinder of his fire.

"I, Nick? Why . . . as well as I might."

Had there been some small catch to his voice? "I am glad to hear it," replied I, going to my Latin, with its datives, ablatives and genitives and finding amongst 'em the following, in Mr. Franklin's hand: *Amicus Plato, amicus Socrates, sed magis amica veritas.* "Plato is dear to me, Socrates is likewise dear—but truth is dearer still," I made out.

I stole a glance at the gentleman, who stood in his dressing gown holding in one hand the flask he had got of the charwoman and in the other the note left for Dudley Midge at Sadler's Wells, looking for all the world as if he were about to juggle 'em like a pantomime clown.

Tell the truth of last night, dear Father, thought I.

My puzzlement was driven away by the early gathering in Craven Street of more than a dozen ragtag fellows astomping their boots and blowing frosty breath and crying out that they must see Benjamin Franklin. Tapping the mole aside of her nose, Mrs. Stevenson held 'em at bay: "None shall come in 'til he come down."

This he did, just at ten, coins aclinking in a leathern purse which he carried for all to see and meaningly shook for all to hear. Forming the crowd into a smart line as he must have when he commanded militiamen against the French and Indians, he took 'em one by one into the front parlor, whilst Polly hung about outside the door. I sat in the room with him, jotting in shorthand what each man said, but this proved of disappointing value, for most had clearly not been at Drury Lane Saturday night, being drawn only by the smell of money of which they got none for their

pains; and the ones who had been there—which Mr. Franklin discovered by sharp questions about the evening's entertainment—could tell little of worth. Aye, they had seen
some fellow fall, but, no, they knew nothing of the circumstances. Many wheedled to discover what Mr. Franklin
wished to be fed so they might dish it up for him, but he
was too slippery for such tricks. Yet we did glean one fact:
all the men who had been seated near Midge had been part
of a claque got up by him to hiss the play.

"He paid you, then?"

"Aye," nodded each and ev'ry.

"But who paid *him?*" muttered Mr. Franklin, when the
last of the line had straggled in and straggled out.

"The claque was not of Midge's doing?"

The gentleman sniffed. "Might've been, if he had the
wherewithal. But, damn it, Nick, he was a penurious,
scraping fellow. No, someone paid him to do it, or I do not
butt my head against the Penns. If we but knew who . . ."

Polly came in.

"Here, now, child," Mr. Franklin wrapped an arm about
her drooping shoulders, "why so down? Come, read Mar-
cus Aurelius, as I have bid you. He will teach you patience."

A quarter of an hour later we watched the shops of the
Strand as we passed by in our coach. "I can feel it, Nick,"
said Mr. Franklin, "some plot being hatched, lines laid,
snares set, but I cannot see through to the whole of it.
These accidents, these near-misses at the playhouse—I
pray me no one else falls victim."

I prayed so too. Carrying my sketchbook and notebook,
I followed him into His Majesty's playhouse. So familiar
was I with it by now that I should have missed its pungent
smell and sounds of music practicing, dancers dancing,
hammers tapping, brushes slapping, voices declaiming—
the soft, continuous thunder of preparation. We wandered
about, Mr. Franklin directing me to make more drawings of
devices. He spoke of reflectors and screens to guide the

light more to the players. "Thus the stage might be made a sort of separate room, on which the audience eavesdrops, as it were." In all this he kept alert. I saw it in the little tilt of his head and the swift dart of his eyes.

He was quick. He spied Lady Linacre before I, and for the second time we followed her upstairs. This time we saw the tail of her pale blue dress vanish into David Garrick's office. She did not thoroughly close the door.

Standing outside, we could hear her voice, in strident fury: "You have compromised me, sir. You have took me, and now you leave me. This may not be. Did you despise the hours you spent in my bed? I thought you liked 'em. Did you but dally? I will not be so used! I remind you that I am a lady, my husband a lord, and London suffers you at the whim of such as we, who may be turned against you if I utter a dozen words, and so—"

A movement of air fanned the door suddenly open, treating us to the tableau of a staring, distrait David Garrick, grinding his hands, and Lady Linacre rigidly before him in a little beribboned hat. At sight of us her icy eyes flashed more with outrage than shame. "Do you listen to what you should not hear?" demanded she.

Mr. Franklin made a small regretful shrug. "You have left the door open. Too, you speak so loud that, passing by, I could not help but hear."

Her gloved hands clenched. "Impudent man."

"Imprudent woman," murmured he, drawing me with him into the room. "Should not this business be kept within bounds?"

"What? 'Tis no business of yours."

"David Garrick is my friend, and—"

Mr. Franklin said no more, for at this moment Richard Cross loped through the door on his long legs. He stopped short; he blinked at our ménage, but the sight did not stop him long. " 'Tis the Cibber and the Pivey," said he, turning upon Garrick. "They are at it again about some part. You must come and smooth their feathers before they draw blood. They'll not listen to me."

"By damn . . . !" Garrick gaped from Mr. Franklin to Lady Linacre. He drew himself up. "Hem, ah, egad, I must—" Muttering, he dashed out, Cross at his heels.

There was a silence, Lady Linacre haughtily regarding Mr. Franklin. He gazed coolly back.

"I know you. You were at Calverly's yesterday," said she at last. "You must have met my husband. Are you acquainted with Sir Angus Bibb?"

"I have not had the pleasure."

"He has two deep scars, one upon his right cheek and one upon his left. My husband put 'em there before suffering Bibb to escape with his life."

"A duel, you say?"

"Yes."

"At what provocation?"

"Some insult to me."

"Dear lady, I have no intent to insult you, merely to say that eyes watch; they observe and know. Would you truly wish your liaison with David Garrick to be revealed at large? Would't not damage your name equally as much as his—perhaps more? Too, can you be so certain your 'dozen words' would have the damning effect you claim? Have you such great power?"

She struck him then, a sharp blow upon the cheek.

The gentleman only peered deep into her face, and her stare faltered under his scrutiny. Doubt showed on her porcelain brow. A sudden seeing of herself as she was? She paled, she bit her lip, her beautiful mouth quavered. Tears burst from her eyes, and she fled the room.

"Ah, Nick . . ." Looking after, Mr. Franklin touched his reddening cheek. "Nay, nay, I am not hurt; such a blow more injures the deliverer. Let us down."

We descended to the stage once more. Upon arriving near noon we had seen many familiar faces: the actors Woodward, Clive, Yates, Cibber; fragile Lucy Drumm, her grumbling husband, her handsome mother. But rehearsals were done, and most actors had gone to whatever the afternoon held. We glimpsed Arabella Prouty still in the wardrobe with Mrs. Goodbody; I did not know what to make of the small glance the wardrobe mistress and Mr. Franklin exchanged. Richard Cross strode about, twitching his fingers. Lacy, Mr. Pritchard, and George Garrick quietly scribbled in their offices.

Mr. Franklin carried about a handful of playbills. He caught Mrs. Clive, just exiting her dressing room. "I so much admire you, ma'am," said he, "that it would mean a very great deal to me to have some few words along with your name upon this playbill. A remembrance? Might you—?" He held out the paper.

Taking it, the Pivey scrawled, "Regards to Mr. Benjamin Franklin from Catherine Clive," before she strode off.

Mr. Franklin tucked this with others which had also been signed by actors. "So we may match 'em against the threatening notes," said he to me.

Coming upon Garrick about to go home to his wife he drew him into the deserted Green Room.

"You see how Lady Linacre is," moaned the actor with a helpless stare.

"I see that in her unwise fury she may effect what the threatening notes only promise."

"Egad, yes."

We were not alone long. A rustling of skirts preceded Hannah Pritchard charging in with a paper. She thrust it wordlessly at Garrick.

He read it, paled, passed it to Mr. Franklin, who held it so I too might see. It was a note, unsigned, which made the same threats to Mrs. Pritchard as had been made to Garrick, hinting at retribution for unnamed indiscretions.

"How dare they!" burst out the tragedy queen, her wattles wobbling. She rolled her sonorous r's. "Why, I am the most vir-rtuous of women. Many a jealous r-rival has censured my acting because she could r-rise no higher than the knees of it; such Grub Street tricks are worked on us all. But to imply I am not vir-rtuous . . . ! Why, all London must know that Mr. Pritchard and I have lived in tr-rue and chaste domestic comfort many years." Snatching the paper, she shook it under Garrick's nose. "Lunacy, I say."

"Some jealous fool . . . a mistake . . . you must pay no heed," mumbled he.

The woman's eyes flashed. "That to such villainy!" And she crumpled the paper and flung it into the fire."

"Dear woman!" cried Mr. Franklin.

Mrs. Pritchard gave him a black look. She gave it double to Garrick. "I shall speak to Mr. Pr-ritchard on this." She stalked out.

Mr. Franklin bent to retrieve the paper—but 'twas curled ash.

In deep concern he faced Garrick.

The actor had gone white. "What comes now? Both Woodward and Mrs. Drumm have also told me that they received such notes today, slipped under their dressing room doors. Is some madman about?"

Mr. Franklin shook his head. "Not mad. A plotting fellow. By the by, does Woodward still importune you about his salary?"

"Damn 'em, they *all* importune me. What a devil it is to be manager as well as actor—how it sucks the life of me! I must go. Good day." He rushed out.

Mr. Franklin gazed at the ash in the grate. "Would that the woman had not burnt it. What did you make of its handwriting, Nick?"

"What I saw of it was even and measured. Nothing like that of the notes Mr. Garrick received, you mean?"

He nodded. "Are *two* people, then, spreading poison? A pair in league? Or do they act separately?" He went to the door. "Let us see if we may discover where Dudley Midge lived."

Abel Drumm stood just outside. Listening? He fixed his sour look upon us. "Midge?" He thrust out his face. "Did I hear you say Midge?"

"You did," replied Mr. Franklin.

"Why do you inquire after a dead man?"

"I wonder at the manner of his death."

"Nothing to wonder about: he fell."

"Indeed he did not go down by the stairs. But one may fall and one may be pushed. I wonder that you show so little sorrow. Were you and he not friends?"

"I despised the dog."

"Enough to push him?"

"Here, now!"

Mr. Franklin smiled. "I jest, sir, for you look in want of a jest. Is your pretty wife well?"

Drumm's face twisted suspiciously. "Well enough."

Mr. Franklin tapped his arm. "Care for her, sir. Treat her gently. A wife is not a crockery jug, she is flesh and bone and heart. Care for your Lucy." He turned. "Come, Nick."

Abel Drumm made a growling at our backs.

"Until now I might persuade myself that this affair meant little true mischief," said Mr. Franklin as we stepped into the passageway to Bridges Street. "The notes to Garrick have produced no revelations; the accidents at Drury Lane may've been unfortunate chance; Dudley Midge might be no victim of foul play. Yet these new letters say otherwise. How they muddy the waters. Let us first see if John Rich be in."

We turned right, to Russell Street, left toward Covent Garden, then up Bow Street, past Number 4, where Principal Justice John Fielding kept his crime-fighting offices.

Five minutes walk delivered us to Covent Garden Theatre. This was a larger house than Drury Lane, opened in 1732, Mr. Franklin told me as we stood before it, "playing Congreve's *Way of the World*—see how much I have learnt from my Betterton?" The only other licensed theater, it was Garrick's principal rival but depended more upon pantomime than Drury Lane. *Harlequin Sorcerer* was advertised on large playbills outside, and John Rich was London's greatest clown. Inside, the playhouse proved much like Drury Lane, with stage, boxes, pit, and galleries, though more elaborately decorated, in Italianate design.

To the dour prompter, guardian of the gates, Mr. Franklin let it be known that he worked for David Garrick. This news must have piqued Rich, for we were promptly admitted to his sanctum, shortly after half past three. There sat the famous Harlequin behind his desk with a great dish of tea before him out of which a cat lapped as if the privilege were his due. Indeed there were many cats in the chamber, I counting more than twenty, lying about, purring, licking paws, rubbing against my ankles, and winding about Mr. Franklin's stick, a veritable carpet of 'em, so that one must watch where he trod. Rich wore a red, tasseled nightcap and blue silk dressing gown pulled close about his neck as if he were cold, though 'twas oppressively warm in the room. He was as lean as a wire, with a face in which the flesh was drawn so tight over the bones one could see the skull beneath. His fingers were long and expressive, his mouth broad, his eyes yellowish slits in leathern skin.

We sat as bid by his flicking gesture. Mr. Franklin came to business: "Do you know a man named Dudley Midge?" He held out my drawing.

Rich fingered it. "Aye, I have seen him about"—this in a dry, croaking voice. "He acted some small parts once or twice but was never in my steady employ."

"He plays a ghost now."

"Dead? We shall all play that part some day."

"He made a fine show of the dying of't. Do you know more of him? Who his friends might be?"

Rich stroked the cat, a pursy short-legged tom. "Garrick's his name," chuckled he, holding out the creature. "As to Midge's friends, I saw him once or twice with that wheedling what's-his-name, whose *Lord* was cried down at Drury Lane o' Saturday."

"Abel Drumm."

"Drumm, aye. He sometime creeps about here to peddle his scurvy plays, but I cannot stomach 'em. A cool head is wanted for true comedy. Drumm is far from cool."

"He is indeed hot." Mr. Franklin probed further but to no avail, and our interview appeared at an end when an amazing sight transfixed me. Rich's bony hands were

clasped in plain view on the desk—yet a third hand suddenly appeared. Its fingers rested for a moment on the
desk edge, then rose and began to nip at his ear, most
dexterously—and I saw that 'twas not a hand but his right
foot, long-toed, nimble. It scratched, it pulled at the pen-
dulous lobe quizzically, as if to ask what it found, then
moved to his nose and after fiddling there a moment, as to
stop a sneeze, began to tug at his lip in a most thoughtful
way. At last it sank from view, leaving me staring.

Rich's yellowish eyes fixed me hard. "Well, boy, well?"

"I wish I might do that, sir!" blurted I.

Mr. Franklin laughed. "O, I wish I might, too. How Mrs.
Stevenson would gape!"

Rich smiled like a basilisk. Creeping upon his shoulder
the fat tom named Garrick batted at his tassel as we
slipped out.

"Was it, then, Drumm who wished to meet Dudley Midge
at Covent Garden, sir?" asked I as we returned to our
coach.

"That was my guess," replied Mr. Franklin, "but the
handwriting of the note at Sadler's Wells is not the hand
that writ Abel Drumm's play."

Squinting into gray sky, I seemed to see notes multiply-
ing upon notes. How to sort 'em through?

Grinder's Court was off Coventry Street, between Leices-
ter Fields and the Haymarket, Peter's smart driving deliv-
ering us there in a quarter of an hour. Would the number
108 writ on the Sadler's Wells note prove Dudley Midge's
lodging? The building stood on the corner, a neat, half-
timbered house, old but well-kept. "A decent looking
place, sir," said I.

The gentleman squinted at it as he leant on his bamboo.
"More decent than befits a penurious scribbler." He puffed
frosty breath. "There is like to prove more to this Midge
than we know. Come."

We went to the oaken door, rapped the brass knocker,

and a wizened dame in a blousy cap, with a nose as sharp as my pencil, soon opened. To her asking what we wished, the gentleman replied that he sought news of Mr. Midge. Pray, did he live here? No. Then did this gentleman? Though my drawing was smudged from much traffic it could be read. He gave it her; she frowned and thrust it back. "Aye," sniffed she, "the cheating rascal let a room from me."

"Rascal, ma'am?"

"He owed me o' Friday, and has not paid, and I have not seen him in above four days. Has run out, I expect, devil take him.

"What name did he give?"

"Figgis."

"Just Figgis?"

"Figgis is all."

"And you, dear lady—?"

"Am Miss Bird."

"Well, then, Miss Bird, I bring bad news, for Mr. Figgis has indeed run out—run out on life, for he is dead: broke his neck Saturday in a fall, so you may never get what he owed you," Mr. Franklin patted a pocket, "unless it be from me."

The woman screwed up her face. "You are his friend?"

"The settler of his accounts. I shall want your help in putting 'em right." He bent near. "May I expect it?"

She considered. "You may expect much—if you pay."

"O, you may trust that I will."

"Well, then—" She beckoned us to follow. Inside, stairs led up from a narrow entranceway. A spare, scrubbed parlor lay to the right, which she took us in.

Mr. Franklin gazed about. "Very nice. Now, when did Mr. Figgis engage rooms in your pleasant house?"

"Six weeks ago."

Mr. Franklin gave a meaning glance: just the time Garrick had received his first threatening note and fire broke out in Drury Lane. "What did he give as his occupation?" pursued the gentleman.

"Writer."

"Of what?"

"He did not say."

"Tell of his habits."

"He came and went at odd hours." She bit back something.

"What more?" urged Mr. Franklin.

"I thought he did not like to be seen."

The gentleman chuckled. "O, Mr. Figgis all over. Furtive, was he? Seemed to think he might be watched?"

"You might put it so."

"What else of his character?"

"Nothing—only he must have that particular room."

"Which?"

"The one just above, alooking out over the street. I made to give him one in back, larger, quieter, by far the better, but he would not have it. I have two in front. One was already let. 'I'll have t'other, then,' says he. 'I likes to see out.' He looks it over, he paces it as if ameasuring, he taps the walls, he peers up and down the hall. He asks about t'other room. 'Its occupant is quiet, is she?' 'Very quiet,' says I, 'not often home,' at which he laughs. 'O, yes,' says he, 'I'll have this room,' and did not even bargain about the price—though he should not, for 'twas fair. And so I took him at twelve shillings the week, with the best landlady in London."

"A gentleman, you would call him?"

"As to that—"

"Tut, say no more. May we see his room?"

We were led upstairs, to a landing where there were as Miss Bird had said two doors, she ushering us with a noisy unlocking through the left. This gave onto a smallish chamber, clean and tidy. A wide bed sat against one wall, a handsome pinewood wardrobe opposite. There were a white glazed basin and ewer, a small table and chair, a candlestand. A figured carpet covered the center of the floor, and a large framed print of a shepherd's revel hung on the wall above the bed.

Genteel—and all wrong, thought I, unable to fit into this clean if plain setting the shabby, pushing man all said had been Dudley Midge.

Mr. Franklin drew aside the casement's white muslin curtain. He gazed out. "A grand view, of near all Coventry Street. And a bit of the court to boot. Did Mr. Figgis sit and watch, that you know?"

A shrug. "May've done." Miss Bird started. "What? Here now, where's my other picture?" Darting to the wall by the wardrobe, she scrabbled at the papered design. "I tell you, my picture is gone."

"What picture, ma'am?"

"One very like that by the bed. It hung right here. It has been removed, it has been took." She shook a finger. "O, Figgis'll owe for that too."

"This picture?" said Mr. Franklin. Reaching behind the writing desk, he pulled forth a framed print of frolicking shepherdesses.

Snatching it, Miss Bird squinted hard to see it was unharmed. She looked bewildered. "But why should he take this down?"

Mr. Franklin pursed his lips. "I, too, should like to know." Suddenly dropping to his knees by the wardrobe, he gathered up what appeared to be a small curl of wood. "Not a fastidious housekeeper, Figgis." Tucking the thing in a waistcoat pocket, he kept his nose moving along the boards whilst Miss Bird stared. "Now, what marks are these . . . ?" He touched scratches in the wood. Rising, he opened the wardrobe to reveal three suits of clothes, rather ragged, a clown's motley, a woman's blue dress.

Miss Bird frowned. "What should the man want with a dress?"

"He was an actor, ma'am, as well as writer. A man of many parts." Mr. Franklin poked at a pair of muddy boots and a jumble of wigs. Then, going to the writing desk, he lifted each of a quill pen, an ink pot and half a dozen sheets of blank foolscap. "If he writ, he left not a word. Did he entertain visitors, Miss Bird?"

"None."

"Talked to you of his life?"

"He was close."

"But paid promptly?"

"Until the last."

Mr. Franklin leant thoughtfully upon his bamboo. "The woman who lives next door, might she tell anything of him?"

Miss Bird gave a dry laugh. "Might, but can't, for she too is gone."

The gentleman straightened. "What? She too?"

"Gave up her room o' Friday, the day before Mr. Figgis died."

Mr. Franklin's lips compressed. "So your lodgings are empty."

"Ready for new occupation." Miss Bird smiled with almost antic geniality. "Might you know any who'd care for 'em?"

"I shall recommend 'em ev'rywhere. But this woman—why did she leave?"

"She did not say, except she must."

"A sudden departing?"

"I did not know of't 'til the day of her going."

"But she paid up?"

"All she owed, and somewhat extra for my troubles."

"Troubles?"

Miss Bird seemed to have said more than she intended.

Mr. Franklin paid no apparent heed. "Tell of her. What name?"

"Mrs. Hart."

"And how long here?"

"Some four months."

"Appearance? Character?"

"Here, what's this to do with Figgis?"

"Answer, ma'am, if you please."

Miss Bird looked ill-satisfied but complied. "As to appearance, she was decent enough to look on, no chick but no old hen. A very lady, I assure you."

"She lived alone?"

"O, yes."

"Had visitors?"

"Some, upon the stair."

"Who?"

"I did not spy."

"And was never tempted to do so? Admirable. Did Mrs. Hart and Mr. Figgis ever converse?"

"Not that I know. Both kept to themselves."

"Then she, too, did not care to be seen?"

"I did not say so."

"There is a great deal you do not say. May we look at her chamber?"

"Why, I do not think—"

Mr. Franklin's jingling of his purse altered her thinking, and she led us next door. This proved a more spacious room, with a larger bed, canopied, and a prettily upholstered sofa and chair in addition to the desk and spindle-legged washstand, all tidy, awaiting new occupation. The same two prints of shepherds and shepherdesses hung on the walls. Mr. Franklin peered out the window, but only Grinder's Court, shadowed by steep slate roofs, was to be seen. "A very private chamber indeed," mused he, poking about in the wardrobe, in the narrow desk drawer, under the bed, whilst Miss Bird frowned. He seemed to find nothing of interest. " 'Tis so very spotless clean," said he at last, "that I believe I might recommend it to any friend seeking lodging."

"O, yes, sir? Then—?"

"Then," he drew forth his purse, "we may settle Mr. Figgis's account."

This quickly done, we left Miss Bird's abode. In Coventry Street I said I thought the landlady surely mistook what Figgis owed, for she had asked more than could be possible, but Mr. Franklin tutted. "I was happy to pay, Nicolas, for 'twas truth I bought. 'Twas half given, or disguised, but I received me good measure nonetheless. What do you make of Miss Bird?"

"She hides something to do with her lodgers."

"And perhaps with herself as well? This grows deeper, Nick. We know that Figgis was Midge—but who may be Mrs. Hart?"

"Not truly Mrs. Hart?"

"Actors play parts ev'rywhere. To what end? It will prove significant that the woman fled just before Midge died."

"To escape killing too?"

The gentleman did not answer. "Damn Mrs. Gout!" cried he with a sudden hobbling. "My aching feet are due another hot bath." He clambered into our coach. "Home, Peter, to Craven Street and succor for Benjamin Franklin's poor, abused toes."

IN WHICH Mr. Franklin picks a pocket,
and we watch the hindside of a play . . .

A new army of clouds massed above London's rooftops as we rattled toward the Thames. A wind swayed shop signs in the Strand, making me shiver and long to sit in the cosy comfort of number 7 Craven Street, book and pencil in hand. I would limn Miss Bird. As for Mrs. Hart—should I ever draw her face?

We were back in Mr. Franklin's rooms by six o'clock, he sitting, feet in a copper tub filled with hot water from Mrs. Stevenson's steaming kettle, whilst he turned over in his fingers the small bent piece of wood he had picked up in Dudley Midge's chamber. Rain began to tap at the window-panes; candlelight flickered on bindings in his tall shelf of books: Plutarch, Locke, Lord Shaftesbury, and the newest acquisition, the Earl of Clarendon's *History of the Rebellion and Civil Wars in England.* From a perch cross-legged on the gentleman's bed, I drew: John Rich in his tasseled cap, awash in cats; Miss Bird peering quizzically. I struggled to convey their quiddities; then, without thought I began to draw Mr. Franklin: his blunt-nosed, kindly face and balding brow, the fringe of longish brown hair beginning to show gray, the quizzical eyes behind the squarish lenses of his steel-rimmed spectacles, his round, sturdy body and stockingless legs planted like two trees in

their tub of steaming water. 'Twas no dignified portrait—it
had its comical side—yet it showed the man as he was:
forthright and plain, aiming to make right prevail. How I
loved the gentleman.

There came three soft knocks. "Begging your pardon,
sir," said Mrs. Stevenson, wiping her hands on her apron as
she came in, "but there is a man wishes to see you. I said
you were ministering to your gout, but he would not hear
no. He was at Drury Lane Saturday night, he says, and is
sure you would wish to hear him. Shall I send him off?"

"Indeed, no. I am always pleased to make double use of
time; thus I shall minister to my feet and hear this fellow,
too. Show him up." Mrs. Stevenson went to do his bidding.

Mr. Franklin winked. "What shall this deliver?" His feet
paddled like a child's in their deep, warm bath.

The man arrived strangely. By the stairs' creaking we
heard him mount, yet he did not appear, though we heard
Mrs. Stevenson's voice from below: "Go in, if you please."
No sign of him. Mr. Franklin and I exchanged a glance. At
last a finger, then two, then four slid round the jamb,
followed by the brim of a battered brown hat, the hat itself,
a creased forehead, spiky brows, watchful gray eyes, finally the whole face, ferretlike, the nose twitching madly.
The man's slitted gaze warily sought ev'ry corner of the
room before an arm poked into view; then the torso in a
dingy waistcoat and threadbare velvet jacket arrived. Last
came two spindly legs, poised to flee. Darting in, the man
shut the door panting as if he had been chased from Temple Bar.

"O, very wise," said Mr. Franklin. "To mistrust is to live.
You are safe amongst us. I am Benjamin Franklin, who
advertised for word of Drury Lane, and this is my young
friend, Nicolas Handy, who would not harm a mouse. Pray
tell your name."

"Harkens," gave out the man hoarsely, flattening himself to the wall and sliding along it as if John Law lurked
under Mr. Franklin's bed to snatch him.

The gentleman merely nodded. "And are come to speak about the man who fell at the playhouse?"

Harkens hovered palely by the washstand. "Just so."

"Then tell your story."

A darting look. "Remuneration will be forthcomin'?"

"For truth and nothing else."

Our visitor peered once more into the corners of the room. "Well, then—" he near bent himself double to give it out: "the man were *pushed.*"

There came the soft lap of water, stirred by Mr. Franklin's feet. "How do you know?"

"B'cause my hand was in 'is pocket."

"*You* pushed him, then?"

"I never! My hand were there to take 'is purse. I be a pickpocket, sir, the very best in London."

Mr. Franklin smiled. "I am always pleased to meet the very best of anything."

Harkens flew forward into the gentleman's face. "Do not mock me, sir!" Just as agilely he scuttled back to his niche by the washstand.

Mr. Franklin regarded the man. He patted his waistcoat coolly. "You mean to return my pocketwatch, do you not?"

"Wot?"

"Come." Mr. Franklin held out a hand.

Harkens hung his head. "Your eyes be quick."

"Not as quick as your fingers."

Half sheepishly, half in pride, Harkens pulled from his left-hand coat pocket Mr. Franklin's gold half-hunter, swinging from its chain. Gingerly he handed it back.

Mr. Franklin tucked it in his fob pocket. "And here is your handkerchief, sir," said he, drawing forth a lace-trimmed cloth from his sleeve.

Harkens' mouth hung open.

"Though," added Mr. Franklin, "perhaps 'tis really Polly's, the charming girl who opened to you not ten minutes ago. Why, yes, here is her mark, in the corner: P.S. I shall keep it, then, to return to her, for she shall miss it. For shame, Mr. Harkens. If you wish coin of me you will leave unattempted any object within these doors.''

"B'gor—!" sputtered our visitor.

Mr. Franklin waved a hand. "Tut, I studied the tricks of the trade when I was a boy in Boston, never thinking to use 'em to steal. Yet they provide a lesson, do they not, that you may *not* be the best pickpocket in London?"

Harkens chewed air. "Y-yer a wonder." His crooked teeth split in an eager grin. "Let us join t'gether! Let us fleece all London!''

Mr. Franklin laughed. "Nay, I have other business. I ask again: how may you be sure the man was pushed?''

"Did I not see the man next him do it?''

"What man? Begin at the beginning.''

"Well, then—" Harkens cleared his throat. "A part o' the gallery is my huntin' ground, as't were. O, there be government amongst thieves, though the covenant of't be not writ down. I does the lower gallery, right-hand side, and Mr. Boggs does the left. This be Satiddies and Wednesdays; t'other nights belongs to others; thus all gets their share, and we are clever fellows, none is ever caught. Well, then, I am in my place Satiddy, second row back, near the center, and I am afillin' the bag which I keeps down my leg with coin and rings and snuffboxes and the like, and I am awatchin' the gent in front o' me, aseein' how best to get at his pockets, when a pecooliar thing happens. 'Tis close-packed and hot, but, just after the play is cried down, along comes another gent, apushin' his way, and has converse on the sly with the man next the one in front o' me, aflashin' him a bit o' coin to get him to move aside so he may stand in's place. None heard this but me. Having gained his place, this new gent proceeds to ply my man with drink. 'See, now, have all you wish!' says he.''

"Drink from this?" inquired Mr. Franklin, picking up the flask from the small round table beside him.

Harkens squinted. "B'gor, very like if not the same.''

"The two men appeared to be friends?''

"Nay, the new man were a stranger to the first, yet this

new man seemed to know my man liked his rum. He made himself seem a friend and seemed to match him swallow for swallow, but I know who drinks and who does not, who is tipsy and a fair mark for the lift, and the new man only makes out to drink, whilst the other man drinks deep, so that in a quarter of a hour he is aslippin' and wobblin'. Thus, when it comes time, when all eyes save mine are fixed upon the stage, he might be pushed easy as pie. But I do not know he is to be pushed, and so my right hand is in his right coat pocket, asearchin'—when there comes a move from the left that gives me a fright, for I am always afeered the hand o' the law will snatch me. But 'tis not the law but the new man's arm and the new man's hand. It grabs the back o' my man's coat and gives a great heave, and I feels my fingers torn from the pocket. In an instant my man's heels are tipped up, and he is gone over the edge."

"And dead," murmured Mr. Franklin somberly.

Harkens wiped his brow. "I was ascared, I tell you. Wot was worse, there was the eyes of the murderer aglitterin' at me. He knows I have seen wot he done. Why, it might be me he reaches for next! I makes to scarper—but no need, for with a look that says keep yer mouth shut, he pulls his cap low on his forehead and turns heel and pushes his way out. I watches just long enough to see 'im through the door, then I goes too, atremblin', and have not dipped a pocket in the playhouse since."

Mr. Franklin sat a moment, then drew forth the same small, jingling purse he had used twice today. "Remuneration, sir. Describe the murderer."

Harkens eyed the purse. He licked his lips. "Of middle size, five and a half feet I should say, youngish, though the true age be hard to tell, for his cheeks were dirty and some peculiar rust-red hair hung low over his face and he had a way o' lookin' down so I could not make him out clear. He had strange, bushy eyebrows and a strange moustache."

"How 'strange'?"

"One brow seemed too high for t'other, givin' 'im a

cockeyed look, and the moustache were so ill-trimmed it did not fit his lip straight. He were dressed like some 'prentice or clerk, in plain stuff. As he ran off I saw very high heels."

"So he may have been shorter than you estimate?"

"May've. And one more thing: I dipped his pockets b'fore I tried t'other man, him who was pushed—and there was nothin' in 'em."

"Odd."

"Aye. All men carry somethin': sixpence, a bit o' right Spanish, a handkercher, but not this 'un. His coat and breeches was empty as a beggar's cupboard."

Mr. Franklin queried more, but Harkens had delivered all his news, it seemed. The purse fell open. Coins fell into an eager palm. "I do not steal 'cause I likes to," murmured Harkens as he slid along the wall toward the door, "but honest work has never fed the likes o' me." And then he was gone.

Mr. Franklin met my eyes. "Ought I to have collared him, Nick? Delivered him to John Fielding? Watched his hand cut off for thievery? Ah, what poverty, what waste, what blighted lives! Think of the man's talent, so nimble-fingered. Why, he might be a politician and fleece the world at large! Nay, 'tis no jesting matter. Devil take it, my water has gone cold! The towel, Nick." He dried his feet. "Midge was murdered then, that is sure. O, I knew it: there is a deadly game afoot!"

"I think on my goodwife Joan," proclaimed Mr. Franklin.

"Do you, sir?" Though his wife's true name was Deborah, he sometime called her Joan, in wry affection.

"Aye, and how she mended her jug."

"Her jug?" Harkens was gone a quarter of an hour. Having assuaged Mrs. Gout, Mr. Franklin might well have slipped into his dressing gown for a quiet evening by his fire, yet he was restless and had leapt up and put back on his stockings and boots, as if he must sally out once more. He wandered from rain-spattered window to door and back, whilst the wind set up a rattling of the panes. "Aye, a jug she loved, a plain crockery thing, got of her mother. It broke one day; the pieces lay upon the table. If I had never seen 'em whole I should not have known what shape they made. Yet she sat with glue and patient heart—I see her now at her task—and fitted 'em back together. The thing would no longer hold water, but she made it pretty much as it had been, to sit upon a shelf. She never passed that shelf without a look; indeed, she may gaze upon it now." He cocked a brow. "You wonder why I think on this? Because we too have a crockery jug to mend, though we never saw it whole and its shards are not made of clay. They are threatening notes sent to David Garrick; they are notes sent to others; they are accidents at Drury Lane, a pewter flask, a toppled man; they are ambition and spite; they are the mysterious Mrs. Hart and Miss Bird who does not tell all the truth; they are a removed picture and marks on a floor and a curl of wood and crooked eyebrows and an ill-trimmed moustache and high heels; they are things we do not know." He drove a fist into a palm. "How I want the glue to stick 'em together! How I long to forge the shape they make! Come, Nick, your coat and scarf and cap. We shall once more to Drury Lane."

"Yes, sir," said I.

Yet, going to fetch my things, I thought on my own broken jug: where had Mr. Benjamin Franklin sneaked to last night?

I followed the gentleman's rapid steps downstairs, passing William coming up and Polly at the door amoaning that we went to the theater whilst she must stay at home. Water poured in the gutters, ships' lamps rose and fell bleakly upon the Thames, and rain cut hard, soaking our cuffs and collars before we made the haven of our coach. Peter was wrapped up against the storm; I did not envy him. His reins flicked, he cried out a drowned urging to our mare, and we pressed through the drenched London streets to the play-house.

Outside Drury Lane the whores damply plied their trade, and the Methodist preacher waited like Cain under a dripping eave to strike down his Abel. Though Garrick had banned him from the playhouse, he hurled his imprecations out o' doors.

Mr. Franklin eyed him. "I wish to see what 'tis like backstage whilst the play is on," said he to me. Relinquishing dripping coats to the porter, we went round by the right-hand corridor and up the side stairs, to the dim-lit area behind the tall, sliding scenes. 'Twas near eight, tonight's play already two-thirds done: *King Lear.* Great metal sheets gave the sound o' thunder, whilst from onstage came a wavering moan, "Tom's acold," so fitting to the night that I shivered to hear it. More than a dozen men, from fresh-faced dandies to leering old lords, hung about and clucked at the actresses going on and off and pinched 'em when they could. This clearly vexed Garrick, for when he blew into the wings in the stringy-haired garb of the maddened old king, he glowered at these hangers-on as if he would toss 'em in the street, but they only smiled back like guests in a private club.

"You're here too, are ye, Franklin?" snarled the actor. "Damn custom! I shall banish these scalawags or do nothing worth in my life." His face altered to that of pathetic, maddened old Lear as he lurched back onstage.

I stood by Mr. Franklin's side. How strange in this shadowy limbo betwixt the life of the play and life at large; here we might be ghosts observing ghosts. Through the slitted spaces between the flats I could see the stage in tall, narrow segments. There in flickering candlelight actors declaimed. A figure would flash by—the Fool or wicked Goneril—or an arm gesture, or Edmund creep and mock. The rakes lounged, legs akimbo, so that Havard as blind Gloucester nearly tripped. I could see the boxes across the stage, Lady Linacre sitting prominently in one, cool and palely beautiful behind her fan. Next her leaned a haughty man with a bored droop of eyes: Lord Linacre, it must be, who had cut a man's cheeks for affronting her. There was

Lord Methuen too, darkly brooding, though he looked more pleased at Lear than at Abel Drumm's jibes Saturday night. Had those jibes to do with Dudley Midge's murder?

About us lay deep and mingled shadows, wherein lurked the many servants of illusion: actors, mechanics, musicians, Lacy and Pritchard, Noverre and five slender dancers limbering up. In one wing hovered the prompter Richard Cross, call boys at his side, a well-worn copy of the play in one hand, his deep-set eyes watching ev'rything. At his signal one of the great machines shuddered and softly creaked, a crouching creature playing out its ropes and wires like things it had spun. I thought of Miss Prouty, nearly strangled, and found her nearby beside Susannah Cibber, who waited to play Cordelia, dead in Lear's arms. Both women had barely 'scaped injury, and Lucy Drumm, standing next Miss Prouty, had received a threatening note. Was no one safe? Lucy leant and whispered something to Miss Prouty, but Miss Prouty scorned her, and I saw hurt suffuse the young wife's face.

Her husband sulked at the rear of the area, eyes pathetically alert. He had no part in tonight's play. His career as playwright was blasted, and he seemed to know that Garrick would soon discharge him. Rich despised him too. Where could he go? He eyed his wife: I must make a success of her, his burning look seemed to proclaim; she is my only means . . .

How could Lucy love such a husband? Yet she seemed to, her eyes following him even now, longing to please. Would it be so very bad if he forged a career for her, which in her frailty and self-doubt she could not do for herself? Yet by English law he would then receive all she made, and she must beg him for twopence. Could this be right?

I looked at Mr. Franklin. His eyes watched the Drumms. Did he think as I? His gaze turned to Lucy's mother, Mrs. Settle, dressed for the sad progress that would end the play. Lord Edmund Calverly stood next her; they exchanged a glance freighted with deep understanding, and I felt a shock at such public intimacy; truly they took no care to prevent the discovery that they were lovers. But then, why should they? Did not many an actress take a lover? Did not three-quarters of London think actresses whores? They made a handsome pair and might carry on for years. Fortunate Calverly, to have home, wife, children, title, mistress.

O, to be a lord in London town.

Yet I could not condemn Calverly. Had not my own father, Mr. Franklin, found companionship outside of marriage? Too, I could discover in Calverly's well-sculpted countenance no arrogance. His gaze was mild, his lineaments grave. His eyes narrowed briefly at Abel Drumm, but why should my lord trouble himself over his mistress's daughter's plight?

Lear came to an end—at some surprise to Mr. Franklin, for Garrick had rewrit it to let Cordelia live. Mrs. Clive stepped out in the interval to sing "The Life of a Beau," a mocking song. Mr. Franklin cast his eyes upon the company assembling for the afterpiece. "Is one a murderer, Nick . . . ?" Lucy Drumm returned in the dress of a sylph, half-masked, to dance with others likewise arrayed. She stood for a moment apart, gazing onstage, where a juggling clown ate fire. Her hands were clasped as if they wrung something in 'em, and her face glowed avidly. She seemed mesmerized by this arena of illusion on which London gazed. Did she imagine it clapping for her? Did she dream of being an actress called for, admired, beloved? Did she hate merely standing in for Mrs. Cibber when the tragedy queen fell ill?

Mr. Franklin slipped near her. "You know me, ma'am? Ben Franklin?"

The young woman started. Pulling off her mask, she gazed at him, at me. I had never seen her eyes so near. They were large, blue, as clear as glass, yet with a ripple of fear marring their gleaming purity. Her voice was mere breath. "I have seen you about, sir. You help Mr. Garrick."

"Shall help him, I hope. To make the lighting better."

"I see."

"I have heard that you received a threatening note?"

"Why . . . yes."

"May I see it?"

She bit her lip. "But, why?"

"Because you are not alone in receiving such a thing. Too, there have been fires, one of which you yourself discovered. And there have been near harmful incidents backstage. The perpetrator must be found. This Midge who died o' Saturday—he was a friend to your husband?"

Reply to this never came, for the husband himself was suddenly upon us—upon his wife, rather, for he grasped her bare arm hard.

Abel Drumm thrust his face into Mr. Franklin's. "What's this about Midge?"

"My dear," replied Lucy, placating, "Mr. Franklin merely asks if you and Dudley Midge were friends." She stroked the fingers that cruelly bit her arm.

Drumm wiped his mouth. "That crawling worm? You know we were not friends." His look bore deep into Mr. Franklin. "Why do you insist that we were friends?"

"Why do you deny it so heartily?"

Drumm whirled upon his wife. "And what's this of threatening notes? You have not told *me* of threatening notes."

"You have had much to think on of late. I did not wish to alarm you."

"The devil with alarming me. You have received such a thing? Show it now."

"I . . . I am sorry, it is no more."

"What?"

" 'Twas so hateful I threw it away. Please, dear, should I have kept it?"

At this her husband growled.

"Come, Nick," said Mr. Franklin, drawing me off, "let us leave Mr. and Mrs. Drumm to themselves. Damned tyrant," muttered he when we had retreated. The afterpiece was just begun: *A Midsummer Night's Dream.* "Shakespeare lopped, as is the fashion," whispered Mr. Franklin as we watched two painted trees pushed from the wings, behind which six forest fairies, Lucy Drumm amongst 'em, gathered for their dance. Woodward played Bottom, Garrick Oberon, Mrs. Cibber Titania. Miss Prouty made a saucy Helena.

No dire incidents marred the evening. When all was done, the audience trailing out, the candlemen creeping with their metal snuffers, the charwomen sweeping and gleaning betwixt the benches, the actors, singers, dancers, and scenemen deserting, Garrick hurried to Mr. Franklin. He had changed into a green velvet suit and tight white wig. "I am glad to see you are still here. I do not know what to do. My two watchmen are indisposed, one of a distemper. The other slipped upon a rope this afternoon and broke his hand. Who will keep watch in the playhouse tonight?"

"There is no one else you can press into service?"

"Not that I trust as much as you. Come to Twickenham tomorrow, to my villa; we may speak freely then. But as to keeping watch tonight—?" His eyes begged eloquently.

"Nick and I shall do it," agreed Mr. Franklin. He looked at me. "What say you, lad?"

I felt a thrill. Stay the night in Drury Lane?

"I should be glad to help in anything, sir," said I.

⚜ 13 ⚜

*IN WHICH we face death, an enemy flees,
and Mr. Franklin spends pleasant hours
by the Thames . . .*

Garrick departed in a swirl of blue cloak. Mr. Pritchard
bobbed his head at Mr. Franklin as he went out with
his formidable wife. Arabella Prouty slipped past with a
veiled look, and bold-eyed Kitty Clive swaggered by as if
she owned the world and would make men pay dear if they
hampered her governing it.

Mr. Franklin watched these departures mutely, one eye
on Woodward's dressing room door. When he saw the
actor emerge, he approached him: "You received yesterday a threatening note, I am told."

Woodward stared down his thin, expressive nose. " 'Tis
I shall deliver a threatening note, to bloody Garrick. I go if
you do not pay me what I am worth!—that is what it shall
say." His nostrils flared as if he inhaled brimstone.

"But as to the other note—"

"What of it?"

"May I see it?"

Woodward sniffed. "Sir, you may have it—for what have
I to do with threats, except to make 'em and then do what
I must when warning is not heeded. The thing is in my
dustbin. It is yours, if you wish to dig for it. I am off."
Swirling his cloak in a manner very like Garrick's, he
stalked away.

Mr. Franklin beckoned. I followed. 'Twas my first time in an actor's dressing room. If I thought to find it a place of wonder, I was disappointed, for 'twas but a cell, furnished with a plain wooden chair, a deal table whereon rested some pots of paint in streaky disarray, a stained mirror, three wigs upon stands, and a costume of motley dangling like a dead man from a tarnished hook. This cold and inauspicious room was the crucible in which James Woodward's alchemy was brewed.

A small, round metal bin sat on the floor beside the table. From it Mr. Franklin plucked a crumpled scrap of foolscap at which we peered, heads together, in the light of a candle. 'Twas indeed a note, indeed threatening, blasting the actor's character and warning him to mend his ways or suffer. Suffer what? It did not say. Nor was it exact as to what was to be mended. The writer despised him, and that seemed all.

"Masks, games," muttered Mr. Franklin, striking the paper, "and yet we learn something from the handwriting. See?" But what I ought to have seen was not then revealed, for at that moment Mr. Franklin caught sight of a dessicated old gentleman creeping past the door, and, stuffing the paper into his coat pocket, he darted out.

"Beg pardon, you are the first gallery ticket-taker, are you not?" asked he in the corridor.

"I be," wheezed the superannuated man so dryly that he seemed to exhale dust. His head wobbled with palsy. "Baggot be th' name."

"You took tickets Saturday night?"

"Aye, 'tis my job."

Mr. Franklin described the dirty-faced, oddly moustached man of uncertain age, of whom our pickpocket had told. "Do you recall such a fellow?"

Baggot plucked at his wispily bearded chin. "B'lieve I do. Th' man should ne'er have been let in, for 'twas long past the hour—the third act, ye know—when 'tis customary for new arrivals to be admitted for half price."

"But he *was* admitted. Why? I assure you that none of what you tell me shall reach Garrick's or Lacy's ears."

"Aye?" The ancient fellow's dry lips spread in a conspiratorial grin. "Well, then, th' man pressed a guinea—a whole guinea!—into my palm!" He softly cackled. "Could anyone say nay to such persuasion?"

Mr. Franklin smiled. "No one." He pressed further, but old Baggot could recall no more and ended tottering out the rear door. We could see as he moved toward Drury Lane that the rain had ceased and a brilliant moon scudded amongst clouds. Then the door shut, and silence wrapped us round. Alone at last in the playhouse?

Not quite, for Lucy Drumm slipped out of shadow wrapped in a long cloak. She did not look at Mr. Franklin and seemed to hope he would neither look at nor address her, as if the merest word might upset some balance.

He cleared his throat as she reached for the latch. "If you need help, Mrs. Drumm . . ."

A tremor ran through her, and her face lifted to his, an alabaster orb set with searching eyes. May I truly trust you, sir? those eyes seemed to ask. Her lips parted, she looked as if she longed to confide, but she kept a lid on longing. "I need no help," breathed she, rushing by.

Her husband waited on the black, wet cobbles outside, an urgent shape, and he took her roughly with him as if she were a bitch dog on tether.

Mr. Franklin scowled "I should like to see her stand up to him," muttered he.

Richard Cross was last out. "I am told you stay," said he. "All doors save this are locked; I shall fasten it when I go—but here are keys, should you need 'em." He handed Mr. Franklin a jingling ring. "Good night." The door opened, closed. We heard the clack of a bolt slid home.

We turned to face our night in Drury Lane.

If I had found standing in the wings whilst the play was played a singular experience, I found this stranger still: Drury Lane silent. I was used to its panting rush to 6:00 P.M.

followed by the feverish exhalation of the play; now the place seemed dead—yet not dead, only sleeping, for as we stood in near darkness I heard the sigh of air in corridors and the creak and crack of wood as timbers settled into rest; too there came the faint squeak of bats. I thought for a moment I could hear the very borers in the walls which would some day bring the playhouse down, but that must be imagination; imagination too the faint roar of audiences past, and the echo of voices which had declaimed within: Nell Gwyn, Mrs. Bracegirdle, Mrs. Oldfield, Macklin, Quin, Colley Cibber, Peg Woffington who had stroked my hair.

I felt momentarily charged by the passion that drove such souls upon the stage. But 'twas not my passion. Mine was for pencil, paper, pictures, words. And so I patted my pockets to assure myself my sketchbook and notebook were there. I turned to Mr. Franklin.

"Let us look about, Nick," said he with a relishing rub of hands, as if he proposed some philosophical excursion into Nature's secrets.

"Yes, sir."

We had been left two candles in glass upon a table next the Green Room door, and a fire in the Green Room grate to warm us. But all the rest of Drury Lane lay dark. We began our traverse, each with his lamp. We made a great spiraling circle, from the Green Room to the right-hand wings, along the right-hand side corridor, which in its black narrowness seemed the intestine of some serpent, across the back of the pit, skirting the spot where Dudley Midge had fallen. From here the stage appeared a black, gaping cavern. Then to the left-hand corridor and left-hand wings, to the scene rooms and dancing rooms. In the wardrobe Mr. Franklin poked amongst costumes, humming a little song. Did he think on Mrs. Goodbody? We peered into dressing rooms, most proving as drab as Mr. Woodward's and all bare of habitation save mice. Shadows receding before us as in some macabre hide-and-seek, we mounted stairs and would've looked into the offices on the second floor had they not been locked, all excepting

George Garrick's, which proved as austere as an eremite's cell. And then up to the long, wide, low-ceilinged attic and more squeaking of bats, who flew in and out the little ventilating windows at either end.

Mr. Franklin tried the door that led to the roof. It yielded. "Unlocked, eh?" He regarded it thoughtfully.

We turned to descend. I believed I heard footsteps, but when we paused they fell silent: more imagining. We ended upon the stage. Behind us stood the two trees where the faeries had hid before their dance. The grooves in which the great flats slid ran beneath our feet. Boxes rose to right and left, next the two broad doors where actors made their entrances and exits. Unlit, the line of floats marked the front of the stage; so did, on either side, the ornate iron screen with its wicked spikes to stay an overzealous crowd. As for pit and galleries, our feeble candles showed little beyond a vast and deepening shadow, seeming to wait, to watch. Did the playhouse even now call for diversion, some canter or song?

'Twas past midnight. Mr. Franklin stretched and sighed. "Let us remain here awhile." The chairs in which the rakes lounged sat by the iron screen. He fetched two, and we rested upon 'em and talked—he talked, rather; I listened. In a ruminating mood, he spoke on his life: how he had been born to Josiah Franklin, who made and sold candles and soap at the sign of the Blue Ball in Milk Street, Boston, and how his brother James had launched the *New England Courant,* "a paltry thing, eight by ten inches, printed in two columns each side. Silence Dogood first gave Ben Franklin voice." He spoke too on his first journey to England: "I saw much—and might've seen more. Henry Pemberton wished to present me to Sir Isaac Newton, but, alas, that never was to be. As to my experience with women, 'twas not only Jimmy Ralph played the profligate." He tapped my knee. "Why, my landlady in Duke Street reduced my rent by half to retain the pleasure of my company." He spoke too on his son William, never far from his thoughts. "Would the boy were more of my mind." At this I nodded. Mr. Franklin was Whiggish in his bent, William leant to the Tory side. I smelt gunpowder in this, but Mr. Franklin turned to a time when they had been great companions, in their campaign against the French and Indians. "My son was of much use to me." William had formed and drilled new companies, led patrols, built fortifications. This gave a new view of the young man whose only skirmishes on these shores were against the ladies of the town. I learnt that he could be resourceful under fire.

Mr. Franklin's voice died after three-quarters of an hour. His head nodded, his chin fell upon his breast, he snored. I was not pleased to be so deserted. Gazing into the darkness that crowded round, I stayed alert, seeking consolation in thinking on London: her twisting ways and watchmen crying the hour and people snug in their beds, as if by so doing I might traverse by mental ways to my own safe bed in Craven Street. I heard the scuttling of mice and groaning of wood. Again I thought I heard footsteps, but when I listened hard could detect nothing but the beat of my heart. Rising, I paced but never strayed far from the island of light formed by our two lamps next Mr. Franklin's outstretched legs. The tallow sank to stubs. Mustn't I wake the gentleman? Oughtn't we to withdraw to the Green Room, where coals would be found in the grate, and more steady light would be assured? We both would rest easier there.

And then I heard a singing. It froze me where I stood a dozen paces behind Mr. Franklin. My eyes searched the darkness. From whither did it come? 'Twas a soft, high-pitched shimmer and seemed to be created in the very air, as if the playhouse had lungs. Hearkening 'til hearkening became agony, I began to know that the sound descended from above and looked up at the six great lusters, hung with their little droplets of glass and supporting two dozen candles each, to illumine the auditorium when a play was played. Massive, heavy, round. One of Mr. Franklin's plans was to move all these over the stage, to light it better. I squinted. One of the six hung above the sleeping gentleman. Its glass droplets quivered; 'twas these that made the sound.

And why did they shake?

I ran, dove, and toppled Mr. Franklin from his chair.

The falling luster shattered in a thousand pieces where he had sat. I felt a sharp pain in my right calf but ignored it as the gentleman and I lifted ourselves from our heap upon the stage. Blinking, we shook bits of broken glass from hair and clothes. Mr. Franklin's spectacles dangled from their cord; he set 'em firmly upon his nose. One lamp had smashed, but the other miraculously still glowed. Lifting it, the gentleman rapidly took in all. "I thank you, Nick. I owe you my life." He frowned ceilingward. "Damn me if I do not wish to lay hands upon whomever has done this." He dashed for the Green Room, found fresh tallow and, replacing the candle in our lamp, beckoned urgently.

I followed his charge upstairs.

We were on the third flight when I felt a breeze I had not felt before. Arriving breathless in the attic showed its source: the sloping door which led to the rooftop. It stood open. We heard running steps above.

"Come, Nick!" As quick as any boy, the fifty-two year old man was in an instant at the door and through it, I scrambling after. To my great alarm I heard a thumping, and poking out my head saw that in his haste Mr. Franklin had lost his footing and rolled some half dozen feet to the level stretch of the roof. Grumbling, he pulled himself up to peer about. I joined him. He had saved our lamp, but we did not need it, for 'twas a night without mist, rain-washed, icy clear, London etched by the ghostly light of a crystalline moon. The foot-high parapet of Drury Lane spread round us; then a landscape of rooftops like close-packed islands fifty feet above the winding ways below. A watchman cried the hour: "One o'clock and all's well . . ." Horse bells jingled. Raucous laughter drifted up.

A figure fled.

"After him, Nick!" Yet I hesitated. Had we any hope, for

our quarry had leapt to the rooftop north and looked like making for the one beyond?

Nothing daunted, Mr. Franklin made off after him.

I set off too.

And then my heart near stopped, for ten paces ahead of me the gentleman jumped upon the low parapet plainly thinking to propel himself across the interval between it and the next rooftop, slightly higher than the one we stood on. Had not the man we chased easily done so? Yet some crumbling masonry gave way, so that Mr. Franklin slipped, yawed, windmilled his arms. I froze as he whirled about, and I saw his startled stare behind his little lenses. Farewell, my son, it seemed to say.

He began to go down.

With a sobbing cry I grabbed, caught his coat sleeve, dug in my fingers, tugged. Yet I felt his weight, inexorable. I shall hang on to the end, I silently cried. Setting my feet against the angle of the parapet, I gritted my teeth and stiffened my back; I pulled and pulled and pulled.

Winning the balance, I drew him back upon the level.

"Dear me, Nick!" cried he, stumbling upon me with a great hug. A brick hollowly struck the cobbles far below. Mr. Franklin peered down at it. Together we gazed across the rooftops, but only looming shapes of mansards and chimneypots were to be seen, no fleeing figure. The gentleman cursed. "Escaped, damn him. Was it he who toppled Dudley Midge? Brr, 'tis cold. Let us in."

Back in the attic he knelt to examine the bolt in the floor that had held the fallen luster. "Deliberately loosed. See? And here you may peer through this small hole, to the stage itself. We were watched."

"And near done in."

"Near is close enough for me. But what is this?"

In a corner of the attic shavings of wood and scraps of torn paper had been scooped into a little pile, with some sticks of pinewood arranged in an expert criss-cross over 'em. "Tinder, prepared for a fire." He kicked the pile into harmlessness. "After doing in Ben Franklin did our man mean to do in Drury Lane? Why, Nick—there is blood upon your leg."

I looked down. Indeed a blot of red spread upon my right stocking, and I felt a sudden ache. Only then did I know that a shard of glass had cut me.

Mr. Franklin tore off his cravat; he bandaged my leg. "Wounded in the Drury Lane Wars." He sent an encouraging smile. "But you will heal." He fumbled with the jingling ring Richard Cross had given him. "Which key will close the oak? This one fits well." He locked the rooftop door. "Now no one may leave—or enter. Come, lad, let us down."

A tune greeted me as, having slept late, I entered Mr. Franklin's chamber at eleven next morn:

"For nothing at night to the playhouse they crowd,
For to mind nothing done there they always are proud,
But to simper and say nothing clever aloud:
Such, such is the life of a beau . . ."

'Twas the ditty Mrs. Clive had performed to much laughter last night. Turning from the bow window, where he appeared to contemplate nothing more perplexing than Hungerford Market, Mr. Franklin regarded me. "And why, Nick, can the beau's brain deliver itself of so little?"

"I do not know."

He raised a finger. *"Ex nihilo nihil fit."*

I parsed this: "From nothing comes nothing?"

"Ha, excellent. And from something comes much. Your Latin progresses well—I fear you have too much brain ever to make a beau."

Of this I was heartily glad.

We had spent the remainder of the night dozing fitfully in the Green Room. Candlemen and workmen had begun to arrive as early as eight in the morning. Richard Cross stalked in at nine o'clock retrieved his keys (upon being

asked how our night went, Mr. Franklin replied only that
we had found little diversion), and our job was done.

The gentleman beckoned me out of his bedchamber, to
his workshop just behind. "Look at this." He had set out on
his workbench the oddments of our puzzle: the flask, the
little curl of wood, the playscript of *A Lord and No Lord*,
the various notes which multiplied alarmingly. He placed
the note to Woodward triumphantly next the playscript.
"*Vide:* the handwriting is the same."

I looked. Both were indeed in identical, perfectly formed
script.

I met his gaze, brightly cocked, like a sparrow's on a
worm. "Then Abel Drumm sent the note to Woodward?"

"More, he is not the man who sent the first notes. Now
see you this." Placing the note asking Dudley Midge to
rendezvous at Covent Garden next one of the earlier notes
sent to Garrick, he looked triumphant again. Both were
hasty scrawls, ink bespattered.

"These also are the same handwriting," agreed I, "but
different from the pair writ by Drumm."

He smiled. "You are indeed too clever ever to make a
beau."

I wished I were cleverer still. "This confirms that there
are two writers of threatening notes. But how, why?"

"How and why, indeed."

I struggled with a thought. "Mrs. Drumm received one of
the latest notes, as did Woodward and Mrs. Pritchard—"

"—and others, perhaps, who do not confess they got
'em?"

I nodded. "But as to hers, if it was also in Drumm's hand,
as seems likely . . . why, then, he has sent his own wife a
threatening note?"

"Oddest of all, eh? How I should like to read the scurvy
man's thoughts! But now, look at this." He pulled a folded
square of foolscap from his coat. It said:

Mrs. Hart, late of Grinder's Court, has left behind
three lady's handkerchiefs with a lady's initials upon

'em, together with other items of some small worth. Wishing only to return these to proper hands, her former landlady begs Mrs. Hart to call upon her at the address which both know well.

I frowned. "I did not know that Mrs. Hart left items behind."

"She did not." He tapped his brow. "Springes to catch woodcocks, lad! I shall ask Peter to place this advertisement in several papers. If 'Mrs. Hart' truly wishes to keep her identity hid, she will in particular want back the handkerchiefs: their initials may not contain an *H.*"

"But surely she will know she did not leave 'em."

"May be. Yet she departed in haste. Ev'ry woman has handkerchiefs; many have indentifying letters embroidered upon 'em. She may *think* she left 'em. The very uncertainty may lure her back to Miss Bird's house, where Peter will keep watch. I know 'tis unlikely, but things grow to a point; we must try ev'ry chance. I shall also place another notice seeking King. The poor man may be gone for good, but we must try to find him. I shall write it now." He scribbled some words, then drew on his coat. "I go to Garrick's villa by the Thames. While I am there apply yourself: see if the nimble fingers of your wit may mend our broken jug."

I paced and thought much whilst he was gone, in particular on the notes we now knew had been writ by Abel Drumm. So many, to so many people, scattershot, as if Drumm had no true target. Yet that could not be. Where did he truly aim? And their handwriting, so regular, so cool, as if writ by a machine, not a being with a heart—it did not suit his temper. Did he disguise his true hand? Again: why?

Our jug still lay shattered when Mr. Franklin returned past six.

He settled himself in his chair by the fire. "Ready to hear of Garrick and Mrs. Garrick and Shakespeare, Nick?" He rubbed his gouty toes. "Fetch your notebook, sharpen

your pencil." He laced his fingers upon his belly. "Here is
my tale:"

Good Peter drove the dozen miles to Hampton. Garrick's villa lies upon the main Kingston road, near
Strawberry Hill where Walpole resides. 'Tis no palace
but handsome. Robert Adam did it up for him: a
white portico with Corinthian columns. Mrs. Garrick
greeted me, la Violette, charming—and staunchly
devoted to her husband. (No wonder he fears to have
her learn of his dalliance.) Winningly, chattering in
her Viennese accent and mispronouncing ev'ry third
word, she showed me round: Hogarth's *Election Pictures* by the fireplace, the medallion decoration of
the staircase, the drawing room painted in parasols
and pagodas, chinoiserie ev'rywhere—vases, plates,
screens. Cupboards groan under the weight of it. In
truth 'twas a gracious house.

Garrick was in his library. Mrs. Garrick brought
me there. Leaving off writing, the actor hurried to
me. He wore a sky-blue coat and wheat-colored
waistcoat with shiny brass buttons. Many may hate
him, but I cannot. He is short and growing stout, but
how sprightly! And his face—how marvelously expressive.

He wrung my hand. "Hem, ah, Franklin, welcome.
But, see what I do." Eagerly he brought forth the
product of his pen. "Dr. John Hill, who writes what
he calls 'comic plays,' attacks me in print. I have
answered him. Do I not put him to rout?"

I read:

    For Farces and Physic his equal scarce is.
    His Farces are Physic, his Physic Farce is.

I laughed. "You rout him well. He will retreat if he
has any sense."

"That is just the problem with these toads, they

have no sense. Thank God I have friends such as you." Eyes crinkling, he clapped my back. "I hope my attachment to friends will be remembered long after my foolscap and bells are forgot."

" 'Tis the best remembrance," agreed I.

Mrs. Garrick nodded approval of our concourse.

Her husband turned to her. "Now, my dear," said he gently, "I shall show Mr. Franklin Shakespeare's temple, and you shall bring us some refreshment in an hour or so, if you please."

"If it please *you*." Pecking his cheek, she withdrew.

Garrick led me to the front of the house where he proudly displayed his grounds, stretching to the quietly flowing Thames fringed by willows. There seemed but one imperfection: the main road cut directly through, but Garrick hastened to show how he had surmounted the problem—subverted it, rather, turning it to a charming point of interest, for in laying out the gardens Capability Brown had dug a tunnel underneath the road, turning it into a grotto that remarkably imitated Nature, with artfully carved rocks and a spring of bubbling water. 'Twas cool as we passed through; swallows skimmed our heads. Coming out upon a slope of lawn, I took in the stone embankment, near it a striking domed building with large windows and a fine Ionic front that faced out upon the river.

"Shakespeare's temple," said Garrick. "Adam designed it." He plucked my arm. "Come, see." Eagerly he showed how one might take refreshment within and pointed out just where Roubillac's statue of Shakespeare would stand, so it would seem the bard rose to greet one when one entered. Garrick waggled a finger. "Never let your Shakespeare be out of your hands!—keep him about you as a charm; the more you read him the more you will admire him." Standing just where his idol would, he looked about with deep satisfaction. This made me sad. He seemed at that moment fully content, but I saw that if the threats made him were fulfilled this content would be blasted. His dear Eva Maria would learn of his infidelity. Could she ever forgive?

Yet murder threatened as well as truth. Meaningly I cleared my throat and saw wariness leap up in Garrick's eyes. He had begged my help—but why must Ben Franklin remind him of things which he either longed to forget or wished not to know?

Yet I must dog truth's heels. Patiently I sketched our evidence: the accidents at Drury Lane—the small incidents he himself spoke on when he first asked for my aid, those since: Arabella Prouty near strangled by the winch which broke the rope-dancer's hip, Mrs. Cibber barely escaping injury from falling scenery. This led to our night in the playhouse: the dropt chandelier, the fleeing man, the tinder expertly heaped, which might by now have brought the playhouse down.

Garrick turned pale to hear it. "Forever farewell the tranquil mind, farewell content!" cried he.

I told, too, of our pickpocket.

He stared. "Someone *pushed* Midge? But surely that was some private vendetta, nothing to do with the threatening notes."

"May be. Do you know a Mrs. Hart?"

"Why . . . I do not believe so."

I told of our discoveries at Miss Bird's.

He made mouths. "But this Miss Bird said Midge and Mrs. Hart never spoke. Why inquire after her?"

"To winnow wheat from chaff. These new threatening notes—I have seen the one writ to Woodward, and 'tis not by the same hand which penned those to you. It is Abel Drumm's hand."

His eyes flashed in outrage. "The damned, scurrilous fellow! I shall dismiss him tomorrow."

I held up a hand. "Pray, do not. Or if you do, do not

say it is on account of anything he has writ. We must play our cards close. He and Midge had some relationship. Perhaps they colluded in sending the notes."

"More likely they than Midge and Calverly."

I started. "Why do you say Calverly?"

"No very significant reason—only that I saw 'em huddled together one time, conspiratorial as thieves. Calverly blanched when he saw me, and strode off."

I urged Garrick to say if he had seen or heard more between 'em which might bear on our mystery, but he was in such an agitated state, apacing and muttering, that he could give me nothing.

His wife arrived gaily and with a maidservant delivered some little sandwiches and cakes and drink, which, the sun being out, she placed on the lawn in front of the portico, where we sat and partook. Garrick dissembled well, he pasted on a smile—yet his hand shook as he lifted his cup, and when his dear wife did not look at him, such paroxysms of dread shook his countenance as wrung my heart.

Poor man. Fame delivers little content.

I was bid to greet three dogs: the monstrous Dragon, a sycophantic hound named Sweetlips, and a minuscule bundle of viciousness called Biddy who snapped at me from Mrs. Garrick's lap. Brother George's children, avisiting, sailed their hats at the wheeling swallows. Eva Maria hummed, her eyes twinkled merrily; she seemed to think life perfect.

Back in the house I was made to admire a portrait of Garrick as Hamlet, and from thence, with much on my mind, I returned to Craven Street.

I put by my book and pencil to place a stout length of oak upon the coals.

Having concluded his narrative, Mr. Franklin watched me. "Well?" urged he.

Proud that he wanted my thoughts, I said, "I wonder, sir, if Garrick tells you all he might."

"As do I."

"Too, does Mrs. Garrick know as little as she seems?"

"Ah."

"And I should very much like to learn what Dudley Midge and Lord Edmund Calverly conspired about."

The gentleman slapped a knee. "You will indeed never make a beau!"

❦ 14 ❦

*IN WHICH I follow Mr. Franklin all unknown,
and murder is once more done at Drury Lane . . .*

I greatly missed King's dirgelike song, which ever and
again had drifted down the attic stairs. Much as I hated
to do so, I began to believe he was indeed gone, never to
be found; and so, whilst Mr. Franklin writ a letter to his
wife, I sat nearby and drew my memory of King. 'Twas my
farewell.

Looking at what I had limned, I saw such sorrow upon
the blackamoor's face that I near sobbed. We were both
cast-off children. I had been saved from drowning; King
had pushed off into London.

I looked out at the city, wrapt in night.

Dear King, do not fetch up upon the shores of death.

Yet I had little time to sorrow, for Mr. Franklin soon
directed me in drawing out sev'ral schemes for Drury
Lane's lighting; some, too, for machines to produce wondrous effects. There was much use of reflecting sheets of
polished metal, but in whatever he proposed I saw the
gentleman's ingenuity. Here was revolution indeed, for if
Garrick built what I drew, the play would (as it were) be
took from the audience; t'would be set apart, in a sort of
box. No more would the outstretched legs of the rakes trip
up any actor.

I labored at this more than an hour, toward the end of

which William looked in. Dressed very fine, he was off for
Drury Lane, he said, to see Mrs. Drumm in the afterpiece.
"She plays a faerie charmingly."

"Still smitten, eh?" Mr. Franklin leant back. "Come,
Billy, speak to me of law. What does it say about married
women? Are they truly their husbands' chattel?"

"The law says a husband may give his wife correction."

"Even to beating?"

"Wives have the security of the peace against their husbands. We English are not barbarians. Wives may have
husbands restrained, if need be."

"If need be eh? But how many wives ask the law to chide
their husbands, tell me that? And if they do, how many are
granted their wish?"

"I do not know."

"And if a wife wish to be rid of her husband?"

"Adultery must be proved. 'Tis customarily the man
who begins a divorce proceeding, but 'tis hard and costly
and may take years. It calls for the assent of both law and
church. Few but the powerful and persistent achieve it."

"And what of the powerless eh?"

When William was gone Mr. Franklin took up a small
volume of plays. "Listen to this, from *An Evening's Love*,
by Dryden:

WILDBLOOD: Then what is a gentleman to hope from
you?
JACINTHA: To be admitted to pass my time with, while
a better comes: to be the lowest step in my staircase,
for a knight to mount upon him, and a lord upon him,
and a marquis upon him, and a duke upon him, 'til I
get as high as I can climb."

He laughed. "Is't not witty? Barbarous too. What a wonder how barbarism may be cloaked in wit." His smile fled.
"I think my son is mistook. I think barbarism resides in
England, in the finest houses. Regard how a woman with a
mind must use it only upon intrigues, since she would be

out o' bounds to use it any other way. May we entirely blame Lydia Linacre? Let us down, for Mrs. Stevenson calls to supper."

After a succulent joint I grew drowsy; last night's wakefulness had caught up with me. A shop boy delivered a brownwrapped package to Mr. Franklin just past nine, which I thought odd at so late an hour, though in my tiredness I paid it little mind. This he took to his workshop whilst I yawned over *Robinson Crusoe*, but after ten minutes or so the lines of print seemed to run like water, and, aching for sleep, I followed the gentleman to say I would to bed.

I found him with the contents of the package, an augur and bit, drilling holes in a pinewood plank.

"Ben Franklin, carpenter," said he. "What think you, Nick? Shall I take up the trade? Carpenters receive no threatening notes."

Why yes, said I, yawning, carpenters were useful to the world. Did I have leave to go to bed?

"Go," said he.

Doing so, I fell promptly asleep.

What woke me? A sound in the night? The soft creak of Mr. Franklin's door just across the way? Though I slept deep, some part of me, alerted by the danger we escaped last night, had stayed wakeful. And so I heard and sat up and crept quietly to my door to peer out.

There went Mr. Franklin, fully dressed, downstairs with his candle.

He moved slow, he took great care. Why? I listened. All the rest of the house seemed asleep: no sound of Polly humming or Mrs. Stevenson rattling pots. I hung fire. Mr. Franklin frequently went out of an evening, to suppers, clubs, the Royal Society. Yet he never slipped out in this manner, secretly.

Quickly pulling on shirt, trousers, shoes, wrapping my scarf about my neck and tugging my cap low on my brow, I followed Benjamin Franklin.

I took care to make no sound upon the stairs. By then his candlelight was vanished; he had gone out the door. Descending the well-known way by touch, I crept out into the chill of Craven Street. At the bottom of the street the Thames gently surged. At the top, past the pump, lay the broad Strand, some carriages upon it, reins jingling, though few windows showed light. The mournful cry of a watchman told 'twas half past eleven. No stars or moon could be seen; I was glad for the concealment this gave. Mr. Franklin's back was a silhouette, moving quickly now, with no stealth. The stench of coalfire thickened the air. I went after.

I thought on my actions. Was't right so to pursue the man who had saved me, my very father? Yet, what did he? I must know.

And so I trailed him, turning right into the Strand and keeping close to shop fronts so I might nip into a doorway should he think to look behind. But he never looked back, only walked rapidly, tapping his bamboo, head up as if he strolled London as free of care as Adam and Eve in the Garden before sin was loosed upon the world.

This was the way to Drury Lane. Was that Mr. Franklin's aim?

But 'twas also the way to Wild Street, number 52: Comfort Goodbody's house. And I felt—knew, with a certainty, when he passed Catherine Street—that that must be his goal.

He turned left and in less than five minutes was there. I watched from a dark corner as he rapped upon the woman's door and she herself opened. I strained to see the look upon her face, but the light at her back shone too bright—yet this same light reached out to where I hovered. I leapt back. The woman seemed to start. Had she seen me? With sudden anger I almost hoped she had, though I shuddered guiltily, as if 'twas I who had secrets to hide rather than they.

And then her house enfolded Mr. Franklin. Her door

shut. Candles were shortly extinguished below, and I knew that no one would soon emerge.

I turned away. Trudging back to Craven Street, I felt betrayed. A lone boy in London on so dark a night was vulnerable to many crimes, but I gave no thought to that; 'twas not the safety of my person that vexed my mind.

It had been five days since Dudley Midge was murdered, but 'twas not Midge who sorrowed me as I dressed at 7:00 A.M., nor Midge who troubled me as I crossed the hall, nor Midge I thought on as I stopped by Mr. Franklin's door as I had done ev'ry morning for six months since my dear father delivered me to the nearest place to home that I had known. I thought only on what I had learnt last night: Mr. Franklin slept in Comfort Goodbody's bed, in Comfort Goodbody's arms. Could it be otherwise? Had he not stole out as if ashamed? Had I not heard him return just before six humming a little song that stabbed my heart?

Yet, as I lifted my hand to knock, I thought again: why should this so fret me? My mother, that was why. Ever and again her dear face floated in my mind. Had not Mr. Franklin loved her? Could he so betray that love?

These were my thoughts, foolish as I think them now—though to a boy, whose life had been 'til then an uncertain thing where he was worked and cursed and beat, they did not seem foolish but felt like blows to make me mistrust all I had begun to trust in Mrs. Stevenson's kindly house. And what should I do when I went into Mr. Franklin's chamber? What should I say?

Why, what I always did and said. And so I knocked and was told to enter and opened to the crackling of a fire already laid and greeted the gentleman in his chair, though 'twas hard to meet his eyes.

He peered at me over the tops of his spectacles. "You look peaked this morning, Nick. Did you not rest well?"

"Well enough," murmured I.

"If you are ill we shall get Dr. Fothergill round to see you."

"I am not ill!" protested I, rather sharply.

He regarded me. "Indeed, I hope not." He sighed. "Alas, no answer yet to the advertisements which I placed yesterday: nothing of King or Mrs. Hart. 'Tis too soon, I guess. Peter watches in Grinder's Court and will send word should any unknown lady call. 'Til then—" He went back to his Betterton, I to finishing the drawings of Drury Lane which I began last eve. As I did so I glanced at the gentleman: his bald brow, his fringe of brown hair, his round, sturdy face bent in study. I had thought I knew him well. Did I? Words of his came to mind: "Let all men know thee but no man know thee thoroughly; men freely ford that see the shallows." Did he keep some of himself even from me?

I rode heavily through the morning on the back of my Latin and my ciphering and some pages of Plutarch's *Lives* but might as well never have mounted for all the distance I got on 'em. Mr. Franklin went out on business and came back disgruntled at all officious fools. "*Aequam memento rebus in arduis servare mentem*," muttered he, tossing down his beaver hat. " 'Remember to keep a calm mind in difficulties.' Horace gives good advice in dealing with the Penns. And with Drury Lane. How I hate to spend time far from the playhouse—what may befall whilst I am gone?" He briskly rubbed his hands. "Some small luncheon, Nick, and then we shall return there, eh?"

Thus we were at the theater by two o'clock, amidst its preparatory bustle: hammering and singing and juggling; fits of temper, shouts of laughter; scolding, praising, hypocrisy fencing with truth. How different from two nights past, when all lay silent save for murder acreeping. Did that same murderer now lurk in innocent disguise?

In David Garrick's office, Mr. Franklin spread out upon the actor's broad desk the sketches I had done of the devices he proposed. His brother, Lacy, Pritchard, and Richard Cross looked on too. Cross glared doubt; Lacy pulled his lip; Pritchard near turned himself inside out in praise: "O, 'tis sure to make all better!"

Garrick tapped his fingers. "Hem, ah, why, yes, 'tis very

fine." He pounded Mr. Franklin's back and thanked him and said they must talk more on how—and if—this was to be achieved, but for now he must to Southampton Street. He seemed cheery; he was truly expert at gainsaying the worst. How I longed to have that talent.

I occupied myself with drawing, so that over the next hour I got down Lucy Drumm and her mother and Lord Edmund Calverly, who hung about Mrs. Settle like a cook about his beef. By this time I had in my book a complete gallery of Drury Lane: actors, managers, scenemen, Swiss dancing master, orchestra leader, even the hangabout rakes and gallants who so plagued Garrick.

I had not drawn Comfort Goodbody from life. I made up my mind to do so.

There was some maliciousness in the decision, and yet I must look, see, examine; I was driven. And so, Mr. Franklin busy elsewhere, I went to the wardrobe where in the long, narrow room I found three girls busily sewing under my enemy's generalship. For her part Mrs. Goodbody poked amongst the many dresses hanging in a row, seeking with her expert eye unravelings, tears, buttons popped. At my coming she turned, and an uneasy look spread over her face.

Smoothing her hands upon her pin-stuck apron, she formed a smile. "Good day, Nicolas. Mr. Franklin is about the playhouse too?"

"Yes, ma'am. I have drawn many people here, but I have not drawn you. May I?"

She flushed. "But, surely—"

"You need not stop work. I shall set you down at work. 'Tis good practice. Mr. Franklin would like it so."

It could do no harm, she supposed with an added pinkness to her cheek. Stepping out of the way in a corner, I strove to look the serious artist whilst the seamstresses peeked up under their little caps and tittered. I drew Mrs. Goodbody's rounded figure, never such a fool as to mistake how it might please a man. I sketched her honest brow; my pencil never denied the wisdom in her fine blue

eyes. (Truth, Nick, truth.) I did not get all down well, but
I saw the quality in my model, her decency and dignity,
and I was ashamed that I secretly mistrusted her. Was I but
a willful brat?

Thus I was glad when Mr. Franklin found me and drew
me off, for we were to return to Craven Street, he said,
before returning tonight with a party of friends. He met
Mrs. Goodbody's gaze, she met his.

"Good day, Mrs. Goodbody," said he.

"I hope you are well, Mr. Franklin," said she.

"I watch my step," said he, and that was all. I stuffed my
book and pencil in my pocket, and we walked out.

We saw a remarkable scene. The wardrobe was to the
left, behind the stage, in the farthest corner from the Drury
Lane exit, an area little traveled, for it led nowhere but to
the wardrobe door. A light burned dimly in a sconce, but
'twas shadowed here nonetheless. In a corner we heard
some struggle, and a female voice cry No!

We turned. There stood Abel Drumm, bent over some
woman. He fought her, he pawed her.

The woman was Arabella Prouty. Drumm bent her arm.
Panting, he fumbled at her waist, her breasts. With her free
arm she struck him hard across the face.

He drew back. "You bitch, I'll have you now!" He was
about to lunge at her—but in an instant, so fast I had no
time to blink, Mr. Franklin was betwixt 'em and pressing
Drumm to the wall with his bamboo, which he held by two
hands to Drumm's throat, so that Drumm writhed and
choked.

"Calm, sir, calm," breathed Mr. Franklin into the man's
empurpled face, "and I shall be happy to let you be."

Drumm clawed the stick, but with his wind gone and
only black unconsciousness to reward him for struggling
more, he gave a pop-eyed gasp: "For God's sake, sir . . . !"
and Mr. Franklin lowered his bamboo.

Clutching his throat, Drumm coughed and spat.

Miss Prouty strode to him. She thrust her face in his.
"Have me? Have your wife, I say!"

Drumm wiped his mouth.

And then there was a third man present, and I felt a chill, for 'twas Lord Linacre with such a look upon his thin-nosed, thin-lipped face as might freeze fire to ice. Drumm blanched.

"You, sir!" Linacre's voice was that of a serpent if a serpent could speak. "You have abused Miss Prouty."

Drumm made mouths. "Why, you cannot think—"

My lord snatched the lace at his throat. "Do not lie. This man stopped you, or I should have done't myself, with less restraint. You owe me satisfaction. I shall send a second round to fix a time. I trust you will not back down. For now, be off."

"But—"

"Off, I say!"

Drumm staggered away.

With great, cool solicitude, Linacre turned to the woman. "Are you harmed, ma'am?" asked he.

Miss Prouty gazed proudly at him, defiantly at Mr. Franklin. "I am well, thank you." She strode off like a queen.

Linacre fixed a speculative stare upon Mr. Franklin.

The gentleman looked in no wise intimidated. "Miss Prouty is an especial friend of yours?"

Linacre's lips curled. "Do not think because you intercede for her that I like you. Benjamin Franklin, are you not? My wife has spoke of you. She says you harry her regarding some private business. Pah, my wife's amours are nothing to me. She would like me to portray the outraged husband, and I have been forced to do so on occasion, when knowledge that might sully my reputation as a man threatened to get about. But for the most part I let her be. I reserve my anger for those who abuse my mistress. I know about David Garrick. The popinjay! I shall deal with him only if he allows his affair with my wife to become public. Then I shall be forced to defend my honor—why, I'll cut his face to mincemeat! 'Til that time let him entertain my Lydia as he wishes; she needs her pets. As for you,

I despise a nosy man. Take care lest you prove to need chastisement too." He strode off.

Mr. Franklin merely smiled. "There is more than one popinjay in Drury Lane, and I wonder if I should not surprise my lord should he attempt to grapple with me." He drew me off. "What we have seen adds a piece to our jug, eh, Nick—but how the devil does it fit?"

The party of friends to which Mr. Franklin had referred consisted of himself, James Ralph, Dr. Fothergill, John Fielding, hopping little Joshua Brogden—and one twelve year old boy, happy to be so privileged. We foregathered at five, at the Shakespeare's Head, where David Garrick had first told of threats and fires at Drury Lane.

I sat by Mr. Franklin drawing Principal Justice Fielding's round, doughy face and froglike chins, whilst he grumbled about the dire state of London's streets: "What is wanted is a force of trained men to police 'em," said he, "so an Englishman may drink his pint without fear of his purse."

"Nay, sir," cried Mr. Ralph, banging down his tankard, "better police the playhouse: keep the riffraff out! keep bad acting and bad plays from the stage!"

Dr. Fothergill turned the talk to a recent anatomizing he had conducted upon the corpse of a thief hung at Tyburn. "What amazement when I slit open the belly of the dog!— coins split from his gut like water from a spring, three pounds sixpence; and I cut from sundry other cavities a gentleman's gold watch, six handkerchiefs of Belgian lace (unfortunately spoilt by bile or I should've took 'em home to my lady), and a handsome emerald ring worth fifty pound."

"Swallowed 'em to hide 'em, did he?" growled Principal Justice Fielding.

"Tut, sir, he did," urged Fothergill, "and a Spanish horn-and-vellum fan, a woolen winter coat, a nightstand, and a large oak chest filled with silver plate."

"Couldn't get down the basin and ewer, eh?" exploded Mr. Ralph, laughing.

We all laughed. How long had it been since I had felt so gay? At a quarter to six we proceded out under Shakespeare's gaze, very jolly—though I spied on Mr. Franklin's face a look that said he did not forget he had been near done in two nights past.

The evening bit with February's chill. Outside Drury Lane the whores wheedled and the Methodist preacher railed against sin. Pressing through the doors we found places in the pit. Had it been less than a week since we saw *A Lord and No Lord* cried down? Listening to the Third Music (we had missed the First and Second), I gazed about. No Lord Calverly or Lord Methuen or Lady Linacre this night. No Dudley Midge to lead a braying from on high. I searched the clamoring galleries. Did the man with the odd eyebrows and lopsided moustache secretly watch? Why had he pushed Dudley Midge? I glimpsed Dr. Johnson, dourly at the end of our row. Then Thomas Arne lowered his baton and Mrs. Cibber floated out to deliver the prologue, which she did in a pure, sweet style far different from Kitty Clive's.

The green curtain rose, in doing so plucking up the sword of one of the stage gallants; in falling it near decapitated a fife-player, and the audience laughed and applauded, but I did not like this omen.

Yet *Lear* went forward smoothly. Though I had seen much of it from the wings two days ago, this was a new experience, and such was Garrick's tragic power as the disprized old king that I forgot all the artifice of lights and flats and winches and gave myself to his performance as if 'twere life. How I hated his two ungrateful daughters! How I wept when Lear railed in the storm!

When the tragedy was done Mr. Franklin bought me a pippin apple whilst Miss Fanny Lawne danced a barcarole. On the other side of us Mr. Ralph pressed Dr. Fothergill to dramatize his comic anatomization for the stage. At last came the afterpiece: *A Midsummer Night's Dream.* The scene was changed before our eyes, to a pretty forest vista, with its painted gnarled oaks slid out in their grooves.

From behind 'em the faeries would emerge. There were three trees. I frowned. Had there not previously been two? No matter. Lovers fled Athens, Oberon worked his magic, Bottom grew ears; and near the end a dozen faeries, their eyes prettily masked, danced.

John Fielding sat to my right, pressing my ribs with his elbow. I felt him start. "What the devil? What the devil, Franklin?"

Mr. Franklin peered across me. "What is't, Fielding? What do you hear?"

The cock of the doughty man's bewigged head showed that indeed his remarkable ears heard something. "A man in pain, a man dying, a man dead," murmured he sepulchrally out of his perpetual darkness.

Mr. Franklin plucked urgently at his sleeve. "But where?"

Fielding sat still and gray. "Somewhere by the stage."

In great distress Mr. Franklin polished his spectacles and fidgeted with his buttons and thumped his bamboo whilst *A Midsummer Night's Dream* moved to its end. "Damn!" snorted he as Garrick and company took what seemed very long bows. Amongst the faeries I noted Miss Drumm third from the left in her blue gauzy wings.

All departed the stage. The green curtain descended, and the audience began noisily to shuffle out. "Come, Nick." At once Mr. Franklin began clambering over benches as he had done when Dudley Midge had fallen, crushing a lady's hat and near toppling an old man, whilst I scrambled after praying Justice Fielding was mistook. Could any ears be so prodigious? Yet clearly Mr. Franklin trusted 'em. We hurried to the side door that led up four short steps. We entered that door, we mounted those stairs. We paused at the top. In the backstage dimness, at the very rear of the playhouse, men and women crowded about one of the giant machines: actors, dancers, musicians, property men, wardrobe women, Mrs. Goodbody amongst 'em. There was a breathless silence, a stunned air.

"O, I pray—" murmured Mr. Franklin, plunging on. Hating to do so, I followed. Wanting not to look, I did.

I stopped betwixt the gentleman and the comic Woodward, who stood as rigidly froze as the rest. The machine which Mr. Cross had last night made to lower clouds sat before us where it always sat, winch handles sprouting, ropes and wires shooting to the ceiling as if they were a spinner's sticky strands. They had controlled the moon above Athens' fleeing lovers and the sun which had lit Pyramus and Thisbe at the wall.

But blood now oiled the thing. A man's head lay crushed amongst the huge gears. I felt sick to my stomach, a nauseous dizziness, and caught blindly at Mr. Franklin's sleeve. He took my arm and gripped it, but when I looked up I saw he too had gone white. This was no clean death, as Dudley Midge's had been; this was gore-spattered. A reddish blackness still dripped from the gears, spreading. Mrs. Cibber looked down. Her shoes stood in blood, and she cried out and fainted into Richard Cross's arms, and all let out the breath they had held in. And then such a caterwauling, of horror, revulsion, dismay.

There came a voice above the rest: "But who the devil is it?"—David Garrick in his garb as Oberon, with dramatically flaring false eyebrows.

James Lacy vomited his supper. Thus did each manager speak to the event. By this time, Dr. Fothergill had reached us, followed close by Joshua Brogden leading blind Justice Fielding, Mr. Ralph on their heels.

The doctor stepped forward. "John Fothergill, physician. We must extricate the body." He looked gravely round. " 'Twill not be pretty. If you have not the stomach, go."

Many moaned but few left. Fothergill and Mr. Franklin bent near the body, which lay with its arms beneath it. The man had not appeared in the play; he wore no actor's garb but shoes and stockings and a coat which might be worn by many men. Upon his stomach, he was no one, and yet he was someone, and all wished to know who that might be.

I thought I knew.

The operation proved more ghastly than Fothergill had predicted, for the very bones of the man's head were caught in the huge gears, their teeth needing to be cranked back to release 'em, this procedure made with such strain and horrendous noises as if the skull were split once more. When this dreadful move was effected, Fothergill and Mr. Franklin grasped the man's bloodsoaked shoulders, pulled him from the machine, turned him. I heard cries, gasps. Again I did not wish to look but forced my gaze to do so. The man's arms flopped back, his toes pointed out. His face was truly ruined, a mass of bruised, crushed, bloody flesh, the features mingled as if mixed up in a stew. Where were eyes, nose, mouth?

I heard more sounds of sickness and fought to hold down my gorge. I longed to sob. How frail was flesh. Yet we knew him by his hair, for though he had worn a wig it had caught amongst the gears and hung there, bedaubed. By his hands too, on one of which stood out on the second finger a plaited gold wedding band.

There came a cry, and Lucy Drumm in her faery costume lunged forward and fell to her knees by the side of the poor dead thing and gave out with a piteous sobbing, aplucking at his garments and painting herself with blood. "Abel . . . my dear Abel!" moaned she.

Her mother dropt by her side. "Is't truly your poor husband?" She held her daughter. "He is at peace then, unhappy no more. Think on that and come away. 'Tis a terrible accident. Come, my child."

I looked at Miss Prouty, who stared as white as flour. She had been a near victim of this selfsame machine. Mr. Franklin met my eye. He shook his head.

This is no accident, proclaimed his steady gaze.

⚘ 15 ⚘

*IN WHICH a ragged wig, three trees
and a burnt scrap of paper lead us on . . .*

Lucy Drumm's mother drew her to an edge of the wings,
where she softly wailed. One of the painters brought a
length of canvas cloth to cover her dead husband's body
'til it might be carried off. People hung uncertainly about,
as if departing might cause 'em truly to contemplate what
they had witnessed.

Justice Fielding trundled forward. "Who saw this happen?" rumbled he.

No person spoke.

"Come," growled the magistrate in a tone which said he
would dig up truth though it be buried deep and sorely
afflict him who made him labor to unearth it. "Who saw,
I say?"

Still no answer.

"What, no one was witness?"

An uneasy murmuring, feet shifting, eyes darting.

David Garrick cleared his throat. "It is, after all, sir,
dim-lit backstage. Your friend Mr. Franklin, has proposed
brightening the area, which this dreadful accident urges us
to do. Too, we are all most busied in putting on the play.
The machine is at the rear, where few people go. The fellow
slipped; he fell into the gears when no one looked, and that
is all. Had someone seen him slip 'twould have been too

late. The accident occurred quick, Drumm died—there is
no mystery in that."

"Hmph," grunted the Principal Justice. "And have you
not suffered a sight too many accidents of late? Why, you
told me so yourself."

There was a stir. All eyes turned to Garrick. "Hem, ah,
but sir—" Wrapping his arm about the justice's shoulders,
he tugged him upon the stage, where I saw him urgently
expostulate.

Those remaining began to depart in murmuring groups
of darkly troubled nature. "Not that any of us loved
Drumm—except his wife," whispered Woodward to Kitty
Clive as they passed. I looked at the pathetic mound of
canvas, a life snuffed, flesh without breath, soon to be dust.
How sad to die so generally unmourned.

Mr. Franklin came to my side. "How do you, Nick?"

I looked up at him. "Well enough, sir."

"Stout lad."

"Is not life the better playwright?" said Mr. Ralph, joining us. "Why, what a turn of tale is here: damned Drumm
dead!—and if he is in heaven he will trouble the angels.
What a sour, mean fellow! But hear now, Ben, I am off with
Woodward and some others to drink. Join us."

"Nay, I shall stay awhile."

"Please yourself."

He strode off, Mr. Franklin's gray gaze following. He
turned to Dr. Fothergill. "What make you of this, John?"

"Murder."

An eyebrow raised. "Think you so?"

"I do. Look." The doctor beckoned us near the body. By
now few people remained, Garrick still urgently commun-
ing with John Fielding out of earshot on the stage, Mrs.
Settle comforting her whimpering daughter, but all else
was unpeopled shadow. "Some light, Nick, if you please."
Bringing a candle from a sconce, I knelt beside the gentleman, at which Fothergill drew back the canvas. He turned
the bloody head. "Closer, Nick. Now, see you," he pointed
with his long-fingered hand, "this reddening on the back of

the skull? The cut flesh? Drumm was struck a blow before he fell—or was thrust—face forward into the gears of the machine."

Mr. Franklin squinted at him. "And you are certain this injury was not done by the machine?"

"Unlikely, given the position of the body. But there is more: have you not asked why at the moment he fell the gears moved? The play was done, no business needed upon the stage."

"I have asked indeed—and found me the answer: because someone unfastened the brake." Drawing us to the machine, he showed the metal arm, slipped from its track.

Fothergill regarded his friend. "Then 'tis truly murder. We must inform Fielding at once."

Mr. Franklin stayed him. "No. Leave it to me."

Fothergill had more than once seen his friend on the trail of mystery. He peered. "What are you about, Ben? Have you—?"

"—found some new puzzle to divert me? I have. Let me piece it together my way."

"You must promise to stay safe."

A small smile. "I have Nick to protect a rash old man."

" 'Tis no jest." Fothergill turned to me. "Keep tight rein on him, Nicolas." He left.

Mr. Franklin knelt as to pull the canvas back over Drumm but, glancing about to make sure his movements were unobserved, he first surveyed the dead man's pockets. There were some paltry coins, a chased snuff box, a cheap brass watch. "What's this?" Pulling forth a greasy reddish wig, he thrust it beneath his coat.

He went to the keening Lucy Drumm. Over her quivering back, her mother's eyes greeted him without tears. Though Mrs. Settle grieved for her daughter, 'twas not likely she felt much sorrow for the husband, and I could not help thinking: would not the young wife be better off now Drumm was dead? Uncontrolled sobs jerked from Lucy's white throat, and both mother and daughter were spotted with the dead man's blood.

"If I may help in any way——?" offered Mr. Franklin.

"Speak to Lucy," urged Mrs. Settle. "persuade her, for the wretched child says she herself killed her husband."

"I did, I did!" moaned the young woman.

Mr. Franklin frowned. "How, child?"

Lucy's head turned, displaying the wet ravagement coursing down her cheeks. "I g-gave him drink," she gulped. "G-gin. He demanded it, and I b-brought it like a fool." She fell back against her mother.

Mrs. Settle patted her back. "Drumm loved his liquor. He was more than usually agitated this afternoon, muttering of some affront. When he was so, he must have drink. He sent Lucy to bring it; she delivered him a pint, which he drank down in half an hour and wanted more. She brought that too."

"Why? Why did I?" came Lucy's recriminating wail.

"Because he would have beat you if you had not," said her mother, tight-lipped. "You know he would."

Mr. Franklin touched Lucy's shoulder. "His besotted state may have caused him to fall into the machine, but you must not blame yourself. If you had not got him gin he would have obtained it another way."

Someone stood nearby. I turned. 'Twas Arabella Prouty. Though the young actress had never shown fondness for Lucy Drumm, she wore now an expression of pale distress. "Dear Mrs. Drumm," her voice quavered. How different from the defiant woman who had struggled with Abel Drumm this afternoon. "May I console you?" Gathering Lucy from her mother, she held her and to my very great surprise began to weep too.

Mr. Franklin beckoned Mrs. Settle aside. "Your daughter and her husband——?"

The mother drew her hand wearily across her brow, as if a long, terrible journey was at last an end. "He was a trying man, but Lucy loved him, foolish girl. He was good to her, in his way, and he loved her too, I think. O, he abused her, and it wrung my heart to see it, but it did not dishearten Lucy. She has a compliant nature; she liked to be led. So, in some strange way, Abel Drumm was a proper husband. And now . . . and now—'' Her reddened eyes turned toward the canvas mound. "What will become of my child? Who will guide the poor lost lamb?"

There came a rapid click of boot heels, and Lord Edmund Calverly arrived amongst us. "I have just heard," said he in prickling agitation. He gaped at the mound, where blood began to seep through canvas. "And that is Drumm? Dear God. Come, let us get your daughter home."

"I thank you." Mrs. Settle shot Mr. Franklin one last look before she and Lord Calverly gathered Lucy to take her off. Arabella Prouty stood stark and alone, then she too drifted away, and silence began to creep upon the echoing playhouse. The undertaker's men arrived as they had recently arrived for another body and scooped up Abel Drumm and carted him away, all his anger and spite stiff on their litter.

Justice Fielding returned from the stage, led by Joshua Brogden. "I do not like letting this go," grumbled he darkly, his great chins trembling, "but Garrick has it that if I press the matter his actors will be so discomposed they will never play any play. Damn me, oughtn't they to be discomposed, if they might have the life crushed from 'em?" He let out breath. "The long and short of't is, I am begged to leave matters in your hands. You are more discreet, Garrick says—ha! Well, I will be content, for cutthroats, plotters, and thieves fill my plate. Will you deal with this, Franklin?"

The gentleman did not reply at once. "Might I have prevented this second death?" muttered he, plainly distressed. "Yet I consent, and shall deal with it 'til I can deal with it no more; then you must show poor Ben Franklin how 'tis done."

The magistrate nodded. "Come, then, Brogden, a dish of eels at the Red Lion, a game bird, mutton pie."

"And gooseberry cream, sir," urged the hopping little man. "Let there be gooseberry cream."

Joshua Brogden led his stertorously breathing master out.

Mr. Franklin looked about. "Where is Garrick?" We found him alone upon the stage leaning against the edge of one of the great flats, his customarily lively expression plunged into dejected speculation. Amongst the empty benches the black-garbed women gleaned.

Garrick looked up. "Well, was it accident, Franklin? Or—?"

"Murder. Carefully planned." Mr. Franklin told why he believed so.

"Dear Lord." The actor flapped Oberon's cloak. "How dare anyone amongst my company—!" He bent forward. "It is someone of Drury Lane? We can draw no other conclusion?"

"Cannot, I believe."

"But who? You will continue to investigate? I will pay you."

" 'Tis lives lost I think on, not coin—though it appears the two murdered men will be missed by few. You will not miss Drumm, eh?"

"Why, I—"

"You need not answer."

The head sceneman appeared, cap in hand, to say that, all being battened down, he and his men would depart.

Garrick shot him a look. "Wait, sir. Why were there three trees in the last scene? There have been two before. I near tripped upon the third one."

The man made mouths. "Did you not ask for three, sir?"

Garrick glared. "I did not."

The sceneman fumbled in a coat pocket. "You did not send this note, near five o'clock?"

Garrick snatched the paper, read. "Look at this, Franklin. I did not write it." He held it out.

I read with Mr. Franklin:

Mr. Dorland,

We shall have three oak trees in the afterpiece tonight, the better to conceal our faeries before they
appear onstage. 'Twill produce a finer effect. See to
it.

D. Garrick

Mr. Franklin solemnly folded the paper. "May I keep
this?"

"Keep it or throw it away. Be off, Dorland." When the
sceneman was gone, Garrick looked more at sea than ever.
"Has this something to do with Drumm's murder?"

"I cannot say. 'Tis writ in Drumm's hand."

"What?"

Mr. Franklin slipped the note in his coat with the wig.
"Perhaps sleep may reveal why. Come, Nick, we both want
rest. Go to your wife, Garrick. Would that ev'ry man might
be consoled so well."

We had swept up two more shards of our jug: a musty wig
and a forgery saying that one more tree was wanted upon
the stage, but sleep did nothing to fit 'em to a wholeness in
my mind. The jug remained shattered whilst I tossed. Who
had so horribly done in Abel Drumm? Why?

I crossed the landing early to Mr. Franklin's chamber but
found him wide awake, greeting the chill, gray morn naked
before his open casement, going up and down in knee
bends and scraping upon his fiddle. Whilst I laid a fire, he
splashed his face at his basin, dried himself, tied back his
fringe of brown hair.

Shortly he stood dressed by a crackling blaze, the wig
and forged note from Drumm resting on the table by his
chair.

He picked up the wig. "Whose is this, Nick?"

"I do not know."

"Think. The wig worn by the man who pushed Dudley
Midge? It is the same singular rust-red hue which Mr. Hark-

ens named. Further, see what is tucked inside." He turned
the wig out, so that into my cupped hands fell two small
lengths of fur, like caterpillars.

"False eyebrows," said I when I saw the stitching on
their underside.

He nodded. "Those worn by a murderer."

"Drumm pushed Midge?"

Mr. Franklin was long in answering. "Much points that
way." Yet the idea plainly troubled him. "Certainly
Drumm was expert at makeup and disguise, as ev'ryone
tells."

"But, why should he wish to murder Midge?"

"*If* he murdered him." Mr. Franklin's voice picked its
way carefully. "There will be reason behind all. Yet is't not
odd that murder is done to those who, to our knowledge,
did *not* receive such threats?"

"Odd indeed."

Mr. Franklin peered out his window. "As to why Drumm
might wish Midge dead—" he rose and fell on his toes, "I
should prefer to discover another thing: why did he carry
the wig and the eyebrows last night?"

"To use again, to murder again?"

"And yet he was murdered himself."

"Was't he who tried to kill you at Drury Lane?"

" 'Tis certain he saw us remain behind. He might easily
have found his way in by the rooftop door—but then so
might anyone."

I felt lost in possibilities.

Mr. Franklin began to pace. "And then there is this
damnable note demanding three trees, which we know was
sent by Drumm, for 'tis penned in the same hand that writ
the play which I keep even now in my workshop. Why
three trees?"

"I do not know."

He made a nettled sound. "If we did we should know
near all." He squinted over some thought, like grit to the
eye, but neither dislodged it nor gave it words. "As to the
time of Drumm's murder, Fielding's ears heard the death

cry a full two minutes before the end of the afterpiece, by my good hunter watch. Garrick was onstage then. Mrs. Cibber. Miss Prouty played Helena. Woodward did Bottom."

"And Mrs. Drumm danced one of the faeries."

"Aye, all of 'em in plain sight. They clearly could not've killed him."

"But all others could?"

He scraped at his jaw. "We must inquire close about the playhouse, to see who was with whom and who saw what that fateful moment. I hope something will come known."

Busying myself about my lessons, I thought on other knowing: Mr. Franklin and Mrs. Goodbody. The knowledge weighed heavy in my mind.

At ten o'clock a hackney coach arrived, hired since Peter kept watch in Grinder's Court. It ferried us through a blustery day—but not this time to Drury Lane. We aimed for the Drumm lodgings, in Castle Street, south of St. Giles.

"How clever a murderer we pursue," mused Mr. Franklin as we dipped in and out of a ditch. He righted his beaver hat. "He makes both deaths look accidents . . ."

We turned from St. Martin's into Castle Street. The Drumm demesne proved to be two rooms above an apothecary. Mounting narrow stairs, we heard voices arguing, a man's and a woman's. Some ghostly echo of the strife that had plagued the Drumm marriage when the husband lived? Yet the woman's voice was not sweet Lucy's. Mr. Franklin's quick, silencing finger said he longed to hear, but creaking stairs had already betrayed us, and the voices abruptly ceased.

The gentleman gave three sharp raps. There came a soft, urgent exchange from within, footsteps. Mrs. Settle opened.

I saw in the woman's lineaments what Lucy would become: a woman lucky to retain youth's look after youth had fled. I also saw an unmistakable wariness. Fear? I felt though she strove to mask it, that its source was the man

in black, polished boots and a fine velvet suit behind her:
Lord Edmund Calverly.

"Mr. Franklin?" said the woman, a bright spot of surprise in each cheek. "You are come to—?"

"—to say again how sorry I am for your daughter's be-
reavement. She is home?"

"Why . . . yes. In her chamber."

"May I—?"

"—see her? Why . . . naturally, since you are so kind. I
shall fetch her."

We stepped into the room. "Lord Edmund," said Mr.
Franklin, nodding, as Mrs. Settle went through a door.
Beyond it I glimpsed Lucy curled like a castoff garment in
a chair by a window in wan morning light.

"Franklin," gave Calverly curtly, shifting on his heels in
an air of ruffled aggravation, as if he wished to be anywhere
but here. How changed from the deep solicitousness of last
night. What had he and his mistress argued about?

He and Mr. Franklin exchanged commonplaces about
last night's death before Lucy trailed out in a blue dress, its
bodice damp from tears, her honey hair, usually ringleted,
pulled back so severely that it seemed a punishment to her
face to frame it so. No rouge or lip color mitigated the
despair which loss had chalked upon her countenance.

"Th-thank you for coming, Mr. Franklin," stammered
she.

"I wished to say again how sorry . . . and to say too, once
more, that you . . . that you must never blame yourself."

The young woman made a whimpering sound. Wrapping
an arm about her, her mother shot at Calverly a reproach-
ful look that startled me.

There followed an awkward silence. Rarely did I see Mr.
Franklin at a loss, but he appeared so now, turning his
beaver hat in his hands, gazing at his toes, then out the
window, at sofa, chairs, carpet, finally clearing and reclear-
ing his throat. "May I, hem, ask a favor? I hate to do so,"
got out he.

Mrs. Settle held her daughter tight. "What might that be?"

"As this is the Drumm household I must ask it of Mrs. Drumm." He gazed at Lucy's bowed head. "Might I, ma'am—if't do not displease—examine your bedchamber?"

"Here, Franklin!" put in Calverly, stepping forward. "What do you say? Do you not know that this poor young woman—?"

Mr. Franklin held up a hand. "I know well enough. Yet I also know that her husband's death was not accident. You must be told that Mr. Drumm was first struck on the head before he was thrust—" A silent gesture completed the tale.

Mrs. Settle shuddered. "You cannot mean—?"

"Dear God." Calverly's fingers opened and closed at his sides. "But why do you think so?"

Mr. Franklin said why.

Lucy lifted swimming eyes. "You say that someone . . . with malice and deliberation . . . ?"

"I regret that I must. I do."

The young woman's pink lips parted, and she stood as if struck dumb.

Mr. Franklin turned his hat in his hands once more. "I come only as he who would discover who did the deed and bring him to justice. Dear Mrs. Drumm," he pulled the reddish wig from his coat pocket, "was this your husband's?"

Her slender arm found strength to move. She felt of the draggled thing.

"It cannot be his," snapped Mrs. Settle.

"But it is, mother," said her daughter quickly. "How can you say that it is not? I know it from his wardrobe. He keeps many costumes. They are hung in our chamber. It is them you wish to examine, is it not, Mr. Franklin?"

"May I?"

"How may prying amongst a dead man's things tell who murdered him?" demanded Mrs. Settle.

Lucy shook her head. "No, mother, we must not pre-vent." Her voice broke, but she went on, "If t'will help to right this wrong, sir, you may search where you please." This proved her limit and, dropping the wig, she buried her face in her hands.

Lord Calverly stirred. He looked like comforting Lucy; he looked, too, like running away—but a shudder resolved his vacillation. "I think you should not be so sad to see him dead," pronounced he with a flaring of his fine nostrils, at which Lucy flinched and Mrs. Settle went white. "I wish you luck, Franklin"—this in keen bitterness. "Truth must out, but I shall have none of it. Good day." He charged from the room.

For a moment no one looked at anyone. Mr. Franklin's knees cracked as he bent to pick up the wig. "May I look into your chamber now, Mrs. Drumm?" asked he.

"Wh-when you will."

I followed the gentleman. The chamber was small, made smaller by two large wardrobes side by side against one wall. Inside 'em Mr. Franklin disclosed a myriad of cloth-ing: a few lady's dresses, yet many coats, shirts, trousers, waistcoats, doublets, sashes, belts clearly belonging to her husband. One or two outfits were as fine as a lord's, the rest stuff which might've been donned by many English sorts, from clerics to costermongers. Mr. Franklin searched for shoes with high heels; he found three pair, yet they did not resolve his doubt. "Drumm played fops upon the stage, mincing courtiers; no surprise he kept shoes for 'em—but no sure proof he killed Midge either." He had half-closed the chamber door, so Lucy and her mother could not observe. Going to the bow-fronted chest, he slid out drawers, searching there too, amongst stockings, stays and undergarments. Nothing. The bottom drawer was crammed with false noses, beards, a ragtag collection of wigs. "Pah," muttered he, desultorily opening the tin of wig powder he found there with little expectation—yet I felt him start. "What's this?"

Inside lay not powder but folded paper.

I smelt lavender as he drew it forth.
He opened it:

Dearest,

Since the first day I met you I have not enjoyed
one hour of restful peace. My beating heart keeps
me wakeful, your image drifts in my mind like
dreams . . .

It went on in this wise for twenty more lines.
It was signed, "Your Passionate Love."
Mr. Franklin's crinkled brown eyes met mine. "Drumm's
hand again. To whom did he write?"
"Lucy?"
"And hid the letter in a snuffbox? No. To Mrs. Hart,
whoever she may be? Miss Prouty? Unlikely. Or—?" He
did not complete this thought. "We shall take it, Nick;
no need to trouble his widow with a later, unpleasant find-
ing." He frowned. "Yet something is wrong about the
thing . . ." Getting to his feet, he cast a dissatisfied eye
about the room, but there seemed no further corner to
search unless we dove beneath the bedclothes themselves.
He led me out.
In the parlor Lucy Drumm and her mother stood mutely
apart. Some discord seemed to have put 'em at odds.
"Did you discover a murderer?" asked Mrs. Settle stiffly.
"No, ma'am."
Lucy shook her head. "It is so hard, especially now."
Mr. Franklin bent inquiringly. "Especially now, child?"
"Yes."
"But why, if you please?"
Mrs. Settle protested, but her daughter paid no heed. "I
am with child," blurted she with fresh tears, "and now that
child has no father."
Mr. Franklin looked grim and pitying. Did he think on
my dear mother and how she had found herself in a like
state, friendless, and had died before I was five? "We can-

not bring back your husband, Mrs. Drumm," said he staunchly, "but we can deliver justice to his murderer. Do you have any idea who that might be?"

"No. M-many seemed to dislike Abel, but that is no reason for m-murder. They did not know him. If they had—O, if only I had made him more happy! What pains he took with me. I tried to be a better actress. I helped him any way he wished. I studied lines past midnight, I aided him in his plays, I acted as his secretary, ever striving to be a cheerful wife when storms blew up. He had many cloudy days. Few understood his torments. He longed to be a man known, sought, admired." She gripped Mr. Franklin's sleeve. "Have you never longed to be such a man?" Her hand fell away. "Could I not have brightened his hours more? But I failed, and now . . . and now . . ."

Sobs halted her words. There seemed no more to be done—Lucy must suffer 'til time healed, and after more condolences and urgings not to blame herself, we repaired to our coach, the gentleman tapping his fingers in no very pleased state of mind. "So Drumm was ate up by ambition," muttered he as we turned toward the Thames. "Many are blighted by that worm. But why this letter?" He snatched it from his pocket. "Was it ever sent? Too, what is Calverly about? And Lucy with child. She understood her husband's torments, eh? Damn me, she understood very little or I am not Ben Franklin. Why is her mother become so unfriendly? What the devil was Abel Drumm's game?"

We arrived at Drury Lane just before noon. Mr. Franklin pressed Richard Cross about the three trees. Had he known beforehand that they were asked for?

"No." The prompter fumed. "Damn the trickster who did it. Garrick near broke his leg on the root of the third as he dashed on." He peered. "Drumm writ the note, you say? He has been aptly rewarded for his mischief then. Now you must excuse me, for I have much to do."

Cross stalked off, Mr. Franklin watching. "Was that the

aim of the tree, to tumble David Garrick? Come.'' I followed him onstage, where the trees still stood in place, fantastically branched, in the fourth of the five sets of grooves which traversed the floor. The addition of the third tree effectively masked the back of the stage from the foremost part, leaving a lane of but three feet where one might pass round. Mr. Franklin walked to the floats, turned, stood with one hand on his chin. ''Hum, thus placed, they effectively screen whatever might occur behind 'em. 'Twas dim-lit there too, as Garrick was at pains to point out to John Fielding. An idea begins to form. Let us examine Drumm's dressing room.''

This he had shared with two other lesser players, it grew out. We were directed to a narrow, mean-spirited chamber that seemed to reek of Drumm's sour character: a couple of dressing tables, a single poorly silvered looking-glass which made our figures yaw and reel, a smell of old leather and greasepaint. There was a metal grate too, clogged with ashes, a half-burnt curl of yellowed foolscap amongst 'em.

Kneeling, Mr. Franklin drew this forth. There had been of late much scrutinizing of scraps of paper, and he and I found our heads close over one again:

> . . . was there, as you know, and the man pulled her upon his knee and fondled her, and soon had her long dress up, and took his part into his hand and placed it betwixt her legs, all upon the chair, and there he worked at her hard, she uttering sluttish cries 'til there came a great shaking upon 'em both. But this was not all, for there soon followed more dalliance upon the bed, hot action, with the same noisy end, all which I shall tell before the magistrate if . . .

Flames had burnt away the rest. I looked at Mr. Franklin. His brow furrowed. ''Like Midge, Drumm writ such stuff for the penny press, Mrs. Settle said—though many scribblers do the same.''

"This then is a sample?" asked I.

"Yet 'tis not in Drumm's hand."

I peered at the rough, hasty scrawl.

"Indeed, 'tis not in any hand we know," muttered the gentleman. "Who, then . . . ?"

"Another threatening note?"

"True, the writer says he'll go to the law if . . . if what? And why should a magistrate pay heed to what passes between men and women ev'ry moment of ev'ry day? Unless . . ." Placing the fragile scrap carefully betwixt a folded playbill, he slipped this in his pocket. His eyes seemed to take fire in the candlelight. "Do you recall what William said on divorce?" He drove a fist into a palm. "O, is that it, Nick?"

There was no time for elucidation. Out in the wings a call boy hurried up. "A message for you, sir."

Mr. Franklin gave the boy twopence. Quickly scanning the paper, he beckoned me along. " 'Tis from Peter. Our advertisement has flushed a pigeon. We must fly to Grinder's Court."

❦ 16 ❦

*IN WHICH we peep through a hole in a wall
and learn more of a claque . . .*

O, O . . . !" cried Miss Bird, flopping like a fish in one
of the brocade chairs in her parlor. Such was her
agitation, flailing and twitching, that she continually
slipped and slid, her sticklike legs finding no purchase in
the carpet, so that she might've flung her thin little body
full upon it and remained there in an agitated, croaking
heap had not Mr. Franklin on one side and Peter on the
other staunchly held her and righted her, 'til her paroxysm
passed to a quavering and from thence to a moaning and
last to an exhaustion. She gasped, she rolled her eyes, she
fanned her cheeks. "S-spirits . . . I want spirits!"

Mr. Franklin regarded her. " 'Twill do no harm. In the
kitchen, ma'am? Fetch spirits then, Peter."

The loyal blackamoor departed.

We still did not fully know what had set her awry. Upon
our arrival Peter had told that, spying at the corner of
Grinder's Court where he set himself up as a begger so he
might see both into the court and along Coventry Street, he
had, somewhat past twelve, observed a scruffy fellow
creep into number 108. Ten minutes thereafter he heard a
commotion, at which, casting aside his false bandages
which had earned him two shillings and threepence since
nine, he leapt up. Finding the door ajar, he hurried in to be

near knocked over by this same man charging downstairs in great heat. The man fled. Fearing someone hurt, Peter dashed upstairs, where he discovered Miss Bird on the floor of Mrs. Hart's former room, head over heels, awailing.

He had got the woman downstairs, where she had progressed from bad to worse, 'til this moment of calm, which a large swallow of gin made calmer.

" 'Tis Mr. Franklin, Miss Bird," said he with great deliberation, prying the bottle from her fingers but holding it near like a toy to entice a babe. "All harm is past, and you are safe. But you must say what occurred."

The woman's nose twitched. Her cap flopped. "Dear me, dear! What occurred? Why . . . why, I heard a sound from above, that is what occurred. What's this? said I, for neither room was let. So I crept upstairs to see what might be. A rat? A rat indeed, for I found in the west chamber a man pawing amongst the bedclothes, with all the drawers out and the wardrobe open and the carpet turned over. He rounded upon me. 'Well, where's the stuff? The three lady's handkerchers, that's what I want, and t'other things as well. You advertised, and I am come for 'em, and shall have 'em or never be Jeremy Jones.' 'I did not advertise, Mr. Jones,' protested I. 'Whose stuff can you mean?' At which he shook me and said Mrs. Hart's and I must stop lying, at which (for I still thought he might answer to reason) I said if I advertised why did he not knock on my door or send Mrs. Hart herself for her things? This infuriated him; he seemed truly intent on doing harm, so I cried out, and after cursing me as I have never been cursed in my life, he ran away. By this time my knees were water, sir, very water, my thoughts unable to conceive. How fortunate that your manservant was near and heard and came, for I . . . O, dear, I grow ditherish. More gin, sir, I must have it to calm my nerves."

"First, dear lady, what did this man look like?"

She gasped. "Not like any gentleman, that is sure! He had a smudgy face and a twisty moustache and a hat pulled low across his brow and patchy clothes—yet 'tis strange, now I think on't, for like some fop or gallant he wore high heels."

"Very high?"

"Four inches if they were one, black and shiny. Do give me my gin, sir, I beg you, for I never drink it except I want it, and I sorely want it now."

Mr. Franklin relinquished the bottle, though he allowed but one swallow before he prised it free once more. "Look you, ma'am." He bid me take out my sketchbook. "Examine these drawings. Are any Mrs. Hart?" I began to show my Drury Lane portraits.

"Why, yes, that is Mrs. Hart," exclaimed Miss Bird after a moment. "Why do you have her picture?" She pointed to Mrs. Settle.

"Why makes no matter," said Mr. Franklin, meeting my eyes. "But we *do* have her. Show others, Nick."

I had turned but three pages more before Miss Bird pointed again. "And there's her daughter." 'Twas Lucy Drumm.

Mr. Franklin nodded. "Her daughter indeed. She visited her mother here?"

"Many times."

"Yet you said in our previous interview that you did not know who visited Mrs. Hart."

"Did I?" Miss Bird was not so far gone as she pretended.

"No matter," said Mr. Franklin. "Look more, if you please."

At my portrait of Lord Edmund Calverly Miss Bird started, though she attempted to cover this with a fanning of her face.

Mr. Franklin looked sharp. He waggled the bottle. "Your tonic, ma'am—but first tell of this gentleman."

She looked at the gin, she looked at my drawing, she squinted hard at Mr. Franklin. She made a face. "Very well, since you will not succor a poor woman except she do your bidding—I do not know his name, but he visited Mrs. Hart too."

"Often?"

"As often as the daughter."

"Which visits you winked at?"

"Whatever can you mean? 'Twas not my business."

"O, winking *is* your business. What more have you winked at in your house, where assignations may be easily made? A man and a woman must have a bed in which to make love; you provide it with no questions—am I right? But I care not of that. Do you know more of this man? No? Then here is your succor." He handed her the bottle. "Whilst Miss Bird calms her nerves," said he to us, "let us above to see what damage this 'Jeremy Jones' has done." We mounted the stairs. "Mark my word, he is never Jones," sniffed Mr. Franklin. "Did he pick the lock to get in?"

"He seemed to do so, sir," affirmed Peter.

Yet we did not go into Mrs. Hart's former chamber, now revealed as Mrs. Settle's. Mr. Franklin merely glanced through its open door, at the disarray Miss Bird had described, before he turned into the room which Dudley Midge had let.

This showed no change, except that Miss Bird had replaced the print of shepherdesses upon its wall.

Mr. Franklin immediately took down the print. "This is the wall adjoining the other chamber," murmured he. "Now, look here, upon the floor." We knelt at his bidding so he might point out the thin scrape marks in the oak planking, where the wardrobe had plainly been slid eight or ten inches from its former position. "Midge did it, so he might have easier access to the wall. This," he took from his pocket the curl of wood he had picked up three days ago, "was made by an auger and bit. Have you not seen such shavings about a cabinet-maker's shop? There must have been others, which Midge swept up; but he did not catch this one. Now, if I am not mistook—" he peered along the wall where the painting had hung. "Aha, see?" He pointed to a round bump, about an inch in diameter. Gripping it with fingers and thumb, he waggled, pulled—

and out it popped: a cork to disguise a hole which Midge had drilled clear through.

"He spied, then," murmured Peter.

"He did."

"The burnt paper in the dressing room grate," said I with a sudden flash of understanding, "Midge wrote it, telling what he saw through this hole."

"I believe so," agreed Mr. Franklin.

"But why did Drumm have the paper?"

A black look. "And was Midge murdered because of what he saw here? Was Drumm done in because he too knew what went on in this house? Would that we knew who cast the paper into the grate last night: Drumm—or his murderer?" Mr. Franklin clapped Peter's shoulder. "Good man! You have led us to truth—or a certain way along the path. Now, transport us to Craven Street."

It had gone half past two by the time we returned home, where Mrs. Stevenson set out a hearty fish stew to warm us. Afterward, Mr. Franklin mused in his chamber. "So that was the room where Calverly and Mrs. Settle met. But why not conjoin in her abode? She has no husband to deceive. Did her own landlady have too waggling a tongue?"

"Midge let the adjoining room for the express purpose of spying?"

"Must have. And was paid to do so by Abel Drumm, or I do not hate the Penns. He then reported to Drumm of what he saw."

"Yet why the threat about the magistrate?"

"Was it a threat? We may be mistook. Could it have been a promise?"

I thought on this. "But why should Drumm care about his mother-in-law's doings?"

"Perhaps he did not. Perhaps 'twas Calverly he spied on. Perhaps blackmail was the game."

"Blackmail?"

"The tribute which certain freebooting Scottish chieftains demand to keep 'em from burning barns and chopping off heads. Did Drumm mean to use what he learnt to wrest money—or something—from Lord Calverly?"

I thought on Calverly's air of decency. A mask? Had blackmail driven him to murder? That he was some sort of deceiver was sure, for he called one woman wife whilst he bedded another.

I shivered. "My lord a murderer, then?" asked I.

"Much begins to point his way." Mr. Franklin turned to the bow window, which showed a cloud-wracked sky. "Yet why high heels? Who is this 'Jeremy Jones'?"

Mr. Franklin must needs work at his *Historical Review* and spent half an hour fitfully at it but ended tossing down his pen. "How this Drury Lane business preys upon my mind! I should hate to trip upon more murder. Come, Nick, to Lord Calverly."

Conjugating Latin verbs had little diverted me. Gladly pulling on my coat and cap, I followed. Peter harnessed the mare, and shortly we were off.

Twenty minutes delivered us to Grosvenor Square. "Am I too rash?" Mr. Franklin chid as we pulled up before a fine brick townhouse. "Does not bearding a lion put one in some danger from its claws?" He sighed. "Nothing for it but to see." Mounting granite steps, he dropped the knocker.

A liveried manservant led us to the same grand drawing room where not many days ago Mr. Franklin had, with David Garrick and others, been entertained by the Calverlys. Rich velvet curtains hung at the windows, brocaded chairs sat about, and a grand marble fireplace rose in one corner, all elegant; Lord Edmund was no less elegant in soft gray breeches and coat and pale yellow waistcoat, deeply absorbed in some paper. This he hastily tucked into a book on a table as he came to greet us. I felt his measured quality: he was calm, he was ready, though his deep blue eyes were watchful. Graciously leading Mr. Franklin to a chair, he bade him sit. "Sit you too," said he to me as if I were quality too.

He settled himself opposite. "It likes me well to see you, Franklin. Since our gathering on Wednesday I have longed to speak to you, to hear you tell of the electrical fluid and of Pennsylvania and of your progress in her behalf. Do the Penns still thwart you?"

"They do, but I shall circumvent 'em." The gentleman wrapped both hands round the head of his bamboo. "I shall be pleased to satisfy you on whatever you will—but first may we dispense with a certain matter: you and Mrs. Settle?"

Calverly's look of pleasant inquiry darkened. Rising, he shut the broad white doors, then reseated himself in rigid contrast to his former easy manner.

"What right have you—?" began he.

"Tut, forgive me, sir. Your relationship with the woman would be none of my business were it not for recent events at Drury Lane, which David Garrick has asked me to look into. Murder, I mean. Deadly stuff. You know that Abel Drumm was murdered. So was Dudley Midge, I believe, and—"

Impatiently: "What can I have to do with these?"

"Perhaps nothing. Yet you may shed light. You know, for example, of a room in Grinder's Court."

Calverly started. "What?"

"Mrs. Settle let that room so you and she might meet there, yes?"

Calverly stared long at this. What did he ponder so hard, abiting his lip? I had the impression he was relieved that his secret was known at last.

"She let the room," conceded he in a manner that remained unfriendly. "But, still, how did you discover—? What right had you to pursue—?"

"No right, sir. In truth, I did not pursue you. I pursued Dudley Midge—or, rather, his course before he was murdered."

Calverly frowned. "Midge? What can Grinder's Court have to do with the scurvy man?"

"He let the room next to Mrs. Settle's. He bored a hole in the wall betwixt 'em. He spied. He saw you with her." Mr. Franklin tilted his head. "You knew none of this?"

My lord's mouth worked. He rose, he paced. "So . . ." said he, as if understanding something at last.

"Sir?"

Calverly returned to us, pale. "No, I knew none of it. But why should Midge—?"

"To use his knowledge against you, what other reason might there be?"

"And yet he worked for me," muttered Calverly, sinking down once more.

'Twas Mr. Franklin's turn to start. "Worked for you?"

Calverly looked at him. "You did not know that too?" His mouth twisted bitterly. "I thought in your pursuit of him you must have . . . well, what does it matter that I have given it away. Yes, though I am not proud to confess it, 'twas *I* paid for the claque which cried down Abel Drumm's play Saturday night."

"But why?"

"Because Drumm is a vile upstart pup!" My lord ground his hands together. "Was such, that is. Now he can cause no more pain. He treated Mrs. Settle's daughter cruelly, he needed taking down. Besides, his play was an attack on a man who, though he has much to answer for, did not deserve so mean and public a chastisement."

"So you took it upon yourself—?"

"I hoped to drive Drumm out of the theater. Ev'ryone hated him. Most of all I hoped to teach him a lesson, which might result in kinder treatment of his wife. What a joke on me, for the play proved so bad a thing, and so despised by Lord Methuen, that 'twould have been done in without my taking a hand."

"Did you have any other dealings with Midge?"

"I sullied myself sufficiently by the one I had. I saw how Lucy's husband treated her. Her mother spoke often of her son-in-law's mean nature. I do not like to see a woman so wronged."

I shifted in my chair. These were noble sounding words, but they might be hypocrisy—or worse. I could not help thinking on Calverly's wife: did he not wrong her? Clearly the best bred of men had blind eyes. Yet it was hard to pass judgment. He had took a mistress, but he had also tried to help her daughter, if by ill-considered means. Could I condemn him for this? Yet 'twas still possible he had pushed Abel Drumm into the gears of a machine to spare his wife of him forever.

If Mr. Franklin wondered so he did not ask. He inquired if Midge—or anyone—had attempted to use what had been spied upon in Grinder's Court.

"To extort money of me? No." Abruptly the doors flew open and two small girls burst in, their golden ringlets bobbing. Scampering across the room, they flung themselves upon their father as if he were a hobby horse.

Whilst Calverly was thus distracted, Mr. Franklin glanced surreptitiously into the book where my lord had secreted the paper he perused.

"You must play with us, Papa!" cried his girls amidst many kisses. "Miss Baffin has the headache; she does nothing but chide us." They patted his cheeks. "*Do*, Papa! Be king of our castle, we want you ever so much."

"There, my Amanda, my Sally, stand and greet Mr. Franklin. This is his young friend, Nicolas Handy." The girls curtseyed.

Mr. Franklin rose and bowed and touched their golden heads. "I shall trouble you no more," said he to their father. "Never fear, I shall keep what I know to myself. Come, Nick, let us leave my lord to play." Calverly's look as we walked out said he knew not whether to take joy in his children or dismay at our visit.

In the corridor outside we met his wife. Mr. Franklin presented me. She was a small woman, pretty, with a high, white brow crowned by hair nearly as gold as her daughters', and she was suffused with such happiness that she fairly glowed. Could this be, given Mr. Franklin's description of her gloom at the recent gathering?

The young wife peeped through the drawing room door, where her husband chattered with their girls, before she turned back to Mr. Franklin, plainly bursting to tell him something. It soon came out: "Yes, I am happy today, sir!" She clasped her hands to her breast. "It is as if my husband has been gone a long while but has finally returned." Her bright eyes shone. "O, to die now would be to die in peace!"

"The letter Calverly secreted in the book as we entered," said Mr. Franklin when we drove through London's streets once more, " 'twas in Abel Drumm's hand."

A chill went through me. "Could you read any, sir?"

"Naught but to note he sent it. The blackmail, which Calverly denies? If so, 'tis a threat that cannot affright him, for Drumm is dead. Did Calverly do him in to shut his mouth? Much still argues against him, and yet—" The gentleman paddled his fingers. "His wife says her husband has finally returned. From captivity to Mrs. Settle? Is that the falling out we witnessed? But why? What has freed him from her arms?"

17

*IN WHICH two women call,
and seven faeries dance . . .*

C alverly *seems* a good man," said Mr. Franklin as we
turned into Craven Street from the Strand, "but even
good men may be provoked to desperate acts. How un-
manned he was. Guilt? Fear of losing all he holds dear? Did
you see him with his daughters? In spite of his pec-
cadilloes, he may truly love his wife." We climbed out at
number 7. "Yet if Drumm truly blackmailed Calverly, what
did he demand? My lord a double murderer? Well, better
men have done worse: Brutus stabbed Caesar, Judas sold
Christ for a few coins; and no one knows how deep conscience may prick 'til after he has took his fateful step." He
winced. "Pah, I hear you Mrs. Gout, I feel you. Let us in,
Nick, for the cold air nips."

Inside the door we learnt surprising news: Lucy Drumm
had come to call.

"I showed her into the front parlor, sir," said Mrs. Stevenson wiping her hands on her apron. "I said I did not
know when you would return, but she insisted she must
wait. She is an actress of Drury Lane? How sad she looks."
Polly pouted by her mother's side. "O, what face is that,
child? What if it should set like stone and you must live
with it the rest of your days? Why, I should have to sew a
bag for your head."

"Mother!" Polly wailed. "Why did you not tell me an actress was here? I must see her!"

"You may not. She is come for Mr. Franklin, and you must let 'em be."

Polly stamped her foot. "Am I never to know of life?" She fled upstairs.

Mr. Franklin led me into the parlor. Mrs. Drumm was indeed there and allowed her small hands to be solicitously grasped. She still looked much down, though she had composed herself and seemed reasonably capable of discourse. She wore coal-black taffeta, a small ebon hat, a black veil, which she lifted. Beneath, her face was a white, fragile moon. Her large eyes sometimes brimmed, but by and large she held back tears. "You said . . . you said I might come to you for help, Mr. Franklin."

"Any time, dear woman."

"I fear Lord Calverly, then," said she.

"Please seat yourself. Tell why."

She settled onto the sofa, Mr. Franklin in a chair opposite, I by his side. She seemed uncertain where to begin. "Calverly had an alliance with my mother. Did you know?"

"I surmised."

"A woman must have a man to get on. Would it were not so, but it is. Yet a woman may not always have a husband. This I learnt young, for, my mother being of the theater, I saw many women take lovers—sometimes married men— who made promises which they rarely kept. I vowed I should never be one of those; so, when I found my Abel," here her voice broke, "when I saw that . . . that I loved him in spite of his angers (mine was no blind love, sir, whatever you think of me), I vowed to be a good helpmeet, and was. Truly, I was grateful to be Mrs. Drumm—had I not attained the name of wife and thus respect in the world's eyes? But I do not blame my mother for taking a lover. In truth I felt glad for her, for my lord did not seem like other men, Lord Methuen, for example, who treats women ill. I thought Edmund decent, I believed he truly cared for mother. But, now—"

"Now?"

She shuddered. "How he misled us! He seemed devoted. He even made promises—some talk of leaving his wife. Of marrying my mother."

"Truly?"

"That is what mother said, though perhaps 'twas what she hoped she might believe (women in love forge truth to their fancy). In any case I do not doubt he led her on. He has proved as selfish as any other man, and now he wishes to discard her."

Mr. Franklin frowned. "Beg pardon, ma'am—but why does this make you fear him?"

"Because I suspect him of being the man who did in my husband." The pale young woman wrung her hands. "Might he then murder me?"

Out in Craven Street a coster's cry cut the air. Mr. Franklin sat very still. "And, pray, why do you think he may be the man who murdered your husband?"

"Because of things he said when he and my mother fought. Things about Dudley Midge and my dear Abel. He let slip that he too had received a threatening letter; though unsigned he believed it came from my husband."

"And did it, do you think?"

She flushed. "I do not want to believe so, yet . . ." her voice fell low, " 'twould be dishonest to deny that Abel sometime acted rashly."

Mr. Franklin stirred. "Who truly writ it may make little matter if, believing 'twas penned by Abel Drumm, Lord Calverly took steps."

"That is what I believe." She searched the gentleman's face. "What do you think, sir?"

"That Calverly had strong motive. A net of evidence draws tight about him. You fear for yourself, you say?"

"My mother still hopes to smooth things over; she will hear no ill of Calverly. But I entertain black thoughts. Calverly knows I mistrust him. I was foolish; faced him, I told him all I suspected. Such a look he gave me then! His

hands opened and closed at his sides so that I thought he
might strangle me on the spot.''

Mr. Franklin looked grim. ''He has much at stake. Look
you, never be alone. You have a maidservant to accompany you? Keep her near. Lock your door. Travel known
ways. Will you to the theater?''

''I wish to mourn my husband, but I must make a living;
Abel left me nothing. I cannot jeopardize my place in Garrick's company. Yes, I must to work, and paint and patch
and laugh and dance and play my parts.''

''You are brave.''

''I do what I must.''

At the window Mr. Franklin watched the beleaguered
young woman's hackney coach bear her off. ''Surprising,
eh?'' He turned. ''Lucy Drumm proves to be more than we
thought, admirable in her way. Truly I pray she'll meet no
harm. Yet Calverly still rankles—in accusing him we do not
answer all questions. Who writ those first threatening letters to Garrick? Who near murdered me in Drury Lane?
We come a distance, but our course is still not clear; we
must tread warily.'' He rubbed his hands. ''But not now. I
am called to Gresham College for a meeting of the Royal
Society; afterward I sup with Collinson and Strahan at the
George and Vulture. Occupy yourself with good works,
Nick: tell Polly tales of Drury Lane.'' He tutted. ''Poor girl.
Women must stay within bounds that never constrain
men. Yet the time may come when they roam free.'' He
shook his head. ''What will the world be like in those
strange days?''

Mr. Franklin gone by six, I did as bid: sat upon the upper
stairs and told Polly many things I had seen and heard at
Drury Lane, including the tale of John Rich and his cats
and his toes. I took care to leave out all that touched on
murder, and I made certain before I spoke that Mrs. Stevenson hummed and clattered in her warm kitchen below;
I had no wish to provoke her by encouraging her daughter.
As for Polly, she wriggled and knotted and unknotted her

fingers and stroked my arm and asked so many questions that I remained for more than an hour replying. Yet I could not answer all. Why exactly had Mrs. Drumm called upon Mr. Franklin? I lied to this and thought: if a small boy may lie with such ease, how much more skillfully might a lord, even a seeming-good one, dissemble too.

The evening drew on, wind sighing about the eaves. London. Seated alone with my candle and book in Mr. Franklin's chamber, I pictured smoke from a thousand chimneypots flying up to a thousand cloud-wracked stars. How far I had come! Wishing to aid him who had saved me, I turned our mystery over and over in my mind: threats, fires, mischief, Dudley Midge toppled by a man in disguise, this man's wig turning up in Abel Drumm's pocket when he too was murdered. I developed many theories, but the three trees fit none of 'em and multiplied into such a forest, from which I could discover no exit, that I ached for Mr. Franklin's wise counsel. I fell into a pet as minutes ticked to hours. He would not return 'til early morn, Mrs. Goodbody's arms would entice him, he would go to her and not to me. I hated myself for being so stung. Was not Mr. Franklin a man? Might he not go his way? Flinging my book aside, I went to the bow window and stared in torment out into the night. The strange thing was that I longed to like Comfort Goodbody.

Mrs. Stevenson walked in. "Mrs. Goodbody waits downstairs," said she.

I turned in numb startlement.

"She wishes to speak to Mr. Franklin, says she. He is not here, says I, at which she asks leave to speak to you." Mrs. Stevenson squinted hard. "Who is she, boy?"

"Wardrobe mistress at Drury Lane, ma'am," I heard my voice.

"Fie, why must these women call on Mr. Franklin? Do they not know he pursues hard labors and may not be abothered at all hours? Well, come and satisfy her, Nick. I have put her in the parlor."

Bewildered, I went down.

* * *

A fire was lit in the parlor grate and a stitchery frame lay by the sofa, a threaded needle poking out of it, telling that Mrs. Stevenson had recently sat here by the lamp. Mrs. Goodbody turned from the window as I entered. She wore an ivory-colored dress and ivory-colored kid gloves and looked a respectable matron save for the sharp pink in her round cheeks and a wary alertness in her fine blue eyes. She might be the wife of some well-to-do merchant, with three servants and a coach. Yet she was no man's wife, she was my enemy.

Mrs. Goodbody's gaze searched me as I came in, as if she read my thoughts and hunted for chinks in my armor.

I said, rather gruffly, "Mrs. Stevenson says you wish to speak to me, ma'am."

"I do. Thank you for coming down."

I waited. The fire hissed.

"May I sit?" asked she.

"If you please."

She settled by the embroidery frame. "And shall you sit too?"

I perched wordlessly on the chair facing her.

She looked at me almost pleadingly. "You love Mr. Franklin, do you? Love him greatly?"

"I do."

"A son should love his father."

My heart beat wildly. "His son?"

"Are you not his son? The gentleman said that you were."

My breath left me. I felt flung down. The gentleman and I had made a pact that my parentage should be our secret. There was no proof of banns called or wedding vows, just the likeness of our lineaments and his outlaw love of my poor, dead mother. Why should we trouble the world—or his wife or his son, William—with the news? This was what we had agreed.

Yet he had troubled Mrs. Goodbody with it. This, combined with wavering memories of my mother, made me tremble to hold back tears.

"I see how it is with you, Nick," said the woman, reaching out as if she would take my hands, though I kept my fists fiercely clenched upon my knees. She sank back in disappointment. "You hate me, do you?" sighed she.

Looking at the wretched regret in her eyes, I wished only to deny this. And yet I hated something, for I writhed in my need to lash out.

Her eyes were moist. "I saw you in the street two nights ago, when Mr. Franklin came to my door. My light fell upon you. You darted back, but I saw. Never fear, I did not tell the gentleman; I did not think you would wish it. But I have wondered since what you thought and felt. Tell me, Nick, for I fear that I too love Mr. Franklin as I have not loved any man. And to have found such a one when I had come to an age to believe that no such man existed—"

I saw in that moment that she had come to renounce Mr. Franklin if need be, for my sake. I do not know how I saw it, but I did, in her tremulous face filled with hope and fear. Yet rather than relieving me, the news made me fear, for a willingness to sacrifice so much gave her great power. Could I thwart her?

She stirred. "Do not blame your father for telling me of you. He loves you; he needed to speak of his love, and I gave him my ear. He knew he might trust. He spoke of your mother. He told how he had loved her, poor creature. I know her well, Nick. We never met, but I too have been set upon by life. Would that I could've taken her in as I took in Betsy, to save one more woman's soul. Yet she died, done in by Hexhams. And you were born. And he came and saved you. Do you understand what I tell you, child? That I know what you suffered at Inch, Printer, for I have suffered too. And I know what you suffer now: you are afraid I may in some way take Mr. Franklin from you." She shook her head. "We who have been taught we deserve little are ever a prey to such fears. Yet I do not wish to take your father. I wish . . . I wish—O, how can I say?—I wish to have him whilst I may. I know that he is married. I know, too, that he must some day return to America. And yet a woman such as I looks for what she can and is grateful when it comes and cares not a fig for the world's opinion." Her whole person trembled. She drew herself up. "And yet, a child . . . you . . . I care for your opinion, I will not harm you." Her breast heaved. "And so, if you wish, I shall no more invite Mr. Franklin to my home, for I have no desire to pain you."

I sat stunned. I believed what she said, and all my anger crumbled. What a fool, what a black-hearted boy, for thinking I could not share my father with her—or with anyone to whom he gave himself! Betrayed? I was not betrayed; he had but spoke of me to the one person in London to whom he felt he might bare his soul. As for Mrs. Goodbody, she had not betrayed him in revealing his words, for she offered now to withdraw.

"Never . . . never," mumbled I.

"Never?" Sadly she rose. "Then I shall say no more but go."

I leapt up. "No, never let me stand between you and Mr. Franklin."

"What?"

I all but fell on my knees. "Dear Mrs. Goodbody, pay no heed to what you think I feel. I do not feel it. I may have, but not now. You are a good friend to my father. Be his friend, see him when you please. Be my friend too."

What joy rewarded me at this, for the woman came to me and held me close and stroked my hair. I burst into tears, she did too, and I was very glad the door was shut so no one might hear our mingled sobs.

Had my mother lived would she have held me thus?

Mrs. Goodbody stepped back and dabbed at her reddened eyes and my damp cheeks. This is how Mr. Franklin found us.

He stood very still in the door in his plain brown stuff, his stick in his hand. "Shall I withdraw?" asked he quietly. "That should please Mrs. Stevenson, for she believes far too many women call upon me of late. No? Then—" Shutting the door, he came to us and searched my face. "Are you well, Nick?"

"Better than I have been, sir," got out I.

"Mrs. Goodbody ministers to you?"

I found a smile. "After a manner of speaking, sir."

"Good. She has a fine way of ministering to a man. Why, she is physic itself." He kissed her hand. "Is your private talk done? Shall we have a pleasant hour by the fire? I am sure Mrs. Stevenson would bring a warm libation."

Mrs. Goodbody mastered her feeling. "I should welcome a pleasant hour—but first I must speak of something else."

"O?"

"It may prove foolish, but—" I had paid little heed to the large handbag sitting out of the way by the sofa. Going to it, she drew forth a white satin dress, to which were sewn two stiff wings. 'Twas one of the faerie costumes, worn in the dance that had concluded *A Midsummer Night's Dream.*

Mrs. Goodbody laid it before Mr. Franklin. "There are eight such costumes, but only six faeries in the dance that was performed last night. Thus two costumes should have hung in the wardrobe—and did, I believed, 'til this afternoon, when I inspected each one as I always do, to make sure they are in good order for their next use. All six which were worn in the dance proved well enough—yet when I chanced to glance at the next in the rack I discovered this." She showed a tear at the back, at the waist, about four inches long. She met Mr. Franklin's eyes. "This tear was not there yesterday afternoon; I am very thorough in my inspections. By the nature of it—see you?—by the way the cloth and threads are pulled I must conclude that someone wore it last night."

"A seventh faerie?" Mr. Franklin peered. "And what did this seventh do whilst t'other six danced?"

"I cannot guess. The wardrobe is often left untenanted whilst the play goes on. At the end the actors take off their costumes in their dressing rooms; then their dressers pile 'em in the wardrobe, where they are not sorted through 'til next morn. 'Twould thus be easy to take out a dress and put it back and never be seen or known.''

"And the faeries were masked," mused the gentleman. "You are certain this is a new tear since yesterday?"

"No mistake. I should say nothing of it—and yet a man died last night. Might this dress be related to his death?"

Mr. Franklin regarded her. "You are a very philosopher, ma'am, and should have been at the Royal Society tonight if the world were just to women. Related? Indeed it may be. Hum, three trees instead of two? Seven faeries instead of six? Where will these numbers lead? Let us add 'em to see what sum they make." He flung open the door. "Three hot flips, if you please, Mrs. Stevenson, delivered as soon as you can."

18

IN WHICH Mr. Franklin refashions a jug . . .

I know," said Mr. Franklin at eight o'clock next morning in his workshop, "that there is some answer at hand, yet damned if I can grasp it. You, Nick?"

"No, sir."

We had turned our mystery this way and that with Mrs. Goodbody last night, making her privy to ev'ry detail; yet though we had all felt revelation within our reach, not one of us had succeeded in snatching it. In gray dawn light Mr. Franklin and I stood gazing at his workbench where lay all those squares and scraps of paper we had come by, with their silent clamor of threats and assignations and spying. But still: who had murdered and why? We wracked our brains at this.

But hours, days, a life could not be spent upon the puzzle, and so the gentleman turned to his business with the Penns: his letter-writing and calling about to make friends for Pennsylvania. He must to Westminster, to the Board of Trade, and took me with him at eleven o'clock. "You shall see for yourself, Nick, the corpses I must prod to life." On the way we stopped into Westminster Abbey; I walked in awe. Amidst the sibilant hush, Mr. Franklin showed me the tomb of Elizabeth, the monuments to Spenser, Chaucer, Newton, the bust of Milton in the Poets' Corner. "Here is

Shakespeare too," said he before a statue with its hand on its chin and its elbow on a pile of books, its cool marble eyes seeming to dream. "The bard is buried elsewhere, but his picture is here; his soul lives on in Drury Lane. Hum, he writ often of bloody murder. What would he make of our tale, could he piece it out? Whose tragedy, do you think?"

I knew not, and shortly we repaired to the place of temporal power, I parsing my Latin in an icy corridor whilst behind thick oak Mr. Franklin strove to breathe life into the stony corpses of the Board of Trade.

Though I felt answer to our mystery hid just out of view, I could not have guessed how soon it should reveal itself. The day was dull and gray, inauspicious for revelation. London seemed shackled by winter, sluggish, slow, her citizens trudging over damp cobbles, heads down, as if the burden of breath became too much for 'em. The hollow, dispiriting clatter of iron-rimmed wheels might've been made by hearses for all the cheer they gave. Church bells dully rang. Beggars held out rag-wrapped hands. Breath frostily blew. Yet revelation came.

From Dr. Johnson, at Drury Lane.

Officialdom had rebuffed Mr. Franklin once more, so he was in a disgruntled mood as he directed Peter to drive us to the playhouse round about one o'clock. He had some last drawings he must show to David Garrick. "Too, I must apprise him of all we know. Yet what is that? That Calverly may be our man? 'May be' is no certainty. How may we prove it, Nick? And if we do, what remedy ought we to take? O, it gives the headache!"

Yet I was not down. As we jounced along I reflected how unbounded was my heart to have its misgivings about Comfort Goodbody dissolved. I felt light, free. Mr. Franklin might have her for his friend and for any other need— might love her too, I cared not. I began to think she might stand in as a sort of mother. Was she not both wise and caring? Had not my life truly changed for the best?

Yet mystery remained. "Three trees. Seven faeries. Pah,

how dull grows Ben Franklin, who cannot make a sum of seven and three."

Walking into the playhouse we were just about to take my last drawings upstairs to Garrick's office, when Richard Cross rounded upon us in his customary rush.

"Mrs. Drumm is allowed by Garrick to take some few days for mourning, so she is not at rehearsal after all," announced he. "She sends this note." He thrust out a paper. "It went to your lodging, but you were not there."

Mr. Franklin watched the man stalk away. "He does his job well, Nick, and must be praised for it, but I wish he took more joy in life. Now, what is this?" Breaking the seal, his eyes darted. "Mrs. Drumm says she takes care but still fears Calverly. She wonders if we may not invoke the law against him, and . . . but what?" He started, and his hand holding her letter trembled. "What . . . what?" He thrust out the paper. "Look you, Nick."

I looked and read, but could find nothing more than the matter he had named, and her signature: Lucy Drumm.

And then I saw. "She could not have writ this, Mr. Franklin," said I, all agape.

He stared into my face. "Then did a dead man write it?"

I could but nod, for the letter was in Abel Drumm's hand.

I was flooded with sick fear. Drumm's face had been crushed; we had known him only by his clothes and wedding band. Had it not been he? Did he now hold his wife hostage? Had he writ this letter as a riddling ruse?

Yet Mr. Franklin did not dash to resolve these questions. Instead his chin sank upon his breast whilst his lips conjured thoughts: "Why, then . . ." murmured he, "and so . . ."

This was interrupted by a shuffling of boots, and Dr. Samuel Johnson appeared round a corner. "Have you seen David Garrick, sir?" demanded he.

Mr. Franklin started out of his revery. "Not above, in his office?"

A snort. "Do you not see that is the direction I come?

No, he is not there, or I should have found him. Gone home to his wife? Hmph, if I had such a one I should go home to her too." A sharp look. "I know you, Benjamin Franklin, the contriver who wishes to make the playhouse better."

A nod. "Come from America, sir."

"That, I find, is what a very great many of your countrymen cannot help doing."

Mr. Franklin only smiled. "And you are Dr. Johnson, the contriver with words. When I write in my people's cause I keep the volumes of your *Dictionary* at hand should I fail to recall the meaning of Whig."

"Ha, you show some wisdom."

"Your *Dictionary* is a goodly piece of work."

"Inquiry led me a hard chase in producing it, for I soon discovered that to search was not always to find, and to find was not always to be informed. But I did not do all of it alone. I employed six amanuenses in my top floor in Gough Square."

Mr. Franklin blinked. "Amanuenses?"

"Scribblers, man."

"Copying out for you?"

"At no other purpose."

"Dear God."

"What, sir?"

"I see, sir."

"See what?"

"Why . . . why . . . you must excuse us, sir, but I thank you, sir." Snatching the gentleman's hand, Mr. Franklin wrung it so hard that the doctor's jowls wobbled. "You have shown me the way. Come, Nick, we must be off." Leaving Dr. Johnson staring, he dragged me from the playhouse.

In our coach he chortled to himself, then thought with a long, slow smile, then laughed again, merrily. "O, Nick, do you recall, when first I told of my study of handwriting, how I asked you to copy out a thing from Dr. Johnson's *Dictionary* and then compare it to other samples of the same copying? Well, that *Dictionary*—or, rather, the method of't—has led me to light. What irony! But you stare. Look you, does this not explain all?" Counting upon his fingers, he laid his thoughts before me. I did not wish what he said to be true, but the more he spoke the more I saw that, though he had not reassembled our jug whole, yet there seemed few pieces missing.

"But what to do about it, sir?" asked I when we were in his workshop once more, gazing at the many pieces of paper upon his workbench, the note he had just received at Drury Lane placed in order amongst 'em to spell out their pattern of deceit.

"That," he gravely tapped his brow, "is what I must think on. But first: a letter to Lucy Drumm: 'Lord Edmund Calverly is great danger!' "

"But should we not go to her at once?" protested I.

He shook his head. "This must be the way."

William returned from his studies at five o'clock. Mr. Franklin promptly drew him into his chamber. I did not hear what passed, for I was sweeping out the hearth for Mrs. Stevenson, but near seven o'clock when I went to him, Mr. Franklin told what they had talked on. "I quizzed him more on English law, Nick, *viz.*: children. Who has governance of 'em? 'Tis the husband. He owns 'em as much as he owns his wife and may do as he please with 'em. Think on it. O, I am very glad to be a man in these times, for if I were a woman I should rebel."

Though he had seemed to remake the shape of truth, there remained cracks, holes. These he paced and muttered over as the evening wore on, I sitting on the edge of his bed like a straw dummy. "The threatening notes in two different handwritings . . . the wig . . . the three trees which should've been two . . . the seven faeries which should've been six . . ." Many names were mixed in his discourse: Mr. Pritchard, Richard Cross, James Lacy, George Garrick; David Garrick and his Eva Maria; my lords Methuen, Linacre, and Calverly; Lady Linacre and Lady Calverly; actors too: Woodward, Havard, Mossop; actresses: Hannah

Pritchard, Kitty Clive, Susannah Cibber, Arabella Prouty, Lucy Drumm, Mrs. Settle. Abel Drumm's name figured often, as did that of Dudley Midge, the buzzing little fly who had been swatted out of life. "And what of Redmayne," asked Mr. Franklin suddenly, with a glint in his eye.

"Who, sir?" asked I.

"Sir James Redmayne. You do not know the rake? One of those hangers-on who lurk backstage to prey upon actresses? To be sure he has a wife, but that does not deter him." Mr. Franklin bent near. "Might not this Redmayne plug a hole in a jug?"

Next morning the gentleman was busy at his desk. He peered over the tops of his glasses as I came in.

"Poor Richard adjures early rising, Nick; thus I am up at his call. We must act quickly, before opportunity congeals like blood on a corpse and we lose our chance. We need more than speculation, we need confession, for no one, not even John Fielding, would accuse a person based upon differently writ letters and a torn faery's dress. Handwriting may some day become a tool of the law, but it is not now; thus we must proceed by other means. *Aut inveniam viam aut faciam*, I propose entrapping our quarry by use of a witness, *viz.:* this same James Redmayne, whom I have named. He saw all, and he shall tell all too, I'll be sworn. But we must take care, for our murderer is driven by strong motive, and we do not want Redmayne—or ourselves—to suffer the fate of others who learnt more than it was wise to know."

Turning back to his pen, Mr. Franklin applied the last words to a letter to Lucy Drumm reminding her to keep a sharp eye out and never be alone. This he blotted, sealed, and gave to me to take to Peter, to deliver to Castle Street. In the following hour before breakfast, I attempted to decline nouns but so mixed up the endings that had Virgil writ as I did he should never have produced the *Aeneid*. I was asked to fetch water from the pump at the top of the way. A sooty wind whirled up from the Thames as I went,

but shopkeepers opened their doors nonetheless. Victual-
ers hung out geese and ducks. Pies and new-baked bread
stood warm behind glass. Standing in a queue, I waited my
turn amidst the gossip of the street. A cat eyed me hungrily
as I returned with my bucket, and I was glad to seat myself
at the round, tidy breakfast table below stairs.

"O, why will you not talk of your new mystery?" protested Polly over her porridge.

"I shall talk of it when I see it clear," replied Mr. Franklin, "And that is that."

By ten o'clock we were once more at Drury Lane, amidst
its bustle. Glancing backstage at the looming machine
which had crushed a man's face, I shuddered. The lengths
to which our murderer had gone!

I did not like Mr. Franklin's plan.

Yet he greeted Woodward and Mrs. Clive and even dour
Mr. Cross with equanimity. He took aside Miss Prouty to
speak to her whilst I watched acrobats balance on a wire,
Thomas Arne at the fore part of the stage driving his musicians through a tarantella. Painters and carpenters jostled
my shoulders. Candlemen hung fresh lights in the lowered
chandeliers.

The luster which had near killed Mr. Franklin looked
thoroughly repaired; I prayed it was now firm in its bolt.

We mounted to David Garrick's office.

"No more threatening notes?" asked Mr. Franklin when
the door was closed.

"No, thank God," replied the actor behind his desk.

"I did not expect there would be."

Garrick hurried to us. "You know something, sir?"

"And shall know more soon. You are acquainted with Sir
James Redmayne?"

"Why, no, I do not believe—"

"He is one of the tribe who plague you by preying upon
actresses."

"Damn all such gadflies."

"Let us rather thank this one—for he saw who murdered Abel Drumm."

Garrick started. "What? Why, who did it, then? Why is not the man in custody this moment?"

"Because Sir James has not yet revealed the murderer's name. Miss Prouty brought him to my notice. He has long pursued her, but she has rebuffed him (she keeps company with another man, as you may know). Yet Redmayne keeps after her. He stood in the wings the night Abel Drumm died; looking for Miss Prouty, he saw instead a murder—how it was effected and who did it."

Garrick gaped. "But why did he not come forth then?"

"His wife. Keenly suspicious, I am told, and pulls the reins hard; Redmayne likes not to provoke her. I have asked Miss Prouty to tell us her story." Opening the door, he showed the woman herself, waiting outside. She came in wearing an almost defiant air.

Mr. Franklin turned to her. "Tell what you have told me, ma'am."

The young actress gazed into each of our faces. She began by describing Redmayne's many ardent blandishments. "But another gentleman presently occupies my interest, so I could not oblige Sir James—though as to that I might have been willing, for a woman must have a friend. Yet you are interested only in Redmayne. He waited for me in a dark corner of Covent Garden after Abel Drumm died. He was greatly agitated. He had seen what happened: Murder, he said. Yet he would tell no more. I sent him home; I went to my rooms—but what he had revealed kept me from sleep. If I did not speak, did I help a murderer go free? So yesterday I sent word to Mr. Franklin, who (it is no secret) has kept close watch on the recent mischief which once near took my life."

"And I," put in Mr. Franklin, "being so informed, took it upon myself to go at once to Redmayne, in Wardour Street. Yet his wife so fixed her eye on him—and on me— that I could get nothing from him. He does not even confess to her that he visits the playhouse. 'I will come to you tomorrow night after the play and tell you what I saw, only on condition that you assure me I shall never be called as witness.' I made him such promises as I could. He comes then, tonight, backstage, secretly. I shall meet him there. He shall tell what he knows, and we may then take steps."

Garrick had turned quite gray. "Murder. Dear God. Thank you, Miss Prouty. Say none of this to anyone. You may go."

Making a curt bob of head, she withdrew.

Garrick looked hard at Mr. Franklin when she was gone. "See here, sir, you know more than you tell."

"I have suspicions, which I will give out only if Mr. Redmayne confirms 'em. Help me—and yourself—by clearing the theater tonight soon after the play is played."

"I shall."

We left the actor standing in deep thought by his window. Backstage I saw Miss Prouty in quiet converse with two of Noverre's dancers. As we passed, the dancers peered furtively at Mr. Franklin.

"Miss Prouty does not seem to keep Garrick's counsel," whispered I.

"She keeps good enough counsel for me," replied he, by which I saw that he meant rumor to fly, so that by ten o'clock tonight all Drury Lane should know that something was afoot.

☙ 19 ☙

*IN WHICH two masks are ripped free,
and a third victim dies . . .*

I spent no very placid afternoon. Mr. Franklin was gone from Craven Street; thus I was left alone with agitated thoughts. He had told me our murderer had a confederate. Did this put him in double danger? I was very glad to know I was to accompany him and to tuck me away where I might watch and hear. Should anything go awry Nick Handy would charge into battle. I peered at myself in the cheval glass in Mrs. Stevenson's back parlor. Could I, but twelve years old, effect any great result? I should try.

Mr. Franklin returned at half past four, grave and snappish. As six o'clock drew near, he made himself ready by putting on a fine suit of fawn-gray stuff, with a cream-colored waistcoat and shiny black boots, which I myself had vigorously polished from two o'clock to a quarter to three.

I dressed too. Just past five o'clock we bid Mrs. Stevenson good eve.

"What, to the playhouse again?" protested she. "Does it not distract from your work?"

"I need distraction, dear lady: some tragedy and comedy, like a doctor's cordial, to take me from the fencing I must do with the Penns."

Peter delivered us to Bridges Street. The eve was chill,

mist clinging about the cobbles, though the sky was sharply black, stars winking round a parchment-colored moon. The passage to the playhouse was thronged, as it had been on our first outing here with James Ralph. The Methodist preacher did not give voice, but the whores still plied their trade.

I had in my coat pockets my sketchbook and journal; I should have little use for 'em tonight, but I fervently hoped that tomorrow, when the sun rose, I should have good news to write in one. Entering the theater, we descended steps, made our way along the side corridor, jostled to seats in the pit. Mr. Ralph was not to be seen. Nor were John Fielding and Joshua Brogden. But Lord Methuen was there. Lord Linacre too, though his wife was not in view. Lord Calverly had come with his lady; they sat together in a box to the left, heads together, intimately conversing. How warmly happy they looked. Was the husband truly reconciled with her? How sad if tonight's revelation blasted their concourse.

And then the Third Music bounded to its close, Mrs. Pritchard declaimed the prologue, the green curtain lifted, and the play began.

'Twas *Jane Shore*, by Nicholas Rowe. One speech stood out, delivered by Mrs. Cibber in ringing tones:

"Mark by what partial justice we are judged;
Such is the fate unhappy women find,
And such the curse entailed upon our kind.
That man, the lawless libertine, may rove,
Free and unquestioned through the wilds of love.
While woman, sense and nature's easy fool,
If poor weak woman swerve from virtue's rule,
If strongly charmed, she leave the thorny way,
And in the softer paths of pleasure stray:
And one false step entirely damns her fame.
In vain with tears the loss she may deplore,
In vain look back to what she was before,
She sets, like stars that fall, to rise no more."

I chafed my hands. A star should indeed fall when Mr. Redmayne revealed what he had seen. Yet did not that star, though it murdered, have its reasons? I turned to Mr. Franklin, but he appeared as lost as I in the wilds where sinners tangled in a web. Dared any of us cast stones?

The play came to its tragic end. Mrs. Settle had a part in it, small. How did she feel to see Lord Edmund Calverly in concord with his wife?

The interval gave us tumbling, ladder-dancing, and jolly Jack Pudding, at which I wished to smile but could not, though the afterpiece, *Tom Thumb*, near made me forget that tricks and traps were yet to come.

And then the clamor of the stage was done, the last clapping hands stilled, the green curtain lowered, the audience murmuring out into the night. A chill seemed to fall over the theater as Mr. Franklin and I made our way by the side corridor backstage. We mounted behind the right-hand wings. Already musicians were filing out the rear door, instruments in hand, the dancers and actors having retreated to their dressing rooms to transform themselves from what they had played to what they were. How grand it must be to strut before the throng, to gesture, declaim, command laughter or tears. But what of banished actors who lost their right to this glory? How it must plunge 'em to despair. Or the new-fledged actor, the first sweet taste of fame wetting his lips, who saw fortune or favor so against him that he should never mount the heights? Might not such knowledge provoke desperate acts if he had the nerve to do 'em?

I set these thoughts aside. The theater emptied. Scene-men departed. Noverre. Thomas Arne. Lacy. Dressers carried costumes to the wardrobe and left. Actors and actresses began to slip out. Mr. Franklin stood near the door, many giving him knowing looks which told that rumor had flown: something was afoot, though no one appeared eager to stay to discover what. Thinking on Abel Drumm's fate, they darted out almost furtively onto the damp, blackly shining cobbles, to coaches, taverns, lovers, havens where they might rest unwrung. Woodward left. Kitty Clive. Mrs. Cibber. Chin outthrust, Mrs. Pritchard towed her husband behind her like a barge towing a skiff.

Out of shadow Mrs. Settle slipped to Mr. Franklin's side.

Softly he asked, "Your daughter takes care?"

"She quakes, sir, 'til this is brought to some end. But she is safe."

"And shall remain so, I pray."

Wrapping her shawl about her, Mrs. Settle crept out.

There remained little more than Richard Cross and Garrick. "You stay again tonight, Franklin?" growled the prompter by the door.

"For a time."

"Take care o' the playhouse, then. See no harm befalls." Pulling on his hat, he strode out.

Garrick came, Mrs. Garrick on his arm; I had not known that she was here, though we had been told she sometimes aided in the business of the house.

"Vot do you tink of my David, Mr. Frankleen?" asked she, bright-eyed. "Did he not show tonight that he iss the best actor in London?"

"The best in the world, ma'am."

A pleased laugh. "The best hussband too. Shall you walk out with us?"

"No, ma'am, I stay. To meet someone."

A coy look. "An actress? Are you smitten?"

"No. I wait on Sir James Redmayne, who has some news which he will not tell any other way."

"How strange." Eva Maria peered at her husband.

He cleared his throat. "I allow Mr. Franklin to indulge this Redmayne's whim, for I owe it to him for all he has done to improve our playhouse. Come, my sweet, for I long for a cup of chocolate made by your dear hand in our very own parlor in Southampton Street."

Mr. Franklin bowed as they walked past. "I bid you good even." His gaze met mine. "You, Nicolas, too."

Though I had known this moment must come, I wished it need not. Yet I nodded and set my teeth and forced my feet to step one before the other. Passing out the door, I accompanied the Garricks as far as Drury Lane, where a carriage waited. "The boy draws well," I heard Garrick murmur to his wife as they climbed in. Jingling reins marked their departure, whilst I trudged Thamesward amongst a thinning late-night crowd, meeting Peter by Tavistock Street, climbing into our coach, being carried off into the Strand. Shop doors were shut, but lamplight lit the cobbles with an evil yellow shine. Iron-rimmed wheels clattered. Drunken laughter burst from tavern doors.

At Catherine Street I readied myself, Peter slowed the coach as we had agreed, and I leapt out into shadow.

After a lowered glance which said, Take care, he sank his chin into his woolen collar and drove on as if I were still aboard.

I crept back to the playhouse. I kept a sharp eye as I went; I did not wish to be seen. I ached with trepidation but would have been nowhere else—indeed I had begged to do just this. Mr. Franklin had very nearly denied me, but, "You have accompanied me far," he had conceded, "and thus have earned some right to see the end—though not to be placed in danger. You must be hid. I must seem to be alone in Drury Lane." To this I readily agreed.

Catherine Street became Bridges Street. Moving warily, I slipped from thence into the passage to the theater, black and deserted in contrast to its thronged character earlier. My breathing sounded loud. Even the soft scuff of my boots seemed to clatter, and I shied at the sudden pattering of drops from a mist-shrouded eave.

A thrashing and squealing nearby told that a cat had got a rat.

Passing the main entrance to the playhouse, locked, bolted, I made my way to the second of the two ground floor windows just beyond. The casement of this second window was shut, but it proved unlocked, as Mr. Franklin had said 'twould be. Opening it, I climbed in and shut it after.

I breathed hard now. Outdoors had been dark, but I had

been able to see by starlight, yet the playhouse seemed pitch black. Had Mr. Franklin forgot it would be so? Must I thus huddle here, helpless? I shrank against a wall but after a moment began to make out the shape of the corridor in which I stood. Creeping a short distance, I learnt why I could see, for I found myself, at a turn, in the passage that led both to the pit and to the flight of six steps which let to the backstage precincts. A single candle in a sconce illumined this corridor. Had Mr. Franklin lit it? Heartened, I crept with renewed faith to the steps and softly up, to discover that the door at their top was ajar so I need make no sound in opening.

Slipping through, I paused in the area behind the wings. I knew this well from many daytime visits, when it was alive with noise and bustle; I had sketched pictures then, whilst Mr. Franklin poked and pried and made himself known to all as the genial gentleman come to help David Garrick. It had never been brightly lit and was even less so now, for only the dimmest of light slanted in long somber bars between the five great sets of flats. All was still. I could make out the squat machine which had crushed Abel Drumm's face and one or two other such devices, their ropes and wires stretching to invisibility in the darkness above, but I could discern little else save odds and ends of property—a table and chairs, a horse cart, a maypole— and no one, murderer or otherwise, seemed to lurk; though as to that, so shadowed was the area that one or a dozen might've hid undiscovered.

Yet this fact was what Mr. Franklin counted on. Skirting the dark periphery, I ended where he had said I should: at the back of the stage, betwixt the vista wall and the most rearward of the great flats, a space about six feet wide. Placing myself there, I could make out twenty paces to my left the back door of Drury Lane. By peering right, round the corner of the flat, I could see the stage. This I did, cautiously.

One of the six great lusters hung half-lowered, lit with a dozen candles quietly flickering. This was all the light, the auditorium beyond the stage an indistinct, looming space where none of the gleaning women moved. Benches, boxes, galleries were untenanted; our play was not for the general audience.

Its main actor, Benjamin Franklin, sat center stage in a straight-backed chair—placed, I noted, where nothing might fall on him. He sat very still, the baldness of his brow softly shining above his semicope of hair, his legs stretched out crossed, his hands resting at seeming ease in his lap. 'Twas a posture of easy thoughtfulness, yet despite the apparent calm there was a waiting about him, an alertness in his eyes only half disguised behind his spectacles' squarish lenses. Thirty paces separated us, but I could almost feel him listening. Did he know that I was here? I wished him to; I longed to whisper, "I have done what you said, I am come," yet I must not speak.

I steeled myself to wait.

How long passed? Time moved molasses-slow whilst I clenched my hands and listened and stood as still as I could in my hiding place for fear of spoiling all the gentleman hoped to bring to light. As during our previous vigil, the playhouse emitted sighs and creaks; there were scurryings of mice, and I seemed sometime to hear the echo of long-ago applause, as if the old wood dreamed on nights of yore. Cold air began to creep as the coals in many fires died. I shivered and sought patience, yet nothing came to succor me. Mr. Franklin sat and waited, one thumb gently rubbing the other in his lap. What did he think on? The leviathans which had breached the sea on his crossing? The true nature of light? The last puzzling bits of our broken crockery pot, which would make it whole once more?

And then there came a rattling, and I started and turned. The rear door, through which the denizens of Drury Lane had recently departed, swung slowly open.

A bulky form appeared outlined against the barely lighter dark of the narrow way beyond. He stood as if sniffing the air. "Mr. Franklin?" came his voice at last, warily.

Did I know that voice?

"I am here," returned the gentleman from the stage.

The man entered Drury Lane. He shut the door behind him.

I was alert now, so much that my fingers tingled and the hair at my nape bristled. It was too dim to make out much of the new arrival, only that he was stout. He moved toward the wings with clumping steps, yet with certainty; he knew where he went. Had I seen him amongst the throng of hot young bloods and aging Lotharios? Drawn him, even?

And then he passed between the second and third flats and came onstage, breathing hard, peering about as if some trap might be laid: his harridan wife informed of his misdeeds and waiting to pounce. He was fat indeed, but well dressed in burgundy cloth, with a handsome black cloak that hung to his calves. He wore a woolly wig that covered his ears. A thick moustache near obscured his mouth. He seemed fifty or fifty-five, though as to that 'twas hard to say his age, so low was his hat pulled over his brow.

I squinted hard. I seemed to know the man, and sudden alarm shook me. Was this some trick to lure Mr. Franklin into solitude, where he might be silenced as Dudley Midge and Abel Drumm had been? I thought on the wig in Drumm's pocket, evidence.

Yet Mr. Franklin calmly stood and said, "I see you are come, Sir James."

"I am." Redmayne rubbed his mouth. "You have done as you promised? We are alone?"

"Quite alone."

"Surely?"

"I have heard only mice this three-quarter hour."

"You say so, do you?" Yet Redmayne did not come near but began to pace in a heavy, noisy way, seeming by this pacing to work out whether he would truly tell his tale.

And then the blow struck me. Peering round the edge of

the flat, I was invisible to the two men onstage, because of the shadow cast by the flat next in succession. There occurred some movement of air near my right ear, warning; then my head was jarred. I heard a kind of crushing noise, my teeth rattled. I do not know if I made a sound. I felt no pain at first, only surprise, and went sharply rigid before slipping sideways, helpless as a babe, into arms that lowered me silently to the floor. Though I did not lose consciousness, I could for a time see nothing but swimming red—I had no idea who had struck me. I was aware of continued conversation from the stage, echoing as from afar, and the continued hollow clump of Mr. Redmayne's boots. At the same time I heard the quick breathing of some person working upon me. Hands—not ungentle—bound my arms back, my ankles too, with deft wrappings of cord. Some cloth was thrust in my mouth and tied there tight. All this I felt as if in a dream. I made no struggle, could not, and shortly, when their work was done, the strangely gentle hands let be; a near-silent patter of steps told that the person fled.

Where? Who had done this?

I lay on my right side on the cold wooden floor. My head began to ache, and I longed for the succor of unconsciousness, yet I knew I must fight the tempting blackness.

Mr. Franklin was surely in danger. I must warn him.

I struggled to hear what passed onstage. "As to Miss Prouty," came Mr. Redmayne's voice after a time, "I wanted her, sir, but she rebuffed me . . ." Nausea surged, an awful gagging, which I fought for fear of choking on my vomit. The moment subsided. My head throbbed violently. Let Mr. Franklin see you, Nick—that will cry danger! Having been pulled far back, I began by a sort of wriggling to work my way toward the edge of the flat that hid me. I gained a few inches, stopped, rested in swimming pain, gained more, rested. All the while I listened. Mr. Redmayne came to the night of the murder—but how long-winded he was. Why did not Mr. Franklin hurry him to the name we wished to hear? The portly man's boots still thumped.

With one last straining move, I brought my eyes where they might peep round the flat, all the while cursing the cloth that prevented me crying out. I saw that Mr. Franklin stood by the chair he had sat in, very still, observing Redmayne lumber back and forth like some lawyer before the bar.

No harm had befallen either man, I might still give alarm. I wriggled more. Surely Mr. Franklin would soon see me.

"I waited in hopes of speaking to Miss Prouty, of pressing my suit," Redmayne said, chafing his hands. "I set myself well back, in a corner, whilst the play went on. I saw Abel Drumm, alive. And then I saw him dead, for—"

Sir James never completed this sentence. He vanished. A stage trap opened. The portly man plunged from view.

There came a thud from below. Silence.

Mr. Franklin leapt to the opening. "Dear sir!" Kneeling, he appeared about to jump down to give aid.

A figure stepped through the flats opposite. We had seen her walk from the playhouse not an hour and a quarter ago: Mrs. Esme Settle.

She looked quite grim. Her long dress rustled.

Mr. Franklin turned. He stood. "Madam," said he, "I regret that we cannot talk. I must below, to see to my old friend. I hope you have not seriously harmed him."

"Mr. Redmayne? Your old friend?"

"He is not Mr. Redmayne."

"What?"

"No time. I must below." Crouching again and dropping his legs through the opening, the gentleman seemed about to leap down, when another voice, soft yet commanding, adjured, "Stop."

He turned toward the side of the stage opposite Mrs. Settle. Her daughter, Lucy Drumm, had come onstage too.

Mr. Franklin did not seem surprised. Lucy held a pistol, hammer cocked; this seemed not to surprise him either, though I stiffened in alarm. It was a large pistol, and incongruous at the end of her white arm, which must be steadied by the other arm.

Despite the pistol Mr. Franklin readied himself again to leap.

Lucy Drumm's large eyes flashed. She shook her head. "The boy. If you wish him safe do as I say. Stand up, sir, but otherwise make no move. I regret the day ever you came to Drury Lane, and I will shoot you if I must."

Alarm paled Mr. Franklin's features. "Where is Nick? You have not harmed him?"

"Stand, sir."

Mr. Franklin raised himself with the aid of his bamboo.

I writhed. How I hated to be used against the gentleman. How I hated, too, the bonds that made me helpless.

Mr. Franklin warily measured the young woman. "You would indeed shoot me. You have murdered twice before." His gaze circled the playhouse. "Nick?" His voice called, loud.

Lucy shook her head. "He cannot answer. But he is well—for now. Do not waste your breath." She called to her mother: "See to the fire."

Mrs. Settle bit her lip. "There is no other way?"

Lucy burst out, "The child, mother! My life! See to the fire."

"As you say." Mrs. Settle vanished through the wings.

A stinging silence followed. Mr. Franklin's gaze was hard, and Lucy seemed for a moment to wish to turn away from it, as if she read shame in it. Yet she held her head high, as to say: I have come this far and shall not falter! We had our proof: it was indeed she who had murdered twice, her mother privy to it all. This was a new Lucy: no slavish, self-effacing wife but a tigress with a pistol in her hand, the true woman rather than the one she had played. Her figure in its dark-blue overcloak was the same small, agile one that had suggested a doe about to flee, but her honey hair framed a face like an avenging angel's. Fierce determination lit her eyes.

A groan emerged from the still-open trap.

Distress puckered Mr. Franklin's brow. "You must allow me to see to my friend."

"Let him see to himself, as I have had to do."

"But he may be injured."

"Have I not suffered injury too? His is small compared to mine—compared to that which my sex, my mother and others like her, has suffered. No, let him have his broken arm. Better by far than a broken spirit."

"The fire you sent your mother to tend—you mean to burn down Drury Lane?"

"That is my business."

"Mine too, if I am meant to burn with it. To cover the fact that you have murdered me too?"

Lucy ignored this. "Why did you say that Redmayne is not Redmayne?"

"Because he is a trick to bring you here. The tables have been turned."

She shook her head. "My pistol says otherwise. But tell me, since you are so clever, how could I murder whilst I danced onstage?"

"By means of three trees. As to Redmayne, he is a creature of my invention, played by an old friend named James Ralph, though I would I had not drawn him into it. You have proved more dangerous than I believed."

"You say you guessed that I—"

"Not guessed, discovered. Your handwriting gave me the clue. It was the same as that which set down *A Lord and No Lord*. I would have seen the thing sooner, yet I believed what David Garrick told me when he gave me his copy of the play: that it had been penned by your husband. No doubt he truly thought it had. Even when you let slip that you did some writing out for your husband, I did not catch the clue. Yet some words with Dr. Johnson nudged my memory. You had copied the play out for your husband; 'twas in your cool, perfect hand. Therefore it must be you who writ the threatening notes that began to come after your husband's death. More to the point, 'twas you who writ the note to Richard Cross saying there must be three trees rather than two. Those trees allowed you to murder."

"How?"

"By hiding the rearward part of the stage sufficiently for your mother to take your place in the faeries' dance. She retains much of youth's bloom; masked, she could be taken for you. Her figure is not so slender, however; in the exertions of the dance she burst the waist of the costume she took in secret from the wardrobe. Your mother would not do the deed herself, yet she would go so far as to tell your husband that you must meet him by the machine. Or did she send word that some other actress had asked to meet him there? In any case, you made the exchange, you slipped into that dark area knowing that all attention backstage would be given to bringing off the final moments of the play. Did you speak to your husband, pleading with him one last time not to reveal that you had murdered Dudley Midge? Or, knowing his adamancy, did you simply strike him down when his back was turned? In any case, you dragged him to the machine, placed him just so, loosed the brake—and the gears did the rest: dreadful! Who could prove it was not accident? More to the point, who should care to? Your husband was little liked; there was small chance anyone would spare him grief beyond the false laments you uttered. You have a brain, Mrs. Drumm. A pity it must be given over to such deadly aims."

Lucy Drumm looked distressed. "Believe me, I did not wish to do it. I hated to see him die."

"I do not say you are without feeling."

"I am not!"

"After all, the child . . ."

"Then you do understand?"

"Never murder."

The woman seemed to gird herself. "And so I must murder again, for you are unlikely to keep what you have discovered to yourself. O, my hands are so far steeped in blood . . . ! But I must hear all you know."

"I do not think that I shall tell you."

She gestured with the pistol. "The boy, sir. You may save him yet."

Mr. Franklin narrowed his eyes. Her arm holding the pistol trembled under its weight. If he dashed rapidly into the wings might he escape its ball?

Yet he made no such attempt. "Very well, for it is your own story. Because your mother was an actress, you grew up close to the playhouse. How thrilling must have been that life. Yet early you saw your fate: to marry a tradesman or merchant. But there was another path, to turn actress, a grander one than your mother if you might. Thus the seed of ambition was planted and grew in the rich, warm soil of a girl's dreams. I imagine you practiced an actress's ways from a young age: mouths, little laughs, dissemblings; you learnt to snap a fan and to take a turn round a room like a lady. You were not a lady, but had not Nell Gwyn climbed high? And so you studied tricks and learnt to lie. I do not say you had the foresight to see where they might lead. You were at first just a child with dreams.

"Yet dreams must meet reality, and you saw when you reached a certain age that you needed a protector: a man who might further your aims. You would far rather have climbed on your own, but the way of the world said a man should deliver you faster. Abel Drumm presented himself.

"You were nineteen then. He desired at first only to bed you. No doubt he sought your mother's aid; such maternal complicity is not new. Drumm made promises. Fine clothes? A furnished room? A lady's maid? But you had a different sort o' mother: she knew your real ambitions; she longed to help you climb. So you did not take Drumm's first paltry offer. You and your mother put your heads together. On the one hand your suitor was unpleasant, you did not love him; on the other he was a rising actor, beginning to be known, a favorite in the sort of comic, creeping roles he played. He was not without ability. Garrick cast him often. He seemed on the way up. 'Twould be advantageous to have such a husband. And so you worked upon him, lured him, played him, made him hot: 'No, but if you would . . .' and at last landed him. You became Mrs. Abel Drumm.

"How long was't before you saw your error? Surely less than a twelvemonth. As his affianced, you had seemed shy, docile, eager to please. As wife you must still play this role, yet he proved mercurial. He even beat you. Yet you little complained, for he began to advance you upon the stage. Smaller roles grew to larger. You learnt that submission got you farthest. O, he learnt a thing too: that you had qualities which the mob liked and that Garrick was disposed toward you. Drumm began to see you were valuable as more than wife, for English law decreed that all you earned came to his hands."

"Curse English law!" spat Lucy Drumm.

" 'Tis vexing to me too. Your marriage then was a using on both sides. How horrible it must have been to be yoked in such a bond.

"Yet you might have put up with his sulking capriciousness, his volatile sense of always being wronged, his pretensions to playwriting, his want of tact—but this latter began to threaten in a way you could not guess it might. He took increasing, unreasonable umbrage at Garrick; he made impossible demands, and when Garrick would not accede to 'em, your husband began to scribble spiteful, threatening notes. How this must have alarmed you. What if Garrick learnt who writ 'em? Yet your husband was . . . how shall I say . . . mad, after a fashion?"

"He showed no thought, no sense."

"Indeed he did not quietly plot and plan like you. What a pair might you have made; you might've ruled Drury Lane. But he was wanton, he struck about like a drunken swordsman. And so, crazily, he writ those notes."

"I was in agonies."

"Yet he showed some method in's madness, for he made his attacks general, so as to hide any clue to who truly writ 'em. He was shrewd otherwise, too, for he became suspicious of you—yet these suspicions arose at a very bad time, for you had just learnt you bore within you a child which might be Lord Calverly's."

"Edmund Calverly was my mother's lover."

Mr. Franklin gazed solemnly over the tops of his spectacles. "*Your* lover, Mrs. Drumm. Do I not speak true?"

She was still a moment, before her pretty face twisted into fury: "The man is a blackguard, like all men!" burst out she.

"You mean that, suspecting you had murdered, he returned to his wife?"

The cords on her neck stood out. "If he truly loved me he would have stood by me."

"He loved only the Lucy Drumm you played. Alas, she was not the real Lucy Drumm, and he could not, it seems, love a woman who would kill a man."

The hand holding the pistol trembled. "Damn Edmund Calverly!" cried Lucy Drumm.

" 'Twas *you* who set your cap for him. After all, a lord! But how to deal with your husband? Would not his suspicious nature easily ferret out the truth? To prevent this you devised a plan: you would make Calverly seem to be your mother's lover. She was handsome, without attachment. Would not Drumm be fooled by such a trick? Thus your mother took a room in Miss Bird's house and welcomed Calverly—though you were always there when he came. Your mother discreetly withdrew. This went happily for a time, Calverly seemed devoted. Did you hope to have him for more than lover? He was a decent man—if you carried his child, would that not bind him? How many lords have raised their bastards to the name of gentleman? You began to have great hopes. Meanwhile your husband was nicely duped.

"Yet not so, for he discovered your trick. Once he began to suspect he proved your match. Given his nature he was no doubt hot to confront you—but thinking that something might be wrung from the circumstance, he held his tongue. Might he not catch a lord in his trap? So he set up his minion in the room next your mother's, where this sneaking fellow took great care he was not seen and bored his hole and watched and writ what he saw, putting in Drumm's hands sure proof and a witness who would testify before the bar.

"He met you with his discovery. He threatened to bring suit against Calverly for seducing and alienating his wife. That would cause public mockery to my lord and pain to his wife and babes, but 'twas not them you thought on but yourself, for it would surely tear Calverly from you. Yet this was not the worst, for Drumm threatened more: divorce. This made you truly desperate, for by then you knew you carried the babe."

Lucy Drumm touched her belly.

"Would Drumm really have shed so lucrative a wife?" went on Mr. Franklin. "You could not take the chance. And so Midge must be got rid of, which you did in disguise. Since Calverly had confided his plan to have your husband's play cried down, you knew you would find the scurrilous fellow in the front row of the gallery. You knew his love of drink, so you plied him with it. Your husband had well taught you his secrets of false moustaches and eyebrows, by which you made yourself a man. Heels gave you height. You wore this same garb when you searched Miss Bird's house. Thus disguised, you tipped Midge to his doom—but you were observed; the man who saw you came to me.

"But what of Drumm himself? He still might divorce you. If he did he might well take your babe, which English law would let him do. Your child raised under that detested hand? This you could not abide. Too, he began to suspect 'twas you who had murdered Midge. Plainly you were not the innocent he once believed. I took from his body the wig with which you disguised yourself. Was that his proof?

"All this cried out that he must be silenced—but by some means whereby you would never be suspected. How better than when you were onstage, in view of hundreds? And so, in the shadow of the three trees (which you caused by your forged letter to Richard Cross), you effected an exchange: your mother danced your part, whilst you crushed the life from your husband in the gears of a machine. Why did you attempt to blame Lord Edmund for the crime? Had Drumm got to him before he died, so that Calverly knew you had done in Midge? Poor Mrs. Drumm, all your plans have come to naught."

Her small chin still lifted. "That is not so. You shall die and never reveal 'em."

"And Calverly? Will you do him in too?"

"I shall tell him the child I carry is his. That will keep him silent." She cast her eyes toward the wings. "Where is mother?"

"She will not come. She is in custody. Principal Justice Fielding has her."

Lucy started. "What do you say?"

"Justice Fielding, ma'am," came this gentleman's rumbling voice as he trundled from the wings and my heart leapt. "I came upon Mrs. Settle in most incriminating sorts, piling up playbills and shavings of wood from the carpenter's shop, and pouring volatile liquids upon 'em. She soon would have lit 'em, I believe, had we not took her—to burn you, Franklin, so we should never detect the hole in your breast." He glowered at Lucy. "The firing of buildings is a great crime."

Slipping from the wings behind the woman, Joshua Brogden wrenched the pistol from her hand. She made a small, despairing cry.

Mr. Franklin's thoughts were otherwise. "What of Jimmy Ralph? Injured?"

Justice Fielding snorted. "Would that he had broke his tongue rather than his arm, for he does not cease cursing Ben Franklin for inveigling him into harm."

"Thank God. And Nick?"

"Nearby. Brogden?"

"Yes, sir." The hopping little man came and loosed my bonds and helped me to rise. My joints cried out, but I hobbled to Mr. Franklin.

He held me at arms length. "So you saw and heard all.

What's this, a bruise upon your temple?" He touched the painful welt. "Curse me, I only meant to allow you to see the end. I never thought they should discover you."

"It makes no matter, sir. I am well, and so are you."

"O, Ben Franklin can still dance a jig. As for you, Mrs. Drumm—" He turned.

The woman cast about wildly, her look saying she saw she was a murderess confessed before the magistrate and must surely hang. Her hand sought her belly; it rested there. Though she did not yet visibly swell, a babe nestled under her heart; she must protect her child. She had murdered twice to do so; she would not cease fighting now.

I read decision in her eye, a flexing of her small, lithe body. Mr. Franklin seemed to read it too, for he made a lift of hand, a warning in his throat—but too late, for in an instant Lucy Drumm had whirled and rushed into the darkness of the wings.

Blind Fielding heard, knew. His three chins wobbled with the shake of his head. "My men guard all exits; she shall not escape."

"Do they guard the rooftop?"

"Rooftop, sir?"

Mr. Franklin met my eye. "Come, Nick. She knows that exit well—it is surely the way she has fled."

He dashed off, I at his heels.

I heard at my back John Fielding bark orders to his men, but the theater was dark, unlit; how should they know where to follow? Mr. Franklin knew where to go—had he not many times in past days marched up and down Drury Lane's corridors and stairs? Had we not together mapped her regions? And so I trailed him in the blackness, hearing fleeing footsteps ahead, Lucy Drumm's spoor. These mingled with our rough breathing and Mr. Franklin's grumbling as he tripped, struck objects, felt for turnings. Rounding by the dressing rooms, the wardrobe, the terrible machine on which I nicked my shin, we began mounting the first flight of stairs. I ran my fingers along the wall for guide, listening to distant stumbling and curses: Fielding's men behind us. Yet these sounds grew fainter, telling that they lost their way in the dark. What of the trundling magistrate? Would his blindness allow him to follow better? As I mounted I reflected: it had been Lucy Drumm who had loosed the bolt which near dropped the great chandelier upon Mr. Franklin; she had then fled across the rooftops. Had the attempt against Arabella Prouty been hers too? Against Susannah Cibber?

Mr. Franklin found the second flight of stairs. "Nick?"

"Aye."

I felt his hand brush my arm. "Keep safe behind me, lad."

We mounted.

This led to the low-ceilinged attic, with its door to the roof. Mr. Franklin moved slow, and I began to hear, above, a sort of frantic panting and thumping, as of fists upon wood. Light began to show, a faint flickering at the top of the stairs; someone had lit lamp or candle.

And then we emerged into the attic.

It was as before: musty, with long, sloping, rough-hewn beams and a broad plank floor inset with the six great bolts that held the lusters. The angled door lay twenty paces away. Lucy Drumm beat upon it.

As we stepped into her presence she flung her body against it, and with a creak it flew open to the night.

Cold air rushed in. A glimpse of stars.

"Mrs. Drumm," called Mr. Franklin.

She jerked about, a chill wind blowing her cloak about her and loosening her honey hair, the same wind which had made the door so difficult of opening.

"Where do you go? Where *can* you go?" pled the gentleman. "You are with child. You must face a court of law, but whatever their verdict, they will exact no punishment 'til your babe is delivered; that too is English writ. Be reasonable, come." He held out his hand.

She shook her head. "And who will care for my child? I have not come so far nor done so much to give it up. I will care for it, I!" At this, the wind snuffing the candle she had lit, she rushed up into the night.

"Foolish woman." Mr. Franklin plunged up through the door. Following, I ended close by his side on the narrow level just below the sloping slates. Stars dotted the sky, and London loomed round, black shapes of roofs, towers, spires in a great circle about us, like some silhouette which a playhouse sceneman might've built. Few windows were lit at this dark hour, and wind blew hard: it had driven the smoke from the sky to make the air clean, keen, biting, as with a knife's cruel edge. Shivering in a gust that near tumbled me back into the attic, I pressed my face against great cold hands that clutched and buffeted. Mr. Franklin peered into the gusting night.

Wind tore at our hair and clothes, tugging, flapping; it tore at Lucy Drumm too. Her small form, wrapped in its billowing cloak, stood upon the parapet from which three nights ago she had leapt to safety. 'Twas perhaps six feet to the succeeding rooftop; she was young and strong, she had leapt it easily once—though not in such a maelstrom. She cast a wild glance back, saw us, and the pale, fated expression that tightened her brow froze me colder than any wind. How she teetered, how she must perpetually wave her arms, to steady herself. I made to go toward her, to draw her down (I had no thought of preventing criminal escape but wished only to remove her from peril) but Mr. Franklin held me back.

"No, Nick, do not provoke her. I pray she does not attempt it."

Yet it was plain she meant to leap; having come this far, to the very edge, she must go on. By now her hair flew free, a great whipping halo, white in starshine, and her cloak lifted blackly, her thin arms visible like pliant sticks. Fragile, so fragile, easily crushed; and all the young, strong life of her, all her will and keen mind, shattered.

She looked at us. Forgive if you can, her large, round eyes seemed to plea. And then she turned and set herself against the night and leapt.

The wind caught her cloak like a sail. 'Twas a moment of triumph, for the wind seemed not her enemy but her friend; it seemed to lift her by that sail, suddenly, in a great breath, across the space she meant to cross, thirty feet above the cold, waiting cobbles. She flew, and I saw that she would succeed, win, flee; in that moment, too, I ached for her to vanish, find safe haven, deliver, suckle, raise her babe; let God deal with her crimes.

But the wind dealt with 'em—and who is to say that God did not drive it? Just as her feet found the farther parapet and my soul cried Yes!, the wind turned, it took her cloak, it tore her about in a kind of frenzied dance. It wrapped her in her cloak; it sent her down.

I heard no sound from the poor, lost woman, no protest; yet there came a lamenting cry as Mr. Franklin gripped my arm, my own anguished protest, torn from my breast.

🜲 20 🜲

IN WHICH Mr. Franklin climbs once more to the roof of Drury Lane, and peace settles upon Craven Street . . .

I awoke in the night, trembling. I had dreamt I was again on that windy parapet. I had held out my hand, Lucy Drumm had grasped it, wanting to be saved. Her eyes had burned with gratitude—but I had not been strong enough, I had lacked the will, and the wind had ripped her hand from mine and sent her down. Shivering in my black, cold room, clutching an aching heart, I thought on my mother, whose profile hid in the locket I wore always round my neck. Hot tears wet my cheeks: I had had no power to save her either; she had died little older than Lucy Drumm. I sobbed long, thinking on what I had witnessed. In numbness I had trailed Mr. Franklin to the windy edge, from which we looked down. A pale blade of light from a street-lamp cut the darkness of the narrow space between the buildings. Lucy Drumm lay in it, her cloak opened in a butterfly shape, at the center of which she was a sketch of ivory, her arms upflung, head to one side, her honey hair spread like a downy pillow. At peace—and who was to say that peace was not best for her?

And yet I cried.

John Fielding had arrived shortly after, clambering out upon the rooftop to stand against the wind. "Tut, fell, did she?" murmured he in the gale.

"Fell," echoed Mr. Franklin.

The portly magistrate shook with sudden agitation. "Drumm! Might I not've done the same had I a babe to keep from the likes o' Drumm!" His sightless eyes seemed to burn. "Who's to blame, I ask? Tell me, sir, truly: who?"

Mr. Franklin found no reply.

"Well, then," sighed Fielding, "we must gather up the poor thing and put her away. Ah, the flotsam of London."

I trembled long before I sank to feverish sleep.

The morning was a somber one: the wind stilled, a gray haze over Hungerford Market, and a thousand chimney pots soiling the air once more. "Dear me!" cried Mrs. Stevenson when I came down to breakfast, "what a dreadful bruising about your forehead." She poked and prodded my temple. "Why, it wants a poultice." She scowled at Mr. Franklin, who descended shortly after. "I heard you come in late. Why did you not wake me to see to the boy? Have you led him into danger? See the result? O, sir, how you vex me! Why, if I did not know you were good of heart (though sometime deficient in judgment), I should turn you out this very day."

He hung his head. "I am grateful you keep me, ma'am, for I do not deserve you. A poultice, that is what is called for. Apply a poultice at once, for I would have Nick well and sound."

Thus I was forced to lie upon my side on a sofa in the back parlor from ten o'clock to one, whilst a thrice-folded white cotton cloth dipped in warm milk and herbs was placed upon my right temple, renewed ev'ry quarter hour. Polly did this service, pressing me unremittingly to hear how I had come to be injured, which I told, Mr. Franklin having said she might now know all. Her eyes saucered to learn that Lucy Drumm, with whom William had seemed smitten, had murdered her husband. "And another man as well? And she fell to her death? You saw this?" Yet rather than gratifying her, the news set her more awry than ever. "O, O, O . . . !" She beat her fists. "Why may you have such adventures and see such sights, whilst I must rest at home?" And she dashed from the room before I could say that I would far rather not have seen what I saw for the injury it cost my soul.

A note had come from David Garrick saying he heard mixed stories about Mrs. Drumm's death. "Her mother is locked in the Fleet awaiting trial? Sir, you must tell what this means." Mr. Franklin had gone to comply, stopping on his way by Lord Linacre's fine house. "Lady Linacre is persuaded," confided he upon his return, "to leave off her seige of Garrick. I should much like to take credit for this, but I may not, for it seems she has boarded a new ship, younger, handsomer, trimmer, a painter of Brook Street, Mr. Cutter, but twenty-two years of age and in great need of patronage, in return for which he paints her naked in his chamber. I saw Garrick too; he is greatly relieved to be free of Lady Linacre and of threatening notes from the Drumms."

We climbed to his chamber. He sank into his chair. I had been privy to nearly all before last night, ignorant only of the fact that Redmayne did not truly exist; Mr. Franklin had withheld that. Yet I had questions. "Drumm writ the first notes, sir," said I, taking my place on the edge of his bed. "But why did Mrs. Drumm write others after he died?"

"To obfuscate. More particularly, she did not wish Garrick to suspect her husband had writ the things, for this discovery might still cast a shadow on her character. Since few besides ourselves know the secrets penmanship may reveal, she imitated only the tone of her husband's attacks, not his hand. But perhaps the most necessary reason was to turn suspicion from her own person; thus she sent notes to herself, to make her seem a victim too."

"And Mrs. Cibber's injury, made by Lucy Drumm?"

"More likely by Mr. Drumm. His wife was not adept at comedy; *A Lord and No Lord* proved so. Her forte was sentimental roles (what a superb Juliet she might've made). But Mrs. Cibber had a hold on such parts, and

Garrick would never set by Susannah Cibber in favor of an untried girl—unless Mrs. Cibber could be got out o' the way."

"Drumm was truly mad."

"He would use any means. He near did in Arabella Prouty for a similar reason: she was of an age with Lucy Drumm, and thus a rival. Did he intend murder—or only nasty injury? We shall never know."

"And the two fires—Drumm set 'em?"

"In anger at Garrick." Mr. Franklin shook his head. "What a curious mixture of sly knavery and foolhardiness. Did he not see that if he burnt down Drury Lane he should kill the cat that fed the kit? Yet twice he laid tinder and struck flint."

"And his wife gave the alarm."

"She could not let him succeed. No wonder she began to believe the only way round him was murder."

Murder. I stared out the bow window at the downcast day. Surely taking a life was bad—yet Lucy Drumm had not seen any other course. Was what she had done truly wicked? After all, she had stopped the man who might've killed Susannah Cibber, Arabella Prouty, others. Had she been wrong? My thoughts were at sixes and sevens.

"And you, Nick—" said Mr. Franklin, "how goes it with you?"

Blinking, I discovered his warm brown gaze upon me. "I did not like to see her die," said I.

"Nor I. But do not lose faith. You are my son and shall remain under my care for as long as you need." He rose. "Now, down to table, for I smell the aroma of a fine pork pie." He chuckled as he led me to the stairs. "Let us be grateful for fine pork pies."

And so our adventure at Drury Lane came to a close. William was much shaken by Lucy Drumm's death, more by learning she was not the sweet, helpless thing he had believed—though this dismay lasted only days, 'til the ringleted daughter of a Tory caught his eye. As for Lord

Edmund Calverly, he was little seen about town 'til May, the rumor being that he had turned the most uxorious lord in London. Lord Linacre kept company with Arabella Prouty, Lady Linacre with her painter. Lord Methuen continued to ravish London's womenfolk, so we heard.

Mr. Franklin called frequently on Comfort Goodbody; sometime we three supped together by flickering candle-light.

As for London's greatest actor, he devoted himself to his wife, as he ought always to have done, and was far happier than in recent days. Drury Lane got on without Mr. and Mrs. Drumm.

Yet I still thought on them. Both had longed to be some-one.

So did I.

When a boy of work at Inch, Printer, I had desired only to be beaten less harshly. But under Mr. Franklin's tute-lage, and with Craven Street's example of kindness to en-courage me, a future which consisted of more than a lessening of adversity began to seem a worthy hope. Was I not Benjamin Franklin's son? Did I not show promise? Hogarth's prints in shop windows cried out their example.

And so secretly, almost fearfully, I thought I might be an artist too.

Such was my dream. Such, too, was Mr. Franklin's thinking, it seemed, for the very day Mrs. Settle hanged herself in the Fleet in grief at her daughter's death and in despair at her own state, the gentleman called me from scouring copper pots for Mrs. Stevenson.

He seated me before him in his chamber. "Should you like drawing lessons, Nick? You are twelve and must seek some path. This one seems to like you. What do you say?"

My mouth fell open. "Oh, yes, sir, thank you, sir," cried I, flinging myself upon him.

When I stepped back he set his spectacles aright. "Um, I see you are agreeable. Good, excellent." He scrubbed his balding head. "We must find you a suitable master soon."

* * *

February, 1758, devolved to March, April, May, the wounds of Drury Lane healing with the uprising of crocuses in Mrs. Stevenson's back yard.

King never returned. We sorrowed long at that.

David Garrick adopted many of Mr. Franklin's ideas, most notably that of shining more light on the actors and less on the audience, which proved a revolution indeed, the theater gradually becoming less a place of assignation and gossip and more devoted to the art of plays. Garrick was some time installing the devices; thus our connection with Drury Lane was not severed, and one day when I walked to meet Mr. Franklin there I caught my breath to discover him upon its rooftop, framed by a vivid blue sky and clinging to an upright stick as if he would fall. Having had much of falling, I cried alarm, at which he smiled and stood easily upright, in no peril. "Hallo, Nick! See you the lightning rod which I have just affixed?" Indeed it was no stick but a tall iron rod reaching above the gable. The gentleman planted his fists upon his hips. "God himself would now be at some trouble to set fire here."

Would not God do as he pleased despite Benjamin Franklin? I smiled back for if any man might get round Our Lord 'twould be my father.

We saw Principal Justice Fielding round about this time, the portly magistrate thanking Mr. Franklin for troubling himself about Drury Lane. "I am hard pressed and spread thin," grumbled he in his small back office in Bow Street. "Yet if one citizen in a hundred were as you, Franklin, London should be a paradise."

Mr. Franklin modestly inclined his head. "And has Mr. Quimp made himself evident of late?" asked he.

Fielding's features squashed in displeasure. "In a thousand ways, damn the devil!"

"It should not surprise me if our paths should cross again."

A week after, in mid-March, a box arrived from Hampton House, Thameside. It proved from Garrick and his wife,

containing a Wedgewood chess set, all the vogue, in which
the pieces were famous actors and actresses: Garrick, the
king, Mrs. Cibber, the queen, Woodward, the knight, etc.
"To our very good and serviceable friend," said the accompanying note. Examining the pieces, I wondered: might
Mrs. Drumm have taken her place here too, if fate had
decreed otherwise? The door was shut on that forever.

Mr. Franklin showed this gift to Mrs. Stevenson and
Polly, who pronounced it cunning; then he carried it up to
his workshop, where he placed it upon a shelf. He began to
scurry about. "It shall be partnered by this . . . and this
. . . this too—" He placed near it *A Lord and No Lord* and
the flask and the wig which he had took from Abel
Drumm's pocket; also the torn Bible that had carried him
the last step in his pursuit of Ebenezer Inch's murderer, the
vial of Opliss Popliss drops that had done in Roderick
Fairbrass, the leering mummer's mask the poisoner had
worn. He surveyed this display. "These shall remind us,
Nick, to take care."

That evening we all—Mrs. Stevenson, Polly, William, Mr.
Franklin, and I; Mr. Ralph, too, his broken arm in stiff
white swaths, which in no way amended his volubility—
gathered after supper by a fire in the front parlor. Mrs.
Stevenson stitched; I sketched quietly whilst Mr. Franklin
talked on his life. This time 'twas of his voyage to England:
fleeing from French privateers and narrowly escaping ship-
wreck off the coast. "I may tell you," said he over his rum
and water, "I thank God for safe arrival. Were I a Roman
Catholic I should have on that occasion vowed to build a
chapel to some saint—but as I am not I vowed to build a
lighthouse." We laughed, I heartiest of all, sitting by the
best and wisest man whom I have known.

ROBERT LEE HALL'S BENJAMIN FRANKLIN MYSTERIES FROM ST. MARTIN'S PAPERBACKS

BENJAMIN FRANKLIN TAKES THE CASE

When Ben Franklin rushes to a printer's shop on London's Fish Lane, he finds the old proprietor murdered and a ragged servant boy with blood on his hands. But Franklin knows the lad is innocent, and together they set off to find the real killer . . .

———— 95047-0 $3.99 U.S./$4.99 Can.

BENJAMIN FRANKLIN AND A CASE OF CHRISTMAS MURDER

A prosperous London merchant, entertaining guests on Christmas Eve, collapses and dies. At least one of those present—Ben Franklin—knows there's more to this than meets the eye . . .

———— 92670-7 $3.99 U.S./$4.99 Can.

MURDER AT DRURY LANE

The constable labels a fatal plunge from a theater gallery a mere accident, but when a number of suspicious incidents begin plaguing the playhouse, its premier actor engages Franklin to investigate.

———— 95112-4 $4.50 U.S./$5.50 Can.